THOMAS CULLINAN

The Beguiled

A Novel

PENGUIN BOOKS

PENGUIN BOOKS

UK | USA | Canada | Ireland | Australia
India | New Zealand | South Africa

Penguin Books is part of the Penguin Random House group of companies
whose addresses can be found at global.penguinrandomhouse.com.

First published in the United States of America by Horizon Press 1966
First published in Penguin Classics 2017
001

Printed in Great Britain by Clays Ltd, St Ives plc

A CIP catalogue record for this book is available from the British Library

ISBN: 978–0–241–32181–2

www.greenpenguin.co.uk

Penguin Random House is committed to a
sustainable future for our business, our readers
and our planet. This book is made from Forest
Stewardship Council® certified paper.

For Helen

THE
BEGUILED

Amelia Dabney

I found him in the woods. Miss Harriet had given me permission to hunt for mushrooms as long as I promised not to go beyond the old Indian trail, which is just before the woods begin to slope down to the creek. Well all that land belongs to the Farnsworths but they never have used it for anything, I guess, which is fine with me. I prefer to have places like the woods kept just the way they are. Anyway on that afternoon—during the first week of May it was—I didn't find very many mushrooms, but I did find him.

He was lying on his face in some dead leaves with one arm around a fallen log, just clinging to it like it was his mother or a raft in deep water. His cap had fallen off and there were half a dozen flies buzzing around a deep scratch on his forehead. He had red hair and freckles and his face in the cleaner places was very pale. I thought at first he was dead but then he moaned very softly and turned a bit on his side. There was a great deal of blood underneath him on the oak leaves and his right trouser leg was just covered with blood.

My first thought was to return to the School and fetch Miss Harriet or Marie or Alice, but then I decided against it. They'd probably make a big fuss about it and decide to wait until Miss Martha returned from the cross-roads and then Miss Martha would say it was too dangerous for any of us to be in the woods and none of us would be allowed to come back. So I knew I'd have to move him myself.

The cannons sounded louder now. They had been booming since early in the morning from some distance to the east of us in that wilderness across the creek. There's still a lot of virgin timber on this property but over there there's nothing but creepers and brambles and second growth pine. It's no good for farming and all the best wood was cut years ago. I couldn't imagine anybody wanting to fight over it but apparently some people did.

His face was turned toward me now so I could get a better look at him. I leaned over to study him a bit closer. He was certainly harmless enough in his present condition and he didn't appear to have a weapon of any kind, though it might be underneath him. But what to do with him? I certainly couldn't drag him back to the school and there was no other way of moving him.

Then he opened his eyes. And almost immediately closed one of them again. I couldn't imagine anyone winking at me under those circumstances but that's certainly what he seemed to be doing.

"Are you frightened?" he asked, very softly but distinctly.

"No," I said . . . then, "Yes."

"That's good," he said. "So am I." And sighed and closed his eyes again.

"Can you move at all?" I asked him.

"I've come this far," he said, "on my feet and on my knees and on the flat of me. I might go a mite farther if there was someplace to go."

"The Farnsworth School is just the other side of these woods," I told him. "The Miss Martha Farnsworth Seminary for Young Ladies."

He considered this a bit. Then, "Any men about?"

"No men. Just five students including me . . . and Miss Martha Farnsworth and her sister, Miss Harriet Farnsworth. I won't say you'll be completely welcome but it will be better than where you are."

"True enough," he said. "I'll accept your invitation. Let's see if I can't make it in on foot. Can you give me a lift up? I'm that light in the head."

I stooped down beside him and tugged at his arm. It was no use, I could get him no more than an inch or two off the ground. After a moment he fell back exhausted. "If I hadn't lost my rifle in the creek," he said. "I could lean on that."

"Here," I said, kneeling beside him. "Put your right arm around me and we'll both raise up at the same time." That got him, trembling, up a foot or more but he couldn't bend his knee to pull it under him.

"Wait a bit," he said. "Can you hold on just a bit 'til I get my breath?"

"Yes," I said, although I wasn't sure I could. But then he didn't seem to be as heavy, holding him that way, as I had expected. He wasn't nearly as heavy as my brother Dick, for instance, or least ways from how I remembered Dick from the summer before last. I told him that and about how Dick and I used to wrestle on the lawn until Mama decided that it wasn't ladylike and I was getting too old for it.

"Where's Dick now?" he asked, still breathing heavily.

"He got killed last year at Chickamauga. That's in Tennessee."

"I know," he said, "but that wasn't none of us. I'm with the Army of Potomac. We was never in Tennessee."

"I wasn't blaming you," I told him. "I know it wasn't your fault." My brother Billy was killed at that battle too, of course, but I didn't see any value in mentioning it. Billy was four years older than Dick and we had never wrestled together, although I liked Billy pretty well too.

Now this was the first time I had ever been close to a Yankee and I suddenly realized something. They don't look a whole lot different from our boys. As a matter of fact that was the first time that anybody, other than a member of my own personal family, had ever had his arm around me.

"What's your name?" he asked.

"Amelia Dabney."

"Mine's McBurney . . . Corporal John McBurney."

"Pleased to make your acquaintance," I said.

"How old are you, Amelia?"

"Thirteen," I said. "Fourteen in September."

"Old enough for kisses then, and old enough to hate."

"How could I hate you," I said. "I don't even know you."

He smiled a bit at that. His teeth were white though a bit crooked in front. "That's a grand philosophy," he said. "Let's teach it to the world and we'll have done with all this squabblin. Now then, shall we try once more . . . ?"

I raised up with all my might, lifting him a bit, then he pulled his knees under him, trying to lean on the good one. The pain made him gasp and the sweat broke out on his forehead but we made it.

"There we are," he panted, "and off we go . . . for what is it now?"

"The Miss Martha Farnsworth Seminary for Young Ladies."

"And with only five students? The title's longer than the enrollment."

"The other girls have gone home," I said. "Miss Martha was going to close the school this year but she decided to keep it open when we five said we'd stay."

"That was brave of you. That betrays the scholars in you."

"Well, it was mainly that we didn't have anywhere else to go." I kept talking, hoping to keep his mind away from the pain. "My home is in Georgia, you see, and my mother decided it would be better if I stayed up here in Virginia for a while . . . what with your General Sherman down there so close to Atlanta and all. And it's practically the same thing with the other girls. Marie Deveraux . . . she's the youngest, she's only ten . . . her home is in Louisiana, and there's practically nothing but Yankees swarming around down there now. And Emily Stevenson's folks have a big place in South Carolina but there's nobody on it, except the hands, because her mother's dead and her brothers are all in the army . . . and her father is too. Her father is a brigadier general. He's probably off there in the woods right now."

"If he's smart, he won't stay," said McBurney. "I've been in battles before but never one like that. It's terrible in there. The brush is burning in a hundred places . . . look, you can see the smoke."

We stopped and looked back. The smoke was rising now above the trees on the other side of the creek. The cannons were still booming, continually now, and once in a while when the wind shifted, you could hear the crack of rifles and what sounded like high pitched singing or whining.

"It's them screamin, do you hear the screamin in there? It's bad enough to be shot but to burn to death . . . and when you can't see a foot in front of you or tell one man from another. . . ."

"Did you run away?" I asked him.

"I wouldn't say I ran exactly. I'm with the Sixty Sixth New York and there's plenty of vet'rans in that outfit and I only did like everybody else. The way it was, we were part of Hancock's Corps and we come across the river last night. Then this morning Captain Weaver told us to form a skirmish line and advance down this road . . . 'twasn't a road at all but only a mud track through the woods . . . and then I was hit and I fell . . . and everything began to blaze . . . the trees and bushes, everything . . . and so I crawled anywhere . . . for an hour maybe. Then I saw an open space and that creek back there at the bottom of the slope . . . and I went down for water."

"And when you left the creek you came out on the wrong side," I told him. "It's very simple. Do you want to go back now? I can show you the way."

"Not now," he said. "Maybe later. When my leg stops bleedin."

We were moving very slowly across the roots and hollows, pausing now and then while Corporal McBurney rested. When I looked back, I could see a trail of little drops of blood behind us.

"Is your home in New York City?" I asked him to keep him awake.

"Not at all," he said, jerking his head up. "I'm from County Wexford in Ireland and proud of it. But tell me about the others at the School. I'd like to know what I'm gettin into."

Well, I wanted to say something nice about Alice and Edwina but I didn't know exactly how. I really don't mind Alice so much. She's really not too mean as long as you don't provoke her, and she certainly can't be blamed for her background. But Edwina is another sort entirely. Most of the time she seems to be completely hateful.

"There are just these two other girls," I finally said. "Alice Simms and Edwina Morrow. I don't know where Alice is from originally but most recently she was living in Fredericksburg, which is about twenty miles from here and which I think your army is presently occupying. There was an almighty big battle fought around that town a bit over a year ago."

"I know," he said. "I was still safe at home but they told me about it."

"As a matter of fact, there was a big battle fought last May, just around this time, in that very woods you're coming from. Our General Jackson was killed in there."

"I heard about that, too," he said. "Some of the fellas in my regiment came across the Rapidan last night for the second time."

One thing he didn't know about; he never heard about how General Stonewall Jackson still rides through those woods at night on his black horse. Our Mattie swears she has seen him. She went up there one night with Miss Martha and Miss Harriet, one night last winter it was, but she never would tell us why Miss Harriet and Miss Martha wanted to go, or what they accomplished, only that she and Miss Harriet were scared half to death. Nothing, of course, bothers Miss Martha.

"Well anyway," I said, "Edwina is seventeen. She's the oldest in the school. She comes from Richmond and her father has a warehouse there. He sells things to the government. And Emily whom I mentioned before, is sixteen and Alice is fifteen. Some people consider her very pretty."

"Ah now," he said, "if she's any prettier than you, she must be a raving beauty. But what about the teachers?"

"Miss Martha's very good and Miss Harriet's very nice. Miss Martha's the oldest, although not much older. I think they also may have been very pretty at one time, but that's hard to tell now."

"I'm sure that sums it all up," said McBurney.

We came to the Cedar Hill road now which divides the Farnsworth woods from the cornfield.

"You'd better wait here a moment while I take a look," I told him.

"This road connects with the turnpike and the other way it angles off to the river and the place you've come from. There were a lot of our troops along here this morning and that's why none of us are supposed to be out."

"Surely your own fellas would never bother you girls."

"I don't know," I said. "Miss Martha says you can't trust any men . . . especially soldiers."

I climbed up the side of the ditch to the road and had a look. There was nothing to the north or east but the smoke from the wilderness. About a half mile to the southwest, down by the McPherson place, there seemed to be a cloud of dust. I went back to Corporal McBurney who was leaning against a tree beyond the ditch.

"We'd better wait," I told him. "There's somebody coming and it's a quarter mile yet across the field to the house."

"Don't you want me to be captured, Amelia?" he asked, grinning though it was all he could do to stand.

"Not until we can at least put a bandage on your leg," I said.

"To be sure," he said. "Once that's done I'll leave immediately and be no further trouble to you. We'd better get down into the ditch hadn't we, and not be standing here in full view of them that pass."

I helped him down. It was a fairly deep ditch and by bending our heads we were below the level of the road. Corporal McBurney still had his arm around me. I didn't think it was entirely necessary since we weren't moving now, but I didn't say anything. There was the sound of horses on the road, coming fast, but that didn't seem to bother Corporal McBurney. He kissed me on the ear. His beard was very rough.

"I'll never be convinced," he said softly, "that you're not the prettiest one in the school."

The horsemen, eight or nine of ours, went by riding hard. They looked as dirty and a bit more ragged than Corporal McBurney. The last one was a barefooted boy riding one of the horses in a team and dragging an artillery piece behind him. The wheel of the gun carriage swerved over the ditch and passed just inches from us. I was really scared then, but McBurney just laughed. It didn't seem as though he could have been telling the truth before when he said he was frightened. It didn't seem as though anything could frighten him. At least that's what I thought then.

After a while the sound of the horses died out. We found a place where McBurney could pull himself out of the ditch. Then we started across the field. I could see our Mattie working in the kitchen garden as we approached the back of the house.

"There's one other person in the household I forgot to mention," I told him. "Our old Mattie, who may well be the nicest person here."

Matilda Farnsworth

I seen her comin with him from out of the woods. I was pickin peas for dinner, lookin up from the row now and then to keep an eye on the smoke to make sure it didn't start to move our way. The boomin and the bangin wasn't botherin me too much by then. It's like a lotta other things. In time you can learn to live with almost anything.

Well I shoulda stopped them right then, but I didn't. I should have gone right up to her and said, "Miss Amelia, you turn right around in your tracks now and take that fella back where you found him."

Later I thought about why I didn't do that. It wasn't because I knew he was wounded bad cause I didn't find that out 'til later. Oh I could see he was leanin on the little girl and kinda hoppin along on one foot but I didn't know he was hurt as bad he was.

In fact I thought at first he was makin her bring him. I thought maybe he was holdin her so's she couldn't get away. I thought maybe he'd caught her out there in the woods and had forced her to tell where she lived and now was makin her walk along beside him so's he could spy out the lay of the land for himself.

I even thought maybe there was others behind him, maybe a whole lot of others like himself, hidin on the edge of the woods beyond the road, just waitin 'til the first one got to the house and sent up the signal that it was all right for the rest to come on.

So I suppose I could say now I was scared, and it's true I was. And maybe that was part of the reason I pretended I didn't see them and why I turned my back and walked away . . . but it wasn't the whole reason. Because to tell God's truth, on top of bein scared I mighta been a little glad about it too.

Because there was a hope in me sometimes that they *would* come, that they'd come and destroy this place, just knock it down with their cannons and then burn the rubbish. Course I never woulda wanted any of the young ladies to get hurt but there was times when I wouldn't've cared what happened to anybody else here, and that afternoon mighta been one of those times.

Oh yes, it's possible I coulda stopped them before they got to the house. For instance I coulda said to Miss Amelia, "If he's hurt so bad you can't take him back to the woods, then put him in my old place in the quarters. I always keep that place swept and clean and we can bring blankets for him from the house."

And Miss Martha and Miss Harriet likely woulda gone along with that too. If he was put to bed in there already, chances are they'd've let him stay there, seein as how they figured he was trash anyway. And then, if he'd never been taken into the house, most likely he would never have gotten so familiar with anybody here.

Well I been thinkin about these things lately—about what I mighta done, or at least tried to do. On the other hand I keep tellin myself I didn't know then what I know now.

I didn't have any notion then how much evil we got in us, all of us. Seems like none of us ever stop to think how evil can collect in us . . . how one little mean thought can pile on another 'til finally we got a mighty load of badness stacked up inside us . . . and then all it takes is maybe one nasty word to set off the trigger in us . . . and maybe that's some little triflin thing that wouldn't even have raised our tempers in a calmer time . . . and then we rush ahead and do things we coulda sworn to the Lord Almighty in the beginning we never had in us to do.

Oh yes, I seen them comin all right, though I pretended later that I hadn't. I seen them comin, but I didn't do anything about it. I just dumped my apronful of peas in the basket, picked that up and went on back to the kitchen.

Marie Deveraux

I was in the parlor that afternoon, at least that's what most of us call it. Miss Harriet usually calls it the living room, I suppose because her mind keeps going back to when she and Miss Martha were younger and it really was the living room of their house. On the other hand, Miss Martha often calls it the "assembly room" or sometimes "the great classroom." The library is "the small classroom" and Miss Harriet's sitting room where the sewing classes are held is called "the upstairs classroom."

Well, Miss Martha had warned us all to stay inside and then she hitched the pony to the cart and went to the crossroads for supplies. That was before all the heavy firing started in the woods. There had been a fair amount of artillery fire early in the morning off to the east and we'd heard the troops and wagons on the road all night, but that sort of thing was going on all the time lately so we'd gotten pretty used to it.

Anyway, Miss Martha would never let a little cannonading stop her. She's seldom able to buy one-tenth of what she asks for—quite often nothing at all—but she insists on going down there every week anyway. I guess she enjoys the trip, or maybe it's just the arguing with Mr. Potter, trying to get an extra pound of salt or sugar out of him.

Sugar is very hard to get nowadays, unless you know someone who might be running the blockade. When I first came to this school more than two years ago—I was barely eight then—I brought a twenty-five pound sack of sugar with me, and I want to tell you I was welcomed with open arms by some of these Virginia girls. Even at that time sugar was getting mighty scarce around here and my Daddy knew it, being in the sugar business himself. So he just had them make up this sack at our Baton Rouge place and he put it under his arm and put my portmanteau on his shoulder and we both got on the cars and came up here to the school.

I didn't really want to come but Daddy and Mama both insisted on it and Louis who might have taken my part had gone off with the Baton Rouge Rifles and so Daddy came and took me, by force practically, out of the Ursuline Convent of the Sacred Heart where I'd been going to school practically all my life and we took the railroad cars to Memphis and from there to Decatur and from there to Richmond. Then Daddy hired a carriage and we came over here to the school. Because that was right after General Lee and General Jackson had whipped the Yankees at First Manassas and this whole part of Virginia was as safe as a church. And New Orleans wasn't because the Yankees had been fooling around with their gunboats between there and Mobile since the first summer of the war. So I came up here to the school and brought the sack of sugar with me. And also some tea and coffee and a half pound of pepper seeds which were hard to get even in New Orleans.

So Miss Martha and Miss Harriet were very glad to see me, and most of the other girls too, except old Edwina Morrow who wouldn't be impressed by any such things as sugar and tea because, according to her, her father could get any of those things all the time. I think her father is a smuggler or something. She seemed a very common person to me right from the start.

And speaking of sugar, it was a piece of sugar candy we were talking about on that very first afternoon. At least the others were talking about it. In this place I'm never permitted to say anything much without being told to be quiet, just like a common child.

Alice Simms was nibbling on this piece of hard candy as though it were the most delicious thing in the world. Emily and Edwina were watching her. I was studying my Latin verbs and ignoring them. It was just about the dirtiest old piece of candy you could imagine anyway.

"All right, where did you get it?" Emily finally asked her. That's what Alice was waiting for of course.

"From an admirer," Alice said. She took it out of her mouth and examined it as though it were a precious jewel . . . just a dirty old red candy ball is all it was. If Mama would have caught Louis or I with a piece of trashy candy like that at home she would have chastised us for a faretheewell.

"There's more where that came from," Alice went on. She took the lace handkerchief with the crooked edges that she had made in Miss Harriet's sewing class out of her bosom. Alice just loves to keep things in her bosom as though anyone here cares to have it called to their attention. She unwrapped the handkerchief and there were four more candy balls. Each one a different color and each one dirtier than the other.

"Aren't they pretty," she said, expecting each of us to beg for one. "And they're very good too."

Well, it didn't look as though Edwina or Emily were going to lower themselves to ask for any. Alice isn't really a bad sort. She's certainly the prettiest one in the school by far, unless you care for Edwina's type, and it's not because Alice takes any great pains with her appearance.

Miss Harriet has to be always after her to even trim her nails or brush her hair, sometimes even more than with me. And she's not nearly as hateful as Edwina or as superior as Emily or as giddy as Amelia. So to save her being disappointed I asked her for a piece of the hard candy. She gave me the one with the most dust on it.

"Who is this famous admirer of yours?" Edwina asked. "Surely not anyone around here."

"It's a Georgia boy I met on the road," Alice said matter-of-factly.

"Ah ha," Edwina said.

"I only kissed him," Alice said, "once or twice. And then he gave me this as a present. He was just a skinny little old Georgia boy about fourteen years old, I'd judge. And let me tell you he was ready to forget all about the war and stay behind McPherson's barn with me just as long as I wanted. But then some old sergeant came back there and found us and he caught Andy by the shirt collar and hauled him back on the road. There was a whole big long line of them moving up there into the wood this morning. Andy Wilkins was this boy's name."

"From the looks of it, he's been carrying that candy in his back pocket since the day he was born," Edwina said.

"Maybe so," said Alice licking it again. "He's had it for a long time anyway. He said he'd been saving it to give to a pretty girl and I was the first one he'd met. As a matter of fact I was the first girl he'd ever kissed."

"I'll bet it was your idea to go behind McPherson's barn, too," Edwina said.

"Maybe so."

"I believe I'll tell Miss Harriet about it," Edwina said. "Or maybe Miss Martha when she comes home."

"Go ahead," Alice told her. "I'll just say I considered it my patriotic duty. And that's just exactly what it was, isn't that right, Emily?"

Because Emily's father is a general she's almost always called upon to decide questions of what is patriotic and what isn't.

"I certainly don't see how Alice is in any position at all to talk about patriotism," said Edwina, "because as far as I know she hasn't got one single solitary relative in the service of our country, and as far as that goes I don't think she has any relatives or family."

That wasn't exactly true, of course, and Edwina knew it. She was just pretending that she didn't know about Alice's mother over in Fredericksburg. From what everybody said Mrs. Simms was one of those what my father used to call a fancy woman. He used to call some of the Market Street girls by that name sometimes when he was having his brandy after dinner with some of his friends in our parlor back home.

I don't know whether the stories about Mrs. Simms are true or not, because Alice has never mentioned her mother to me personally and so all I know about her is what the other girls say. As far as that goes I don't know anything about Alice either except the fact that she's very poor and Miss Martha and Miss Harriet are letting her stay here. Anyway I was so happy with Emily right then I could have hugged her. Even if I can't tolerate her half the time I could just have hugged her then.

"Why certainly Alice has a family," Emily said. "She not only has her mother in Fredericksburg, whom I'm told is a very charming person, but she also has a father who is a high-ranking officer and who has just been cited for extra brave conduct during some of the recent fighting around Chattanooga."

"And where is he now?" Edwina asked suspiciously.

"He's just recently been captured by the enemy, isn't that what you said your Mama told you in her last letter, Alice?"

Now I knew, of course, that Emily was making it all up because Alice Simms is the one girl in the school who never does get any mail from anywhere. Edwina must have known that too, but she wasn't about to get into any arguments with Emily. She just sighed wearily, as though she were giving up on all of us, and went back to her Bible history.

Alice's eyes had started to water a bit, which certainly proved that the girl had some feelings, but she dried them now. "Here, Emily," she said, "have a piece of this candy. You can have the cleanest one."

Emily took the candy ball very graciously and set to picking some of the hairs and bits of lint off of it. Emily worries more about cleanliness than some of the rest of us. She's a good bit like Miss Harriet in that respect.

"It's very delicious," I said, thinking I ought to put in my pennyworth. "Once you get past the outer layer and down to the meat of it."

"If you girls really like it," Alice said, "it wouldn't be much trouble to get some more. Next time any of you spy any of our troops out on the road, just let me know and I'll go out and hail them. I'll guarantee you, if they're young ones just off from home, there'll be a few of them with hard candy in their pockets."

"I wouldn't go out there any more, Alice," Emily told her. "You know Miss Martha doesn't like us outside when there's troops around."

"That means enemy troops, doesn't it?"

"It means any kind of troops," Edwina said sharply from her corner. "Just as Miss Martha says, any kind of strange men are capable of doing harm to women."

It was true, of course, that Miss Martha was continually warning us about allowing soldiers or any strangers near the school. I don't know whether this is mostly to protect us or to prevent them stealing our little Welsh pony or Lucinda, our poor old cow. Anyway on two different occasions around this same time last year when they fought that big battle over east of here near the old Chancellor house, some of our boys came in the yard and asked for water . . . one time it was when they were going to the battle and the other time a day or so later when they were coming away . . . and both times Miss Martha stood out there by the well with a hay fork and made them drink quickly and get off the place. We all thought it was a pretty mean thing to do even after she explained again how afraid she was those boys would do some harm to us.

Normally no strangers ever come near the school anyway since we're not on the main Spottsylvania road. Even the neighbors very seldom come around because Miss Martha is not regarded as a very friendly person. And I swear the rest of us will be getting that reputation too because we're not supposed to mingle with or talk to anybody in the neighborhood. It used to be one or two of us could ride to the crossroads sometimes with Miss Martha when she went for supplies, but even that is not permitted anymore. The only place we ever get to go nowadays is up to Saint Andrew's Episcopal Church on Sundays. And that's no particular pleasure for me because I happen to be a Roman Catholic and I don't exactly go along with the way they run things in the Episcopal Church. However, I usually go on Sundays anyway, just for the change of scenery.

Because even a war can get dull if all the news you ever get of it is what your family tells you in their letters, and those becoming scarcer every month in my case because it's very difficult for Mama to get any letters out of New Orleans, even with all the shipowners we know, and Daddy's in the Army with little time to write. Anyway, for the past year it just seemed as though the interesting part of the war was going on everywhere in the country but around here, until this particular day when the cannons started up again and the troops began to march again along our back roads.

We had watched them all morning from behind the curtains in the front room. There were even more of them this time on the Cedar Hill road than there had been a year ago, except that this time they were a little more weary looking and a bit more ragged, if that was possible. There wasn't as much shouting or singing and they were all moving a lot more slowly than before. I expect they knew what they were headed for and they weren't in any hurry to get there.

Then about noon they seemed to have all gone past, and if it happened this time like the last time, we wouldn't see any more of them for a day or two. That was the argument that little Amelia Dabney used anyway when she told Miss Harriet she knew where there was a nice patch of mushrooms in the woods on our side of the creek and that it would be a sin to let them waste there and that's what would happen because the first rainfall would destroy them and everybody knew that all this cannon fire would surely bring on rain.

Amelia will use any excuse at all to get into the woods, of course. It's her favorite pastime to roam around in there and study all the trees and rocks and birds and whatever. In some ways she even looks like she belongs there, she's such a very plain looking little sunburned thing who sometimes reminds me of a chipmunk or a frightened little deer. And it's very strange that I think of her in that way because although we're about the same size, she's three years older than I.

Alice was the first to see her coming back that afternoon.

"Well I will declare," Alice cried. "Do you girls see what I see? That shy little Amelia Dabney has captured herself a Yankee!"

Alicia Simms

First, my name is not Alice but Alicia. They call me Alice, all of them except Miss Harriet, but I was christened Alicia and Miss Harriet has the certificate to prove it. I sometimes really and truly believe that Miss Harriet Farnsworth is the only friend I have in the whole world. She is certainly the one person in the world who cares from one day to the next whether I live or die, and that's more than you can say for anybody else around here.

They think because I wasn't born on a big plantation in Louisiana or Carolina or in some fine town house in Richmond or Atlanta, I'm not worth anything and I don't know anything and I'll never amount to anything. But they're wrong about that. I'll amount to more than the rest of them put together. I have more to work with than any of them . . . much more. And I think Miss Harriet realizes this even though she's never told me so.

I've been at this place three years, since the first summer of the war. The way it was . . . that spring my mother and I had gone to Washington. We had been living in Fredericksburg, Virginia, and thereabouts for a good long while before that, in the Jefferson Hotel mostly, which was not the worst hotel in town but I guess you certainly couldn't call it the best.

My mother, I ought to say, is the most beautiful woman in the world and she is also very kind sometimes, but she does have one serious drawback. Most of the time she is not very clever. It's not that she's unintelligent; it's just that she doesn't think very clearly in times of emotional strain. And this, as my mother herself is always the first to admit, is a serious weakness in a woman . . . especially a woman who has to support herself and her daughter.

Well, we were living in this Jefferson Hotel in the spring of eighteen and sixty-one. We had two nice rooms on the fourth floor overlooking the Rappahannock River, compliments of Mister C. J. Moody, the owner of the hotel. We might have been there yet, if Mister Lincoln hadn't decided to interfere in our business and those fools in South Carolina hadn't decided to test their cannons on Fort Sumter and Mrs. C. J. Moody hadn't decided she'd have to rush back from Mobile. Alabama, where she had been visiting her Mama, to check on the safety of her husband.

She came back to town on the Richmond, Fredericksburg and Potomac cars, only it was very late when she arrived owing to the fact that some Yankee sympathizers had ripped up a bit of the railroad track. It was after midnight by the time she got a carriage from the station to the hotel, and consequently I guess she was very surprised to find Mr. C. J. Moody in my mother's room. The walls aren't very thick in the Jefferson Hotel (I should say, weren't very thick because I believe the entire building has been destroyed now by Yankee cannon fire) and therefore I was awakened very shortly after the argument started. Mr. C. J. Moody claimed that my mother was a bookkeeper he had hired during Mrs. Moody's absence, which might have been true to begin with. I mean that, although my mother certainly knows nothing about bookkeeping, it might have been her original intention to learn the trade and Mr. C. J. Moody's intention to teach her. However,

I guess there is something about my mother that prevents men from keeping their minds on business very long. And obviously from what Mrs. C. J. Moody was saying, there wasn't any evidence of any bookkeeping going on when she entered the room.

Anyway, that next morning my mother and I went down to the railroad station ourselves and boarded the same cars that Mrs. C. J. Moody had ridden into town very likely, since the trains sometimes waited in Fredericksburg for several hours, and we set off for Washington. At that time, of course, hostilities hadn't really started in earnest and there was a good deal of traveling still going on between the United States and the Confederate States.

Our objective was to find my father. My mother said, as she had said many times before, that she had borne the burden of my upkeep long enough and it was time now for my father to lend a hand. We had gone through several campaigns of looking for him in past years in and around Virginia and Maryland—once we had even gone as far as New York City—but every time we'd be interrupted by people like Mr. C. J. Moody. But now, my mother stated, she was settling down to search with all her might. She was going to start off by going directly to the United States War Department. At that time neither my mother nor I had really made up our minds whether we were for the Yankees or the rebels.

The War Department seemed the most logical place to go because my mother knew my father was a soldier. As a matter of fact, that's about all she did know about him except that his first name was Clint and that he had a brown mustache, when she knew him, and that he was a second lieutenant, when she knew him. She reasoned now that he ought to be at least a major by this time, and with the war about to start in earnest, he might go even higher. So we got a room in a boarding house on G Street and that same afternoon walked down to the War Department.

Several people, including a general and two or three colonels, were very cooperative and attentive to us at the offices but not very helpful considering the small amount of information we had to give them. They said that our description of the man we wanted would fit about half the officers in the army. We didn't tell them it was my father we were looking for, of course, but just that it was a dear friend of our family whose last name we had forgotten. Well about all that came of it was my mother got invited out to dinner by a colonel of engineers and I had to go home by myself to the house on G Street.

We stayed in Washington until July of that year, spending every afternoon walking the streets down around the capitol, going out to the parade grounds to watch the drilling, waiting at the railroad stations as regiment after regiment came into town. It didn't seem hardly likely that my father could have been attached to any Ohio or Indiana volunteer regiment, for instance, since he was definitely in the regular army when my mother knew him, but she felt that he might have been reassigned to recruitment duties for one of the state militia regiments. And she was certainly making friends with a lot of officers, and some non-commissioned officers as well.

By the middle of July, I was about willing to concede that my father must be dead or retired from the army and, frankly, at that point I didn't much care. Then the Yankees decided if they were going to have a war they might as well get on with it, and so they decided as a first step they'd whip all the rebels in Northern Virginia. General McDowell—whom my mother knew but not well—was put in charge of the expedition and he got on his horse and led the whole army across the Potomac and down to Manassas Junction. A lot of other gentlemen and ladies—including Congressmen and Senators and their wives and such like—packed picnic lunches and drove down there in their carriages on the morning of the twenty-first of July because they figured the war was going to end with this one big battle and if they didn't see this battle now, they might never see one again for the rest of their lives.

My mother and I went along in the carriage of a Congressman from Iowa. We weren't going just for the picnic, of course. We figured if most of the Union Army was going to be present at the battle, the chances were very good that my father might be there too.

Well, if he was there, we didn't find him. And if he ran like most of the other Yankees on that afternoon, I'm certainly glad we didn't. We didn't see much of the battle itself from the hillside where we stopped for our picnic, but we certainly heard plenty of cannon and musket fire and a lot of yelling. Then the Yankee troops began to retreat along the road where we were, with our boys pouring a lot of fire after them. I say "our boys" because it was just then that my mother and I definitely decided to take sides.

Anyway, all that excitement was too much for the Congressman's horse. The Congressman was standing in front of the carriage, trying to hold the horse's head when the animal suddenly bolted off across a field, trying to get away from all the noise and smoke and dragging the carriage and my mother and me behind him.

That was how we came back to the Confederate States. We were half-way to Warrenton before the horse got tired and we could quiet him. Then a company of Mississippi Cavalry came along headed by a handsome young captain. He unhitched our carriage and had one of his men walk our horse around for a spell to cool him off, and meanwhile the captain himself got in the carriage next to my mother and became acquainted with her. She told him we were sisters on our way to visit relatives in Richmond.

Well, the captain escorted us to the home of some of his relatives in Warrenton and we spent several enjoyable days there. At least my mother and the captain enjoyed themselves and most of their dinner companions did too. They were all vastly entertained by my mother's story of the battle— which of course we had happened upon accidentally—and the running Yankees. Naturally I grew rather tired of the whole thing after I heard it several times and I was happy when the Mississippi boys were ordered out of Warrenton and my mother decided to take up once more the search for my father.

By that time, she had decided my father must be somewhere in the Confederate Army. It was really something we should have considered right from the first, since there were plenty of regular Union officers who converted over at Secession, including General Lee himself.

Therefore, when Emily Stevenson suggested on that first afternoon— the afternoon when McBurney came—that my father was a high ranking Confederate officer who had been captured by the enemy, it could very well have been true, even though Emily thought she was lying when she said it.

Of course, I really don't want any sympathy from Emily or anybody else, although I will admit that she has treated me a lot nicer on some occasions than most of the other people around here. That's with the exception of Miss Harriet, of course.

And the best I can say for most of the others is that I probably don't hate them now as much as I did when I first came. That's partly because I've learned to disregard them almost entirely, and partly because there aren't as many girls here now as there were in that summer of eighteen and sixty-one when I came.

There must have been all of twenty or twenty-five girls here at that time, and it was said there had been even more students here in previous years—some northern girls even—before people began to talk seriously about war.

The family with whom we had stayed at Warrenton had directed us to the school. My mother had decided she could get on with the search for my father much better if she weren't encumbered with me. Also, although she didn't say so, I think she had made an engagement to meet the cavalry captain in Richmond. My mother is always capable of transacting business like that right under my nose, seemingly without saying a word, the whole matter being handled with sighs and smiles and downcast eyes. I must say I have learned a great deal from my mother . . . much more than I ever have at this school.

Well, we came to the Farnsworth school on that day in July a few days after that first battle of Manassas and my mother told Miss Martha Farnsworth somewhat the same story she had told the cavalry captain, except that this time she did admit she was my mother. She told Miss Martha we were from Fredericksburg and that she was on her way to Richmond to claim an inheritance and that she would be back to get me in a few weeks and would pay my tuition and board at that time. Privately, she said to me very much the same thing, except that instead of an inheritance it was a gentleman in Richmond who had promised to loan her a large sum of money whenever she needed it. So she drove off that day in the Congressman's carriage. And never came back.

I think Miss Martha and Miss Harriet sort of suspected the story right from the beginning. Miss Martha, I know, wanted me to leave very shortly after I came because, as I heard her tell Miss Harriet one time, she felt I was not a desirable influence in the school, even apart from the fact that I wasn't paying anything. As a matter of fact, I don't know how I could have been undesirable because I had hardly anything to do with any of the other girls, at that time or any time since. Unless it was because I looked undesirable.

Anyway, Miss Harriet kept defending me in her very quiet way. Now ordinarily what Miss Harriet has to say on most subjects does not seem to mean a great deal to Miss Martha. Miss Martha always seems to have her mind made up before Miss Harriet begins to speak and nothing Miss Harriet can say will ever change it. However, in my case there was another factor to be considered. The enrollment kept falling off so badly as the war continued in this part of Virginia that the school could just not afford to lose any more students, whether paying or non-paying. I mean if you're going to have a school, it stands to reason you've got to have students. And with so many girls leaving of their own free will, it was just not sensible to force any girl to leave . . . even if the girl happened to be me.

I have thought many times about leaving on my own, especially at those times when I am having particularly bad trouble with Miss Martha. I am quite an independent person and most people think I look older than my age so I would have no fear about maintaining myself. I don't get along too well with women, it's true, but with men . . . well, I'm sure in time I could do quite as well as my mother. But then at those times when I am thinking these things at night, Miss Harriet will quite often come to my room and comfort me and ask me please to be patient and that although I may not realize it, she has problems too and by my presence I am a comfort to her, too, as well as she to me.

I have a room of my own on the third floor. It used to be a storage room and when I first came I guess it was the only place they had since the school was certainly crowded. There is plenty of room now, of course, on the other floors. None of the girls share rooms now except by choice. Amelia and Marie, the youngest ones, share a room but Emily and Edwina each have their own. But this doesn't matter. I wouldn't come down now to join any of them even if they asked me.

There is another reason why I stay. This is the place my mother left me and the only place she knows to get in touch with me. Most times I wish she would come back or at least write. Other times I hope she doesn't.

I was thinking some of these things on that afternoon as I ate the candy that Andy Wilkins gave me. I was really feeling very bad about taking it from him, even though I would never let the other girls know that, after he had carried it all that way from Georgia. He was really very likely hoarding that old candy to eat at some moment when it would bring the most comfort to him. Well, I could only hope that what he got in exchange was a comfort too.

I was looking out the window right about then and I saw Amelia coming with McBurney.

Emily Stevenson

He looked half dead when Amelia brought him in. My first impression of him was that he wasn't much bigger than Amelia and she's rather a frail little person. However, as we grew to know him later, he seemed a bit larger.

He was hopping on one foot and half stepping on, half dragging the toe of the other. Amelia was beaming as though, for the first time in her life, she had done something right.

"Ladies," he said, smiling rather pathetically I thought, "I give you greetings." And made it to the settee and collapsed there.

Lord, I thought, if they're all as weak and defenseless looking at him, why has it taken us this long to beat them? I thought I might mention that to my father the next time I wrote him. Of course, I know my father has his hands full with them—their soldiers are better fed and better clothed than ours for instance—but they don't have the sprit or the common purpose that our boys have and that is what will defeat them in the end. Our boys are all native born citizens of the Confederate States, while the Union army is made up of foreigners and immigrants and even some Negroes now they say, and the Lord only knows what else. Just like this creature that Amelia brought in—who was obviously from Ireland or some foreign place like that. Not that we don't have a good number of respectable Irish people in Charleston, although they are somewhat the poorer class, but at least they are native born citizens of the South and not complete strangers hired or impressed to take part in a quarrel that is not their own.

"He's not dead is he?" Amelia cried rushing to the settee. It was apparent that Amelia had made up her mind to add this Yankee to the collection of other odds and ends she had found in the woods—the rocks and leaves and butterflies and beetles—which she keeps in her room to the distress of all of us but most particularly to Miss Harriet who is a rather timid person and who got a severe shock on one occasion, I remember, when she found a huge spider in a pickle jar under Amelia's bed. At any rate, Miss Harriet gathered her courage and accompanied Amelia to a spot sufficiently removed from the school where Amelia set her spider free. Even Miss Harriet would not have considered killing the spider, which indicates that she is a somewhat more gentle person than Miss Martha who, without any argument permitted, would have squashed the spider instantly underfoot. Well, it takes all kinds to make up a world, I suppose, or even a school. Amelia in time forgot about her darling spider and set about gathering other pets, one or two of which I'm sure she had in her room at the time McBurney came.

Well he looked as though he wouldn't last another moment. His face was as white as the linen antimacassar on the back of the settee. I took a closer look at him and saw that he was still breathing but in very quick and shallow gasps. It was obvious that he had to be given medical care immediately or not at all, and even then it seemed likely that nothing any of us could do would help him.

"His leg is bleeding . . . all over Miss Martha's Persian rug," said Edwina, who always is the first to notice and report such things.

"Soap and water will take it out," I said. "But we won't worry about that now. Amelia, fetch Mattie from the kitchen. Marie, go find Miss Harriet."

Marie and Amelia obeyed me but I must say not willingly. Miss Martha and Miss Harriet more or less depend on me to keep things in order when they're not around and I do my best to carry out their wishes even though I realize that some of the girls resent it. Edwina Morrow resents it terribly, of course, because she is a year older than I and she has been a student at this school longer than anyone else here. Of course, that's not entirely of her own choosing. Like Alice Simms, Edwina has nowhere else to go. She has no near relatives except her father and he's too busy selling shoddy goods to our poor government to be concerned with a daughter like Edwina.

There was an old copy of the Southern Illustrated News on the table. I opened the newspaper on the settee and then proceeded to lift our prisoner's legs up on to it.

"I believe there are some poems by Edgar Allan Poe in that newspaper which Miss Harriet is desirous of saving," Edwina commented.

"She'll be glad to sacrifice the newspaper, I'm sure," I said, "rather than the settee. Be quiet now and give me a hand, one of you, while I straighten him out."

He was only barely conscious then, but I'm sure he heard us. His eyes moved slowly from Alice to Edwina and back to me, asking silently for help. I really and truly felt sorry for him then, the way the very life was draining right out of him. His face was gray behind the freckles wherever it wasn't covered with soot, and his lips were turning as blue as his eyes.

Alice poured a bit of water in a glass and brought it to him, but he couldn't open his mouth enough to drink it. When Alice tried to pour it in, he just slobbered it out like a month-old infant.

"Try it this way," Edwina said. She dipped her handkerchief into the water and then gently squeezed the water drop by drop between his lips.

"That's good material, isn't it?" I asked her.

"It's Chinese silk," she said. "My father brought it back from Shanghai after one of his trading voyages."

Well, I privately doubted that her father had ever been on any voyages to China or anywhere else of any great distance other than, if the stories were true, some frequent trips up and down the river before the war. I don't spread rumors usually, but one of the girls who didn't come back to school this year—perhaps it was Leonore Fairchild or Martha Willis—has stated as a positive fact that for several seasons Edwina Morrow's father had presided over a card game in the main salon of the Memphis Queen and had been called out and caned several times and once thrown into the Mississippi as a result of irregularities arising from those activities. Be that as it may, however, the handkerchief was definitely rich goods and I must admit that I would have thought twice about it before soaking it in water to comfort a Federal soldier.

"That was very clever of you to think of that, Edwina," I said. I usually try to compliment her whenever I can, though the Lord knows there's seldom much opportunity. "Now don't give him the water too fast," I told her, "or he may go off in a choking fit even before he bleeds to death."

Amelia Dabney came back in then, dragging old Mattie who had an apron full of peas that she had been shelling. Poor Mattie took one look at the figure on the settee and then let out a terrible shriek and scattered those peas all over the living room.

"You chil'ren have brought destruction in this house," she cried. "Take him back! Take that critter back where you found him. Let his own take care of him. He ain't no concern of ours."

"There were none of his own around," Amelia said defiantly. "He was all by himself."

"Take him back anyway," Mattie insisted. "Take him away off somewheres and let him die a good ways from this house. Don't let him pass away in this living room so's the Yankees can come around here bangin on our door and accusin us of murderin him."

"Nobody's going to accuse us of anything, Mattie dear," Alice said soothingly. "Nobody knows he's here but us . . . and the Lord. The Lord probably sent him directly to us intending for us to take care of him. That means all of us, Mattie, you too."

That was enough to settle Mattie down. I believe the mere suggestion that the Lord was asking her to take a hand in His affairs would have been enough to send Mattie marching off to face those very cannons that kept rumbling their unearthly chorus off there in the woods.

"Where's Miss Harriet?" Mattie asked, venturing a closer look at our prize.

"She's napping, I guess," said I. "Marie has gone to fetch her."

"If anything is gonna be done for this boy, it's gonna have to be done mighty quick," Mattie said as she felt his brow. "Though I wouldn't be surprised if it warn't too late already."

Well, I guess we all burst into tears at that, Alice and Amelia and I, and even Edwina, I noticed, managed a drop or two.

"Now, now girls," I told them. "Compose yourselves. It's only natural to feel some pity for the fellow, but after all, he's no worse off than if Amelia hadn't found him."

"That's right," Amelia said as a new thought came to her. "Or perhaps that's part of the Lord's will too. Maybe we're not supposed to be able to do anything for him. Maybe I was just supposed to find him and bring him here and that's all." Dead or alive, he was still a forest specimen to Amelia, a rare specimen which she had found all by herself.

"What's keepin Miss Harriet?" said Mattie, joining in the weeping. "What's keepin that poor lady?"

"She's coming now," announced little Marie Deveraux re-entering the living room. "She only waited for a moment to fix herself up a bit. I saw her pinching her cheeks to bring the color to them and she also put some lamp black on that gray streak in her hair. I expect she figures it isn't every day we get a man in this house."

Harriet Farnsworth

As I recall now, it took some moments before Miss Marie Deveraux's news began to penetrate my numbed mind. I had taken to my bed with a severe headache after sewing class and at first I thought what she was telling me was just some childish nonsense of her own invention. The younger girls especially are not adverse to playing little tricks on me occasionally, knowing they can count on my good humor. I will tolerate all sorts of silliness which my sister would not countenance for one instant. Martha claims that this laxity on my part causes the girls to lose respect for me. That's possible, of course, but I think sometimes they like me better for it.

"All right, I'll have a look at this prisoner, Miss," I said, arising. "And if it is only more of your foolery, you shall go without your dinner."

I tidied myself a bit and threw the black lace mantilla over my shoulders—the mantilla Father had brought home from the Mexican War—and then I followed the impudent little Miss Deveraux down the stairs.

As a matter of fact, I did half expect to find some visitor in the living room, some relative of one of the girls—a brother possibly, or a father, stopping by on his way to the battle. That was in furious progress now by the artillery sounds, but still a mile or more away from us—much too far, I thought, for any wounded straggler from it to come wandering through our woods.

But one had. And he would never wander farther by the present look of him.

"He's still alive, Miss Harriet," Alice Simms said, as though saying it would insure it. "You see how he clouds my mirror when he breathes on it?"

Over his half-open mouth she held her cheap little pocket glass—a relic of her unfortunate mother—and then presented it for me to examine.

"Blood is still seeping from the wound in his leg, too," said the practical Emily Stevenson. "I believe that means his heart is still functioning— though I have felt his ribs several times and can detect no tremor."

"This sort of thing is quite beyond my experience," I told them. "But of course we must do whatever we can for him, at least until Miss Martha comes home."

I could imagine what Martha's reaction was going to be when she set eyes on him. I knew what she would say about the safety of our charges and this breach in the walls of our defenses. Nevertheless, until she did return, the responsibility was clearly mine, and I resolved to do my best to handle it.

"One of you girls run up to my room and fetch my sewing basket. Mattie, is there any old cloth that we can spare?"

"There ain't no cloth at all that I know of," Mattie declared. "I want to dust around here any more, I got to do it with corn husks. You know Miss Martha has given most all of our sheets and pillow cases to the ladies who been collectin them for bandages."

"The damask tablecloth in the linen cupboard then," I said. "Get that, Mattie."

"Your Grandma brought that from the Tidewater place," Mattie cried horrified. "And the Lord knows how many years it was in the family before that. You ain't gonna stain that tablecloth with enemy blood, Miss Harriet? Miss Martha sure ain't gonna like it."

"Fetch it," I said. "I'll explain it to Miss Martha when she comes."

I am sometimes surprised myself at how authoritatively I can act in an emergency. Of course, it helps if Martha isn't around.

Mattie brought the cloth with no further protest and Amelia came back downstairs with my sewing basket. I took my scissors, breathed deeply, and began to slit his trouser leg.

It was ghastly. From the ankle nearly to the knee it was one long lacerated trench with the bone exposed at the calf and pieces of dark metal embedded in several places.

"Miss Martha will have to 'tend to this," I said between my teeth. "I'm not qualified to fool with this. Any of you girls who are about to faint, go elsewhere and do it."

I cut the tablecloth in strips and bound the leg as tightly as I could above the knee, getting Emily who was the strongest to tug at one end of the cloth while I pulled on the other.

"That ought to stop the bleeding somewhat," I said, "if there's any blood left in him."

Then I went to the wine cabinet. Martha generally keeps it locked because in the past we have had one or two girls who liked to filch a sip or two of sherry in the afternoon, more out of mischief, of course, than anything else. Luckily I knew a way of opening the cabinet with my scissors blade and more lucky yet, inside the cabinet and hidden behind the sherry there was half of a bottle of plum brandy which Marie Deveraux's father had sent to us two Christmases ago and which I had forgotten about completely.

I poured a small glass of brandy for myself to stop my hands from trembling, then brought a bit of it over to the poor fellow on the settee. The girls stood and watched with great interest as I ever so gently poured a drop or two of brandy between his lips.

"He'll only choke on it," Edwina predicted. "That's what happened with the water when Alice tried to give it to him."

"Brandy may have a different effect on him," said little Marie. "I believe he's an Irishman from his way of talking and many of those people have a great liking for alcoholic spirits. I know Mister Patrick J. Maloney, who was our overseer at home for a brief period before the Yankees invaded us, used to say that he had nine lives like a cat and that in case of death, he could be revived with one of my Daddy's special toddies which he dearly loved. I'm only sorry you've never tasted one of those toddies, Miss Harriet. I really believe you would enjoy them too."

"A toddy is not a lady's refreshment," I told her sharply. I thought to say more but she seemed so guileless, as she always does, that I let the matter drop. It quite astonished me the way those girls could just stand there gazing with such fascination at that apparently dying boy and his terrible wound. When I was a young girl, the mere sight of a finger pierced by a thorn was enough to make me swoon, but these students of ours seemed to have no such sensibilities at all. That, I think, is one of the uncalculated evils of our times—the way these years have hardened our young ladies.

I poured another small glass of the plum brandy, swallowed a tiny bit more of it myself and then, again very cautiously, fed the rest of it to the boy. If it was doing him any good at all, there were as yet no visible effects, but at least he was keeping it down.

"Stand aside now, girls, if you please," I said. "Let the poor thing have what air there is on this stifling day. If he's going to die, let him be as comfortable as possible until it happens."

They obeyed me and did move back a bit. Marie tittered nervously and Emily reprimanded her, Amelia and Alice looked to be the most woebegone, the first, I guessed, because it seemed she might be losing her prize trophy, and the second because she was beginning to think, like her unfortunate mother, that the loss of any man diminished a woman's world. I wondered idly if either Alice or her mother had ever heard of John Donne.

All of the girls had tears in their eyes, I noticed now, including Edwina Morrow, one girl in whom I had never expected to find any pity. She saw me looking at her then and quickly blinked away the tears. And then smiled and winked at me.

Edwina Morrow

The drunken old busybody . . . the stupid old tippler! I suppose she thought I wasn't aware of what was going on but she was wrong. As far as that goes, I'm sure all the girls in the school knew of Miss Harriet Farnsworth's frequent trips to the wine cabinet and, formerly, to the cellar where the larger stocks of wine were kept. I say "formerly" because I expect the supply that Miss Harriet's father put in years ago must be exhausted by now. In any case, I haven't seen Miss Harriet sneaking down there lately, but of course that might be because her sister has put a new padlock on the cellar door and Miss Harriet as yet hasn't figured out a way to open it. Not that the wine supply or lack of it affects the students in any way, since none of it was ever served to us, except occasionally during Christmas holidays to those who didn't go home.

One Christmas Eve, as a matter of fact, when Miss Harriet and I were sitting alone by the fire in the parlor, after Miss Martha and old Mattie had gone to bed, Miss Harriet and I consumed quite a bit of wine together. As I recall, that was the first winter of the war. I was fourteen at that time and I suppose Miss Harriet assumed it would be an easy thing to loosen my tongue with wine, so she could learn all the things about me which she doesn't know, and never will know!

She made one great mistake on that occasion. One thing she didn't realize about me was that I had learned to drink wine at a very tender age. When I was only six or seven, my father used to hold me on his knee in various clubs and taverns and in the salons of various steamboats from St. Louis to New Orleans, at which times he would pour wine into me as though it were my mother's milk. This was partly out of kindness, I suppose, and partly in an effort to quiet me so he could get on to more interesting affairs.

At any rate, I was still clear-headed on that Christmas Eve long after dear Miss Harriet had begun to nod and slur her words and spill her sherry in her lap. She wanted me to tell her of my past life with my father—where my mother was and about my family generally—all the facts which she and her sister had been unable to learn in previous questioning. Again I told her nothing, but I added considerably to my store of knowledge about her, which knowledge I will be very glad to reveal to anyone who seeks it. And there will be no charge for this information.

All the Farnsworth sisters know about me now is practically no more than they knew on the day I came. That was that my family name was a good one, that my letters of recommendation (including one signed by an important governor and another by a gentleman who is now a member of Mister Davis' cabinet) were excellent, no matter how the letters were obtained, and the quality of my money could not have been improved upon.

My school accounts have always been paid in advance, which is something I dare say cannot be said about the accounts of the other girls in this place. When I came here four years ago, I brought sufficient money to take care of my needs amply for much longer than I ever intended to stay. When I entered this school for the first time, my Indian beaded handbag was filled to the brim with Federal gold coins, a kind of species of which, I soon found out, Miss Martha Farnsworth was particularly fond.

Therefore my credentials being of the finest, I am constantly deferred to in this school. Although the girls all hate me and the Farnsworth sisters love me little more, still I am treated here with the utmost civility, at least by Miss Martha and Miss Harriet. When there is an extra serving of Mattie's pudding left at dinner, or an extra rasher of bacon at breakfast (I am speaking of the past now since we have not had any bacon for some time), it is generally offered to me before anyone else.

Oh yes, Miss Martha is definitely partial to the sight and sound of gold coins. The only times I ever see any animation in her eyes are these occasions twice a year when I drop my little stack of double eagles on her desk. It seems to be the one thing in life that gives her pleasure. "There, Miss Martha," I sometimes say on those occasions. "I hope you are not too patriotic to accept this Yankee money. If you are, I will be more than glad to go to a store or bank and try to persuade some gentleman to exchange with me for Confederate paper. Or perhaps you'd rather wait until my father has the opportunity to send me some of our own legal tender."

"Oh no, Edwina," Miss Martha will always answer. "I won't put you to that trouble. This will serve our purposes as well as any other."

This patriotism is a tricky thing these days, you see. She really never knows when I bring it up whether I am mocking her or not. Of course, I am sure Miss Martha is no more patriotic than some old cow in a pasture. In fact, she probably doesn't even care who wins the war as long as the outcome has no effect on her personally. What she would like is to have the thing done with, one way or the other, so the enrollment can return to normal and once again the money will pour into the Farnsworth School.

I know Miss Martha, as well as the other students here, would give anything to know how much money I have left. I'm sure that on one or two occasions some people have searched my room. This was done very cleverly, of course, and both times everything was almost restored to its proper place, except the first time the position of a book on my night table was altered and the second time a black thread was removed—a thread which I had suspended from a knob on a cabinet drawer.

Anyway, there aren't enough of my Federal double eagles left now to pay for another year at this place, but that doesn't matter. I have settled with the old crows for the present term and long before the leaves have fallen, my father will be here to take me away.

They know nothing about me and my father, but I know a great deal about them. I know of Miss Harriet's problem with the wine and Miss Martha's greed and many other things about their lives now and in the past. I have heard the quarreling in the night. I've heard Miss Martha's bitter accusations and Miss Harriet's weeping. She weeps, like all the weak people in the world, for the lost days, for the way things once were and will never be again.

She turned away from the wounded Yankee on that first afternoon and looked at me with a smile of satisfaction. I couldn't imagine what was on her mind until I realized she must be thinking I was shedding tears myself, for the soldier presumably. Miss Harriet was happy because she thought she had found another bleeding heart.

Well, once again she was wrong about me. I was not weeping out of any pity for the Yankee. If one were to begin bewailing the wounded and the dying, even those who had been struck down on one solitary day, there would be no end to weeping. I didn't know this fellow. He wasn't wearing the uniform I was supposed to be supporting, and for all I knew, he deserved what he got. At least that is how I felt, as far as I can remember, on that first afternoon.

I doubt very much that I was weeping at all on that day. It was probably only some trick of the sunlight from the garden which caused Miss Harriet to think so. Or even if my eyes had watered slightly, it was very likely the result of some passing thought about my father. In a way, the Yankee reminded me of him. My father is long-limbed and thin, and sometimes, after a sleepless night, very pale too, like this fellow was. In fact, there was a time—not so very long ago either—when my father didn't look much older than the Yankee on the settee.

"He would be far better off if he died right now," I remember thinking, "and was free from all his misery. I wish him well. I wish he would die." This sorry mood and the sunlight caused my eyes to fill up again and so to avoid giving Miss Harriet any more pleasure, I turned and left the room.

I went out on the front portico and sat there alone, considering my way of life and how it might, conceivably, in the near future take a turn for the better. I took out my Chinese silk handkerchief to wipe some perspiration from my brow and found it still wet from some water I had spilled on it. The handkerchief belonged to my father—a souvenir of one of his many lady friends. I rolled the useless little piece of cloth into a ball and threw it into the forsythia bushes beside the porch.

The artillery fire was continuing in the woods and there was a great deal of smoke in that direction, covering the whole eastern and northeastern sky. It occurred to me that I was not the only person with trouble in the world. Each rumble of the cannons, each swirl of smoke, was a sign of great trouble, starting at the spot in the woods where the metal landed and spreading like ripples in a stream to villages and towns and solitary lonely houses all over the land. Perhaps the trouble of the wounded boy inside would spread and infect people far away from here—a mother possibly, or a sister, or a sweetheart. I wondered if he had a sweetheart.

I also wondered vaguely if anyone would be concerned if I died. If, for instance, a misguided shell should fall on the school and kill me, would anyone really care? Would my father care—or did he have more pressing problems of his own?

Time passed—perhaps an hour—while I was thus occupied. Just before sunset, I saw Miss Martha with the pony and cart turn off the Cedar Hill road and start up the school drive. "Here comes the cannon ball that will decide the Yankee's fate," I thought. "His life is in her hands." Subsequent events proved that was only partly true. His life was in all our hands, as ours were in his.

At any rate, I decided I'd walk down the drive to meet Miss Martha and tell her the news.

Martha Farnsworth

I had warned Amelia Dabney a hundred times to stay out of those woods. Now, I decided, there was nothing else to do but punish her for this latest act of disobedience.

"Will you ask her parents to take her home?" asked Edwina Morrow. She had climbed into the cart, uninvited, and was riding beside me to the house.

"I believe that will hardly be possible at the present time since her home is in a battle zone." I had no wish to discuss the matter with Edwina.

"That's true," she said, determined to continue the conversation. "I'd forgotten that. As a matter of fact, it's my impression that Amelia has not heard from her family for some time, as I have not heard from my father."

It was my impression that her father might just possibly have been detained by the authorities for some illegal speculations in cotton. At least, I had seen his name in a Richmond newspaper several weeks before—we no longer receive the papers at the school, but this was a copy owned by Mister Potter at the crossroads store—in which her father was mentioned as one of several people being questioned by a government commission set up to look into such activities. However, the girl could know nothing of this and I was not about to tell her.

"Also, I imagine in times like these, Miss Martha," she went on, "with all your additional expenses—food prices being so high and all, you would naturally be reluctant to expel any paying student—even an irresponsible little person such as Amelia Dabney."

"There is no present question of expelling anyone," I told her sharply. "And if there were, the school would not be dissuaded by any financial considerations."

I knew from three years' experience it was not a wise thing to enter into debate with Edwina Morrow. She apparently takes a malicious pleasure in twisting anything I say to fit her own purposes—childishly evil whims for the most part—born of her own loneliness, Harriet insists. Born of the devil, I am more inclined to think.

"What do you plan to do about the Yankee soldier?" she asked now.

"I plan to do nothing," I said, "until I can get in touch with some of our own troops and deliver him up to them."

"It may be some time before you can do that," the girl said. "The way it looks now, our boys are otherwise occupied."

She was right in that respect. It looked as though they would continue to be occupied for quite some time, considering the sounds and conflagration which seemed to be advancing nearer to us. "If the wind doesn't change before long," I thought, "we may have much more to worry about than one wounded Yankee soldier."

The thought of fire reaching our buildings had been with me since the last battle, and before I was ten minutes on the road that morning, I was sorry I had decided to go for supplies. There had been troops moving eastward on the turnpike the afternoon before—hordes of them by the dust— and in the morning, still more of them even on the Cedar Hill road beside our place. That road, of course, is on private property where it crosses our land, though we've never interfered with its use by anyone on legitimate business.

That used to be the old logging road when my father was cutting oak and cedar out of our woods. Most of the best timber is gone now, though we still have a few good trees. To the east of us on the other side of Flat Creek, it's all scrub pine and sweet gum and thorn bushes, whatever wasn't burned away during the battle which began that first week in May of this year or wasn't consumed during last year's fighting around the old Chancellor place.

At any rate, the firing had begun while I was still on the Cedar Hill road before I reached the turnpike. I had hoped to be able to cross the Pike without incident and continue down to the old Plank road which, being narrower, might be hoped to contain less military traffic. However, the firing to the east caused such confusion and piling up of troops at the crossroads—with some of those on horseback trying to move more rapidly down the center of the Pike and some of those marchers on the sides deciding to slow down instead of speeding up—that it seemed we might be isolated from Potter's Store for the remainder of the summer.

I pulled up as close as I could to the edge of the turnpike and called out until I got the attention of a boy who wheeled his mount against the traffic and rode across to me. He was about seventeen, trying to grow a beard, and as brown and bony as his horse.

"Lieutenant Depew, Sixth Alabama," he shouted. "Can I be of service, ma'am?"

"I have to get across this road," I said, "immediately."

"No civilian's allowed on this road today, ma'am."

"I don't want to get on the road—I want to get across it to the Plank road."

"You can't go down there either. There's Yankees a couple miles to the east of here. They've crossed the river and are headed for Richmond."

"Well that's your business," I told him. "I have my own to attend to. Who's the general in charge of you soldiers?"

"We got a lot of 'em, ma'am. General Rode, General Battle, General Ewell . . ."

"Dick Ewell will do. You tell him that Miss Martha Farnsworth wants permission to carry out her urgent business. Tell him Miss Farnsworth begs to be remembered to him because she thinks she had some young lady cousins of his in her school one time."

There was a momentary break then in the line of troops. I gave the pony a slap of the reins and moved across the road.

"Ma'am . . . come back here, ma'am," the boy shouted.

"You just tell General Ewell what I said," I called back. I was across the Pike by then and moving down the Cedar Hill road on the other side. I reached the Plank road without any more trouble, but found that highway nearly as congested as the Pike. It was jammed with the men of General Hill's Third Corps who advised me, with accompanying profanity, that there was a battle now in progress at the Brock road crossing and that they were moving up to it. I told them I wasn't going quite that far so they let me fall in behind one of their ammunition wagons.

It took a couple of hours, I guess, because the Plank road is narrow, with boards only on one side. The heavy wagons were constantly slipping and sliding in the mud and the mounted men kept trying to ride around and in between the marchers. It was noon or after before we reached Potter's store. I turned into the yard and found Mister Potter outside putting up his shutters.

"You can't close just yet," I told him, tying the pony to his porch. "You've got a customer."

"I haven't the time to argue with you today, Miss Martha," said Mister Potter nervously. "Grant and his whole Potomac Army are crossing the river right now up at the Germania Ford. I can't leave this place open for them Goddam German mercenaries to loot."

"Please watch your language," I told him. "I don't know what you're so worried about anyway. Why should the Yankees take anything from you? Those people are probably carrying more in each of their wagons than you've got on all of your shelves."

Some people in this locality declare me unpatriotic and unsympathetic to our cause because of sentiments like these, but I affirm it's only being realistic. The Yankees have all the goods and all the money and and therefore, it seems evident to me, they will eventually win the war. Money is your great and ultimate weapon. With money you can buy steel and gunpowder and salt pork and all the courage you need.

I said these things in eighteen and sixty-one and I do not hesitate to say them now. Nowadays I don't see how anyone can be uncertain of the outcome. It is no longer a question—if it ever was—of who will be victorious, but only how much longer we can continue to bleed. (The same thought occurred to me later when I saw the Yankee in my living room and the results of Harriet's poorly applied tourniquet on my needlepoint settee.)

Well, if I cannot be sensible and popular at the same time, then I will always choose the virtue rather than the friends. We prefer to live in isolation at our school anyway. We've managed by ourselves until now and with the help of the Almighty—Who makes less demands than one's neighbors—will continue to do so.

Of course it is one thing to have sensible convictions and another to fly them from a flag pole. I realize that many of our girls have lost near relatives in the war—I lost a brother myself—and it sometimes causes grief to think that dying serves a purpose. Therefore, as much as possible, I avoid entering into any discussion of military events with the students—or even with my sister, who is often as ostrich-like about the situation as they are.

As I have told Harriet lately, our prime concern right now must be to keep the school in operation, so that we may capitalize on the resurgence of the spirit that is bound to follow the ending of the war. When normal travel and communication is once more established in the South, I expect Farnsworth School to be crowded to the doors. We may even have to build an addition to the house and hire another teacher—perhaps some recently widowed or fatherless young lady who, under the circumstances, might be willing to work for very little or no money—perhaps merely for her room and board.

Money . . . if my father had only managed to save more of it, if my mother had not wasted it on my brother, Robert, if my sister had not spent her portion on a foolish flight to Richmond at the age of eighteen—to marry a certain New York gentleman named Howard Winslow, she thought, but found out differently after Mr. Winslow had departed with some eighteen thousand dollars of Farnsworth money. If all of these things had not taken place, it might never have been necessary to start the Farnsworth School. Not that I can honestly say I have ever regretted that part of it. In a certain sense, I gain a great deal of satisfaction out of forming, and sometimes reforming, young lives.

These feelings have made me less bitter toward my sister in recent years.

Harriet usually does try her best to carry out my wishes and if she does not always succeed, it can be blamed on weakness rather than on any perversity in her character. Harriet is not an unintelligent person; she is just not wise in the ways of the world.

I have never discussed the Howard Winslow affair with her at any great length. I was too angry when it happened and in late years I haven't really cared. I don't know the exact circumstances of her parting with the man—whether she gave him the money or if he took it from her by force—although that would scarcely seem necessary, considering my sister's gullibility. I am sure that she expects Howard Winslow to come back some fine day, riding on a white horse and prepared to carry her off to some golden land of romance.

Thoughts of that nature—and the little wine I sometimes allow her—keep her in reasonable control. She seldom leaves our grounds, except to attend Saint Andrew's on Sunday, although I've discontinued our church going while the war remains in this neighborhood. Well in spite of all, Harriet is a good teacher, as I am too, I think. We both received good private educations as children and we are able to communicate our knowledge now.

When we were children . . . when we had money. "Money," I said to Mister Potter. "Hard money is the only answer." This was after I had managed to extract from him a pound of sugar, ten pounds of pork, ten pounds of wheat flour, a sack of assorted and unmarked vegetable seeds and the end of a bolt of white muslin—all the while ignoring his lamentations on the lack of any of those articles.

I returned to the school by the way I had come but with even more difficulties and delays than in the morning. This time, of course, I was moving against the traffic and even Southern soldiers, I found, were reluctant to move off the boards and into the mud to let a lady's carriage pass, especially when they had a battle on their minds.

I was cursed audibly several times, once or twice by officers, and at one point of absolute impasse, it seemed as though the cart and Dolly and I might be overturned. Then a cadaverous, tobacco chewing soldier in a tattered straw hat came to my rescue. "You're keeping North Carolina troops from the war, ma'am," he said, taking Dolly's bridle and leading us on to a stretch of fairly dry ground. "But there's some of us don't mind a little interruption."

"You stay with me now," I told him, "until we come to a less crowded part of the road."

"Yes ma'am," he said genially. "I'd rather be goin in this direction than the other anyway."

The firing to the east had become much more intense and rapid now. "Most of that ain't cannons," said the North Carolinian, in answer to my question. "That's about a million Springfields and Enfields and squirrel guns all goin off to once. There couldn't be much artillery in that band concert cause they say that brush is so thick up there a man has to go into battle sideways just to get himself kilt. That's why the Confederate Army likes skinny volunteers like me."

He stayed with us all the way to the Cedar Hill crossing and even led us part way up the side road until we were out of the path of the marching columns. Then he winked and saluted and started off, but I called him back.

There was a small piece of salt pork in my parcel, separated from the large slab. "Here," I said, "for your trouble. The next time you come up here for a battle, try to let us know in advance and we'll clear an open space for you."

"You're a joker too, ain't you, ma'am," he said grinning, "as well as bein a lady who knows exactly what she wants. I noticed that about you when I seen you comin down the road expectin the whole army of Northern Virginia to divide before you like the Red Sea. Well, that's the way to be. Know exactly what you want . . . and to blazes with how you get it . . . and with everybody else."

He fell back into line then and moved off, chewing philosophically on the raw chunk of pork. I often wondered after if he knew what he wanted and if he stayed alive to realize it. Some of his fellows stared enviously at him and then hopefully at me as they went past but I had no more meat to spare. I had the school to maintain and keep in operation until a better time. I had young girls to shelter and provide for and shield from harm. Let the generals and the politicians take care of everything else. The school was my first and only responsibility.

With these thoughts I continued on my homeward journey and reached the school without further incident.

"Even if our boys didn't have other problems on their minds right now," said Edwina Morrow as we stepped out of the cart, "you might not want to bring them to the school in force to arrest our prisoner anyway. A force of healthy soldiers might be more dangerous for the school than one wounded one—no matter which side each is on. Men are men, I'm told, no matter what their uniforms. Isn't that the way you think, Miss Martha?"

"I have no set way of thinking," I said. "I am an empiricist like John

Locke whom you have studied lately in your philosophy. What we will do
with your Yankee ultimately depends entirely on what we need to do." Then
I went in to have a look at the stranger in my living room.

Matilda Farnsworth

I suppose in any parade somebody's got to do the leadin and somebody's
got to follow. If Miss Martha was born to be an organizer, I suppose it ain't
her fault. She's been a good lady most of her life, that's got to be admitted.
She's always been good in time of sickness, for instance.

In her Daddy's time when the quarters were filled and the place was
being worked—like it ought to be today if there was a man around to see to
it—in those days it was always young Miss Martha who helped her Daddy
tend to the sick in the quarters. Her Mama was generally always ailin herself and her brother and sister were too young for anything but foolishness
but little Miss Martha from the time she was about ten would be out there
in the quarters every morning with the jugs of calomel and root tonic that
she wasn't hardly able to carry, and the roll of bandages and the scissors in
her little apron pocket, and her Daddy going along behind her laughin fit to
kill as she dosed them sick niggers and bandaged their cuts and bruises and
gave them all kinds of advice on how to care for themselves.

I was in the kitchen then—I always been in the house and my mother
before me—but my man was in the fields and what I couldn't see out the
back door he would tell me about at night. Sometimes some of those sick
hands wouldn't take so willingly to Miss Martha's treatments, so her Daddy
would always have my Ben standin by to hold them down while she poured
her medicine into them.

Her Daddy always depended on my Ben to be his right-hand man since
we never had any regular overseer on this place. It was big enough all right
for a hired manager, but ol' Master always liked to take care of everything
himself, or liked to think he did. That's the reason, some folks around here
will tell you now, Farnsworth went to seed.

It's true I guess, what they say, that for the last hundred years or more
the men in this family ain't been much account. From the time the first of

them lived on the Tidewater, it's been the Farnsworth ladies who've been mainly in charge of hangin on to the family money and property.

They had a lot of it, I guess, back in the days when they lived in the big place on the James River, but then one of the men folk got into some kind of trouble and scandalized the neighborhood and so Miss Martha's Grandma decided they better come out here and make a fresh start. Well I guess the land wasn't good enough for their roots, or their roots were never deep enough for the land, because the Farnsworth money, and the name too, I guess you could say, has been slippin slowly away ever since.

Miss Martha's Daddy was a good and kind man but he'd rather go hunt quail or fox or read a book or just watch the sun set over the rim of his whiskey glass 'stead of payin any attention to his crops or fences. And his son, Robert, was just like him, or maybe even worse. Master Robert didn't only sit and watch the money flow away, he threw it away as fast as he could on cards and horses and whatever other kinds of sportin and high livin he could find for himself.

Course this was a while after he grew up. When he was younger he was much more settled and obedient—to his Mama until she was gone and then to Miss Martha who started to keep an eye on him. Miss Martha and Master Robert were very close when they was children. They used to ride together and go on picnics in the woods together and sometimes they'd just sit long hours on the porch playin checkers or dominos, or sometimes just sit there and talk the whole afternoon away.

Then all of a sudden Master Robert grew up and got wild. He spent all his time runnin to parties and gamblin halls from Washington to New Orleans and never came home at all except now and again for a night or two to talk his Daddy out of some more money, and then off he'd go again, before morning, and we wouldn't see him for maybe another six months or maybe more.

His Daddy didn't see anything much wrong in it. As a matter of fact I heard ol' Master say one time it was a good thing for the boy to get away from his sisters for awhile. It would maybe make a man out of him, ol' Master say.

Well the last time Master Robert came home was right after his Daddy died and he didn't stay long that time either. Now I don't want to talk about any scandals in this family but I will say that Master Robert and Miss Martha had a terrible argument that night. Miss Martha was beggin him to stay to home but he wouldn't listen to her. I won't repeat everything I heard that night, but that was the meat of it. I wouldn't have been listenin at all except the noise of it carried down to the kitchen and woke me up and I heard little Miss Harriet cryin and went up into the hall and found her sittin on the floor outside Master Robert's room. They was all weepin that night, the three children weepin. I'll tell you that was the first time I ever heard Miss Martha weep. And I don't ever expect to hear it again.

Master Robert left the next morning before his sisters were out of bed, takin everything of value he could cram into his saddlebags, includin all the money there was in the house and a lot of his Mama's and his sisters' jewelry. And as far as I know nobody in this house ever heard from him again.

Miss Martha did her best to find him. She wrote letters and hired people to hunt for him in every town he'd ever mentioned bein in. She made trips herself to Richmond and Charleston and a half dozen other places but it wasn't any use. Master Robert had disappeared just like the earth had opened up and swallowed him.

I think that was one reason Miss Martha wasn't too upset, at least at first, when Miss Harriet ran off a while later, chasing after some rakehell friend of Master Robert's who had come here with her brother a year or two before. I guess Miss Martha figured that Miss Harriet might get together somewheres with Master Robert and at least get back some of the money and valuables. But that didn't happen and after awhile Miss Martha found out Miss Harriet had taken another batch of money herself.

Well, I won't say any more about that poor child. She's had her share of misery in this house—a lot of it before and more of it after she came home. She was allowed only that one big mistake with Miss Martha, and she's been made to pay for it ever since.

Then after the war started, a lot of stories used to come back to us— third and fourth hand stories mostly—about people who knew people who had seen Master Robert at the battle of Manassas or at some officer's ball in Roanoke or lyin sick in some hospital in Richmond. Miss Martha investigated every one of the reports but if there was ever any truth in them, the bird had always flown by the time we heard them.

Finally one day last winter—along about the middle of December it was—Miss Martha met a soldier at Mister Potter's store who told her he had seen Master Robert the previous spring at the big battle they had up there around the Chancellor house. "He looked the same as always," the soldier said. "'Cept he was dead." Master Robert wasn't too popular with a lot of the folks who live around here.

Well, everybody knows that most of those dead soldiers up there were never buried after that battle because the fires were ragin so hot the generals had trouble gettin the live soldiers out let alone the dead ones. By the

time the fires had died down, everybody on both sides had decided to clear
out of the vicinity and so as a result, there's plenty of poor unburied bodies
up there lyin naked to the sun and rain, waitin for the Day of Judgment
that's bound to come for all of us.

Anyway that same night after the girls were all in bed, Miss Martha
hitched ol' Master's Arab stallion to the cart, told Miss Harriet and me to
get in behind her and started off down the road for Chancellorsville. I sure
wasn't too happy about going off on any winter night's journey even though
at first I didn't know where we were headed.

By the time we got to where the Germania Ford road crosses the turnpike, I had a pretty good idea of our destination. That's near the old tavern
where the Fredericksburg stage used to stop and just beyond there is where
General Jackson got the wound that killed him and where most of the unburied bones are lyin in the brush. If it hadn't been so dark and we hadn't
come so far already, I would have jumped out of that cart right then and lit
out for home. Miss Harriet felt the same way, I know, and she pleaded with
her sister to turn around and go back but Miss Martha wouldn't listen.

I guess she must have got some idea of where to look for Master Robert
from the soldier she had talked to during the day because she turned on to
the Ford road without stoppin and went south toward the old Chancellor
house. When we got near to the Wilderness Church and the Fairview
Cemetery, she pulled off the road into a field and tied the stallion to a broken fence.

"Come along, Harriet," she say gettin out and takin the lantern and the
shovels she had brought. "You, too, Mattie."

"Miss Martha," I say, "I ain't never refused you before but even if the
Lord Himself offered to lead me by the hand, I couldn't walk into them
dark fields tonight. Even if my spirit was willin, my feet wouldn't be."

Miss Martha saw how nervous I was so she didn't say any more. Poor
Miss Harriet was scared to death, too, but I guess she wasn't as afraid of the
darkness as she was of her sister so she went trudgin off through that mud
behind Miss Martha, carryin that heavy shovel that Miss Martha had given
her. Into the darkness they went, through the mist rising from that swampy
ground, across a ditch where a wagon was upended and a busted cannon
was pointin at the moon.

If I ever prayed to the Lord in my life, I prayed that night. When their
footsteps had faded and the little speck of lantern light was gone, I closed
my eyes and prayed. I was afraid of the darkness and afraider still that the
clouds would leave the moon and I'd see worse things than I could imagine.

There were terrible things in that mist—marchin men, led by General

Jackson on a black horse, weepin women, ugly birds and bats and other hellish creatures—all movin silently across the fields, with the only sound the wind rustlin through the ruined trees and our poor old stallion whinnyin and stampin in the chill night air.

Well, the Lord was merciful that night and kept the ghosts away from me. And an hour or so before dawn, Miss Martha and Miss Harriet came back out of the mist and got into the cart and we started home. Whether or not they found Master Robert and buried him, I couldn't say. I didn't ask them and they didn't tell me. In fact, Miss Martha said nothin at all and Miss Harriet cried all the way home. Neither one of them ever mentioned Master Robert's name in my hearin again.

A day or so later, Miss Martha sold her Daddy's Arab horse. She said we had no further use for it and that she needed the money. It seemed to me it might also be because she didn't want any more males of any kind on the place.

That same thought had come to me once before right after her Daddy had died and Master Robert had run off. That was the day that Miss Martha brought the dealer in from Richmond and sold all the hands on the place. I stood in the yard that day and watched while the people were bein loaded on the wagon.

Miss Harriet saw me and came over. "They'll be well cared for, Mattie," she said. "Miss Martha gave orders that they're to be sold to only the best places. She says she wouldn't do it, Mattie, but she's going to start a school here and she needs the money."

I wanted to yell out and tell her what I thought of Miss Martha and what her Daddy and Mama would think if they was still alive, but I didn't. She hadn't made any deal for Ben yet and I thought maybe there was a chance she wouldn't if I kept quiet.

She waited until the very end with Ben. I remember how she looked at me and then at Ben and then at the dealer. I wanted to call to her and say, "Send me away too if you're going to send Ben," but I didn't say anything. I couldn't. There was a pride in me that made me keep silent, a pride almost as strong as Miss Martha's own.

Well she didn't sell Ben that day. She finally sent the dealer away with his loaded wagon and then she went into the house without sayin anything and left Miss Harriet and Ben and me standin there. I don't know what it was she felt in her heart that day but whatever it was, she repented of it because a week or so later she sold Ben to a farmer over at Locust Grove.

It was for less money than she was offered on that first day, I found out later from Miss Harriet—not much less but some—and it was to a place nearby so that Ben was able to come and see me now and then until he died. I guess maybe that was as close as Miss Martha could come to kindness when money and her pride was involved.

My Ben always claimed she held him back that first day for a different reason. He said it was because she was afraid of me—because I knew her better than anyone else knew her, even Miss Harriet. Ben knew about the talk I'd heard that night in Miss Martha's bedroom, the night before Master Robert ran away. I told Ben about it but I never told anybody else and I never will.

Maybe she was a bit fearful of me once, but that was long ago. We all change in our feelings toward each other as we get older. I don't even hate her any more like I used to. I know that she's the way God made her and I suppose she can't help it and she can't change.

Well those thoughts all came to me on that afternoon the Yankee soldier was brought into this house. I was standing there in the living room watchin poor Miss Harriet tend to him as best she could and askin myself, "What is Miss Martha going to do when she comes home and finds this young man in her house—a good lookin young man who is just about the age that Master Robert was when he went away. Is she gonna tell us to get rid of him or what? Will she make us tote him down to the road and leave him there so's our soldiers can pick him up when they go by?"

"Well," I figured, "she might do that later but she won't do it right at first. The first thing she'll do is come stormin in here, blamin and threatenin everybody for the Yankee's bein here . . . and then she'll take a good hard look at him and decide that we've been tendin to him all wrong and she'll have to show us how to do it."

I remembered Miss Martha in the quarters as a little girl and I knew she'd welcome the opportunity to work on a really sick person. I was pretty sure she wouldn't want to pass up this chance to practice her nursin once again.

And I'm not sure I even wanted it that way. I wasn't so scared of him then, only sorry for him, but I think now I wouldn't've been opposed to Miss Martha if she had decided to hand him directly over to our soldiers on that first afternoon. It sure would have been better in the long run if she had done exactly that, or even if she hadn't done anything at all but just let him lie there without touchin him. Just gone off and taken us with her and closed off the living room and let him pass away by himself.

There was the smell of death on that young man. It wasn't so much his bleedin or his paleness or the way he lay there so still, but a kind of mark on him that I could tell for what it was even if he had been unwounded and was marchin down the road. I was sure when I first set eyes on him there wasn't nothing on earth could ever save him and it wasn't going to be any use to try.

Miss Martha came in then from the porch with Miss Edwina Morrow behind her. There was no use to wonder any more. What was goin to happen, would happen.

Emily Stevenson

It was obvious as soon as Miss Martha came in the door that first afternoon that gossipy Edwina Morrow had given her a complete account of how little Amelia Dabney had found the soldier in the woods and brought him home. That sort of tale bearing was about what you could expect from Edwina. It was typical of her to strike out blindly in any way she could, hoping to get as many girls in disgrace as possible. Therefore, I determined to defend Amelia to the best of my ability.

"The Yankee couldn't walk, Miss Martha, and Amelia helped him," I said. "She did find him in the woods, it's true, but I believe it was not very far inside the woods and I am also informed that Amelia went there with a very good intention."

"What intention was that, Miss Amelia?"

"To collect some mushrooms," I said, "with which to supplement our table."

"Please let Miss Amelia answer for herself, Miss Emily. Were you on a food-gathering expedition, Miss Amelia?"

Poor Amelia was frightened half to death. She lives in mortal fear of all human authority anyway even when she hasn't done anything wrong. All Miss Martha has to do is turn her gaze on Amelia and the poor little thing is liable to faint dead away.

"Well," she stammered now, "it's like Emily says. I was gathering these mushrooms. . . ."

"For the table or your collection?"

"Well actually both, I guess."

"What kind did you bring back?"

"Well . . . some *amanita phalloides* . . ."

"The common name for which is death cup. Any other kinds?"

"Some *amanita muscaria.*"

"That is also a poisonous variety. Any edible kinds, Miss Amelia?"

"She has brought back edible mushrooms several times, Martha," Miss Harriet put in, "and also nuts and crabapples and wild berries. You know that yourself."

"I know that she has been warned repeatedly to stay out of those woods during these perilous times. Does it occur to you, Harriet, that you and I are responsible in this situation? These young ladies have been entrusted to our care—their parents have put them in our charge in the expectation that we will look out for them and protect them from all moral and physical harm."

"There really didn't seem to be any danger on our own property, Martha."

"No danger? There are thousands of young men passing on the roads outside . . . young men for whom most personal moral laws have been suspended. They are going forth to violate the Sixth Commandment with the blessings of their leaders. Do you think very many of them would hesitate to violate the Seventh on their own initiative?"

"In the Roman Catholic religion that would be the Fifth and Sixth Commandments," bratty little Marie Devereaux interjected.

"Be quiet, if you please, Miss," Miss Martha told her. "I realize that most of you girls have family connections in the military service and I do not necessarily refer to that kind of young man or any others well bred like them. However they are not the kind who make up the bulk of the Confederate armies now. Nowadays our banners are being carried by the moppings of the Richmond streets, by hill boys and illiterate tenant farmers and parolees from Atlanta jails."

I felt I had to speak up then. "Does that mean, Miss Martha, that you think our boys are any less courageous or dedicated to their cause than Yankee conscripts like the one on our settee?"

"He may not be a conscript," said Amelia, determined to defend her treasure. "Possibly he volunteered for his army."

"I think you have made yourself enough trouble for one day, young lady, without adding more," Miss Martha told her, and then added quite unnecessarily, "I'd be obliged if you'd keep quiet too, Miss Emily. I am not defending the Yankees. Individually, I'm sure they're as bad as any of ours, and collectively, of course, they're supposed to be our enemies."

Supposed to be! Good Lord, I thought, what kind of talk is this from a teacher in front of young children like Amelia and Marie to say nothing of impressionable people like Alice. If the Northern invaders are not the most dastard foe that any civilized nation has had to face then all our training and upbringing has been for naught.

"What do you think we should do with him, Martha," asked Miss Harriet cautiously as Miss Martha went over to look at him for the first time.

"My first thought," said Miss Martha, "is to load him into the cart and take him down to the main road and let the troops deal with him. This is a military matter and none of our business."

Now even though Miss Martha had spoken rather nastily to me, I was inclined to agree with her in this. I tried to imagine what my father, Brigadier General John Wade Stevenson, would have advised under these circumstances and I had to admit that he, too, would have declared it a matter for soldiers and nothing at all suitable for the attention of young ladies. I was about to mention this and in fact some later events made me wish I had when Miss Harriet spoke up in a way unusual for her.

"I think it is a humanitarian matter," she said. "Would you turn a grievously injured boy over to the rough care of soldiers on the march?"

"They very likely wouldn't take him anyway, Miss Martha," said Alice Simms who has already considering the benefits of having a young man in the house. "What could they do with a wounded boy like this? There aren't any prison camps near here they could put him in. Very likely they would just order us to take care of him, at least until the battle is over."

"Also," said little Marie Deveraux who welcomed the sort of excitement this guest of ours promised to bring, "also, if our boys find this Yankee by the roadside, they may just be curious as to where he came from and they may wonder if there are any more like him around. That may cause great hordes of them to come poking around here to see if we have any more wounded Yankees and, Miss Martha, I believe that is just exactly the situation you are trying to avoid."

"We could wait 'til after dark," said old Mattie, "and maybe take him further down the road where this place wouldn't be connected with him."

"How can you be so heartless, Mattie," Marie said, "and here this poor boy has been fighting to set you people free."

"I ain't heartless," Mattie said. "I'm just afraid."

Mattie very likely had been seeing strange signs in her herb tea again or listening to the wild dogs baying at the moon, either one of which would have been to her a sure sign of impending doom. I was accustomed to old Negro women like Mattie at home on our place and I knew there was often a lot of truth in the terrible things they predicted. These people are so used to living with trouble, it seems they have a special eye and ear for its coming.

"He could be taken back to the woods," said Edwina Morrow, "like Mattie suggested awhile ago and we could just forget we ever found him."

"You didn't find him—I did!" Amelia shouted. "And I will not take him back even if I am absolutely ordered to do so!"

"You will go without your dinner tonight, young lady," said Miss Martha, "for that remark and for your conduct this afternoon. This creature's leg is still bleeding. You've got this tourniquet all wrong."

"You fix it, Martha," Miss Harriet told her. "You know all about such things."

"I know you have seen fit to ruin a damask cloth—the lace border alone of which was worth at least twenty-five dollars one hundred years ago—and would cost ten times that amount today, if obtainable at all."

"It was worn and old, Martha, and the lace was torn."

"If that is an excuse for destroying it, then the Yankees must be right. They say that all our customs are old and worn down here, don't they, and they propose to teach us new ones."

Miss Martha unloosened the bandage on his leg and began to unwrap it gently. As she had said, the blood was still seeping from the wound though perhaps not as rapidly as before. In any case, there was probably very little blood left in him now. Miss Martha ripped the remainder of his trouser leg away without ceremony and then proceeded to wrap the cloth around again, only this time higher up on his thigh.

"I think the main leg artery divides somewhere close to the knee and it's best to pinch it off before that point. One of you hand me that baton."

Miss Martha took the baton, which is used in our music lessons, and, inserting it between the cloth and the Yankee's leg, began twisting the stick until the bleeding had slowed to a trickle. Then she tied the stick in place with another bit of the cloth and leaned over to examine the wound, prodding it and probing it with her finger as professional as some old army surgeon. In spite of my anger at her, I really had to admire her. The Yankee, mercifully, was still quite unconscious.

"There's enough metal in there to shoe a horse," she said. "I doubt whether it's possible to get it all out, even if we had the instruments. And it's quite possible it would not be worth the effort anyway."

She felt his pulse as we had and could detect no tremor. Then she put her ear to his chest and listened. "He's still breathing, but not much more than that," she said finally.

"Then you're not going to turn him over to our troops?" Miss Harriet asked.

"Unless he lives, which seems very doubtful at the moment, the question is only academic. If by some miracle he lasts the night through, we'll decide what to do with him in the morning. Now all of you, pay attention. Get me some needles—several sizes—and some silk thread. Mattie, fetch me as much water as you can. Boil it quickly. I'll also need some soap and towels . . . and more cloth for bandages. There is some white muslin in that bundle in the hall. Bring it to me and also a pair of scissors. I had intended some of you to have new shifts this summer but if you must bring wounded Yankees in here, you can do without new undergarments. I'll also need some sharp instrument for probing his leg. Find something in the kitchen, Mattie."

"How about that little pickle fork?" old Mattie asked her.

"That may do—we'll try it anyway. And also maybe a small paring knife. More swiftly all of you, if you want your Yankee to be alive at bedtime."

Mattie went off to fetch the kitchen implements and Miss Harriet set about supplying the needles, thread and scissors from her sewing basket, which was already on hand. I brought the muslin in from the hall and Marie went to get the towels and the pot of tallow soap which we are forced to use nowadays, and very sparingly at that. However, before Marie could complete her errand, Edwina, as unpredictable as ever, rushed off to her room and returned with a sliver of scented toilet soap.

"It's boudoir soap," she said offhandedly. "My father brought it back from one of his journeys to Paris."

"It's French soap all right," Alice said, examining it. "My mother uses it all the time."

Well, I thought, I suppose she'd have to, in her reputed business, but I made no comment. Edwina could not refrain, however, from crowning her act of charity with an unkind remark.

"You mean your mother used this kind of soap when you saw her last."

"If you like," Alice retorted. "If you must be so exact about it, I think that was probably some months or maybe even years after the time you last set eyes on your father."

"Enough of that," Miss Martha told them. She had completed examining her patient and was ready to set to work. "Get behind this settee all of you and shove it to a place of better light."

We shoved the settee and its uncomplaining occupant over to where the last rays of the sun were coming through the garden door, or at least as much of the setting sunlight that was not obliterated by the smoke from the woods.

Mattie returned then with a bucket of steaming water and the kitchen implements. Miss Martha threw the knife and fork into the water along with the needles and thread and, while they steeped, she took the scissors and began cutting up the muslin and the remaining piece of her valuable tablecloth. Then she threw a bit of the cloth into the water, let it soak a while, withdrew it on the point of the scissors, grasped it in her bare hand and after dipping it into the tallow soap began scrubbing the Yankee's leg.

"You may save your scented soap, Edwina," she said. "We may need it another time. At any rate, it's thoughtful of you to offer it. Now this may become more unpleasant as we continue, girls. Anyone present who thinks she may faint or do anything else nonsensical will please leave the room now. That includes you, Miss Harriet."

No one left. Miss Martha smiled grimly and continued her work. That hot cloth must have burned her hand terribly but she gave no sign of any pain. I thought then as I have thought before, if Miss Martha had only been born a man, she would have made a great contribution to the Southern cause.

When the leg was thoroughly cleansed of its mud and gunpowder and dried blood, Miss Martha straightened up. "I'll need more light now. Bring the lamp."

Mattie went out to fetch the living room lamp which is kept in the kitchen nowadays to prevent its being unnecessarily lighted. Like everyone else, we are reduced to using cotton seed oil instead of kerosene in our lamps these evenings and even that is in very short supply. Meanwhile, Miss Martha was fishing the pickle fork and paring knife from the hot water with the point of her scissors.

"Here," she said, dropping the knife and fork on a towel and handing the towel to Marie. "Hold these until I ask for them. Now I'd like the assistance of two more people. One to lift this gentleman's leg and hold it steady and the other to stand over him and watch him closely, and in the event he regains consciousness, to hold him down."

I volunteered to be the leg holder and Miss Harriet, who was quite pale by this time, said that she would stand by and guard against his sudden movement. Mattie returned with the lamp then and held it over the settee where Miss Martha directed. Then Miss Martha took the knife and pickle fork and began picking the bits of shrapnel out of the Yankee's leg.

As she had said, there was a great deal of metal embedded there and it took a long time. Miss Martha was quite colorless herself before she finished. A wisp of her usually carefully pinned dark hair was hanging on her forehead and trickles of perspiration were running down her cheeks. "She is not a beautiful woman," I thought as I watched her with great admiration, "but she is attractive in her own determined kind of way." I thought she was probably the most determined looking person I had ever seen.

When the metal was all out, or as much of it as Miss Harriet could find with her crude instruments, she applied more hot cloths to the leg, reshaped the splintered bone as well as she could and then, taking a needle and a length of black silk thread from Marie, she began to sew up the wound. Before two stitches were taken, Edwina Morrow had crumpled to the floor.

"Alice . . . Amelia . . . take her out," Miss Martha said without so much as looking up. "Help them please, Mattie. Miss Harriet will take the lamp. Lift the leg a bit higher, Emily. There's nothing to this part you know. It's just like sewing up a Thanksgiving turkey."

Well, it was certainly more complicated than that. Although it wasn't the neatest job of sewing I had ever seen, considering the circumstances under which she was working and the condition of that leg, Miss Martha would have won the gold thimble in any seamstress competition in the world. That boy's leg was not only torn, it was mangled, and the excavation work Miss Martha had done for the imbedded metal certainly didn't make the repair work any easier.

It must have taken nearly an hour and almost all the thread in the spool before she tied the final knot. Then she sent Marie up to her room to fetch an old hoop skirt which she or Miss Harriet or someone in their family must have worn in far bygone days. It was of fine lavendar taffeta with embroidered pink roses on it, altogether a very handsome piece of goods, old as it was. However, Miss Martha didn't hesitate one moment, but ripped the skirt apart and removed the stays and used them as splints for the Yankee's leg. Then she bound the whole with strips of the new muslin and the remaining piece of damask table cloth.

"There . . ." she said, "there you are, young ladies." She sighed and stepped back and mopped her dripping brow in most unladylike fashion.

Little Marie was so overwhelmed she applauded and Alice and I joined in. "That old Yankee had really better live now," Marie cried. "After all the hard work we've put in here."

"Very good, Martha, very good," Miss Harriet said, quite overwhelmed herself.

"It's not very good at all," Miss Martha said, although I'm sure she was pleased at our approval. "I really wouldn't have attempted it, if I hadn't felt I couldn't do him any harm. Well, now we must wait and see what the next few hours will do to him. At least we've stopped the flow of blood. If the spark of life is strong enough in him, a good night's rest may help it glow a bit. Now then, young ladies, back to your separate duties. Those with lessons, attend to them. The others, set yourselves some worthwhile tasks. Has Miss Edwina recovered yet? Get a small onion from the kitchen, one of you, cut it and hold it underneath her nose. Mattie, Harriet . . . let's clean up here and see to dinner."

"Miss Martha," Amelia Dabney said shyly. "I would like to thank you for your kindness to this Yankee. Incidentally, his name, in case you've wondered, is John McBurney."

"I didn't wonder about it at all, Miss Amelia," our headmistress told her. "And I'm afraid he won't be here long enough—dead or alive—for his name to make any difference to us. Now, Miss Amelia, since you won't be dining with us, you are free to go to your room."

Marie had started for the kitchen to get the onion for Edwina, who at this point was still lying unconscious or close to it, on the settee in the entrance hallway. Obviously there is nothing most of us in this school would like better than the chance to shove an onion in Edwina Morrow's face, but of course only the more childish students can afford to be so eager about it. However, Marie was willing to risk losing even this golden opportunity for a chance to cause a bit more disturbance for Miss Martha.

"Miss Martha," she said, "I think it is unfair of you to punish my roommate, Amelia Dabney, for going into the woods today, since she has explained to you that she had good educational reasons for doing so. Even if we all do not share her queer interests, I don't think she ought to be punished for them, especially since it was not her fault she was caught today. Now I myself went into that very same woods one day about a week ago, and I had no particular reason for going except that I wanted to be alone, and I was not caught or even suspected."

"You're caught now," said Miss Martha, "and you may join Amelia in her punishment."

"But, Miss Martha, for pity's sake . . . I am admitting it!"

"Then your conscience will be at ease, for which you should be grateful. Go to your room, the two of you. Miss Alice, get the onion and attend to Miss Edwina."

Alice went off with great alacrity and the little imp, muttering and making terrible faces at us all, followed her roommate up the stairs. She certainly is the strangest child and I believe her Papist upbringing is to a great degree responsible for it. She is frequently guilty of the most stubborn and outrageous conduct—very often, apparently, for no other reason than sheer deviltry—and then is willing to confess all quite cheerfully as though that will wipe the deed away. Oh, Marie and Miss Martha are old adversaries at this game. Fortunately, Miss Martha is on to Miss Deveraux's strange little system of morality and Miss Martha doesn't hesitate to rule her with an iron hand.

As I have said, I do not always like Miss Martha, but I do admire her strength of will. I must repeat that our army has lost a great soldier in the person of Miss Martha, and let me tell you, her mettle and her coolness under fire were tested even further in the weeks ahead.

Marie Deveraux

Well, I did not mind at all being sent to my room without dinner on that first evening. It had happened to me many times before and I expect it will happen many times again. After all, it is really not as serious a catastrophe as a stranger to our school might suppose.

For instance, Miss Harriet usually manages to dare the wrath of her sister on these occasions and will slip up to see me later in the evening with a portion of dinner concealed beneath her shawl. As a matter of fact, it is quite possible for a person to fare better at this kind of secret meal, than when one must face the nightly competition at the table down below. I suppose Miss Martha and Miss Harriet would hold up their hands in horror at the suggestion that there is any mealtime competition between the polite young ladies at this school, but nonetheless, it most certainly exists.

Now it might be thought that Amelia and I, who are the youngest, would be given some sort of preference at the table but such is not the situation at the Farnsworth school. Here, lately, it seems to be more of a case of "to the oldest belongs the spoils" with no thought or consideration for those students who may have brought valuable and nowadays very hard to get food and other merchandise with them, when they came to the school in the first place . . . without mentioning any names, of course.

Anyway for a while I thought I had discovered a method of winning these mealtime contests. I began in various ways to cause mild commotions at my end of the table. Sometimes I would kick Amelia or speak loudly to her or perhaps I would spill a glass of water or reach long distances for some article instead of asking to have it passed to me. In these and many other general ways I would just exhibit such terrible table manners that Miss Martha in desperation would all but drag me from my chair and bring me up to the seat next to her and across from Miss Harriet.

Well that plan worked very well for some time. Up there at the head of the table I was served right after the teachers and before any of the other girls and I was faring much better than I had for several semesters until Miss Martha finally realized that my bad conduct was intentional and then she began to send me away from the table altogether.

I might say that I think if Miss Harriet was in charge of the dining room here we might not have all these problems. Miss Harriet is generally much fairer than her sister about younger students getting their share of the food, but Miss Harriet, as my father used to say, is not piloting the steamboat. Also she is always daydreaming so much that she doesn't even notice what goes on. However, it is a different situation altogether when someone is sent away from the table. That person who is banished immediately gains Miss Harriet's total sympathy and as much of her support as Miss Harriet can afford.

I explained all this to Amelia Dabney who, like Miss Harriet, lives in a world of her own. They're not very similar worlds, of course. Miss Harriet's mind is generally in the past and is preoccupied with balls and parties she attended in the old days, or believes now that she did. I know this because the poor thing quite often talks to herself when she thinks she is alone.

On the other hand Amelia's world includes no human beings at all. It's filled with bats and bugs and all the wiggling, crawling creatures that live in logs and under rocks and in the crevices of trees. I believe Amelia Dabney would not care one whit if the whole human race was destroyed tomorrow as long as her dear woodland creatures were preserved from harm. I confess I sometimes wish I had another roommate because I am not all that fond of living in a room in which you are liable to find worms in your bureau drawers and bats on your bedposts.

"Don't worry about your dinner," I told her now. "Miss Harriet will be along in a bit with some yams and greens and possibly even a rasher or two of bacon because I think Miss Martha managed to bring some home today."

I was trying to comfort Amelia because she is not used to being in disgrace as I am. However, although she does live in mortal fear of a cross word from Miss Martha or from anyone else for that matter, she has less reason to worry about missing dinner than anyone else in this house. That girl has a trunk full of nuts, herb roots, berries and mushrooms, some being the poisonous ones, I suppose, which she had picked that afternoon and some others which could be eaten safely. I guess they were safe to eat because on this occasion Amelia was certainly eating them.

She offered me some but I refused politely. There's no doubt she knows a great many of the secrets of nature, but as long as I was certain that Miss Harriet would be coming along shortly anyway with whatever she'd been able to save for us from the table, I decided I wouldn't take a chance on the mushrooms. I did accept a handful of blackberries and a few walnuts and hazelnuts which were left over from last autumn.

"What in your opinion," I asked her, "is going to be the final end of this Yankee affair?"

"In all the orders that I know of in the animal and insect kingdoms, the intruder is never accepted peaceably by the existing species. That's stated very plainly in a book by an English naturalist which I have in my trunk."

"What happens to the intruders in these other kingdoms?" I asked her. I was trying to crack a walnut by slamming it in the bureau drawer and trying to accomplish it quietly so that Miss Martha wouldn't hear.

"Well," said Amelia thoughtfully, "sometimes they win out. I've seen a hunting wasp invade a nest of grasshoppers and kill or at least paralyze all of them with his stinger, so that each of them could be hauled away at leisure to be eaten."

"My goodness," I said, finally getting the walnut cracked but also splitting the side of the bureau drawer a bit, although not too noticeably, I thought. "I'm certainly glad I'm not a grasshopper."

"On the other hand," Amelia went on, "quite often the intruder doesn't win. I've seen a caterpillar invade a nest of tiny red ants and be charmed by them or diverted in some way until he was entirely at their mercy. The little ants seemed to be stroking the caterpillar with their feelers until he was quite relaxed and after a while he released a few drops of liquid from somewhere near his tail, and then all of the ants partook of this liquid which they seemed to enjoy very much. Then, having milked him, they joined together to drag that helpless caterpillar underground, intending, I suppose, to use him for future feedings."

"Good heavens," I said. "Was that caterpillar permanently injured?"

"I'm not sure, although that's not too important from a naturalist's point of view. The caterpillar would have died in the spring anyway when he became a butterfly and meanwhile he was providing food all winter for that little colony of ants."

That girl certainly entertains herself in the weirdest fashion. I don't think I've ever met another person who will spend her time as Amelia does, crouched for hours over an ant hill or a grasshopper's nest, and then draw a moral lesson from the activities of those insects, if it was a moral lesson she was trying to pass on to me at this time.

"You still haven't said what you think Miss Martha will finally do with your Corporal McBurney," I told her.

"I don't know," she said. "I hope he gets well soon and goes away. Or else dies."

"Amelia Dabney," I cried somewhat shocked.

"If he's going to be treated meanly here, I'd rather have it that way," she said. "In fact if I thought he was going to be treated meanly, I believe I would take him back to the woods tonight."

"I doubt if he can walk," I said.

"I'd help him like I did before."

"He's unconscious now."

"Maybe he'll come around after a while."

"Well if he does," I said, "that's due to Miss Martha's taking care of him and stitching up his leg. That certainly doesn't seem like meanness to me. 'Give Satan his due,' is what my mother always says and I think what's good enough for Satan is good enough for Miss Martha."

"How he is treated now is no guarantee of how he will be treated later," Amelia said. "I would like you to promise me something, Marie. Promise me that if I decide it's better that Corporal McBurney leaves here, you will join me in helping him escape."

"What help would he need?" I wanted to know. "He's a grown man of at least eighteen years of age, isn't he, and maybe even more. When his leg heals he can just walk right out of here and go back to the Federal Army or the North Pole or anywhere he likes."

"Promise me anyway," Amelia insisted.

To quiet her I did. I couldn't for the very life of me see what possible harm could come to Corporal McBurney from five girls and three old women but to comfort that nervous child I agreed. I call her a child even though she is three years older than I am, because I am certain I will be a grownup adult long before Miss Amelia Dabney.

Shortly after that she decided she would go back downstairs and see how Corporal McBurney was getting on. That was perfectly all right as far as I was concerned because if she didn't return before Miss Harriet came with our secret dinner, it just meant that much more for me. Of course Amelia had eaten so many of her woodland delicacies that she undoubtedly had no appetite for normal food by this time.

"If you are not otherwise occupied," she said, pausing by the door, "I wish you'd keep an eye on my *chelydra serpentina*."

"Your what?"

"My little snapping turtle. He's underneath the bed in that old jewel box of yours, which was empty and which you weren't using anyway."

"If anybody ever gave me any jewels they would have to be put in that box," I told her sharply. "I believe that is why my mother presented me with it. I don't think she would be happy at all to hear that some dirty old snapping turtle was occupying my teakwood jewel box." My Lord you just have to be on your guard every moment with that girl if you don't want every one of your possessions used to shelter the monsters she collects. In any case I absolutely refused to have anything to do with her snapping turtle.

She left the room then, moving very quietly as she always does, and went down the stairs. That girl certainly would have no trouble, I thought, escaping from anywhere or anyone she pleased. She can come and go like a summer shadow without anyone hardly ever taking notice. I suppose if someone really wanted to get away from the Farnsworth School without attracting attention the best possible person to go to for advice would be Miss Amelia Dabney.

Amelia Dabney

The rest of the School was still at dinner when I came down the stairs to have a look at Corporal John McBurney so that I was able to enter the parlor without disturbing them.

He really seemed to be quite a bit improved. He was still very pale and as motionless as before but his hands seemed warmer and his breathing was becoming almost regular and quite audible now. I went to the garden door and opened it slightly to give him a bit more air.

The day had ended by this time and most of the sounds of battle with it, but the woods to the east of us were still on fire. What was happening to all the birds and animals in that part of the woods, I wondered. Would God permit them to escape the flames? Would He protect their dens and nests until the armies moved on?

I had found a quail's nest a few weeks before in that part of the woods. It was a wonderfully well-constructed thing, sheltered in a clump of high grass and concealed from the eyes of passing hawks by a covering spray of wild grape vine. There were eleven little eggs in that nest on the afternoon I discovered it and I wondered now if those baby quail had all come out of their shells and left their nest before today. A God who could permit those baby quail to be destroyed, I thought, would be a most cruel kind of God and I don't believe I would ever be able to warm up to Him.

In fact sometimes I feel more concern for those innocent animals that are suffering in this war than I do for all the soldiers on either side. The soldiers are at least to some degree responsible for their own fates. Most of them have probably volunteered to be where they are, or even if they haven't, they can still escape the burning woods like Corporal McBurney.

Whether I would feel this way if my brothers were still alive is something I cannot say. I do know that Dick and Billy both would probably laugh at my sentiments if they were present now, the same way they used to laugh when I cried at their hunting quail and pheasant in our fields at home. Also I know that if they were both to be allowed back from the grave tomorrow, they would surely volunteer again, for fear they had missed some noise and excitement the first time. And no animal would ever be foolish enough to do that.

Well I suppose whether you prefer animals or people depends a great deal on the individual circumstances. I do know that I never felt very close to anyone at Farnsworth—except very occasionally Marie Deveraux—until I found Corporal McBurney and brought him back here. And that was because, I decided on that first night, he was a person very much like me. I am what you might call a very alone person and I had the feeling Corporal McBurney was that kind of person too.

The night sounds on the place were beginning as usual, war or no war. The cicadas in the oak tree out back started it and then the crickets joined in, followed by the frogs in the creek. The voice of one big bullfrog was missing for a while and I was beginning to think that something might have happened to him but then he began to speak his mind . . . galump . . . galump . . . galump. Then a tree toad put in his whistle and some nightingales joined in and finally the old owl, who lives in the eaves of this house and who is very quiet during the day for fear of being discovered, realized that night was safely on us and added his screech to the chorus.

These natural sounds were punctuated now and then by the crack and echo of a rifle from way off in the woods. The pickets on both sides were still nervous, I suppose. It is probably difficult to leave off anything, even killing, when you've been hard at it all day. "Poor lonely pickets," I thought. "I do wish all of you could find your way out of the woods tonight." And came back then to Corporal McBurney who had found his way.

Was he sleeping normally now or still unconscious from his weakness? He didn't stir at all when I sat down on the floor next to the settee and put my lips very close to his ear.

"Corporal McBurney," I whispered. "You may not be able to hear me but I want to tell you anyway that I intend to help you in any way I can. I am your friend, Corporal McBurney. If you are mistreated here you must come to me and I will help you. There may be some people here who will hate you because of the uniform you wear, but I don't feel that way. I like you and I want you to get well again. Remember that, Corporal McBurney. I am your friend."

"What are you doing there, you little vagabond?" It was Edwina Morrow standing in the doorway. Apparently she had recovered from her earlier fainting spell.

"I was telling Corporal McBurney something private," I said.

"Come away from him, you grubby little thing. He's not one of your birds or beetles to be fondled by your dirty fingers."

"My hands are reasonably clean, Edwina," I said. "And I'm not touching Corporal McBurney anyway. I'm only talking to him."

"How can you talk to him when he's in that condition, you little fool!"

Edwina always calls me a lot of names, prefacing each one of them with "little." I don't know if a little something is worse than a big something but Edwina always makes it sound that way. Of course, I don't really mind what she calls me. I know it is Edwina's nature to say these things and I'm sure it indicates no personal dislike of me, at least not of me more than of anyone else.

It's true that I sometimes get a bit more of it than the other girls, but I think that may be because I don't retaliate. When she made a particularly nasty remark to Alice Simms one time, Alice walked right across the room and slapped her. Again, one time when she said something which Marie Deveraux took amiss, Marie, who—like a good many of those Louisiana people—has strong ideas about personal honor, bided her time for a week or more and then on a Sunday morning before church services dumped a pail of dirty water on Edwina who was walking in the garden. Naturally Marie was punished severely for this, but punishment on those occasions means very little to Marie. And it certainly made Edwina wary of crossing her in the future. Marie may be only a ten-year-old girl but all the same she is an extremely revengeful person.

Edwina entered the room now holding something behind her back. "Go upstairs to bed as Miss Martha has instructed you," she told me.

"She didn't instruct me to go to bed," I said. "She only told Marie and I that we had to go to our rooms without our dinner. What is it you have there behind you, Edwina?"

"Nothing," she answered quickly. "It's none of your business."

"It seems to be a bowl of potato and leek soup," I said, "and you're spilling it on the rug."

"Oh well," Edwina said, "if you must be so nosy. It's simply that I got tired of listening to all the stupid chatter in the dining room, so I brought my soup in here to finish it."

"Go ahead and finish it then. I won't bother you."

"I shall when I am ready."

"The soup will be quite cold if you don't hurry."

"It's really none of your concern, Amelia," she said angrily. "It's quite possible, isn't it, that I prefer it cold!"

I thought of something then—something that might have come instantly to mind had it been anyone other than Edwina bringing the soup from the table. I resolved to test my suspicions.

"Perhaps I will go back upstairs," I said. "As long as you are here to keep an eye on Corporal McBurney."

"That's the first intelligent thing you've said. He needs to get his rest. He doesn't need little children bothering him."

At least I had progressed to being merely a little child now, which, coming from Edwina, was practically a compliment.

"Well, goodnight, Edwina," I said, walking slowly out of the room.

"Good riddance," she said, watching me.

I went only part way up the stairs and then paused and waited there for a moment. Then I came down again as quietly as possible and returned to the living room doorway. I don't really like to spy on people but I had to make sure of this situation, since Corporal McBurney was concerned.

Sure enough Edwina was over by his side trying to feed him soup. I wanted to call out because I was mortally afraid she would choke him, but on the other hand I did appreciate her taking an interest in him and I was also afraid that if I were to trap her in this generous act, she might turn her back on him forever. And right now, I decided, Corporal McBurney needs every friend he can get in this house.

Surprisingly enough, some of the soup seemed to be staying down. Most of it was dribbling over his chin and every time that happened Edwina would very patiently take the spoon away and ever so gently wipe his chin with her handkerchief. I noticed it was a different handkerchief than the one she had told us earlier was of Chinese silk. Well, she was certainly donating a lot of handkerchiefs to the cause of Corporal McBurney. And

Corporal McBurney was very definitely swallowing some of that potato and leek soup.

"Well," I thought, "if this is what you're really like, Edwina Morrow, you can call me any names you please and I won't mind one bit. Also I will keep your secret, if that's the way you want it. After all, the only important thing now is that Corporal McBurney gets well."

Therefore, being satisfied that my Yankee soldier was in good hands, at least for the time being, I came away from the doorway and went back up the stairs to the room I share with Marie Deveraux.

Harriet Farnsworth

After the dinner dishes had been cleared away, I decided it would be only charitable to take a bit of food upstairs to Amelia Dabney and Marie Deveraux who had been sent to their room in disgrace. My sister would disapprove of my actions, I'm sure, and I know she is well within her rights in disciplining these girls for their impertinent conduct, but an entire night is a long time for a growing child to go without nourishment and the Lord knows they don't get as much of it as they should anyway in these days of shortage.

With the help of our good Mattie, I managed to garner a part of a loaf of bread, some peas and some salad greens. A bowl full of these items, together with a bit of bacon I had saved from my own plate, I thought might tide the two young sinners over until morning. They accepted my gifts in their usual off-handed manner—like tribute brought to royalty rather than dole to the needy.

"Eat quickly, girls," I told them, "and then out with your light and into bed with you before Miss Martha comes by on her rounds."

"We can handle everything all right, Miss Harriet," said Marie casually as she nibbled at her food. "We have a system in this room whereby we can allow Miss Martha to come all the way up the stairs and even start down the hall, and then we can blow out our candle in an instant and be in bed looking as though we had been asleep for hours before Miss Martha reaches our door. Our main defense in this system is the fact that Amelia here has very good ears and can hear the faintest movement from anywhere in the house."

"It doesn't seem a very honest system to me," I said. "Also candles wasted now may be regretted at a later time when you really need them."

"We have extra ones," said that child who never lacks an answer. "Amelia has brought a store of beeswax from the woods and we've made our own."

"Save some of the bread for me please, Marie," said Amelia, picking at her greens.

"There's plenty for both of you," I assured her. "You can share it equally."

"She doesn't want it for herself," Marie explained. "It's for her turtle. She says her turtle's ailing and she forgot to bring him any flies today because of the trouble with McBurney."

"I see," I said, wanting to see but finding it rather difficult. "Well, God made all of us . . . you and I and Mister McBurney . . . and Amelia's turtle."

"Do animals go to heaven when they die?" asked Amelia, turning that elfin little face to me.

"I don't think so," I said. "I believe God permits them to have their happiness in this life."

"What about the animals that are dying in the woods tonight?"

"Well," I said, "first of all we've not sure they're dying, are we? Perhaps they're all escaping the fire. And even if a few are trapped . . . I'm sure they're the old ones who are ready to pass on anyway. And I'm sure God makes certain that it happens painlessly."

"What about us?" Marie asked. "Don't we ever get our happiness in this life?"

"Not very many people do."

"I intend to have mine," Marie said. "I'm not at all sure I'll care much for heaven, especially if they have a lot of rules and regulations, so I think I'll take a bit of mine on earth."

"You will be very lucky then, if you accomplish it," I said. "You are more fortunate now than Amelia. She has already had great unhappiness in the loss of her two brothers."

"Well," said Marie, "my father is in the army too and so is my brother Louis, and they could both be dead for all I know—the way the mail is nowadays. Have you ever been truly happy, Miss Harriet?"

"Yes, once . . . a long time ago . . . but it didn't last very long."

"What caused it to end?" Amelia wanted to know.

"Reason and common sense," I said. It is difficult to know how far to go with children such as these. One wants to be—must be—kind to them and yet there is always the suspicion that they know more than they ask. I often think they know the answers and are only interested in your reaction to the questions.

"Is Corporal McBurney happy, do you think?" asked Amelia now.

"If he isn't, and he recovers, we must try to make his stay here as pleasant as we can. Although I should think the mere fact of his being out of the war for a while would make him quite happy."

"Yes, that's true," said Amelia thoughtfully. "He said as much today."

"What was your happiness like when you experienced it long ago, Miss Harriet?" asked Marie, the chief inquisitor.

"Very nice."

"Do you think it will ever come to you again?"

"I no longer count on it."

"Would you be glad if it did?"

"I . . . yes, I suppose I would . . . but it could not be the same, because you see the knowledge of unhappiness makes it impossible to ever more experience unalloyed bliss. That's only possible in a state of innocence."

Innocence? Yes, they seemed completely innocent—watching me quietly—Amelia with her sad brown eyes and Marie with her guileless blue ones.

"Scrub your faces and your teeth and brush your hair now, both of you. One hundred vigorous strokes each, so that when you are beautiful young ladies your hair will glisten and shine as you are whirled around the floor at your first ball."

"Did your hair glisten at your first ball, Miss Harriet?" Marie inquired.

"It did, yes. It was jet black and shining—very much like Miss Edwina Morrow's hair now. I wore it in a chignon . . . with a gold clip, I remember. . . ."

"Who escorted you to your first ball?" asked Amelia.

"My brother."

"He's dead too, isn't he?" said Marie.

"Miss Martha believes so."

"But you don't?" wondered Amelia.

"I don't think about it."

"Your hair has a gray streak in it now," said Amelia. "Is that from sorrow or disappointment?"

"More likely old age," I said.

"Why do you have gray in your hair?" inquired Marie. "While Miss Martha who is older has none."

"Perhaps you had better ask Miss Martha that," I said. "Now do as I have told you, then say your prayers and get to bed."

"I'm not much interested in balls myself," declared Marie. "I know I shall never be a raving beauty, so I feel it is all a great waste of time."

"I'm not very interested in balls either," Amelia said, "unless maybe I could attend one sometime with Corporal McBurney. Do you think he would accompany me to some such affair, Miss Harriet . . . after the war is over, of course."

"He might be very happy to do so," I said, "but I suggest you don't mention it to him right now."

On that note I closed their door and came back downstairs to the living room. The lamp was still lit on the table by the settee and our patient was still unconscious. Seated in a chair drawn up beside him now was Edwina Morrow of the vixenish disposition and the hair of my youth. She looked up defensively but without comment as I approached. Corporal McBurney still seemed a long way from attending any balls with young Amelia.

"Has he come around at all?" I whispered to Edwina.

"He opened his eyes once," she said, "and his lips have moved several times as though he was trying to speak."

"Well, that's something," I said. "Perhaps by morning he'll be much better. You may go to your room now, Edwina, and I'll sit with him for a while."

"I don't mind staying." She stated it flatly and waited for my protest.

"I know you don't dear, but you need your rest. It's really very good of you to be so considerate of the young man. I'm sure he'll be most grateful when he recovers."

"Do you think he will recover, Miss Harriet?" she asked.

"He seems to be making progress. We can only pray that he continues to do so."

"I don't set much store by prayer," she said. "I don't recall ever getting anything through prayer."

"Did you ever pray for anything?"

"Once—long ago. Did you ever pray for anything, Miss Harriet?"

"Why certainly," I said.

"And was your prayer answered?"

Should I tell the truth? No, it wasn't granted. In fact I haven't really prayed for years. I just go through the motions to keep my sister happy and to maintain the image of a devout teacher in a Christian school. I fear God—as I fear many things—but I don't pray to Him. Because I know the thing I would ask for, if I did pray, would not be granted. Indeed, I suppose if I were God, I would not grant it either.

"They say that no prayers are ever wasted," I said circumspectly. "If you don't always get what you pray for, sometimes you get something better."

"If we prayed that the Yankee might live, and he died, would that be something better?"

I had been too quick with my reassessment. Edwina was being her usual difficult self. "I don't see how—and please don't ask me, dear—but I suppose it could be."

"Oh I can see how it could be." She smiled at my impatience. "If what happens to you while you are living is bad enough, then you are better off dead . . . don't you agree? In any case I don't intend to pray for this Yankee. I'm content to let nature take its course—since I'm sure that's what's bound to happen anyway."

"As you please, my dear."

"He looks something like my father," she went on unexpectedly. "Did you ever see my father, Miss Harriet? He's quite a handsome man."

"I'm afraid I've never had that pleasure," I said. She was quite aware that I knew Mister Morrow had never visited the school, but if she wanted to pretend that he had been here on some occasion and that I had unfortunately missed him—well, it cost me nothing to tolerate her sad little whim.

"You must take after your mother then," I remarked and meant it well—meant nothing at all, in fact, beyond an attempt to introduce a topic which would not result in argument. "I assume your father must be of fair complexion."

"No, he is not. My father is dark—darker even than I," Edwina said quickly. "I only meant that this boy resembles him in feature."

"Well then, your mother must be most attractive, and you must have features like her, since you don't look anything like this young man."

"Why must you pursue this point, Miss Harriet? Why must you harp on such a trivial matter!"

"I'm sorry, dear. I've forgotten, if I ever knew—is your mother still alive?"

"Certainly, she's alive!"

"Please. . . ." I said, "I didn't mean to upset you, child."

"I'm not your child! Stop acting so ridiculous, Miss Harriet!"

"But it was you," I said, befuddled, and then realized there was nothing I could say. Once again I had learned the folly of trying to be nice to Edwina Morrow.

"You may go to your room . . . at once, Edwina."

"Yes ma'am." She gave me a mocking little curtsy.

"Oh please . . ." I said. It's the word I seem to use most often, but I find I just cannot be severe with anyone for very long, even Edwina. She did look like such a lonely little girl as she turned away. "Please wait a moment, Edwina."

"Yes ma'am?"

"How old are you, Edwina?"

"It's in Miss Martha's enrollment book."

"I don't have that with me at the moment."

"I'm sixteen."

"Almost seventeen?"

"Not quite seventeen."

"It's strange how elastic ages are," I said, amused. "If I were to ask Marie—who is ten, I think—the same question, she would surely answer 'Eleven,' meaning that she was in her eleventh year, but advancing herself all the same. Would you like to remain sixteen, Edwina?"

"I have no preference."

"You are the oldest girl here, I think."

"Possibly . . . but only a few months older than Emily. This again is very trivial conversation, Miss Harriet."

"I know," I said. "I just wanted to—well, send you away less abruptly."

"I accept your apology."

"I'm not apologizing, Miss!" I'm afraid I shouted, angry again.

"Yes ma'am. May I go as you have suggested?" Now I would have sworn she was deliberately baiting me.

"What would you like to do, Edwina? I'll leave it up to you. If you would rather stay in here for a while, you may do so."

"Alone?"

"Well, with Corporal McBurney. And I thought I might take advantage of the lamp to do some sewing."

"I think now I'd prefer to retire, Miss Harriet."

"All right," I said, as gently as I could. "Just one more thing—and this is not trivial—at least to me, it isn't. I was reminded tonight that your hair is almost exactly the shade and texture that mine was when I was your age, or at least I like to think now that it was."

She stood there quietly for a moment, seeking the snare in the compliment, I suppose, and then finally decided if it was there, it was not a dangerous one. "Thank you, Miss Harriet," she said quite graciously.

"You are a very attractive young lady, Edwina. You should be very happy to be growing up. You are without any doubt the most attractive young lady we have had in this school for a very long time."

"Thank you again," she said, with no malice at all in it now. "It doesn't really make any difference to me, but it's very kind of you." She smiled wanly—one of the few times I have ever seen Edwina smile—turned to go, then paused. "If I can help with the nursing of the Yankee, I would be obliged if you'd ask me. You may have noticed my turning a bit faint here this afternoon, but that was due to the severe headache I've had all day."

"I assumed it was something of the sort, Edwina. And we shall certainly call on you as soon as help is needed."

She smiled again and left the room, passing and ignoring old Mattie in the doorway. Mattie watched somberly as Edwina went up the stairs, then she came over to me.

"I've just done something that makes me feel good," I announced. "I have turned away wrath with a compliment. I've just told that little lady how good-looking I thought she was."

"Oh she's good-lookin all right," Mattie agreed. It showed the dear soul's inherent humanity, since she has always had more difficulty with Edwina than with any other student in the school.

"She's sometimes an extremely vexatious young person," I said, "but I have hopes now that kindness will eventually win her over."

"Kindness won't rub out her troubles," said Mattie.

"Well I know she's unhappy over her family situation. She and Alice Simms are somewhat alike in that respect. Alice is looking for her father and Edwina is looking for her mother."

"I don't think she's lookin for her mother," Mattie said.

"I meant it figuratively. I don't know exactly what the situation is but I gather that her parents are not living together. And of course she doesn't see much of her father either. He has never come to visit her and she's never been home since she's been with us. I must say he keeps her well supplied with money, although that's strange too, since she never seems to get any mail from him."

"She brought the money with her," Mattie asserted. "She keeps it hid in her room and in other places around the house. Leastways she did. She might not have much of it left anymore."

"Perhaps that's bothering her too, if her money's running out."

"It could be part of it, but it ain't the big part."

"All right," I said, humoring her. "Give us your solution, Mattie. What is the chief cause of Edwina's misery?"

"It's because she don't know who she is—she don't know what she is."

"How do you mean, Mattie?"

"She's got black blood in her."

"Mattie . . . Mattie," I whispered, horrified. "You must never say a thing like that."

"I wouldn't say it if it wasn't true."

"But, Mattie, she's no darker really than little Marie Deveraux, and her features are almost as sharp as mine . . ."

"Take another look at her, Miss Harriet. Take a good look at her eyes. That's why her Daddy keeps her here. That's why he never lets her come home."

"Now, Mattie," I said as firmly as I could. "No matter what your personal opinions are, you must never repeat a word of this to anyone else."

"No ma'am I ain't gonna."

"Not even to Miss Martha."

"I ain't gonna say any more about it. I wouldn't've said it to you, only you brought it up."

"Even if it were true—and I'm not prepared to accept it, Mattie—but even if it were, it wouldn't make any difference. Maybe the child doesn't even know it herself."

"She knows."

"Nevertheless we must never mention it again—to her or anyone. Nobody else in this house shall hear of it from either one of us."

"Maybe one other person has already."

"Who?"

"That Yankee over there. He had his eyes open a minute ago and maybe his ears too."

I turned instantly but he seemed exactly as before—pale, motionless, breathing regularly but hardly noticeably. "You're mistaken, Mattie," I said after a long moment. "He's still unconscious. It may have been the way the light played on his face."

"Yes ma'am . . . whatever you say."

Alice Simms entered hesitantly then. A little Dresden figurine is the way I always think of her. However low the estate of her forebearers, there could certainly be no doubt of her racial background. With those blue eyes and blond hair she needed only a staff and a green hillside behind her to play the lovely shepherdess.

"We're omitting evening prayers tonight, Alice," I informed her. "As a group, I mean. You may say your prayers in your room. We want to keep it as quiet as possible in here for the sake of our patient."

"Yes ma'am," said my little pastoral maiden, coming in anyway.

I have long been determined to make something of this child. It is my theory that a girl like Alice can grow beyond her beginnings to the loftiest of estates, and it is for that reason I have stood by her and taken her part on several occasions when my sister was becoming most discouraged with her deportment and her ability and desire to learn, and was once or twice at the point of putting her out of the school. Alice is not the most difficult of students by any means but there is the financial problem and that, unfortunately, adds to her sins in my sister's eyes. However one of the problems in Alice's case has lately proven to be a blessing. Even Martha cannot send a girl away in these days if she has nowhere to send her.

"I believe he looks more handsome now than he did before," my homeless one observed.

"That's probably only because he's cleaner," I said. "I washed his face and combed his hair a bit before I came in to dinner."

"He needs to be shaved too," said Alice. "His beard is too boyish to be really distinguished looking and the way it is now, it's only scraggly."

"Well I suppose I could find an old razor of my father's or my brother's but I wouldn't attempt any such operation in his present condition. We're not putting him on exhibit . . . we're only trying to make him well."

"He probably ought to be given a thorough washing though, don't you think, Miss Harriet?"

"How do you mean, 'a thorough washing'?"

"Well . . . a bath maybe."

"If the young man recovers, he can take his own bath."

"Yes ma'am," said the golden one unabashed.

Emily Stevenson, our cadet sergeant-major, came in then. "Miss Harriet, Miss Martha would like to see you in the kitchen. At once," Emily reported.

"All right. We're not having evening prayers in here tonight, Emily, so you can go to your room any time you like."

"Thank you, Miss Harriet," she said, not quite saluting. "Did you mention that to Miss Martha? She told me we would have our prayers in here as usual in ten minutes and she desires me to inform the other girls."

"All right," I said, a trifle peevishly I suppose. "Miss Martha has apparently forgotten that some of the girls have been sent to bed already."

"No, she remembers that. I am instructed to summon the punishment girls to the living room so that they may pray for forgiveness."

"I think that is very unfair," Alice commented. "If one is sent to bed without dinner, one should certainly not be required to repent in public later."

"What you think will not change the course of history, I'm afraid," Emily observed. "Also there seems to be some doubt as to whether the girls in question have gone without their dinners. Miss Martha has discovered that some food is missing and she believes that Marie and Amelia may have plundered it."

"Oh now, now," I said. "I must speak with Miss Martha about this."

"Yes, ma'am," said Emily cooly. "She would like you to do just that."

My sister has sometimes declared that she could leave Farnsworth in the charge of Emily Stevenson and be secure in the knowledge that Emily would run the school as efficiently as she ever could, and very likely much more efficiently than I. It is probably a fair enough estimate of Emily's capabilities. Unfortunately, Emily is also aware of her talents for leadership and this, at times, makes our relationship a rather awkward one. However I had no time to worry about it at the moment. I was too busy trying to think of ways to explain the shortages in the kitchen without involving Marie and Amelia.

"Come with me, I need you," I told Mattie. "Emily, inform the others as you have been instructed. Alice, keep a watch on the young man—but don't touch him."

"Touch him?" said Alice, wide-eyed. "Why in the world would I ever do that?"

Alicia Simms

Did I touch him? Well, yes, when I was alone with him, I leaned over the back of the settee and touched him ever so gently with my finger on the tip of his nose. Then I touched his forehead, then I touched his cheek. He really ought to be shaved, I decided. He would be ever so much more handsome if he were clean shaven.

I had a rather crazy thought then. It was that I would like to kiss Corporal McBurney. I would kiss him ever so gently, I thought, not hard enough to awaken him but only just enough to make him aware that someone was kissing him and to make him dream of that person, so that when he finally did awaken he would remember and would seek that person out and say to her, "Alicia Simms, I remember you from my dreams. I have come for you now, Alicia. I have come to take you away from here forever."

Then he would propose to me and I would accept, and we would be married right here in this parlor. And my mother would come to the wedding and all the girls and their parents and their brothers in uniform.

There would be officers of all ranks from our armies . . . generals and lieutenants and captains, and maybe some handsome common soldiers too. And beautiful ladies in velvet and silk and brocade dresses, trimmed with lace and gold ornaments, and wearing rings and necklaces and jewels in their hair, and on their heads the latest and most fashionable hats from Paris, every one of which would be surmounted by a gigantic ostrich feather.

And my father would come too. Perhaps my mother would bring him. Maybe she would find him again just in time to bring him to the wedding, and he would come to the parlor of the Farnsworth School on that afternoon—it would be a late spring afternoon when the jonquils and the lilacs were in full bloom and we could smell them through the open doors and hear the bees in the fields and the bobwhites in the woods—and he would see me for the first time, standing here, and he would simply not believe it.

"I positively cannot believe that this is my little girl," he would say to Mother. "She is even more beautiful than you are, Sarah." And then he would grab hold of me and hug me and lift me off the floor as though I really was still a little girl. "And then," I thought, "my father will take me by the hand and lead me over to the garden window where you will be waiting, Corporal McBurney."

"I love you," I thought, and said it. "I love you, Corporal McBurney," I said. "I would like to kiss you." And did. I leaned over and did it—quickly the first time and more slowly the second.

The second time I would have sworn he kissed me back. It startled me, I will admit. I drew back and looked at him, but he seemed the same—still very pale, eyes closed, breathing very softly. Or was it quite as softly? The other girls came in then for evening prayers, which prevented my checking Corporal McBurney's reactions a third time.

"Hurry along, hurry along," Miss Martha was telling them as she drove them forward with her Bible. "We don't want to keep this lamp burning all night."

Miss Harriet and old Mattie were leading the procession, the two of them red-eyed—from recent weeping, obviously. In fact Mattie was still sniffling a bit. Apparently Miss Martha had been reprimanding them in the kitchen over the problem of missing food. Very likely Miss Harriet had been up to her old tricks again of begging food from Mattie to take upstairs to the punishment girls and Miss Martha had trapped her at it. If that were the case, however, I couldn't think ill of Miss Harriet, since the dear old soul had done the same for me on several occasions when I was being punished, and even several times when I hadn't broken any rules but when Miss

Harriet simply thought I wasn't getting enough to eat. And that is all of the time recently, if anyone is interested.

"What are you doing there, Miss Alice?" Miss Martha demanded now.

"She's watching the injured young man," Miss Harriet said in a somewhat broken voice. "I left her here to watch over him. Did I do wrong there too, sister? Did I exceed my authority in that?"

"Harriet, you will please control yourself," Miss Martha told her. "If your emotions are such that you cannot pray quietly with us, then I suggest you leave the room. That applies to Mattie too."

They didn't leave because they didn't dare to leave. Evening prayers have always been a very serious matter with Miss Martha. Had Miss Harriet and Mattie gone off as she suggested, very likely they would have had something worse to weep about on the following day.

"Now then," said Miss Martha, "if you will take your places. Miss Amelia and Miss Marie may stand for prayers this evening."

The rest of us took our chairs and the two culprits and Mattie stood in back of us. That, of course, was perfectly all right with Marie because she never takes any active part in our services anyway, since she is a Papist, except for maybe muttering a grudging "Amen" once in a while when she is feeling particularly sociable, which isn't often. Most of the time she is in some kind of trouble with Miss Martha anyway by the time evening prayers come around, and she therefore tries to make herself as quietly offensive as possible.

"Stop fidgeting, Marie," Miss Martha directed her now. "Bow your head and fold your hands like the others. I'm sure the Pope won't mind. Amelia, what are you eating?"

Amelia, frightened as usual, gulped and choked and had to be pounded on the back by Marie. "It was a hazelnut," Marie reported. "It's gone now."

"Almighty God," Miss Martha sighed, and paused just long enough to make it seem a curse. "Almighty God, we ask thy special blessing on this school tonight. The troubled times continue—the hardships increase, but we can endure if Thou will but give us the strength. Our chief prayer is that this school and its occupants will escape Thy total wrath in the days ahead. We ask this in all humility, knowing that we are not worthy of Thy attention. Some of us are weak, very weak. Some of us who should be strong and capable of giving good example to the children in our care have not enough of Your wisdom in us to enable us to see that good discipline is the greatest kindness we can offer to our charges."

As Martha paused for breath Miss Harriet began to weep again. "Amen," said Emily, leaping into the breech. Emily is always ready to second any call for discipline.

"Spare the rod and spoil the child is as true now as it ever was," Miss Martha went on. "Now I will impose no further punishment on the two girls who were given their dinner after I had sentenced them to bed without it. I cannot see that this is in any way their fault. May the Lord forgive the person who is guilty and make her see the error of her ways."

Miss Harriet stood up then. "The Lord isn't the one offended here," she cried. "Or if He is, He isn't complaining about it. I'm afraid you are the only one who is offended, Martha."

Well we all practically went right through the floor at that. That was the first time in the memory of any students at the Farnsworth School that Miss Harriet had ever had the gumption to speak back to her sister.

"It is all well and good to talk about troubled times and hardships," Miss Harriet continued in a trembling voice, "but there is such a thing as unnecessary hardship, and also something called the virtue of mercy, which ought not to be out of place at a school for children."

Then she started to weep again which more or less spoiled the whole performance. Miss Martha told her that kind of conduct was disgraceful and asked her to please sit down and be quiet and not interrupt the prayers again. Miss Harriet sat down but she did continue to sob a bit.

"I am inclined to be somewhat tolerant of these irregularities and emotional outbursts," said Miss Martha when she had everyone's attention again, "because of the unusual state of excitement brought on us today by the coming of our wounded visitor. However, it is precisely because of the presence of this person that we can have no more of it. If he recovers, there might come a time when we may need all the steadfastness and strength of purpose we can summon in order to preserve our welfare here. Of course I don't anticipate his being with us long enough to cause us any real difficulty, but in these times, it is well that we be prepared for any eventuality. And a great part of that preparation is self discipline."

"Amen," said Emily again.

Well I thought remarks like that were foolish but naturally I made no comment. It just seemed ridiculous to me that a harmless-looking boy like Corporal McBurney would ever cause us any injury. But thinking about it later, I guess it was not physical injury Miss Martha had in mind.

She leafed through her Bible then, reading us some appropriate passages which applied to her remarks. I can't remember the exact verses but I know they had to do with sinful people and the destruction of Jerusalem and the importance of being watchful in the night.

Then, as was customary, Miss Martha asked if any of the girls—"or more particularly any of the faculty," with a hard stare at Miss Harriet— would like to confess any of their errors of the day and ask God's forgive- ness for them. There was no response to this invitation. There seldom has been during my years at Farnsworth School.

"Then," said Miss Martha after a pause, "if you all feel you are inno- cent of any misdeeds today, I can only pray that God will enlighten you. Now we'll move on to the petitions. Does anyone wish to ask for special blessings?"

Edwina held up her hand. "I pray that the Lord will see fit to restore the health of the wounded Yankee," she said, looking at all of us quickly as though she expected an argument.

"That is a proper prayer," Miss Martha said. "We will pray for his re- turn to health and for his early departure."

We all lowered our heads—even Marie participating in this—and asked for blessing for Corporal McBurney. I prayed especially hard for his recovery, but not his departure. I wanted Corporal McBurney to get better and stay here with us more than anything I had ever wanted in my entire life. At that moment I wanted it more than I wanted my mother to come back and take me away from Farnsworth, and even more than I wanted to find my father.

"Are there any more petitions," said Miss Martha, deciding that Cor- poral McBurney had received enough of God's attention.

"I ask God's blessing on our armies," said Emily. "I ask that General Lee's army emerge victorious from the battle in the woods. I pray that this may be the final crushing blow against the enemy and that our boys may then return home to their families and that our great Confederacy may prosper and live in peace forever." She paused and then continued, faltering a bit. "Also I pray that those who are already gone will be the last to go."

"On both sides," said Miss Harriet, wiping her eyes. "I pray for the safety of all our relatives and friends in the field, especially those in posi- tions of great responsibility, like Emily's father and Marie's father. I also pray for our deceased kindred. Amelia's two brothers . . . Emily's brother . . . Miss Martha's and my brother . . . who is missing. . . ."

"And who we are certain now is dead," said Miss Martha. Miss Martha cannot refrain from correcting a mistake even in a prayer.

"May they be in happiness somewhere . . . waiting for us. . . ." It seemed like there was more to it but Miss Harriet's voice is so soft at most times it is difficult to hear her and now the prayer just trailed off into silence.

"And may we conduct ourselves in such a manner in our daily lives," said Miss Martha, determined to have the last word, "that we may be worthy of joining our relatives in Heaven. Are there any more subjects for our prayers?"

Amelia raised her hand shyly. "My snapping turtle is ill," she said.

"Your what?"

"My little snapping turtle. He won't come out of his shell."

"I'm afraid that is not a proper subject for prayer," said Miss Martha coldly. "Pray for your departed relatives and not sick reptiles. If there are no more proper petitions we shall close by asking for God's continued help and blessing for tomorrow. May we all be kept from harm throughout this night."

"Amen!" said Mattie loudly. Mattie is always allowed to say the final Amen. I believe this has been the custom at our school for a number of years, although Miss Martha is always threatening to dispense with it because Mattie has the habit of shouting her Amens before Miss Martha is quite ready.

"Amen," I said to myself. "May Corporal McBurney also be kept from harm tonight." I remember distinctly saying that to myself on that first night. I don't know what in the world I thought might harm him but I said it anyway. However I don't remember ever saying it on any night after that.

Miss Martha and Miss Harriet went over to have another look at him before retiring. "He does seem better, sister," Miss Harriet observed, quite subdued now.

"He doesn't seem good to me at all," said Miss Martha.

"He's sleeping quietly."

"That's weakness."

"His color is much better."

"That is fever."

"The bleeding has stopped."

"And the leg is beginning to swell. Do you see? Here and here. . . ."

"That could be from the tightness of the bandage, couldn't it?" asked Miss Harriet hopefully. "I'm sure his breathing is much more regular than before."

"Possibly," Miss Martha conceded grudgingly. "In any case there is nothing more we can do at the moment. Mattie, you may sleep in here tonight. Get your blankets and fix yourself a bed on the other settee. If he awakens during the night and attempts to move, summon me at once."

"And me," said Miss Harriet. "You must notify me too, Mattie. It's good of you to be so concerned about the boy, Martha."

"It's not alone the boy," said her sister flatly. "It's the whole house that concerns me. It's true I've done my best today to aid his recovery, but I shall sleep tonight with Father's pistol on the table beside my bed."

Well I don't know whether this was said for Corporal McBurney's benefit or not, but if he heard he gave no sign. If Miss Martha could fire that old flintlock pistol she certainly was better than any of us. It used to be kept in a case in the library together with a supply of powder and ball and Marie had taken it into the garden one afternoon during Miss Martha's absence to show us how her father had once won a duel in Baton Rouge. However Marie could not manage to fire the thing and neither could any of the rest of us, our military expert Emily included. Shortly after that episode Miss Martha removed the pistol to her own room.

"Come along, girls, come along," Miss Martha ordered us. She waited, holding the lamp, in the doorway until we had all filed out and then she preceded us up the stairs in the usual fashion, with Miss Harriet and her candle bringing up the rear to prevent any straggling. Thus ended the first day of Corporal McBurney's residence at our school.

Amelia Dabney

I awakened early on the next morning as is my custom. I am usually the first of the students to arise in this school. Miss Harriet says it is not ladylike or good for the complexion, since it encourages wrinkles, to be out of bed before eight and although Miss Martha doesn't worry much about the complexion of her pupils, she does not insist that anyone arise before that time. However I have never been able to sleep very long after the sky begins to lighten and on that particular morning—the day after Corporal McBurney came—I was up and dressed especially early.

I tiptoed out of the room, very carefully so as not to disturb Marie, and came down the stairs, half expecting to find that either yesterday had been a dream and there had never been a Corporal McBurney or that he had been here but had become frightened of us and had stolen away during the night. But he hadn't.

"Good morning," he said, opening his blue eyes and then winking one solemnly at me. "It is morning I take it."

"Yes, about six o'clock, I think."

"I thought as much from the larks I heard singing out there in the back."

"Do you like birds?" I had been sure from the first he would.

"Love them. Anything wild I love . . . anything wild and free."

"Those aren't larks, I think. I believe I hear some robins and possibly some thrush."

"Oh. Well you must have a different sort of lark here than from what we have in Ireland. Those birds I hear trilling and twittering away out there now sound very much like Irish larks."

"That's very possible," I said. "It may be some variety of the species we don't have here. I wonder if you would mind describing that Irish lark to me—the coloring and so forth—and the nest, if you're familiar with it—and the eggs."

"I will," he said, "with the greatest of pleasure . . . when I feel a bit stronger. There's nothing I enjoy more, when I'm feelin up to it, than a good old chat about the birds."

"You do remember me don't you?" I asked him, a bit worried.

"But how could I forget you? You're the angel who saved my life."

"Well," I said, "I'm sure I don't exactly deserve that much credit. I only brought you here and then Miss Martha attended to your leg. If anyone saved your life, I guess you might say that she did."

"She's the older one with the look of authority about her?"

"Yes. Do you remember seeing her?"

"Vaguely," he said. "I also have a vague recollection of a number of others . . . very attractive young ladies they were too."

"Everybody in the house was here. We were all terribly worried about you."

"Oh isn't it wonderful," he sighed, "to have such charming people takin an interest in an old rough sort like myself."

"Corporal McBurney. . . ."

"Johnny."

"Johnny, can you remember my coming in here last night around dinner time and talking to you."

"It seems like somebody did."

"What I said to you was that if you were ever in any trouble or danger here and needed to escape, you should come to me and I would help you."

"What sort of trouble would I be gettin into here? I'm a peaceable man, darlin. . . ."

"Amelia. . . ."

"To be sure, Amelia. Darlin Amelia, I intend to conduct myself in a quiet and gentlemanly manner, so there couldn't possibly be any trouble, and as for danger—what sort of danger would there be to me in a houseful of charmin and well bred young ladies. You did say there were no men here, didn't you? Well then I'll be as safe here as in my old mother's arms, as long as somebody doesn't take the notion to go off and notify the Confeds of my presence—or worse, the Yankees."

"You don't want the Yankees to know you're here either?"

"Why would I want those New York toughs and Dutch farmers to hear of this place, the way they'd be comin in here pesterin and annoyin you and maybe even committin worse depredations. When my leg is better, I suppose I'll have to rejoin 'em, but until that day, if anybody comes lookin for me, you can say you never heard of me."

"Well Miss Martha will be very glad to learn that you have that attitude, I'm sure. I'm certain that will make her feel much more sympathetic toward you. And it may take a while, don't you think, Johnny, before your wound is better."

"When I look at you, I hope it's years, Amelia." He winked again so I knew he was only teasing me.

"How does your leg feel now? Is there much pain?"

"I can tolerate it."

"I only wish we had some medicine we could give you to relieve it."

"That's very good of you. If you had a drop of spirits it might help."

"Let's see," I said. "Miss Harriet gave you some brandy yesterday and I think she put the bottle back in this cabinet."

"It isn't there now," he said before I could open the wine cabinet. "I asked the darky woman about it a while ago. She said it was gone."

"I guess Miss Martha must have taken it."

"She didn't look like a drinking woman, as I remember her."

"Oh she wouldn't have taken it for herself," I said. "If she removed the brandy from the cabinet, it would have been to prevent Miss Harriet from getting it."

"Oh ho."

"I'm sorry," I told him. "I really shouldn't gossip about things like that."

"Information exchanged between friends isn't gossip, my dear. I'll need to know everything I can about these people if I'm to spend some time here—in order to fit in as quiet and unobtrusively as possible, don't you see? In order not to make any false steps in the parade."

"That's true," I said. "Well you can always call on me for anything you want to know, Johnny. Except there are other students who are better informed than I am. My roommate, Marie, for example, knows just about everything that goes on in this place."

"Well, I'll have to get in touch with Marie then, won't I?"

"That won't be difficult. She'll certainly be in to see you some time this morning. I want to warn you however, that although Marie is very nice, she is a very shrewd person. Even though she is the youngest, she may be the most shrewd person here. It's almost impossible to deceive her about anything."

"Oh," said Johnny. "I hope I don't ever deceive anybody here. I hadn't planned to do anything like that."

"I know that," I declared, "but all the same I thought I'd better tell you about Marie. Now perhaps, when Miss Martha comes downstairs, I can ask her to bring you some brandy."

"Don't bother yourself. I'll manage without it."

"Are you comfortable otherwise? Did Mattie take good care of you during the night?"

"Is that the old darky? Sure she's not the most friendly chambermaid in the world but she attended to my needs quite satisfactorily. Then she brought me a bowl of soup this morning. Someone else brought me a bit of soup last night as I recall."

"That was Edwina Morrow."

"A black-haired girl—very pretty?"

"Yes." I hesitated and then decided it was really not jealousy, but a sincere interest in his welfare. "You must be very careful of Edwina too—more careful than with anyone else. She can be quite mean, if she ever decides she doesn't like you."

"Then I must try not to give her any reason to dislike me, mustn't I? As a matter of fact, I hope nobody in this house dislikes me, Amelia, I'm really not the worst sort in the world, you know." His voice was growing weaker now and he seemed on the verge of dozing off again.

"I'm positive you are a very good sort, Johnny," I told him. "And I'm sure that everyone in this house will agree with me."

"Ah that's grand . . . that's what I need to get my health back. The confidence o' me friends . . . the knowin that they'll stick by me through good times and bad . . . through fair weather an' foul . . . through sunshine . . . and storm. . . ."

I thought he was asleep and had started to tiptoe off but he called me back.

"Wait a bit, dear little Amelia, 'til I tell you about a strange bird . . . the like o' which I know you've never seen . . . in your young life."

"What kind of a bird is it?"

"A very small one . . . very fragile . . . but with great determination . . . and with more strength than you might suppose from looking at it . . . if you ever got close enough to one to see it at all. It's a very rare bird and very shy, and it can only be found in the most remote and inaccessible parts of the world. On high mountains you sometimes see it . . . or in the heart of dark forests . . . or sometimes floatin on the wind above the most untraveled ocean. . . ."

"What is its natural habitat?"

"The entire earth, I guess . . . for it has no real home. Nobody knows where it comes from since it's almost always on the wing. It flies from dawn to sunset, and since it can travel at such great speed, it often follows the sun around the world. It never stops anywhere long enough to build a nest . . . or raise its young. I guess that's why its kind is dying out. One of these days there won't be any of the species left. . . ."

"My goodness," I said, "that certainly is a strange bird. What's it looking for, do you suppose?"

"That's the great mystery."

"What is this bird called?"

"I don't know what it's proper name is . . . but I call it the lonely bird. . . ."

I waited but he said no more. This time he evidently was asleep.

"Whyn't you let that poor boy alone?" said Mattie from the doorway. "You gotta get up before daylight to pester him?"

"He says the most interesting things, Mattie. He's just told me about the most amazing bird."

"I think he's an amazin bird hisself, never mind the kind he tells you about."

"What sort of a bird would you say he was, Mattie?" Mattie is a very good judge of people, white or colored, although sometimes her first impressions are swayed one way or the other by a person's background. Therefore it wasn't to be expected that she'd feel favorable immediately about Corporal McBurney.

"I'd say he was a crow, an old big-mouth crow. Crows like to talk all the time and strut around and they take a fancy to anything bright and shiny."

"Well there's nothing wrong in that," I replied. "There are plenty of people here who are fond of talking, and I'm sure that Corporal McBurney is no more taken in by appearances than you are. As for strutting, I fail to see how anyone can strut when he's lying on his back."

"He can strut without movin a hair. I know what that boy is thinkin lyin there. He's thinkin he's the only rooster in the yard and the coop is filled with fat young hens."

"Is it so wrong for him to think that? From a biological point of view that seems rather natural."

"I declare to the Lord," said Mattie, "if Miss Martha heard you say that you wouldn't get no meals for a week. And if your own Mama heard you, she'd likely smack your face."

"But is it wrong or not?"

"It ain't wrong, I suppose, if he don't go no farther than thinkin. And speakin of talkin too much, it seems to me you got more to say since this Yankee come in this house than you ever had before all the while you been here. Used to be you never spoke 'less somebody ask you a question. Now you're expressin biological opinions all over the place. Now get outside and help me with this hoein."

"He really is very nice, Mattie," I said following her out to the kitchen. "He says he wants nothing more than that everybody likes him."

"Oh I know that. He'll do his best to make that happen. You know what he told me a while ago? He said when the Yankees win the war he would see to it personally that Mister Lincoln made me the head of this school."

Well we both had to laugh at that. Mattie is a dear old soul and very intelligent too, and she can appreciate a joke as well as anyone else.

"I'll bet my breakfast that Johnny was winking when he said that," I told her.

"He winked all right," she conceded, "but he was watchin me to see how I was gonna take it before he winked."

"Well, Mattie," I said as I took my sunbonnet from the kitchen peg where we keep them, "if the Yankees do win the war, you just start your own school and I will enroll in it. However you must promise me you'll let me devote my entire time to the study of nature."

"You'll get all the nature study you need in that pea patch. You just move on out there now and study all them bugs you find on the vines."

Before we went out however, Mattie gave me a cup of acorn coffee—which I believe I prefer to the real kind, although no one else here feels that way—and a biscuit she had saved for me from the previous night's dinner. Since I am always the first pupil to begin her daily gardening chore—we are all expected to do a certain amount of it before breakfast—Mattie usually has a little treat for me.

As I had told McBurney on the way from the woods, sometimes I think that Mattie is the dearest person in this school. In fact I wouldn't be surprised if she is the most honest and unselfish person too. It occurred to me that I should also have told McBurney to place his complete trust in Mattie and I resolved to do so at the next opportunity.

We went out to the garden then. I am always happy working in the garden in the early morning, but as I recall I was happier on that morning than I had been in a very long time.

Martha Farnsworth

Our visitor seemed much improved on the second day. He was awake and smiled quite cheerfully when I went in shortly after eight o'clock to have a look at him.

Several of the girls had crowded around the door and were staring in at him with much tittering and giggling. I gathered that he in his turn might have been waving or gesticulating to them, but if so he ceased when I entered. The girls made way for me and then advanced behind me, but at a discreet distance.

"Go back," I told them sharply. "Go on about your business. You have work to do in the garden . . . get on with it."

"Please, Miss Martha," said Alice Simms. "Shall we have classes in here this morning?"

"No, we shall not. The classes which would normally convene in here—French and History of England I think—will meet instead in the library."

"What about the music class, Miss Martha?" asked Marie. "Will you move the harpsichord into the library?"

"And Miss Harriet's dancing class, which is scheduled for this afternoon," said Edwina Morrow. "There's hardly room for dancing in the library."

"We'll cross those bridges when we come to them," I informed my charges. "If necessary we can postpone the music lessons and as for Miss Harriet's instruction in the dance, I think we can dispense with that for the time being anyway. Now move along, all of you, to your work in the garden."

They went, but unwillingly, with more tittering and whispering and staring over their shoulders. It was evident that we were going to have our problems with this young man in the house.

"I'm disrupting your place here . . . that's plain, isn't it, ma'am," said the gentleman in question when I turned back to him.

"Indeed you are," I told him.

"You don't mince words, ma'am. You speak right up. I like that."

"Do you indeed," said I. "And do you think it makes a great difference to me whether you like it or not?"

"I'm sure my opinion means nothing to you at all, ma'am. I'm not looking for your approbation."

"Are you not. What are you looking for then?"

"Whatever care you can spare me. You've given me plenty now and I'm
most appreciative. I don't know how I can ever repay you, except, of course,
by recovering my health as rapidly as possible and quitting your company.
That was the answer that just popped into your mind now, wasn't it, ma'am?"

As a matter of fact it was. The fellow had a genuine facility for antici-
pating your thoughts.

"Aren't you afraid that I will hand you over to our soldiers?" I asked him.

"No, I don't think so. I don't say that you won't do it, but very
likely worse things could happen to me. Of course I don't relish the prospect of spending the next few months in Libbey Prison or Andersonville,
but it's better than being dead. And that's what I would be, if you hadn't
helped me."

"You can't be certain of that. Even if the girl hadn't brought you here,
very likely your own men would have found you. Or even if you had been
taken prisoner, some of our surgeons would have attended to you."

"From what I hear, your surgeons have more work than they can keep
up with nowadays. And our own sawbones don't have it much better. Anyway your ministrations are much to be preferred to whatever care I would
have gotten in a hospital tent. Any army doctor would've whacked the leg
off and had done with it."

"And you wouldn't like that."

"Would you? To be spendin the rest of my life as half a man . . . hobblin
around on some old stick . . . unable to earn honest wages and dependin on
alms and charity most like. No ma'am, I've seen what goes on in those hospital tents and I'll tell you I'm very glad to be where I am. For you must
understand, ma'am, that I've always made more use of my legs than most
fellas my age. I was always a great one for runnin and jumpin and hoppin
and leapin. And dancin the clock around too. I heard you mention dancing
classes a bit ago. Why I could instruct your pupils in any kind of dance you
could mention . . . Irish, English, American . . . reels, waltzes, polkas, anything at all. Let me tell you, ma'am, I can wear out the arm of any fiddler in
the world with my legs!"

It was hard to dislike him. He had such an open friendly look about
him, that even when you knew for a positive fact that there was guile
behind his innocence, it was difficult to think of it as anything but a boyish trick.

And the guile was there, no doubt about it. Whatever Corporal John

McBurney said, you had to ask yourself—is this the way Corporal McBurney really feels?—or is this the way he wants you to think he feels?—or is he even more clever than you suppose and is allowing the edges of the trick to show, hoping that when you see it, it will make you feel superior to him in cleverness. And you're really not. Or at least he thinks you're not. Because what he really wants is your misjudgment of him.

How deep do the layers of deception go, I wondered one day. But not that second day. On that morning I found myself—at least for the moment—beginning to enjoy the company of young Corporal McBurney. I had no intention of allowing him to stay, of course, once he was able to move about. And I likewise had no intention of permitting him any commerce with our students.

"Well I'm not sure that a radical operation wouldn't have been the best medical procedure in the long run," I told him. I uncovered his leg and prodded the flesh gently above the bandage. "I'm sure your army surgeons know more than I do about these things. Although the condition of your leg doesn't seem to be any worse than before. Is there any feeling in it?"

"Enough."

"Pray that it continues to pain you. When numbness sets in, as I understand it, it is an indication that the member has begun to putrify."

"That won't happen. The way it feels now, I'd swear you were cookin it for your dinner."

"We don't eat Yankees here," said I. "We cure them, and in the process hope to civilize them, and then send them on their way. The pain should lessen after a bit. The important thing is that the stitches hold and that we keep all infection out of the wound. That means that you must not attempt to walk on it. You must not move at all, except with help, when I am with you or when Mattie is here. Do you understand that?"

"Perfectly."

"If the pain is too great, I might bring you a small glass of wine. I understand you were given some of my brandy yesterday—in fact quite a lot of it."

"To tell you the truth, I don't remember much about yesterday."

"I can believe that. If you had as much of the brandy as my sister claims, I wonder that you remember anything. At any rate that bottle is empty but there is a bit of my father's wine left in our cellars. I'll send Mattie down for some in a little while."

"Oh don't bother, ma'am."

"All right. Just as you say."

I turned away, smiling to myself. I was sure I knew my man and that he'd change his mind before he lost his chance. However when I had moved off a step or two and looked around, the young devil had closed his eyes and was feigning drowsiness.

"I wouldn't have taken you for a temperance man," I remarked.

"Ma'am?"

"I have always heard that an Irishman will drink anything."

"So he will. Or at least almost anything. On the proper occasion."

"Mister," I thought, "if you want my wine, you'll ask for it."

He opened one eye at me then and grinned, conceding me my small triumph.

"And this does seem like a good occasion, come to think of it. I'd dearly love a sip of your wine, ma'am. I've no great fancy for the grape—the juice o' the grain is more to my likin—but I'm sure whatever stock you have here is excellent."

"It isn't being offered for your pleasure, but only your comfort," I said coldly.

"To be sure. Sometimes they go together though."

"I must remind you, Corporal McBurney, that you are not our guest but a somewhat unwelcome visitor. We don't propose to entertain you here."

"I wouldn't expect it, ma'am . . . in times like these. Although you'll find I'm easily amused."

He grinned again and looked beyond me. I turned and found Edwina Morrow in the doorway.

"You were sent to do your gardening, Miss," I told her.

"Yes ma'am. I've finished the hoeing in my row."

"You must have worked at a remarkable pace then," I said. "What is it you want here?"

"Nothing important. I just wondered if there was anything I could do."

There was a low chuckle from the boy on the settee. "Mister," I thought grimly, "if you say one word, you'll find yourself out on the edge of the road before noon." But he said nothing. He was lying back, his eyes closed again, still grinning.

"There is nothing you can do here," I informed Edwina. "Now I want you girls to remain out of this room for the time being. You have enough school and other work to keep you well occupied without interfering with this sick man."

"I didn't intend to interfere. I only thought to help with the nursing."

"That won't be necessary," I said. "The adults in the school can take care of it."

"But young ladies my age are usually considered adults, or at least that is what Miss Harriet is always telling me." She started to withdraw, then paused. "I really did only want to be of service."

"And when have you before, Miss?" I said to myself. And then felt a twinge of remorse. If the girl really wanted to do something unselfish for once in her life, it did seem a shame to refuse her the opportunity. However without much reflection I decided I had more to worry about than whether or not Edwina was to be allowed to practice charity even—and on second thought it seemed most unlikely—if she were sincere.

Edwina was hardly gone before another one of the Corporal's well-wishers appeared. Alice Simms was back this time and of course that was to be expected. She could hardly have been the offspring of her mother otherwise.

"Please, Miss Martha," said that least-innocent one, as innocently as only someone very practiced could be. "Shall we have our breakfast in here instead of in the dining room? Miss Harriet wants to know."

"Why in the world would we have our breakfast in here?"

"Well since Corporal McBurney is unable to leave his bed this morning, Miss Harriet thought it would be nice if we all had our breakfast in here together."

There was another low chuckle from the settee.

"Did you say something, Mister?" I asked, wheeling swiftly.

"No ma'am," said he, and with no smile this time. He knew just about how far I could be pushed.

"It is well for you that you did not," I said. "And, Miss Alice, you may tell Miss Harriet that we will have our breakfast in the dining room as usual and that this room is out of bounds to students until further orders. Is that clear?"

"Yes ma'am, quite clear," said she with an insolent little curtsy. Then looked beyond me to smile conspiratorially at McBurney and slipped away before I could reprove her for her impudence.

I turned back to him again and stood there watching him for quite some time. He was expressionless now, his eyes closed again, but I knew he had not fallen asleep.

After a while he sighed. "Will ye have a deadline like at the prison camps? You could mark it off there in the doorway. Then you can stand in here yourself on guard."

"Don't be flippant with me, Mister. It could prove quite unpleasant for you."

"I'd take my chances on that. You don't seem the sort to act out of anger or petty irritation." He paused again. "It's not my fault, is it, that I wasn't born the same sex as you?"

"I'm not opposed to men, if I've given you that impression. I'm not even opposed to you. If it were just you and I in this house, you might have the run of it—providing I was convinced you wouldn't steal anything."

"And you're not convinced of that at the moment?"

"How could I be? I don't know you."

"It would do no good for me to swear that I've never stolen anything in my life?"

"I don't know you."

"You said, 'if you and I were alone here.' Does that mean you think I'm going to attack your pupils?"

"No, I don't think that. I intend to see that you don't get the opportunity."

He half sat up. "I could make the opportunity, lady, if I was that kind of fella!"

"Lie back and be quiet. I don't permit shouting in my house. Besides you're going to disturb that wound."

"Do you think me that sort of fella?"

"I can't judge you yet. If I decide you are, you won't be with us long."

"It would do me no good to swear I wouldn't dream of harming your young ladies?"

"Again I don't know you."

"How long will it take to know me?"

"You won't be here that long."

"Well," he said lying back and breathing heavily from the exertion, "I'll give you a few quick facts so's I won't be a total stranger to you, in case you decide to throw me out this morning. Name . . . John McBurney. Age, twenty. Colonial citizen without rights of Great Britain. Born in the Country of Wexford of Patrick McBurney, deceased, and Mary McBurney, still living . . . if you can call it that nowadays in Ireland. No money, no prospects, no worries. No contagious diseases, no physical defects, except a recent war wound. All my teeth and hair, fingers and toes. A sound mind, I'm told, and a good memory. No troubles, no grievances, no hatreds—which may surprise you, considering where I've come from. No curiosity, except about the whole world. No wishes, except to be my own man. Entered the city of New York, December twenty-third, eighteen-and-sixty-three. Enlisted in the Union Army, January fourth, eighteen-and-sixty-four. Promoted to the rank of acting corporal, April fifteenth, eighteen-and-sixty-four. Captured by Confederate ladies, May fifth, eighteen-and-sixty-four. Now ma'am would you say you still don't know me?"

"I know what you've told me."

"Meaning I could be lying?"

"Yes, you could be, but even if you told the truth, all you've given me are some biographical statistics which could fit anyone from a clergyman to a criminal. I still don't know what you're really like."

"I don't suppose you'd learn that if I stayed here a lifetime. Nor very likely would I learn what you're like in the same length of time. Except that I know a bit about you already."

"Do you indeed," said I. I must admit I was somewhat beguiled by his earnestness of manner, if not his audacity. "You said you didn't want anything except to be your own man. To be free and footloose, I suppose that means. And that's all you want?"

"I want to live my own life in the way I choose. I want to be beholden to no one—take orders from no one. I came to this country because of that. If you knew what it was like in the old land, you'd understand me. And I suppose maybe I want the usual things . . . the wife and toddlers and the place to hang my hat . . . that whole lot, you know. And also right now I'd like a friend."

"Only one friend?"

"A friend is not so easy to come by in a strange land."

"You were four months in the Union Army. What about your companions?"

"Some of the native borns made fun of me—my brogue, you know, and I suppose my country ways. Well I had to fight them or retreat, and even if I had a mind to run, there's very little place to hide in an army company. And either way it doesn't gain you many friends, especially when it's a veteran outfit that has been together for a long time and has shared a lot of common trouble. Those oldtimers don't take too kindly to the newcomers and bounty men."

"Bounty men?"

"I got two hundred dollars bounty for enlisting."

"That's a lot of money."

"The rebs all enlist for God and country, don't they, and the grubby Yankees sell themselves for money."

"That's what some of our people say. And I wonder that you were promoted if you were so much disliked."

"You haven't got it exactly straight. It wasn't that they all disliked me, I'm sure of that. It was just that they weren't entirely friendly. And I'll tell you the truth about the stripes. I won them in a fair fight. I bet all my pay for one year against the corporal's stripes that I could whip him. And the captain, who was truly an evil man and who wanted to see me beaten, agreed to it. Well I will say he was fair about it when I won, though he didn't expect it. Anyway he let me sew the stripes on to wear—until the corporal had recovered, he said, and there was time for a rematch. Also, with due humility, the captain knew I deserved the rank. And about the bounty ... I sent the two hundred dollars to my mother."

Had he, I wondered?

"Do you believe me?"

"I don't disbelieve you?"

"That's not quite the same thing, is it? Go away, lady, and let me sleep."

He turned away, facing the back of the settee. I thought then that there were tears in his eyes. Suddenly, lying there, he looked very much like my departed brother. There was really no similarity of feature and McBurney was much slighter than Robert, but the back of this boy's head on the settee pillow and the hunch of his shoulder reminded me of Robert on one of the last occasions I had seen him.

He was in his room lying on his bed with his back to me and he said, as I recall, very much the same thing. "I don't want to talk with you. Go away and let me sleep." I had rebuked him, as I often did, for some foolishness or other and that was his response.

Robert's hair was very like this boy's also, in its curliness and tawny color and the way it usually grew over the edges of his collar, much the same as this boy's. I wondered if Harriet had noticed this. I also wonder now what would have happened had I not noticed it.

Because I believe now that was what prompted me to say, "I have changed my mind. I think we shall all have our breakfast in here after all."

It was not that my pity for him had blinded me altogether to the dangers of the association. I was still aware of the potential evil. As for that, there was evil in my brother too and I'm sure I would have hesitated before permitting Robert the run of a house full of young women.

But at that moment it did not appear that our visitor was about to run anywhere for a while. And I thought, "At least we can test him in this manner. We can see how he behaves in company. And if he shows the least sign of any forwardness, I will not hesitate to send him away immediately."

"Well, what do you say?" I asked him. "Are you agreeable to breakfasting in company?"

He turned around and stared at me. "I'd like a bit of soap," said he. "And a comb. And a razor if you have one."

"I'll see if I can find my father's razor," I told him. "The comb is easy enough and Miss Edwina Morrow had a small piece of soap last night which she may be willing to part with again today. I'll send Mattie in with everything and expect you to be ready to receive us in exactly fifteen minutes."

"Yes ma'am," said Corporal McBurney grinning happily. There was no devilment in the expression this time but only boyish pleasure.

The sun was high now and the cannons were beginning to rumble experimentally in the woods. It seemed the battle was commencing again as I went out to notify the others of the change in our program.

Edwina Morrow

Miss Martha came out of the parlor on the morning of that second day and announced that Corporal McBurney had won her over completely and that she was going to throw the house open to him. It wasn't exactly that, of course, but it did sound as though that might be what she had in mind. What she actually said was—and I'll swear she was blushing—that she had thought it over and decided that it was only Christian charity for all of us to have our breakfasts with him.

We were all seated at the dining room table, with Mattie standing in the kitchen doorway, waiting for Miss Martha to come in so she could begin serving what was passing at the moment for human food. Well when that announcement came you might have thought a Yankee shell had fallen on the table the way those proper young ladies leaped up and flew off in all directions, giggling and snickering, and pinning their hair and unpinning it, and demanding "Who has my ivory broach?" and "Who has my mother of pearl necklace?" That was Alice Simms, as I recall, shouting as she ran up the stairs to change her dress.

The patriot Emily declared that no enemy soldier was going to cause her to change from her customary black muslin—which had been sent by her family when her brother was killed and which she has been wearing as her personal banner ever since, and which has been growing a trifle musty this summer, if the truth must be known, since she has no cologne to sprinkle on it and probably wouldn't stoop to that sort of frivolity if she had. However, Emily's declaration to remain in mourning notwithstanding, she was at the dining room mirror as she said the words, pinching her cheeks to raise some color in them.

Even Miss Harriet was caught up in the excitement and hurried toward the stairs following Alice, Marie and Amelia. I don't know what sort of beautifying Amelia was planning to engage in, since she always looks like she has been climbing trees in whatever clothes she wears. She had a mourning dress too, sent to her from home, but I believe she fell off a fence or something and ripped it irreparably the first time she had it on. Of course Miss Martha and Miss Harriet wear black almost all the time in honor of their brother. I might say, with no disrespect intended toward dear Master Robert, that the color does nothing for either one of them, but then what color would?

"Where are you going, sister?" Miss Martha called out now.

"Only to tidy myself a bit," said that person, flushing to the roots of her hair.

"You are tidy enough," Miss Martha told her. "For Heaven's sake, Harriet, act your age." However Miss Harriet continued up the stairs anyway and Miss Martha followed her, announcing to the world that she, at any rate, was not going up to do any foolish primping but merely to look for her father's razor which it seemed Corporal McBurney had requested. She also mentioned that he wanted some other items which I happened to have in my skirt pocket at that moment, my bar of scented toilet soap and my tortoise shell comb. I had intended to offer them to the Yankee earlier in the morning, but at that time Miss Martha, apparently desiring private conversation with him, had prevented my entrance into the parlor.

Well anyway I wasn't about to do a lot of primping and fixing myself in the Corporal's honor. If I didn't suit him as I was, he could go and find a better game, as my father used to say. I did decide, however, to avail myself of the present opportunity to slip in and see Corporal McBurney and present him with the toilet articles.

I was preparing to do this, only pausing in the doorway to smooth my bun a bit, when Marie Deveraux came hurtling back down the stairs, carrying a Bible or prayer book in one hand and some jewelry in the other.

"Excuse me, won't you, Edwina," she said, almost running into me. "I have some personal business in here." And then rushed into the parlor and over to Corporal McBurney on the settee.

Well I am not one to listen to the conversations of others but for the life of me I could not comprehend how that child of ten or eleven or whatever she is could have any business of any consequence with a total stranger and enemy soldier. Therefore, since I had legitimate business myself with him, I determined to wait by the doorway until the unmannerly little person had finished whatever it was she had to say. I made no attempt to eavesdrop, but of course that is hardly ever necessary in order to hear the remarks of Marie Deveraux, since she is seldom capable of speaking in anything lower than a shout.

In this instance, with no preamble, she flung the book on Corporal McBurney's lap and announced, "There's something for you. I wanted to bring it to you last night for fear that you might die before morning, but then I thought since you were unconscious you wouldn't be able to read it anyway."

"That's very logical," he said.

"I assume you are a Catholic. I hear that almost the entire population of Ireland is Catholic."

"Not quite," he informed her. "But you've picked me out. I was baptized in the faith."

"Well then, there's a Catholic prayer book for you to browse through while you're not doing anything else. It belongs to my mother and it's in French but you can probably puzzle out the Our Father and the Hail Mary. You don't want to go to Confession, do you?"

"To you?"

"Hardly. But I could run out on the main road and probably find a Catholic Chaplain with one of our regiments who would very likely be willing to assist you. That is if you feel on the verge of death and can't wait much longer."

"I think I can hold out for a few hours yet."

"You probably have done some pretty horrible things in your life and you ought to get your soul in order before anything happens. You have done some horrible things, haven't you?"

"I suppose that depends on your point of view."

"Well then, examine your conscience while you're lying there and if you want a priest a bit later, just let me know. By the way, I'm Marie Deveraux."

"I'm John Patrick McBurney."

"Pleased to meet you," she said and came rushing out again, revealing now what she was carrying in her other hand. It was a pair of earbobs and she was trying to attach one in her ear as she hurried along.

"Just a moment, Miss," I said, blocking her. "Where do you think you're going with my jade earbobs?"

"Oh Edwina," she said, giving me what she considers her most captivating smile and which she only uses when she is trapped in some misdeed. "Don't be hateful, Edwina. Everyone is dressing up for breakfast."

"Not in my jewelry they are not." I reached for her but she ducked away. "Where did you get those anyway, you little thief?"

"Why I merely saw one on the floor in your room."

"The door was closed!"

"The breeze must have blown it open. Anyway I retrieved the one from the floor so that it wouldn't get stepped on and crushed and then I saw this other one on the stand and I was going to return them both to you, but then I realized that I had no finery to wear for Corporal McBurney's first breakfast here, and I was sure you wouldn't mind. . . ."

"You little devil!" I almost had her then but she dodged around a chair and tipped it over in front of me, almost tripping me.

"After her, after her . . . that's the way," the Yankee shouted gleefully, pulling himself up on the back of the settee. "Which d'ye choose, ladies and gentlemen, the little brown squirrel or the big black cat? Step up and make your choice, folks, before the bets are closed. The bigger one has the reach but the small one the experience. Oh did ye see that nimble little twist as she slipped away! After her, Blackie . . . after her, girl!"

"Please Edwina," the little vixen cried. "You have scads of beautiful jewelry. You don't need these two old pieces. You'll wear yourself out, Edwina. I can keep this up all day."

"She's right, Blackie," said the Yankee. "In an open field you'd have a better chance but in an enclosed place like this you're no match for her. Ah let her have the trinkets. That pale shade of green don't suit your raven tresses anyway. Rubies would look better on you, Blackie."

I realized then how unseemly I must appear and halted, on the verge of capturing the nasty thing, and let her get away.

"Oh how beautiful you look this morning, Edwina," she yelled from the doorway. "You're all dressed up yourself, aren't you?"

"I am not!"

"Well perhaps you are a bit disheveled now. However I have not seen that gorgeous silk brocade dress on you since last Christmas, if I can remember correctly."

"Get out of here!"

She scampered off howling with idiot laughter. I felt so ashamed of my unladylike conduct that I turned to leave the room myself.

"Wait a bit, Blackie," the Yankee said then. "Don't run off when you've only just come. Did you want to see me about something?"

I nodded and went over to the small parlor table which Mattie had drawn up beside his settee. I put my scented toilet soap and tortoise shell comb beside his pitcher of water and backed away, suddenly embarrassed and not knowing what to say to him.

"Thank you very much, Blackie," said he.

He was reclining again and attempting to clean his fingernails with a Union ten cent piece. His nails certainly needed cleaning. I said so. Those were the first words I ever spoke to Johnny McBurney.

"They look as though you had been trying to dig a pit with them," I said.

"I was," he said. "In the battle yesterday. When all that iron was flyin overhead, my first thought was to bury myself, Blackie."

"And when you couldn't bury yourself deep enough, you ran."

"I did. I surely to God did, Blackie."

Was he mocking me by repeating that? His eyes were smiling and his voice was friendly.

"My name is Miss Edwina Morrow," I said.

"Ah yes. Howdy do."

"It wasn't very brave of you to run."

"Maybe not. But it was smart, I think."

"Because you're still alive?"

"Not only still alive, but as an extra reward, I've met you."

"You don't even know me."

"I know your name . . . Miss Edwina Morrow."

"What have you been told about me?"

"Nothing besides your name. It's a lovely name. If I was old Edgar Allan Poe, I'd write a poem called 'Miss Edwina Morrow.'"

"Are you sure nothing else has been said about me?"

"Well, dear girl," he said, setting to work on his grubby nails again. "I have not exactly been in the proper condition to listen to gossip about anybody. What are you afraid of anyway?"

"I'm not afraid of anything."

"Then what do you care what is said about you?"

"I don't care."

"That's my girl."

The words he used, if said by anyone else, would have convinced me I was being derided, and I paused again, not at all certain that this wasn't the case. But he looked up at me and smiled—such a warm and friendly smile—and I thought, after all he is a stranger and not even an American. The words and expressions that he uses aren't exactly our way of kindly speaking, but that doesn't mean he's trying to be unkind.

"I just didn't want you to start with the wrong impression of me," I finally said, "before I'd even had the opportunity to talk with you myself."

"Then you do care what I think about you."

"Not at all! You're a stranger here, that's all, and I don't want you to be misled about me. Otherwise I don't care a fig what you think." Strangely enough, even at that point I believe I really did care, but of course I couldn't tell him that. Then.

"Well I must make very sure that I'm not misled about you, mustn't I,

Miss Edwina Morrow. Perhaps you'd better set me off on the right foot immediately by giving me a complete and accurate account of yourself. For instance, where do you come from and how long have you been here?"

"I've been here four years," I said. "And my father's home is presently in Richmond."

"And where is your mother's home?"

"In Savannah, Georgia. My parents do not reside together."

"Ah, too bad. And how long has it been since you last saw your mother?"

"If you must know," I said, "I have never seen her. Or at least I cannot remember seeing her." I would have been very irritated by these questions, but he had a certain childlike directness which made it seem that he wasn't trying to bare any of your personal secrets, but only attempting to expand his own knowledge of this strange world in which he now found himself.

"My father took me away from Savannah when I was quite young," I went on. "And then we lived in many places afterwards. My father has engaged in many enterprises and has been very successful in most of them."

"I'm sure he has been. This is a great land for success. You can smell it in the air. Now take myself, for example. I've been here less than six months and just look how successful I've become. I've seen a good bit of your country. I've been promoted in the army, and now I'm enjoyin a grand holiday in the care and company of the most genteel ladies. How much more success would a poor bog-trotter want? But tell me more about yourself, Miss Edwina Morrow."

"There isn't time now," I said. "The others will be here in a moment."

"Well you must come back later then when we can have a private talk. I'd like very much to know you better."

"Why are you so interested in me?"

"Because, Miss Edwina, I think we're much alike. Something tells me we're both really out of place here. Me, for obvious reasons. And you, for reasons that maybe aren't so plain to the naked eye, but all the same I can guess at one or two of them."

"What are they then?"

"One big thing is your looks. The little Frenchie wasn't lying before when she said you were beautiful."

"That doesn't matter to me."

"I'll bet it matters plenty to some of the others here. I'll bet there's some here who're very jealous of you."

"Even if that is so, it still makes no difference to me."

"Does it matter to you that I agree with the little Frenchie?"

I paused and thought this over very carefully. Then I told him,

"Yes, I guess I am glad you do."

"Why let me tell you, Miss Edwina Morrow, you've got it all over these other girlies here like a bright star floatin over the empty sea. And it's not only these few here you overshadow. Why I've been to some of the largest cities in this world and I can tell you truthfully, you beat the finest female creatures in them all."

"Please don't mock me."

"Mock you? Oh my dear, I wouldn't dream of mocking you. Do you know what your big trouble is, Miss Edwina? You haven't been praised enough. You don't appreciate your true worth, because I'll bet no one has ever told it to you. Isn't that so?"

"Perhaps it's so."

"Don't underestimate yourself, Miss Edwina Morrow. Be glad you're not like all the others, even if it does get a bit lonely sometimes. That's the second reason you're out of place here, Miss Edwina. I'll bet you're the independent sort who speaks her mind and the devil take those who don't agree with it. Ah that's the best way to be after all. What one thing do you want most in the world, Miss Edwina?"

"What do I want?"

"That's my question. Did you ever hear of the little people with magic powers in the place I come from? Pretend I'm one of them and that I have the ability to grant you anything you choose. Now what's your wish, my dear?"

"Nothing. I don't want anything."

"Oh come now. You must want some little thing. Would you like the war to end immediately and your sweetheart to come back to you safe and sound?"

"There is no such person. I have no one in the military."

"Aren't you lucky then. Well what else would you like? To see your mother?"

"No."

"What then? Just tell me the first thing that pops into your mind. Quick now . . . have you thought of something?"

I nodded.

"Tell me what it is."

I told him.

"And that's the thing you want most in the world?"

"Yes."

"All right then," he said solemnly. "I'll have to see that you get it."

The others came into the parlor then to have their breakfast and so that was the end of my first conversation with Corporal McBurney.

Emily Stevenson

Quite a little ceremony was made of Corporal McBurney's first breakfast at this school. I must say I was not in complete agreement with the idea at first, considering the flag the Corporal represented. However he was wounded and he was a stranger and if Miss Martha wanted to demonstrate how generous and hospitable we could be in victory, I decided I could not object too much to it.

Mattie arranged a table for us on one side of the room while Corporal McBurney remained on his settee opposite but at some distance from us. He was propped up with pillows and the settee was turned around so that North and South, as Marie put it, could have an unobstructed view of each other. Conversation was not prohibited. In fact, up to a point Miss Martha tried to encourage it but at first very little of any consequence was said, except for some general remarks about the weather and the garden and conditions at Farnsworth when Miss Martha and Miss Harriet were young.

This, of course, is a favorite topic at every meal—the way things were and the way they are now. I suppose the poor dears feel they must console themselves occasionally and at the same time impress their poorer students by reciting the history of their family's glorious past. I don't object to it but I am not overawed by it and I don't think some of the others are either, Amelia and Marie, for two examples.

Marie's father owns two or three large places in Louisiana and Amelia's family has one of the largest plantations in the northern part of Georgia, which I understand has been overrun by Yankees now, and also a large new home in Atlanta. As for our own place in South Carolina, you could put Farnsworth and all its land in one corner of it and never see this little school again, unless you happened to ride across it on a hunt or something.

Well I suppose the account of balls and levees and various other social activities at this house and at the old Farnsworth place on the James, or wherever it was, might have been of some interest to our visitor but he didn't exhibit much enthusiasm. He was certainly polite enough and he nodded and smiled agreeably whenever anyone looked at him, but he made no attempt to enter into this part of the conversation. He just kept on eating what finally added up to an enormous amount of food.

Everyone was trying to avoid mentioning the war, of course, for fear of causing him embarrassment, although this was somewhat ridiculous, as we all finally realized, with the battle raging furiously once more to the east of us even closer now, it seemed, than yesterday. It is very hard to avoid speaking of something that is making your garden windows rattle and the coffee cups juggle precariously on your plates.

"My goodness," I said finally. "If they must have wars in the morning, you'd think they could be more quiet about it."

"I'm in favor of that," said McBurney cheerfully. "I suggest we go back to the good old days of pikes and lances and broadswords. Then, you'll see, the Irish will rule the world."

"Do you really believe so, Mister McBurney?" asked Miss Harriet.

"Oh yes ma'am, there's no doubt of it. There never was a nation better at individual close-hand combat than the Irish. Didn't we keep the Roman legions at bay when they had all the Britons hidin in their caves or roostin in the trees. We beat off the Angles and the Saxons and the Jutes, and the Picts and the Gauls and the Norsemen, and after that we held our own with the Normans too. Yes ma'am, your maps of the British Isles would look a bit different today if it wasn't for gunpowder. It was the invention of gunpowder that ruined us."

"That's an interesting theory," I remarked. "And if you want to carry it a bit farther, you might anticipate some other interesting results. I'll bet your Northern armies wouldn't be in Virginia now, if this war could be fought entirely with the weapons which the Greeks and Romans used."

"You're absolutely right, Miss," said he. "Didn't that same thought occur to me only yesterday when I saw how valiantly your boys were conducting themselves and against such overwhelming odds. There was this road, d'ye see, we were told to cross—a whole bunch of us—and a little group of your fellas were defending it—Georgians, I think they were. . . ."

"I'm from Georgia," Amelia told him. "Although I don't have any relatives in those Georgia regiments any more."

"Was it the Seventy-First or Seventy-Fourth Georgia Volunteer Regiments?" I asked him. "Those regiments are part of my father's brigade although it's possible they're still fighting with General Longstreet in the West."

"If it was the Twenty-Third Georgia," said Marie, "you might have been shooting at my own Uncle Philip. He lives in Macon and I'm sure he's with that regiment unless he's already dead."

"To tell you the truth," McBurney said, "I don't know what regiment it was. They didn't say. They just yelled out that Georgians were never gonna let the Yankees pass and by God—excuse me—by George, they didn't. They were dug in behind some rocks and fallen logs and they stood off a dozen charges of the best we had. I don't know what might have happened later because there was artillery coming up behind us, and then our bunch was sent off to support an advance in another section of the line, so whether those Georgians are still holding out or not, I couldn't say. In a way, you know, I kinda hope they are."

"Those are hardly the proper sentiments of a loyal Union soldier," Miss Martha felt obliged to put in then.

"Oh my goodness, Miss Martha," Alice said. "He's just paying tribute to our boys. Anyway I'm sure Corporal McBurney wasn't in any position of command where it would make any difference to him whether those boys held out or not. Isn't that so, Corporal?"

"Quite so," said he, giving Alice a quick flicker of his eyelid. Already, I thought, he has Miss Alice sorted out and classified. Most young ladies might feel insulted if a person like McBurney winked at them, but one sort of expects those things to happen to someone like Alice Simms.

"That's exactly right, ladies," he continued now. "I don't mean to low rate the Union Army at all because there are a lot of fine and courageous fellas in it. I only mean that mechanical contrivances have taken all the sport out of war. There's just no fun in it any more like there might've been a thousand years or so ago. Oh it must've been a lot different when you could ride off to a battle, secure behind your visor and your suit o' mail, depending only on the strength of your arm and the quickness of your eye to save you from anything worse than a few missing fingers or an ear or a dent on your helmet and a sore head for a week or two. And even if you did fall in them days, you had the consolation of knowin you had been bested by a better man than you, and not some skinny nervous dry goods clerk with his hand twitchin on a cannon lanyard maybe two miles or more away. Oh ladies, when I saw your fellas yesterday guardin that muddy piece of road, I realized it was in the best and most noble traditions of the heroes of old. Oh when you think of what gunpowder has done to the knighthood of the world. Why those fellas behind the walls at Troy wouldn't have lasted through one sunset if those outside would've had a mortar or two or even a three inch rifle. The whole history and literature o' the world would've come out entirely different. What's that book the Greek fella wrote?"

"*The Iliad* by Homer," Edwina Morrow supplied, her eyes shining as she watched him.

"That's it," he said. "Now that fella would've had no plot at all if the city had come tumbling down on the first day. Well they don't write poetry about wars any more, do they, and it's no wonder. There's nothin very poetic about being destroyed by a machine. . . ."

He paused here, lowered his gaze, as though he felt he might have spoken out of turn, and returned to his food.

"Interesting, very interesting," said Miss Martha.

"Extremely interesting," said Miss Harriet. "You have a fine philosophic turn of mind, Mister McBurney."

"Thank you, ma'am," said he modestly. "I try to find a helpful lesson in the experiences of each day." And winked at me, the devil, behind his coffee cup. You rogue, I thought, you unmitigated red-headed rogue.

Well, he had succeeded in those few words, and while completing his breakfast which consisted of three bowls of barley porridge, four stacks of corn cakes and molasses, about a dozen beaten biscuits with drippings and several cups of acorn coffee, in completely charming the entire company, to a certain extent myself included. I believe if a vote could have been taken right then, with no time out for consideration of the thing, Corporal McBurney would have been elected a permanent resident of this school.

Of course I suppose some of our students would have voted that way even before that first breakfast. Some of the giddier ones had gone to fantastic extremes to make themselves look pretty for the Corporal. That included Edwina, whom I would have considered to be above such frivolities, but who came to breakfast wearing her finest red brocade dress, and Alice, who of course has few dresses of any sort and nothing very fine, but who managed, nevertheless, to bedeck herself with a collection of gaudy trinkets—rings, wrist bands and other baubles—which I gather are some of her mother's lesser trophies.

Little Marie, who will not be left out of any gala occasion, entered regally, wearing a pair of jade earbobs and looking for all the world like some kind of midget woman of the streets, and would have stayed at table that way had not Miss Martha, realizing that this was the ultimate in absurdity, ordered the child to either remove the jewelry or leave the room. Marie removed the earbobs, ungraciously, of course, and throughout the entire meal thereafter was as sullen and unmannerly as only she can be.

"Perhaps we have all been taught a lesson this morning," Miss Harriet said now. "Perhaps we have all learned not to judge anyone too quickly."

"There's more to any man," Corporal McBurney said soberly, "than the color of his coat, or for that matter, his skin." And looked at each of us in turn as he spoke—to test our reactions, I suppose, to that question which the Yankees seem to feel is the only thing we think about down here—and ended his inspection with old Mattie who was just entering with a fresh pot of acorn coffee. "Is that the way you feel about the situation?" he asked her. I could have sworn he was on the verge of saying "Miss Mattie" but recollected where he was and thought better of it.

"I don't think about such things," she told him shortly in the tone she reserves for white people whom she considers not quite up to her standards. "Nobody knows any of us but the good Lord. And He's the only one can ever judge us proper. I 'spect He knows there's plenty of hatred behind the most friendly faces, and plenty of love too, I s'pose even in them that never smile."

"Amen to that." It was Edwina, surprisingly. I had never known her to agree before with any of Mattie's little comments which she sometimes offers to us, free of charge, at mealtimes, or any other time she is given the opportunity. For that matter, I couldn't remember Edwina ever saying an agreeable word to Mattie, which is not surprising, I suppose, when you consider that she seldom says anything agreeable to anyone.

Well the breakfast party ended shortly after that. Miss Martha invoked the blessing and our visitor bowed his head with the rest of us and meditated as ordered, though whether on religious matters or other topics I cannot say.

"Is there much attention given to prayer in the Northern camps, Mister McBurney?" Miss Harriet asked him as we all arose.

"Very little, ma'am," he said. "It's all card playing and cursing and general loose talk, except, o' course, on the eve of a battle, and then you can't move an inch from your blanket without trippin over courageous Christians on their knees."

"Don't you suppose the same situation may exist as well in the Confederate Army?" Edwina asked him.

"I suppose it does, Miss," said he, staring thoughtfully at her. "The only difference being that since most of the Confederates seem to know what they're fighting for, they may have their minds on their jobs more often than the Yanks."

"Did you know what you were fighting for, Corporal McBurney?" I inquired.

"Put it this way, Miss," said he, "I thought I did, but I've been having my doubts ever since the day I boarded the cars and set off for Maryland."

"And what changed your mind?" Marie wanted to know.

"The fact that we were invaders," he said promptly. "Whatever the merits of the Yankee cause, it can't be denied that we are invaders. And since I'd come from a land that has been living under the heel of invaders for several centuries, I began to lose heart in the whole venture. That's God's truth, ladies. I give you my solemn word."

It seemed he had an irreproachable answer for every question. I wondered whether he really believed in every statement he made, or whether he might be merely feeding us a little sugar, as the saying goes, in order to insure a pleasant stay with us. Therefore I resolved to hang behind a bit as the others were leaving and examine him a bit further.

Young Marie waited behind for a moment too. "Let me give you some advice," she told him as softly as it is possible for her to speak. "Don't get too involved in these Protestant prayers we have here all the time."

"What's the best way to avoid them?" he asked her, grinning faintly over her shoulder at me.

"Oh you can't completely avoid them. You just have to go along with them. The thing to do is count sheep or say a Hail Mary or something whenever Miss Martha gets started on one of those long winded blessing she's so fond of composing. You don't have to be openly nasty about it. Just don't let yourself get caught up in it. Otherwise you might be in great danger of losing your faith."

"Thanks very much, Miss," he told her solemnly. "I appreciate your interest."

"You don't need to thank me," she said. "You and I have to stick together against these heathens." And with that she marched out, ignoring me.

"Well, Miss," he said cheerfully to me. "It seems you're next in line. Do you have some advice for me too? Don't come too close to me, however, if you're one of those heathens the little lass has mentioned."

"If you plan to guide yourself according to the wisdom of that child," I said, "you will very likely find yourself in serious difficulties before the day is out. Marie is a great one for telling others how to conduct themselves but she can never manage to stay out of trouble herself."

"Oh she's a regular little barracks lawyer all right," he said laughing. "I had her number the first time I clapped eyes on her."

"No one is going to interfere with your religious beliefs here."

"I know that, Miss. Though as a matter of fact, I don't feel very strongly about religion one way or the other."

"Do you feel very strongly about anything?"

"How do you mean that, Miss?"

"Is there any belief or cause to which you are dedicated? Is there anything you would be willing to die for?"

"To be honest with you, Miss," he said after a pause, "I don't think so. Unless it was some person—my mother maybe or a girl who was very close to me. I might be willing to sacrifice myself to protect a person like that. Of course you must understand that not everyone who puts on a uniform has any thought of spilling his own blood on it. In fact I'd wager to say that very few fellas in this war, whether they be from North or South, have any thought of dying when they march away."

"I suppose you're right," I said. "Even my father, I suppose, doesn't want to give up his life if he can avoid it. Of course that doesn't mean he won't be quite willing to do so if it becomes necessary. But feeling as you say you do about the gallantry of our boys, it seems to me you joined the wrong side."

"I've thought that many times myself, Miss," said Corporal McBurney with unwavering gaze. "It came to me when I began to learn the story of the war and how the North had started all the fuss. You see I knew nothing at all about it when I stepped off the boat. Oh I'd heard there was some kind of fightin goin on but I didn't know the first thing about the argument. One side looked as good as another to me then, and there were no Confederate recruiting stations on Broadway Street in New York."

"You mean you joined the Union Army just for the adventure of it?"

"Mostly, I guess," said he steadily. "O' course a very good line was handed me by the recruiting officer—a smooth-talking oily sort—who told me how you were torturin and mistreatin all the blacks down here."

"That's a vicious lie!" I told him angrily.

"Well it would seem so," said he, "from the little evidence I've seen. This Mattie woman you have here seems to be treated well enough."

"Of course she is. And so are most of the others. Why the darkies on our place in South Carolina are just like members of our family."

"You mean they're related to you?"

"No, not that of course. I just mean they're treated about as well as the rest of us."

"You don't ever intermarry with them though."

"No, of course not."

"But now I did hear somewhere though, that some people in the South are of mixed color . . . that they have black blood in them."

"I guess there is a certain amount of that sort of thing among the lower classes," I admitted. "But most of our people, of both colors, are every bit as respectable as people anywhere else."

"Oh I know that. You don't need to convince me on that score. Well as I say it's just the story of the war itself I didn't know before. Otherwise I can tell you I would've set sail for Charleston instead of New York."

"I don't think you would have made it," I informed him. "Charleston is blockaded now and it's very difficult for any ships to get into the port. However if you're really thinking seriously of changing your allegiance, I'm sure it can be easily arranged. I'd only have to send a letter off to my father and I'm sure he could take care of it immediately."

"Oh that's very kind of you, Miss," he said, and he honestly did look as though he was appreciative. "I may just accept your offer . . . once this leg of mine is healed again."

"I could write my father now and your leg would be healing while we were waiting for his reply."

"That's so, isn't it. Well let me give the whole matter a good thinking over. It's not a nice thing, you know, to be a turncoat, although I guess a person is allowed one honest mistake in a lifetime. However I'd still like to study the proposition very carefully. You understand that, don't you, Miss?"

"Yes, certainly I understand it. And I think it's wise. Also I'm glad you mentioned the word 'turncoat.' I wouldn't care much for a turncoat either, but as you say, an honest mistake can't be helped."

"Ah grand, we're in agreement then. And just as soon as I've thought the whole thing out—that ought to be as soon as the pain in the leg eases and my mind is clear—I'll send you off to your pen and ink to compose a nice letter to Dad offerin him my humble services for what they're worth. All right, Miss?"

"All right."

"Good enough. But now to get back to what we were discussing before— what about these people of mixed color? Are they accepted as white people?"

"No!"

"Never? I mean in cases where they might have only a little black blood. Say one quarter or one eighth or maybe even less."

"They are still considered black."

"But you don't mistreat them."

"Certainly not. Those mongrel people are very highly prized as house servants—chamber maids and butlers and so forth."

"I see, I see."

"The Yankees are the only ones guilty of mistreating people, though I'm sure they've never told you anything about that. The way they've burned homes and stolen negroes and cattle and brutalized women and children right here in Virginia in their cavalry raids in Westmoreland County and in other places as well."

"Hanging wouldn't be good enough for fellas that'd do a thing like that."

"Well I'm sure Miss Martha and Miss Harriet will be glad to know you feel that way."

"How do you feel about me now?"

"Better than I did before, I guess."

"You know, I said to myself yesterday, when I came into this house, 'That rosy-cheeked one is the leader here. She's one you've got to sell.'"

"Sell what?"

"Myself."

"Why should you think it necessary to sell yourself?"

"Well maybe not McBurney lock, stock and barrel, but just the fact that he didn't mean you any harm."

"I didn't think you were conscious enough yesterday to make any such assessment of us."

"Well I wasn't hardly. It was only a quick guess. Lord, but you're suspicious, Miss."

"My name is Emily Stevenson."

"Stevenson . . . is that an Irish name?"

"English."

"Ah . . . but generations back, o' course."

"I guess you might say that my family has been in South Carolina for a long time. My great grandfather served under General Washington."

"And fought the British? Well now, we do have something in common, don't we?"

"You haven't served in any war against England."

"No, but I'd like to. That's the war I would've joined, if there had been any going."

"The British are almost our allies now. The blockade runners bring in a lot of our supplies from England."

"Oh I suppose some of them are all right. The common people are the same everywhere. It's the kings and queens and all the fancy dukes and lords that are continually causin trouble. They can't bear to let a piece of property go, you know, once they get their claws on it. It broke their hearts to lose this country, and they're very fearful now of losing Ireland."

"That's something you're dedicated to, isn't it—your own country."

"Yes maybe so. I suppose you could say that."

"Well I'm glad. I think every person ought to be dedicated to something. Otherwise I don't think that person could be of much value."

"The fella who becomes dedicated to you will be a lucky man."

"Thank you."

"I mean it. You're a fine, plain-speaking, upright young lady. A great many of the women of the world, you know, are deceivers by nature. They can't help it. They say one thing and mean another and they'll lead a fella up the garden path for their own sport and think nothing of it. But I get the impression that would never be the case with you. You seem to me to be a very honest young lady."

"Well I hope I am. I've never had any reason to be dishonest about anything."

"Reason or not, I don't think you would be. Do you know what you remind me of, Miss Emily? The girls at home. You're so sturdy and steady-eyed . . . and neat and clean and healthy looking."

"Well I'll take all those adjectives as compliments."

"They're meant as such, Miss Emily. Something else I'll tell you. I don't know whether you trust me yet or not, but, Miss Emily, if there was one person in this house I'd put my faith in, that person would be you."

"Well thank you again. You haven't met everyone in the house, have you?"

"Most of them. And sized up the others. Oh they're all nice people, I expect, but I get the impression there's none of them as straightforward as you. If you said you'd stick by a fella, he'd know he could believe it."

"I wouldn't say it unless I meant it."

"That's my point. You're still not ready to buy the merchandise, are you?"

"Perhaps almost ready."

"You just think about it some more, Miss Emily. I can guarantee you wouldn't be getting a bad bargain. You'd be purchasing a good friend, if that's worth anything. You think about that, Miss Emily, and meanwhile I'll be thinking about you writing that letter to your father."

Mattie entered then to clear away the dishes.

"Miss Harriet say you to come to the French lesson in the library," she informed me. "And Miss Martha say this Yankee's not to be bothered by anybody for the rest of the day."

"I'm sorry," I said. "I didn't realize I was holding up the lesson. And if I've bothered you, Corporal, I'm sorry about that too."

"You couldn't possibly bother me, Miss Emily," said he as gallantly as one of our own. And smiled, but didn't wink this time.

Now I must confess that upon leaving the room I did something which ordinarily I would consider despicable, and I suppose that is exactly what it was, although I told myself I had sufficient reason for it at that time. I was still not entirely sure whether or not I could accept Corporal McBurney, and so I waited for a moment just outside the parlor door to hear if he had anything to say about me to Mattie.

He did. "There goes a very nice young lady," he said.

"Uh huh," said Mattie.

"She'll make some man a grand wife," he said. "Of all the lassies in this school, I'd say she'd make the best."

"I don't think Miss Emily is figurin on marryin up with no Yankee," Mattie said.

"Oh I didn't mean that at all," said he. "She's way out of my class, I'm sure. I may have the brains and beauty, but not the wealth to enter a competition like that. All I meant was that if some suitable fella came along to examine the stock here, I believe Miss Emily would be the number one choice."

"It don't seem exactly right," Mattie replied, "to talk about Miss Emily and the other young ladies that way."

No, it isn't right, thought I, but it's very funny. Corporal McBurney, in his rather unpolished way, had paid me just about every compliment one could think of—with the exception, of course, of saying I was pretty. Of course, if he had said that, I would have known he was not being honest himself.

I waited by the door no longer, but hurried along to the library. That was the first time in my three years at the school that I had been late for a class, and, strangely enough, I was not very concerned about it.

Matilda Farnsworth

He seemed mighty chipper next morning for a man who most died the night before. That was after Miss Emily had left the room and I was pickin up the breakfast dishes. He also seemed mighty anxious to know whether Miss Emily was out of hearin or not the way he was tryin to lean over the end of the settee to see if she might still be waitin in the hall.

Well he said some nice things about her and then he asked a question that didn't sound so nice. It might not have been anything comin from some people but from him—a stranger, in this house for less than a day—I didn't care much for it.

"Which one of these little gals got the most money?" That's what he called them—not young ladies or young misses, but usin the colored folks' talk.

"None of these young ladies got any money," I told him, "'cept what their families send them for the school. Young ladies don't generally carry money round with them."

"Which family has the most?"

"I don't know."

"The Stevenson family?"

"Maybe. I don't know."

"That little one who brought me here—Amelia something or other—I'll bet her people have money too."

I got so mad then I had to speak up. "Most all their folks got money or they wouldn't be here! This is a quality school!"

"All these girls aren't quality, are they?"

"I got no time to waste now," I say. "I got my work to do."

"I'm sorry, Mattie," he say. "I don't mean anything by it. I've just got a great curiosity about the world in general and seeing all these young lassies, and confined here as I am with nothing else to think about, I only began to wonder about them. Now just between you and me, I'll make a few guesses and you tell me if I'm right. Now I would bet that very good looking blond girl—Alice—is not quality. Am I right?"

"I don't know what she is. Miss Martha keeps her here out of the kindness of her heart, and what's good enough for Miss Martha is good enough for me."

"I thought so. And that darlin of them all, Miss Edwina Morrow, is not quality either, I'll bet. Right? Quick, quick, speak up."

"Her Daddy maybe got more money than some of the others here."

"I didn't ask you that. I asked you to tell me if she is or is not quality."

"I ain't sayin one word more. You ask Miss Martha or Miss Harriet anything else you want to know."

"They're quality."

"You know they are! Don't you ever say this family ain't quality!"

"I wouldn't dare to say it, Mattie. Don't strike a wounded man now, I beg of you. I was only foolin with you, Mattie old darlin. I don't care who is or isn't quality and whether or not anyone has money. I'm only grateful for being here, safe for the moment, out of the storm. I'm far from quality myself, Mattie, if you're judging by blood lines. I'm descended from tinkers and gypsies and people of no name. I've no land and no fortune and doomed to sit, I am, on the very outermost edge of the fire, where you couldn't read a prayer book with the biggest print and on a cold night your back would never be warm."

"You talk awful funny, Mister."

"I'm an awful funny fella, Mattie. But I mean no harm. I'm a wanderer and a rover and a great dreamer of wild dreams . . . and a great liar too, I suppose. I'm seldom seen when I pass and I won't be missed when I'm gone. But believe me, Mattie, I mean no harm. Do you have a bit of tobacco, Mattie?"

"There's still a patch growin out there in back."

"Don't you ever cut any of it? Haven't you got any hung up and dried?"

"You got a pipe?"

"I lost it somewheres. I'll use yours, Mattie."

"You sure ain't quality."

He laughed then, fit to kill. He sure was the strangest man.

"If Jesus Christ walked in here, Mattie, and asked you for a smoke, what would you say? I'll bet you'd say, 'Lawd, you ain't quality!'"

And then he howled again. He laughed so hard I had to laugh myself.

"After a while you ask Miss Harriet if she got an old pipe around here," I told him when I got my breath back. "She might give you one of them old pipes of her Daddy's or Master Robert's."

"Thanks, Mattie. Who is Master Robert?"

"He was the brother of Miss Martha and Miss Harriet."

"Is he dead?"

"Well, Miss Martha thinks he's dead. She thinks he was killed at that battle in these woods last year."

"Chancellorsville."

"I don't know what the Yankees call it. We just say the battle in the woods. Now we probably call it the first battle in the woods."

"Why does Miss Martha only think her brother was killed? His regiment ought to know what happened to him."

"I don't know if they do or not."

"Even if he was reported missing at first, it's been a whole year now. Your War Department must have some kind of records. They must have him listed dead or captured by this time."

"The thing is Master Robert might not have joined the army under his own name."

"Why would he do a thing like that?"

"Maybe he didn't want Miss Martha to know where he was."

"Then if that's the case, maybe he isn't dead at all. He might just have run off somewhere and no one will ever find him."

"Like you?"

"How do you mean, Mattie?"

"You ran off, didn't you? Nobody knows you're here but us. Maybe nobody else will ever find you either."

"That's so, isn't it. Wouldn't that be grand? I could just spend the rest of my life here, surrounded by charming young ladies—my every need attended to, my every wish fulfilled. It would be sort of an exchange, wouldn't it. Myself for Master Robert. I'll have to tell Miss Martha."

"I wouldn't 'vise you to mention it to her at all."

"What was the trouble between them, Mattie?"

"I don't know."

"You mean you don't want to tell me."

"Whatever way you like."

"Tell me this then. Why is it that two good lookin ladies like that never got married?"

"Man, you do ask questions."

"It passes the day, Mattie."

"You like to pass right out the door when Miss Martha find out how nosy you are."

"Tell me, Mattie."

"I expect Miss Martha never wanted to get married. Miss Harriet might have wanted to once, but I guess she changed her mind."

"Why?"

"How do I know. Ask her yourself. But don't say I told you to ask. You're worse than a three-year-old child the way you pry at a person. Well I can't fool no more with you. Half the morning's gone already and I got plenty of work to do."

"You won't have to do anything at all after the Yankees take over down here, Mattie."

"I ain't gonna live long enough to see that day. Nobody gonna live long enough."

"It's comin, Mattie, it's comin sure as you're born. The great Day of Jubilee is what they call it. Then you'll be ridin up North in a private railroad car that Mister Lincoln is gonna send down here for you. You'll be wearin a silk dress and diamonds on your fingers and drinkin champagne outa gold goblets. Old Mister Lincoln will be at the station in Washington to meet you and all the other black folks and he'll lead the big procession down the street to the White House. Only the name'll be changed to the Black House then, Mattie. And you folks will move in there and stay there just as long as you want. Each one of you will have a fine bedroom with big soft beds and silk blankets and there'll be white maids and butlers to take care of you. You can stay in bed all day, if you like, and have all your meals brought in to you on silver trays. You can order anything you want to eat. Even if it isn't on the menu, they'll cook it special for you. You can have ham and gravy and ice cream and chicken at every meal, if you like, and cakes and pies and cherry tarts, just anything at all. And each evening there'll be a band concert on the lawn outside your window, and all you'll have to do is give a shout and that band will play any number you request instantly—jigs or hymns or marches, or anything you ask for. Then, before you turn in for the night, there'll come a very polite knock on your door, and when you open it, Mister Lincoln will be standin there and he'll say, 'Mattie, was everything satisfactory today? You got any complaints with the way things went? We know you folks been havin a hard time for quite a spell down there in Dixie and we aim now to make it up to you. So you just be thinkin about that, and if there's anything at all your heart desires, you just write it down on a bit of paper with that solid gold pen you'll find over there on the desk. You'll notice it says "compliments of Old Abe" on the pen—I had 'em made up special. Anyway you just write down on the paper whatever it is you want, and even if you can't write, make a big X—we got a mind reader out here who can decipher it—and then slip the paper under the door and we'll take care of your order first thing in the morning. And now, good night to you, dear Mattie. Sleep tight, don't let the bugs bite. I can promise you that tomorrow will be even better than today.' And you know something, Mattie? It will be. How's that for a jubilee, Mattie?"

"You are the craziest man."

"When the jubilee comes, I'm gonna tell 'em I'm colored too, so's I can get in on the celebration with you. Now don't you tell 'em any different, Mattie."

"All right," I said. "You better lay back now and get yourself some rest. You look like your fever's comin on again."

"Mattie, what was the name of Miss Harriet's boy friend—the one she almost got married to?"

I told him. "Howard Winslow," I told him, and five minutes later I was sorry. But at that time it didn't seem it could cause any trouble and I don't know for certain that it ever did. Anyway, at that moment, there didn't seem to be any harm in the Yankee boy. About the worst you could say about him then was that he was like some crazy puppy worryin an old rug.

That's just the way he seemed. He just wouldn't let up foolin and teasin and tormentin. Sometimes you'd figure he didn't ever have a serious thought about anything. And then other times, behind all that foolin, he seemed to be havin a whole lot of them. I started carryin the breakfast dishes out then, just as Miss Harriet was comin in.

Harriet Farnsworth

It was not until about ten o'clock on his first morning with us that I had an opportunity of conversing privately with our guest. For her first class in the mornings, my sister teaches the French language and as much of the literature of that country—some of the essays of Montaigne, a play by Racine and parts of the less atheistic writings of Voltaire and Rousseau—as our charges can assimilate. My assignment at some of these periods is to take Miss Marie Deveraux aside for private tutoring in other subjects. Marie can read and speak French like a Parisian and has devoured all the French texts we have, although with little understanding of their philosophic contents. I had set her to reviewing some pages in her English grammar and while she was thus occupied I decided to visit the living room and see how Corporal McBurney was getting on. My object was to reassure him of our interest in his welfare and to tell him that as far as I personally was concerned he was welcome to stay at Farnsworth until his health was completely restored.

I would like to state now that in describing this and other meetings which I had with Corporal McBurney I want to be as exact as possible. When I recount something I said or, more particularly, something he said, I shall endeavor not to let subsequent events affect my memory. Indeed I want to be particularly careful in relating the way he said things because that, as I soon came to realize, was quite often more important than the actual words he used.

Mattie may have realized this, I think, before any of the rest of us.

"How is he?" I asked her as she was coming out of the room with the breakfast dishes.

"He's feverish," said she. "You best not pay much attention to him, no matter what he says. In fact maybe you better not talk to him at all."

"Let me be the judge of that, please, Mattie," I told her somewhat peevishly. As I have said, Mattie is a treasure, but she does take an irritating joy in giving me orders at times. It is a habit not easily overcome, I suppose, when you are Mattie's age and have been in a family longer than the children, although she never seems to forget her place in her relations with my sister.

He was reclining with his eyes closed as I entered the room, but the faint smile on his lips led me to believe he was only shamming sleep. I went to him and placed my hand on his brow. He may have been a trifle feverish but no more than that.

"Do it again, ma'am," he said. "It feels awful good."

I obliged him.

"It makes me think of one time I was sick at home. . . . I had a winter cough or something and was kept in bed. . . ."

"And your mother took care of you?"

"No. Or at least not in the daytime. She couldn't. We were only renting a small corner of a great estate, you see, and after my father died my mother went to work as a maid in the big house. It was one of the ladies at the big place who learned I was sick and came down to visit me one day. She fed me broth and said kind words to me, and put her cool hand on my brow. She was an English lady but very nice."

"I'm sure she was. She probably had children of her own."

"No, she was too young for that. She was a daughter of the family. I was about eight or nine at that time and she perhaps five or six years more. She was a striking girl, I remember . . . rather small and slender, but fine boned and with lovely dark hair and the palest, kindest face. But of course, she was not for the likes o' me."

"She was too old for you anyway."

"Ah no, do you think so? Does a few years mean that much? I've never felt that way."

"I suppose it's a matter of opinion. Still I'm surprised that a boy of eight or nine would be thinking of such things."

"Maybe we begin earlier than the lads over here." He grinned now. "In actual fact I probably had no such thoughts on my mind at that moment. Very likely it was nothing more than being grateful for her kindness, and it was only later, probably, that the romantic part occurred to me."

"That seems more logical."

"Anyway her hand felt just like yours does now."

Listening to him, I had forgotten how long my hand had been resting on his head and I snatched it away—too quickly, I suppose in my confusion. He laughed. It was a soft, highly amused laugh and I cannot say even now that it was derisive.

"I think my fever must've risen suddenly and burned your hand," he said.

"No, no . . . it wasn't that."

"What then? Did I embarrass you? I'm sorry if I did, if for no other reason than the fact you might've soothed my forehead longer. It was very nice feeling your hand there and thinking of that young English lady. You look a great deal like her too."

"You shouldn't feel obliged to pay such compliments to someone of my age."

"Oh I don't feel any obligation, ma'am. And they're not really such grand compliments. I can think of much better if I put my mind to it. And also I don't think of you as being that old."

"Please, Corporal McBurney. . . ."

"You're not old enough to be my mother, are you? Is that what you were going to say?"

"No, I wasn't going to say that. And it is possible that I am not that old—at least not in civilized society."

"That's the great trouble with the world, do you know it—civilized society. That's what keeps us tied down and locked up and smothered. Haven't you ever felt a small little uncivilized spirit in you, batterin at the walls of your heart, cryin in a tiny voice, 'Let me out, Miss Harriet Farnsworth . . . let me out, let me breathe!'"

"Yes," I told him. "I have felt it."

"But never let the spirit out."

"Yes, once I did."

"Good for you! You must tell me all about it."

"I don't think I want to tell you," I said.

"You're folding your hands ever so tightly, ma'am, as though you might be afraid that one hand would get loose and burn itself again."

"I certainly didn't mean to give that impression."

"Sure I know you didn't, ma'am. It was only in the way of a joke. And maybe some other day you'll tell me about the time you let the spirit loose—someday when you get to know me better."

"I don't see why I should ever tell you anything as personal as that."

"Oh don't look at it that way, ma'am. I'm not interested in any of your secrets. I only want to hear about a time—no matter what the place and circumstances—you can leave out all names and dates, if you like—but I only want to hear you tell me of how you hurled caution to the wind, and braved all the gods and elements and furies, and shouted out, 'I am Miss Harriet Farnsworth and I want to do this thing and by Heaven I will do it!' That's all I want you to tell me. I've told you of how I did a similar thing myself, haven't I?"

"I don't remember that you have. You've only said a nice young lady came to nurse you."

"Oh, I didn't finish it. Well when she left, you see, I kissed her."

"You did?"

"Yes. I was so grateful to her, I sat up—like this—and pulled her to me . . . and kissed her."

He demonstrated. I withdrew—flustered, admittedly—but not quickly enough.

"I had to do that, ma'am, and I won't apologize," he said. "I wasn't sorry the first time I did it—with the young lady—and I'm not sorry now. You may stand there and think all the things you like—that I am ungentlemanly and coarse and whatever else is customary. But I say one thing to you, Miss Farnsworth, I meant you no dishonor. The situation was the same as that first time, when I was a child, and I felt that I must do the same as I did before. Obviously, if I had asked you, you would not have permitted it. So I didn't ask you. Now you may do as you like. You may inform your sister, and then summon the reb soldiers outside, if you like."

"I could do one thing worse to you, I think."

"What's that, ma'am?"

"I could ignore it. I could pretend it never happened."

"By all the saints," he said delightedly. I am still certain that was exactly his reaction. He wasn't shamming this time, but was genuinely delighted at my words. "You've hit the barrel right on the bung, ma'am. You've found my weakness, so you have. That would flatten me indeed. That would stretch me out and paralyze me—to have you walk away from here, disregarding me completely. Can you do it, d'ye think, ma'am?"

"No, I don't suppose so."

"Ah, too bad . . . for you, but good for me. Well I could give you another go at it. I could repeat the whole performance, say at this same time tomorrow."

"I don't think you'll get the opportunity."

"Do you mean you'll have your sister put me out, or that you'll merely stay away from me."

"You are still our patient. And I wouldn't be so certain, if I were you, that your fate is entirely in my sister's hands."

"Now you're angry."

"You are a coarse person . . . really you are."

"I come from coarse beginnings, Miss Farnsworth, I make no secret of that. Go away then and ignore me. It won't happen again, I give you my word. Pretend you never came in here at all today. That's what the young English lady did. She just smiled gently and walked out the door with her spoon and bowl and I never saw her again—except at a distance once or twice when she was riding her horse across the field, and one time when she was passing in a carriage on the road . . . with a handsome young fella in a Guard's uniform."

"I'm sorry," I said.

"Ah, you needn't be. I wasn't out anything, except a bit of pride. Shame is a great weapon, ma'am. It'll do more damage to a soul than a war can ever do to a body."

"I know . . . I know that."

"It struck me that you maybe felt the same. Well go away then and we'll both forget it. Only don't glance in a mirror for a while yet. You look somewhat feverish yourself."

"You *are* coarse."

"I said I was, didn't I? But perhaps, if you keep me company, you'll smooth away the rougher edges. Do you know, Miss Farnsworth, I think we're much alike. Although we're poles apart in class, we have some things in common. Our pride, for one thing, and maybe the fact that neither one of us is much like anyone else around here."

"Do you sense that about me?" I asked him, somewhat surprised.

"I do. I think you've a great fondness for the finer things—things that might, to plainer folks, seem useless and trivial and maybe even showy— but to you they're more important than the ordinary facts of life we have to deal with everyday. I think you love the fragile, delicate stuff that's so easily shattered in the hands of the clumsy world. Fine pieces of china, I'll bet, and old lace . . . thin crystal goblets and bits of polished ivory. . . ."

"I have some!" I told him. "I have some little religious figurines that came from China and have been in our family for many years. I'll show them to you, if you like."

"I'd be greatly obliged."

"I have an Oriental painting on a screen too, which is centuries old, and which belonged to my mother . . . and some old Spanish lace which is supposed to have come from the court of Philip the Second. Oh it makes me very happy to know that you are interested in such things."

"Let's be honest, ma'am. I didn't say I was interested. I said I'd guessed that you were. I was born under a thatched roof, ma'am, and lived there most of my life. I know very little about quality, but I'll admit I'd like to know more."

"Then I shall teach you," I declared. How he could have provoked such enthusiasm on my part by means of a very simple and I suppose not at all difficult assessment of my personality—especially after what had happened only moments before—is completely beyond me now. Of course it did seem that he was eager to elevate himself and that kind of desire on the part of anyone has always been most appealing to me. And perhaps he was eager to improve himself. Perhaps that was not a sham either.

"Is that a book of poems over there on the table?" he asked now.

It was the collected poems of John Keats and was so labeled in large letters on the cover.

"Do you like poetry?" I asked bringing the volume over to him.

"I know very little of it," he said. "What I know I like."

"Can you recite a poem that you know?"

"Well there's one by Mister Shakespeare. Let's see . . . how does it go?

> Let me not to the marriage of true minds
> Admit impediments. Love's not love
> Which alters when it alterations finds,
> Or bends with the remover to remove:
> Ah, no! It is an ever fixed mark,
> That looks on tempests and is never shaken.
> It is the star to every wandering bark,
> Whose worth's unknown, although his height be taken.
> Love's not time's fool, though rosy lips and cheeks
> Within his bending sickle's compass come;
> Love alters not with his brief hours and weeks,
> But bears it out even to the edge of doom.
> Now if this be error and upon me proved,
> I never writ, nor no man loved."

"That's very good . . . very, very good, Mister McBurney."

"John."

"It was a perfect recitation, John."

"Well we had this old book of Shakespeare at home, you know. It was the only book we had, in fact, besides the prayer book. I read that old Shakespeare a thousand times, I'll bet."

"Did you really? You must recite some more to me . . . something from a play perhaps."

"I'd like to do that. Maybe in a day or two I'll be more up to it. Thank you for your interest, ma'am. That does sound elderly, doesn't it. I'll call you Miss Harriet as the girls do. Read me something out of that Keats book, will you, Miss Harriet?"

He reclined again and closed his eyes. I leafed through the volume and selected the "Ode on a Grecian Urn," perhaps my favorite of all the author's works—which I read quietly aloud and then waited. There was a long pause during which I began to think that this time he might really be asleep.

But then. "Beauty is truth, and truth beauty ... that's true, that's very true. Though some people would deny it. In fact, I'll bet most people would say that truth is that sound you hear outside there in the woods. Truth is thunder and fire and death, they'd say, and anyone who thinks that's beauty must be mad. But I agree with the poet. I think that truth is this peaceful room ... and a kind lady ... and that butterfly in the sunlight out there in the garden."

"You have a nice soul, John McBurney," I said impulsively. "You may have rough edges, as you say, but I think your soul is as nice as it can be." Those were my exact words then, and if we could take one or two days from the calendar and obliterate one or two incidents, I believe it would still be possible to say those words about Corporal McBurney now.

"Fine thoughts are easy," he answered. "They come easy to the likes of me. Fine poems will bring them on ... or fine wine. Now there's something else I'll bet you appreciate ... a good glass of rare wine."

"I do enjoy a small amount of it on occasion," I admitted.

"Your sister said she was going to fetch me a glass or two to ease my leg," said he, "but I guess she forgot about it. Perhaps when you see her, you could mention it."

"She did promise it to you?"

"Oh yes. Ask her if you like."

"There's no need to do that. I'm quite satisfied to take your word for it. However it might be difficult to get the wine right now. You see, when we turned our home into a young ladies' school, we felt it would be better to keep the wine cellar locked. We have kept it locked ever since and my sister has the key."

"She carries the key with her, does she?"

"Always. It is on a ring with all her other keys."

"And she's giving lessons now, isn't she. I guess she'd hate to be disturbed."

"Yes, I suppose she would. It's a pity. There is some very old Madeira down there which I know you would enjoy."

"I wouldn't care so much about enjoying it, as long as it eased the ache in my leg."

"I'm sure it would. I sprained my wrist one time many years ago, playing at some game or other, and do you know, that wrist is still very painful sometimes—especially at night and in damp weather. And a small glass of wine always eases it."

"There's nothing better for any kind of bone ache than good wine. My mother, God bless her, always said that. It's too bad you don't have another key to that place."

"When the war is over perhaps we can have a second key made. Perhaps I will suggest that to my sister."

"Maybe I could make one for you right now, if I had a file and a small bit of iron. I'm fairly handy at that sort of thing. A barn nail might do it if it was long enough. What does that key look like anyway?"

"It's just an ordinary key. Very much like all the other keys."

"If I could see the lock, I might not even need a key to open it. I might be able to fix it with a knife blade. There was a fella in our company had been a turnkey in a jail and he showed me a trick or two he'd learned from the prisoners."

"My goodness, I'd like to see a demonstration some time."

"I wonder. . . ."

"Oh you mustn't move, you mustn't! You'll tear the sutures."

"I've got to move sometime, Miss Harriet. It may be a month before this leg heals. I can't stay on my back that long. If I only had a crutch or cane or something. . . ."

"We'll find some kind of support for you, as soon as it's safe to move your injured leg at all. Meanwhile I'll make a confession to you. The wine cellar lock can be opened without a key. I have done it once or twice myself . . . with a scissors blade . . . when my wrist was paining me and my sister wasn't here."

"You don't say. Well of course she's here now though, isn't she. But occupied, eh?"

"Yes, and I would not want to interrupt her class. Moreover she has another class—history of England, I believe—which follows in the library immediately after this one. Is your leg paining you now, John?"

"Like the devil himself was sticking darning needles in it. And your wrist?"

"It twinges now and again. I'll get the Madeira for you, John. However there is something I should tell you. My sister is rather opposed to my taking wine as a sedative. She feels that the pain is all in my imagination. Therefore I won't have any wine with you today . . . unless you insist. . . ."

"Oh but I do insist. I can't drink good Madeira by myself."

"Very well then. I shall have a small glass with you. One more thing. If you think you should tell my sister about this, feel free to do so."

"I see no need to mention it."

"As you wish. However, if she asks you, you must tell her the truth, John."

"I always try to be truthful, Miss Harriet."

"I'm sure that you do."

I went upstairs then for my sewing scissors and, making no attempt to be surreptitious about it, descended to the wine cellar and obtained a bottle of Madeira. I returned to the living room with this and two glasses and while Corporal McBurney watched, I poured the glasses exactly full.

We toasted each other and sipped the wine. He asked to hear more poetry and I read several more selections from the volume of Keats. It seemed obvious that the wine was easing the discomfort of his leg.

Before he had finished his second glass, and while I was still reading, he fell asleep. I arose and felt his forehead and once again concluded that he had no fever. Then I took the bottle and the glasses—in this time of shortage I am not ashamed to state I finished his myself—and went upstairs to my room.

I had no further conversation with Corporal McBurney on that day. Since I had developed a slight headache, I sent word down with Mattie that my classes would be cancelled—English literature and English grammar—and that I would remain in my room until dinner.

Alicia Simms

"Where've you been?" he said.

I explained to him that there just hadn't been any chance for me to come in and see him earlier. Miss Martha had watched me like a hawk for the entire day, making sure I was kept busy all morning and afternoon.

To make matters worse Miss Harriet decided she was sick halfway through the morning and therefore Miss Martha had to take over all of her classes. Well it sometimes isn't too difficult to slip out from under Miss Harriet's gaze for a few moments, but no one—with the possible exception of Amelia Dabney—can ever accomplish it with Miss Martha.

"Excuses, excuses," said Johnny. "Come here to me now, you bold girl, and stop wastin my time." He pushed over to make a space for me and I joined him on the settee. There wasn't too much room because that settee isn't as large as some and I wanted to be careful not to jostle his wounded leg, although that possibility didn't seem to be worrying Johnny.

"Here, we'll get rid of some of this to make us more comfy," he said, tossing some books on to the floor, one of which was our large volume of Shakespeare which had been under his pillow.

"What in Heaven's name are you doing with that?" I asked him.

"Just polishin off a few rough edges," he said, "just addin a touch of culture."

"You don't mean to say you've been reading it?"

"A drop or two of it, my dear. Don't look so shocked. It ain't half bad."

He seized me then and kissed me. I must say I never expected that to happen. That suddenly anyway.

"How do you feel now?" I asked him after a while.

"Marvelous, now that you're here. How did you manage to slip by the old lady then, if she's that beady-eyed?"

"Classes are over now. It's almost time for dinner. I can only stay for a moment while the others are upstairs."

"Is it that late? Have I slept all day?"

"I guess you have. Mattie told Miss Martha that you were asleep at lunchtime and Miss Martha said not to disturb you."

"That was good of the old girl, wasn't it, but it's left me terrible hungry now."

"Hungry for what?" I asked him.

"Oh all sorts of lovely things."

Well there wasn't much talk between us for a while after that. I believe the next thing that was said was said by me. It seems to me that was some trivial remark like, "My goodness, will you let me get my breath?" and then I added, "I don't believe we have been formally introduced. My name is Alicia Simms."

"Oh I've known you for years," he said. "I used to dream about you when I was a boy."

"Did you really?"

"Every night. For a while I even took to goin to bed before sundown to get an early start with you."

"You devil."

"It's the truth. I went to bed early and got up late for a long time there, until my mother beat me with a broom for it, for she said all that dreamin would hamper my growth."

"It didn't seem to do that. You seem pretty well developed."

"Thank you. The same to you."

"Oh that's not the same. I meant your shoulders and arms. You seem to be all bone and muscle. There don't seem to be any soft places on you."

"Sorry I can't return the compliment."

"Now stop that! Stop that pinching and poking! Supposing someone should look in here."

"I'd say you were teaching me anatomy."

"I don't think anyone could teach you anything, Mister McBurney, especially any young lady."

"Are you a lady, Alice?"

"Alicia. Certainly I'm a lady. Or at least I hope I am. What kind of a question is that?"

"It's a joke is all. I was teasing you."

"Well I don't think it's a very nice subject to joke about. One time my mother told me that if anybody ever suggested that I wasn't a lady or that I wasn't as good as everybody else, I should not hesitate but should slap that person right across the face just as hard as I could. And if that person persisted in his insults, I should scratch him and kick him and do just anything at all to silence him."

"By golly, I believe I'd hate to be put in a ring and asked to go the distance with your mother."

"Oh she's not vicious. She's very kind and gentle most of times. She just feels that all girls should learn to protect themselves."

"Mum must've been in some tight corners, eh? Anyway she's produced a very handsome daughter. That's one thing to her credit."

"Thank you."

"Don't mention it. And if anybody says you're not a lady in my hearing, I'll give them a good kick myself—once my leg is better. Who do you get your yellow hair from, Mum or Dad?"

"My father, I believe. My mother's hair is red."

"Why do you only believe? Don't you know what color hair your father has?"

"Oh of course, his hair is fair. He's been gone for such a long time, that's all—he's in the army—and when you haven't seen a person for a long spell like that, you begin to forget what they look like."

"That's true enough. And sometimes you don't have to be away from them for very long either. As for instance, I was very friendly with some of the best looking girls on Broadway when I left New York, but after spending these few minutes with you, I know I wouldn't even recognize them now if I went back there and passed them on the street."

"You're quite a soft talker, Johnny McBurney."

"Ah now I've never been accused of that before. If there's one thing I've always prided myself on, it's the way I've always been able to keep a latch on my tongue. I've always been a firm believer in the old saw, actions speak louder than words . . . as so. . . ."

And with that he demonstrated some actions which really made me rather annoyed.

"Stop that, I told you! They'll be coming downstairs any minute now!"

"You don't care what you do as long as you're not caught at it, is that it, Alice—excuse me, Alicia. Come down tonight then after the others are asleep."

"I will not."

"Where's your room? I'll come up and visit you."

"You will not! Do you want to have me sent away from here?"

"That's the last thing I want, darlin. What would life be for me here at old Farnsworth without you."

"Well I know you're only joking anyway, because how could you walk upstairs with the way your leg is. And I'm certainly glad you feel that way about our school, and about me too, of course. We must make your stay here as pleasant as ever possible. We must be nice to you . . . and gentle with you . . . and bring you back to health . . . and fatten you . . . because you are so pale . . . and bony . . . and thin. . . ."

"Now you stop that, you forward girl! What would Miss Martha say if she caught you feeling my ribs like that?"

"I was only looking to see how thin you were."

"Well you can't do that without a doctor's ticket. Only Miss Martha and Miss Harriet are permitted to examine me without a ticket . . . in daylight. Of course any pretty girl is free to have a look at my ribs after sundown—that's by appointment o' course."

"It's after sundown now."

"Ah so it is. Well I'll have a look in my engagement book then. I'm havin a terrible time here lately without my private secretary. Where is your room anyway, pretty bird, just in case when my leg is better I'm strollin around some night and want to pay a social call."

"On the top floor—in the garret."

"Way up there? Are you alone?"

"Yes, now I am. When more girls were here, some of them had their beds up there too."

"What about the black-haired one? Does she have a room to herself?"

"Why do you want to know about her?"

"Just curious, that's all—I just wondered how big the house was, and how many bedrooms you had."

"This house is very large. There are six bedrooms—some of them with sitting rooms—on the second floor, and each bedroom has space enough for several beds. At one time there were at least twenty girls enrolled at this school."

"By golly, I should have come earlier!"

"Well, of course, some of the girls weren't terribly attractive."

"I'm sure none of them could beat you—or the black haired one."

"Why must you keep talking about her?"

"Now you've got to admit she is good looking."

"I don't think she is at all. She looks like an Indian or a Mexican or something."

"What something?"

"Never mind. Do you think she's prettier than I am?"

"It's hard to compare you, you're such different types."

"I should hope so."

"Does she sleep alone though?"

"Yes, now are you satisfied? She used to share a room with Emily, but since she has never been able to get along with a single person in this house, she asked Miss Martha to give her a room to herself. Edwina is so afraid someone is going to spy on her, and examine her precious belongings, and find out how much money she has."

"Does she have money?"

"She must have. No one ever sends her any and she always pays her school charges on time. Miss Martha always makes a big point of letting me know that. Now will you stop talking about her? I'll make you stop!"

Then I covered up his mouth—with mine—so he couldn't speak . . . for a long while.

"Please, darlin . . . I'm a sick man."

"You're not that sick."

"All right then. If I die, 'twill be on your conscience."

He was grinning when he said that, of course. Then neither one of us said anything—or at least nothing worth mentioning—for another long while. I don't know how long we would have gone on like that, or what would have happened eventually, had I not looked up and seen Marie Deveraux standing in the doorway, watching us.

"I have a short announcement to make," she said, "if you two have time to listen. Dinner is prepared in the dining room, Alice, if you would like to join us. Corporal McBurney's dinner will be brought in here shortly, if he is not too ill to partake of it. I have been instructed to deliver those messages to both of you, although I am quite sure that the person who gave me my orders never dreamed that I would find the two of you together. Well, *c'est la vie*. Get on with what you were doing . . . whatever in the world it is."

Then she smiled unpleasantly and, humming a little song went out. Of course I had to follow her just as soon as I had made myself half way presentable.

Marie Deveraux

I was not surprised to find Alice in the parlor since I had observed her slipping down the stairs. I was a bit astounded at how quickly she had become engaged in *amour* with Corporal McBurney, but I suppose that is a result of her early training. As a matter of fact when I entered the parlor, Corporal McBurney was in the act of removing her dress and it looked very much as though Alice was helping him.

Well as you can imagine, they were both rather flustered at my appearance. Corporal McBurney did manage a small wink at me, but his heart was not in it. In fact his cheeks took on quite a bit of color—much more, I noticed, than the slight flush which arose on Miss Alice's face. Of course he was still a stranger here, whereas Alice is used to my popping in and out of rooms unexpectedly.

If you want to know, this occurrence didn't make me feel any less sympathetic toward McBurney, because in all honesty I didn't give him credit for having very many brains anyway, right from the start. Why anyone in their right mind would want to undress an uninteresting person like Alice Simms is completely beyond me. What in the world could they expect to find—some great hidden treasure? However, everyone to their own choice. All men are strange creatures, I guess, and Corporal McBurney was probably no worse than many others.

I went back to the dining room then and after a few moments Alice joined us. She took her seat at the table quietly and since no mention was made of her tardiness by either Miss Martha or Miss Harriet, I had no excuse to bring the subject up myself.

It's funny how sometimes those things go. Sometimes if you are one minute late to table Miss Martha will devote the whole mealtime to a lecture on punctuality. Then other times she doesn't seem to care a copper cent. That happens most often, of course, when she is concerned with other things such as money matters or holes in the roof or something of that sort. Since she was smiling too pleasantly this evening to be worried about business problems, I could only decide that the presence of Corporal McBurney was humanizing her.

Another indication of the mellowing of her temper was the fact that she had apparently not noticed how brooding and sullen Miss Harriet was this evening and how resentfully she was spooning her soup. These little bravados on Miss Harriet's part are always a sure sign that she has been at the wine but Miss Martha did not seem to be aware of it.

"It has occurred to me," Miss Martha said, "that we might all profit by Corporal McBurney's being in this house—until his leg heals, of course. What does each of you think of that?"

She was looking at Alice as she asked this question and that unfortunate girl really did blush this time, all the way down her front which she had forgotten to refasten.

"Well, Miss Alice?"

"Yes, ma'am . . . I'm sure we can."

"In what way would you say, Miss, his presence here may benefit us?"

"Well," said Alice—hoping desperately, I imagine, that it wasn't some kind of trap—"maybe the sight of Corporal McBurney here will help us to remember that there is something else in the world besides lessons."

"It seems to me that is all there should be for any young lady your age. If we learn our lessons properly when we are young, we can expect a calm and happy life later when we are faced with the distractions of the world. Is that not so, sister?"

"I cannot answer that," replied Miss Harriet sourly, "since I have encountered very few such distractions."

"It seems to me you have met up with one this very day," Miss Martha said, apparently taking a good look at her sister for the first time. It is a mystery to Miss Martha how her sister gets into the wine cellar since the door is always kept securely locked. She doesn't know that Miss Harriet can force the lock with her sewing scissors and since it would be of no obvious benefit to me, I am not about to tell her. Of course Miss Harriet doesn't visit the wine cellar too often nowadays, because she knows that would set off a full scale investigation. Also when she does remove a bottle, she always rearranges those remaining, sometimes replacing those on the upper shelves with bottles which I think are filled with water and then as an additional precaution, she always sweeps away her footprints in the dust, if she has made any.

These measures, I guess, cause Miss Martha to wonder whether Miss Harriet does not have another supply of spirits hidden away somewhere and, naturally, this is just what Miss Harriet intends. I know that on several occasions when she has been obviously tipsy, Miss Martha has searched for such a supply in her room and elsewhere, but, of course, there is never any to be found. When Miss Harriet takes a bottle from the cellar, she consumes it immediately, as she must have done on the present occasion. Sometimes I wonder if Miss Harriet really enjoys her drinking, or if she only does it to discomfit her sister.

Anyway Miss Martha didn't press the subject at this time—she seldom does in front of us—but went on to ask Emily how she felt we might gain by the presence of the enemy.

"He will be a constant reminder to us that the war is still going on," Emily answered. "Although I personally am almost beginning to think of him as not an enemy at all, since he doesn't seem dedicated to the Union cause. Still, he wears their uniform and every time we look at that we will be reminded of the sacrifices we must continue to make and the prayers we must offer to Heaven that the Lord will grant us a glorious victory."

That is not all she said, of course, but it's all I can remember now. Sometimes I think Emily is wasting her time at this school. She ought to pack her belongings and go to Richmond and run some government office. She would make a wonderful politician because she can give you a speech instantly on any subject, and if she can't compose one long enough to suit her, she will recite the words of someone else, until sometimes I think if she doesn't just shut up, she will drive me right out of my mind.

I just get so tired of it all that here lately I have taken to saying the Rosary to myself during Rhetoric class. One day recently I got through five and a half decades while Emily was reciting the Washington speeches of someone named Henry Clay.

Well Miss Martha went on with her questioning of each of us about the value of having McBurney in the house. Amelia told her that she had found Corporal McBurney to be a student of nature like herself and that she expected to learn a great deal from him about European wildlife. Edwina said that she agreed with Alice—something of an event in itself, Edwina agreeing with anyone—that any breath of air from the outside world was welcome, and also it seemed to her that Corporal McBurney was a very sensitive person whom she thought knew her better now than all of us did with whom she had lived four years.

This comment seemed to revive Miss Harriet a bit.

"How do you mean he knows you better, dear?" she inquired.

"He knows I am not considered here to be of any value," Edwina said.

"And he does set value by you?" Miss Harriet asked gently.

"Yes, I believe he does."

Now that was the first time I had ever heard Edwina suggest that she cared what anyone thought about her. It certainly was a little crack in her character and as a matter of fact it melted a tear which ran down her cheek and dropped into her bowl of turnip soup. Then ashamed of her weakness, she got up and left the table without even asking to be excused.

Surprisingly enough, Miss Martha did not make an issue of it, but instead decided to ignore the whole thing. She merely declared that since the subject seemed to be an upsetting one for some people, the discussion was over, and then, bowing her head, she whipped right into the dinner-ending prayer of thanksgiving without ever allowing me the opportunity to express my opinion. I was all prepared to speculate on the possibility of the Lord's having sent McBurney to our school in order to increase the Catholic population, and I was going to state that although I certainly did not consider Corporal McBurney the best possible Catholic or even a very good Christian, I hoped to be able to improve him, but I was not able to say two words of this before everyone began leaving the room. It is really disgraceful sometimes the way I am always the last one called upon to speak at table and, contrast wise, the first one asked to recite in class. If I am ever enrolled in any other school, I intend to lie about my age in the hope of getting a little simple justice.

As we left the dining room Mattie reported that Corporal McBurney had also finished his dinner and in response to a suggestion by Miss Harriet—to whom she was being unusually amiable, considering Miss Harriet's condition—Miss Martha agreed that we might have our evening prayers as usual in the parlor and before the prayers a few moments of light conversation with our guest.

He didn't seem much in the mood for any kind of conversation as we all entered the parlor immediately and stood in a little circle around his settee. In fact he seemed to be pretending that we had interrupted a nap to which he would like to return without delay.

"My, you certainly do look well-rested, Corporal McBurney," I said in order to get the discussion going. "Doesn't he look well rested and invigorated, Miss Alice, after the peaceful day he has spent all by himself here on the settee?"

Alice made no answer but only scowled defiantly at me. Corporal McBurney, on the other hand, looked as though he had given everything up for lost and appeared to be thinking very rapidly of throwing himself on either Miss Martha's mercy or mine. Unfortunately, Miss Martha, unaware of this little personal issue, interrupted it.

"Corporal McBurney is undoubtedly more rested than he would be had you been allowed to plague him all day with your nonsense," she remarked quite unfairly.

"Ah, no," he said, making his choice. "She's been very good to me, that little lady. She's offered me all sorts of kindnesses today, and I'm sure her little heart is full of much more of the same. I only hope I can repay her goodness some day."

"She quite often can be a terrible nuisance," Emily felt obliged to put in. "But of course I suppose one must consider her age."

"Well, now," McBurney said. "I never thought of her as being any younger than the other students here. She seems to be a very sensible and serious minded person, Miss Marie does."

"Do you really think so?" Alice asked him, evidently genuinely amazed. Now when Alice, who is not entirely stupid, was moved to question his flattery, I began to wonder if, just possibly, he might not really believe it.

"I do indeed think so," he said. I watched him very closely and he didn't wink at her.

"I agree," Miss Harriet said. "Marie has many good qualities and it's time we realized that."

I thought it would not have hurt her to go on and name a few of those qualities. Still, it was nice of her to pay me such public recognition even though I knew it was partly because she was still in her mood of disagreeing with Miss Martha on every possible issue. Nevertheless, I did feel a lot more kindly toward her for a long time after that and toward McBurney too. He was seemingly not as unintelligent as I had first thought.

"Now I have a suggestion," Miss Harriet put in. "Since our music lessons were suspended today in order to permit Corporal McBurney to have his rest, why can't we have a little music now—if Corporal McBurney will not be too disturbed by it."

"Not at all," said he. "It's a grand idea. I'm very fond of music."

Miss Harriet went immediately to the harpsichord. In Louisiana we have been playing pianos in our homes for a hundred years or more but here in Virginia it seems that the best families must use the same old out-of-tune harpsichords which their ancestors brought to the colonies and which, in my opinion, they might better have left behind.

We began by singing that old standby, *Lorena*, with which McBurney was already very familiar since it seems that the Yankees sing it all the time around their campfires. McBurney said he thought it had been written by a Northerner, but Emily said no that could not possibly have been the case. She was peeved already because she had wanted to begin the program with *The Bonnie Blue Flag*, but Miss Martha had overruled her, feeling that McBurney might be sensitive about such things. Frankly I don't think he cared much one way or the other because when we finally did get to *The Bonnie Blue Flag* after *Lorena* and *Flow Gently Sweet Afton* and *Drink to Me Only with Thine Eyes* Corporal McBurney joined right in with, "We are a band of brothers" as loudly as the rest of us and considerably more in tune than some us.

We were just about through the second chorus of it when there came a very loud pounding on the front door. That ended the song abruptly.

"Yankees," said Emily, ready to gird her loins.

"Possibly not," said Miss Harriet. Her voice was trembling and her hands were still poised above the keyboard. "It could very easily be some of our own."

"There is only one way to find out who it is," Miss Martha said "Mattie. . . ."

Mattie, who had been singing along with the rest of us, looked as though her eyes were just going to fly right out from fright. Visitors at any hour were an unusual occurrence and practically unheard of at night.

"Do I have to go alone?" the poor thing asked.

"Yes," said Miss Martha, "but I will be in the hallway behind you. Whoever it is, you will ask them to wait on the porch while you inform your mistress. It is not polite, I know, but these are not polite times. Harriet, you will remain in here with the girls. If it is Yankees or unruly soldiers of our own army, I will rap three times on this door. Then you will take the girls out through the garden to the woods and stay there until I come for you. Do you understand now, all of you?"

"What about Corporal McBurney?" Amelia wanted to know.

Corporal McBurney, sitting up on his settee, looked as terrified as any of the rest of us including Mattie. He certainly was considerably paler than he had been even on the previous day.

"Corporal McBurney may remain where he is, since he is in no condition to leave anyway without assistance. I'm going upstairs now to get Father's pistol. You can pretend some difficulty with the bolt on the front door, Mattie, to give me time to return to the hallway. Be quiet in here, all of you. Mattie, come along."

She went out with Mattie trailing unwillingly behind her. The pounding on the door continued. It was undoubtedly several fists pounding now.

"Even if you must remain here, Johnny," said Amelia quite calmly, "you needn't be all that conspicuous. May we cover him with the rug, Miss Harriet?"

"Yes, certainly," said Miss Harriet, glad of something to do. "All of you may help with this."

We took up the Persian rug and threw it over the settee and Corporal McBurney, leaving him only a small opening for air at one end.

"Don't make any noise in there now, Johnny," Alice told him.

"I don't think you need to remind him of that," I said. "I don't think he's going to make any voluntary noise, but he should do something about the way his teeth are chattering."

Then we waited quietly watching the door until after a few minutes Miss Martha returned from the hallway. She was very white but triumphant and she was carrying her father's old Mexican War pistol which at that time she was keeping in the bedside chest in her room.

"It's all right," she said. "There are just two of them, a captain and a sergeant . . . two cavalry men of our own. Mattie is giving them something to eat in the kitchen."

"Why did they come?" Miss Harriet asked.

"To offer their assistance before the army leaves this vicinity. It's thought that General Grant may break off the fight in this area tomorrow and start South again. This captain says our army will have to get to Spotsylvania Court House before the Yankees in order to protect the road to Richmond. Therefore by tomorrow we may be behind the Yankee lines."

"How did those cavalry men find out about us here?" Amelia wanted to know.

"Someone at Potter's store told them about the school. Their troop is scouting along the turnpike tonight so these two men decided to ride up here and see if they could be of any help to us."

Then Miss Martha noticed the rug covering the settee and guessed what we had done. She paused for a moment and thought about it while we watched her.

"I haven't as yet mentioned anything to them about Corporal McBurney," she said finally. "It occurred to me to do so and then I thought I might speak with all of you first. However what I see here leads me to believe you have already decided what you would like me to do."

"And you will do it, sister?" asked Miss Harriet gently.

"Not necessarily. But let me remind you of the possibilities. First, we could ask them to take Corporal McBurney away with them."

"But he couldn't ride a horse without hurting his leg," Amelia said, "even if they had a spare horse which they very likely don't."

"He could ride behind one of them," Miss Martha said, "but it's true it might cause his wound to reopen. That brings us to the second possibility. We might tell them about Corporal McBurney's being here, but suggest that, since he is wounded, they come back for him at a later time."

"I thought you said our boys were going to retreat," Alice put in.

"So they are, but this captain feels they'll be back this way before long."

"That's wishful thinking," said Miss Harriet. "It might be weeks or even months before they come back again, if they ever manage to do it."

"Why, Miss Harriet, I'm sure you don't mean that," Emily declared. "However I do agree that it might take some time to mount a counter attack and it might be a few weeks before we see them around here again."

"And so if you tell them, they'll very likely insist on taking Johnny along with them right now, and he'll probably die before they ever get him to a hospital," said Alice. "They won't have any time to 'fend to him and so they just won't care what happens to him."

I had taken no part in the conversation up 'til then and I felt as if I should offer some comment. "If he proves to be too much of a nuisance for them," I said, "they'll likely just shoot him and leave him along the road." I said this very distinctly and I noticed it caused some obvious shivering under the rug.

"The third possibility is that we allow Corporal McBurney to stay here until he is recovered and then send him on his way alone." Miss Martha paused again and studied us. "Probably I should not even be discussing this with you. As head of the school and the one responsible for your welfare I should decide for myself what ought to be done."

"Then do it, sister," Miss Harriet told her. "Make up your own mind to do it. Whatever your decision is, we will not hold it against you."

"Of course I know I am not infallible," Miss Martha continued as though she had not heard Miss Harriet. "And there is the question of Christian charity to be considered. That weighed against the risk."

"You keep talking about Corporal McBurney as though he were some old piece of baggage," said Amelia close to tears, "and not a good and kind person who is present in this very room. Anyway there is one more thing that ought to be considered. He's not really your prisoner and therefore it's not right for any of you to be even thinking about handing him over to the soldiers. None of you captured him and he didn't come here of his own accord. I found him and brought him to this school without even asking him if he wanted to come."

"Also," said Alice, "I believe Miss Emily mentioned having some doubts as to whether he could even be considered our enemy."

"That is correct," Emily agreed although somewhat doubtfully. "In many ways he does seem to be in sympathy with us."

"There isn't much more time," Miss Martha said. "It won't take those boys long to eat the little food we can spare. All right then, if you all think Corporal McBurney should be permitted to remain here until his leg is healed, I will be guided by your wishes. However if any one of you thinks otherwise, let her raise her hand. If any one person is opposed to his staying, I will tell the soldiers and let them decide whether to take him now or later."

No hands were raised. I thought briefly of raising mine just to see if Miss Martha would consider my opinions of any consequence, but then I decided against it. I wasn't really opposed to Corporal McBurney at that time and, after all, only a few moments before that he had promised to re-pay my goodness.

Miss Martha waited for a moment longer, then smiled as though she was considerably relieved and started out. It was only then she realized that she was still carrying the old pistol.

"When the soldiers saw me with this," she said, "I believe they were more frightened than either Mattie or I. In fact one of them remarked, 'I've faced thousands of Yankees in my day, ma'am, but I don't think all of them together would be as dangerous as one nervous lady holdin a cocked pistol in her two hands.' 'Well,' said I, 'if you prove to have legitimate business with me, I will permit you to lower the hammer on this contraption. I man-aged with great effort to raise it, but I'm afraid I could never get it down again without pulling the trigger.'"

We all just screeched with laughter at that, Miss Martha included. I had never seen her enjoy herself so much before.

"And did they uncock it for you, Miss Martha?" Alice asked.

"You can see they did. If they hadn't I'm afraid we might have been faced with the problem of another wounded soldier, or, at the least, a great hole in the hallway ceiling."

That set us off again and I think we would have been laughing yet if Corporal McBurney had not begun to cough and choke and make all kinds of sputtering noises underneath the rug. We removed it hastily and thumped him on the back and it wasn't long before he was breathing more normally. As a matter of fact he may have been only pretending to be chok-ing in order to insure our sympathy. He had it at that time, of course, but he also had no way of knowing how long it would continue.

Alice suggested that she wouldn't mind accompanying Miss Martha back to the hallway in order to say a word of cheer to our brave soldiers and

Emily said that she'd be glad to go along with Alice on that kind of mission. This prompted me to mention that I'd like to have a look at the two cavalrymen myself but all three of us were rejected quickly and firmly by Miss Martha who said that, although the captain and the sergeant were nice young men and members of fine Mississippi families—something she had certainly found out in a hurry—at the same time there was no need of putting temptations and longings in their way.

Now this was a very clever thing for Miss Martha to say, since it flatters Alice no end to be thought a temptress and as for Emily, it was probably just about the greatest compliment she had ever been paid. Emily is not an exceptionally ugly girl, but she is obviously a very plain person of the sort my father used to describe as having been born to be someone's maiden aunt. Also if Emily did not drive boys away with her unattractive appearance, she certainly would do so with her tongue. No one, unless he was completely witless, would want to spend his entire life taking orders from and being continually corrected by Emily Stevenson.

I don't suppose Miss Martha was intending to include me in the enchantress category, since I assumed I would be considered by experts in such matters to be either too young or too small to tempt anyone. Not that I'm really interested in such things, thank you.

Well, no matter. Miss Martha left the room and the others turned their attention once again to McBurney, who was starting another performance of his coughing and choking, out of jealousy this time, possibly, because our thoughts had strayed from him. Therefore, while the others were fussing over him, I decided to follow Miss Martha anyway for a quick peek at the cavalrymen, because for one thing I have many relatives in Mississippi and I thought one of these boys might quite possibly be my cousin Geoffrey or my cousin Edmond from Biloxi.

Well, it wasn't. It was just two weary-looking country boys who were coming out of the kitchen still chewing on biscuits and cold turnips with Mattie behind, escorting them along. They were so ragged and dirty I'm sure their fine families would never have recognized them at their own front doors and they were so skinny in the bargain, I'll bet you could have taken off their coats and shirts and counted every one of Mattie's turnips and biscuits inside them.

I was standing on a lower step on the stairs, where it curves, peering over the rail at them as they said their farewells to Miss Martha at the door. Then I heard a noise beside me and turned to find Miss Edwina Morrow. In the excitement we had forgotten all about her.

"Are they taking Corporal McBurney with them?" she whispered.

"No," I said softly, "we decided to keep him."

"What do you mean 'we'? I wasn't asked."

"That's your fault," I said. "You shouldn't have been so rude and rushed away from the table."

Miss Martha evidently heard one of us talking—it might have been me—and turned then to scowl at us over the shoulder of one cavalryman.

"You're sure everything's all right here, ma'am? There's nothing we can do for you?" This was from the captain, or at least I assumed he was the officer because his coat had more buttons on it than the other's, and was not worn quite so badly at the elbows. "If you're afraid of being molested by the Yankees, we maybe could spare a few of our boys to sleep in your barn for a night or two," he continued. "We could send one or two of them up here right now."

"I wouldn't mind staying on here with the ladies, captain," the sergeant volunteered. "In fact all of you could just go on ahead and I'd catch up with you in a few days—soon as everything was safe around here. I could just unroll my blanket right here in this hallway."

"You're very kind," said Miss Martha, "but we couldn't let you do that. We cannot take you from your duties in the field."

"Oh, it might even be some advantage to us, ma'am," said the captain, "having somebody behind General Grant keeping an eye on him, least 'til we see what he has in mind. In fact maybe I ought to stay on here myself, sergeant, and you could ride back to the road and tell the colonel what I'm aiming to do."

"No, no," said Miss Martha very firmly. "I cannot permit it. One or two of you would be no protection against the whole Yankee army and your presence might just call attention to us and provoke them into setting fire to the place. Thank you for your kind interest, gentlemen. Good night."

"I'd be proud to pay my compliments to your students," said the captain.

"Thank you again. I'll tell them."

"There was singing before, wasn't there," said the sergeant wistfully. "I enjoy good singing."

"I'm sure you do," Miss Martha said. "I would have guessed that instantly. Good night, gentlemen. God be with you. Good night." And she all but pushed them out the door and slammed it after them.

"How come you did that?" Mattie asked her. "Even if you didn't want to say nothin about the Yankee, it don't seem to me it would've hurt to let one or two of them stay in the barn."

"You're forgetting that the Yankee is fairly helpless at present and they are not," said Miss Martha. "Also when I didn't tell them about him immediately it didn't seem wise to let them find out about him now. We are not that far from Washington here, you know. There have been known abolitionists and Yankee sympathizers in this region and General Lee's army can burn houses and commit other depredations as well as General Grant's."

"I could've sworn to them you weren't no abolitionist."

"Don't be impudent!"

"You may find out later you made a big mistake."

"If I do, I will take the consequences," Miss Martha said. "I know I made one great mistake in not selling you South years ago when I could have made a dollar on you!"

Then she opened the front door again and followed the soldiers out, announcing that she was going to make sure they left our premises without taking our pony and cow along. Mattie wasn't too disturbed by Miss Martha's remarks because she gets that sort of thing all the time.

"That poor lady just don't trust nobody," Mattie declared.

"With one exception," Edwina said. "She has evidently decided to trust Corporal McBurney."

"Would you have voted for his staying here, if you had been with us earlier, Edwina?" I asked her.

"I'm not sure," she said thoughtfully. "I like him, I think . . . but I'm not sure that his staying here will be a good thing for him . . . or for us."

Well naturally if everyone else at the school was in favor of something Edwina would have to be opposed to it. It was very unusual, however, to hear her say she liked anyone or anything. I don't ever remember hearing her make such a remark before and as far as I know, she never made it again, even about McBurney.

We went back to the parlor then, where I was reprimanded for disobeying orders, first by Miss Harriet and later by Miss Martha when she returned from outside. This is the price one must pay for independence and I have learned to put up with it. I don't know what else anyone could expect from a member of a family which my father says has a history of arguing with the headsman even while the blade is falling. I am just a person who has always been accustomed to making up her own mind—if the truth must out, my own dear mother and I quite often disagreed over this and it happens to be one big reason I am in attendance at this isolated Protestant school—and I am too set in my ways now to ever change them.

I mentioned this out of the side of my mouth to Corporal McBurney. It was after Miss Martha had ended her lecture and Miss Harriet had gone back to the harpsichord. I also asked him how he was planning to repay my goodness.

"How's that again, little darlin?"

"You said a while ago you hoped you could repay my goodness someday."

"Oh yes," he muttered. "Well then, when's your birthday?"

"July eighteenth."

"The same month as mine. Mine's the third of July. All right then, you'll get a fine present on your birthday as a reward for being so nice to me."

"What sort of present will it be?"

"Oh I can't tell you that. It's going to be a surprise."

Well I couldn't imagine where he was planning to get this wonderful present since there are no good shops of any kind nearer than Richmond, and he didn't seem to have brought anything of any value with him. However I didn't consider it mannerly to question him any further and also there was no immediate opportunity because the singing was about to begin again.

For the first selection after the intermission we had a volunteer solo by Miss Emily Stevenson who sang *Somebody's Darling* which, if you are not familiar with it, is a fairly recent and very sad song about a young soldier with blue eyes and curly hair who is dying in a hospital. Emily, I can tell you, brings nothing but enthusiasm to any song she attempts but this particular number is so very sad, I suppose it would cause tears to flow if it were performed by a flock of crows.

We had hardly recovered from Emily's selection when Corporal McBurney offered to try something similar which it seems is popular with the Union troops. This one was called *Just Before The Battle, Mother* and it told the story of a young man who was preparing to go into battle, apparently without any hope of surviving, and was thinking that he would much rather be at home with his mother than where he was, which I guess was a natural enough desire under the circumstances.

Corporal McBurney really had a surprisingly good tenor voice together with a very dramatic way of rendering a sad song and as a result we had just about all broken down by the time he reached the final chorus and that included Miss Martha Farnsworth, Miss Edwina Morrow—and believe it if you can—me. I don't know when I ever wept before at an evening song recital but I must admit I was sobbing right along with the loudest of them on that occasion.

Well, McBurney paused only briefly to survey the destruction he had wrought and then began a very brisk and jolly number, without accompaniment this time, since Miss Harriet's eyes were too wet to see the keyboard. Now, amazingly, this second song seemed so funny and McBurney himself was so comical as he sang it, making all sorts of exaggerated faces and at one point leaning precariously over the back of the settee in the manner of an intoxicated Irishman, that we all just turned instantly from tears to laughter. I don't suppose the song really was so awfully clever—in fact I heard Miss Harriet say some time later that she thought it rather vulgar, except of course on that evening she laughed as hard as anyone else, even while she was still mopping her eyes from the Mother number—but McBurney just performed it like a veteran of the music halls.

If I can recall it went something like this—in McBurney's brogue, of course.

> Arrah, none of your boardin school misses,
> Your sweet, timid craythurs for me,
> Who rave about cupid and blisses,
> Yet know not what ayther may be;
> I don't feel at all sintimintal,
> For romance I care niver a rap,
> But give me a plump, jolly and gintle
> Young widdy in weeds and a cap.
>
> Oh her thremors o' girlhood are over,
> Love's blossom has ripened to fruit,
> And her first love, asleep under clover,
> Is the sile where my passion sthrikes root.
> It is pleasant to know the departed
> Was so tindherly cared to the last,
> And that she will not die broken-hearted
> If I should pop off just as fast!

There was much more of it but that is all I can recall right now.

After that, Alice, who loiters at the gate so much she knows all the marching songs, struck out with *Yellow Rose of Texas* and *Goober Peas* with the rest of us trailing along where we could, and following that Edwina, whom we also found to have a nice clear little voice and who had never bothered to exhibit it much at prior singing sessions, offered us a solo version of *Virginia, Virginia, The Land of the Free*, and then blushed so much when she was finished that I just felt awfully sorry for her.

Next Corporal McBurney announced that as far as he was concerned the greatest song of the entire war was *Dixie* and he led us in several rousing choruses of that which I'm sure must have rang in the ears of the poor cavalry sergeant were he as far away away already as the Orange Pike Road. And what may have seemed more unusual to that troop cavalry was the song we moved to next, *John Brown's Body*, which Emily, in a burst of good will, suggested, and which we all went to as willingly as to any songs of our own.

Then our guest very generously called for a reprise of *Bonny Blue Flag* with which we really shook the rafters and finally we closed the evening with *Home Sweet Home*, which brought on the tears again but they were sort of smiling tears this time, if you know what I mean.

I don't believe we ever sang so well or cried so much or felt so happy either before or after that particular evening. I must say in all honesty that the people in this school are not individually or as a group the greatest singers I have ever heard, but that evening I believe we could have brought down the house at the Opera in New Orleans.

Furthermore I think everyone here could testify that we never felt so warm and good and friendly to each other as we did on that night. Everyone was kissing and hugging everyone else and murmuring compliments about each other's fine voice and remarking on each other's particularly nice appearance, which it seemed everyone had just noticed for the first time—all this in a way that I would normally have found quite sickening, but on this occasion I was right up there in the thick of it myself, just jumping up and down in my eagerness to be nice to somebody, I just didn't care who.

And of course Corporal McBurney was the hub of all this good fellowship. It seemed as though everyone present was standing in line to tell him what a marvelous singer and good Christian and brave young man he was, and similar loose statements like that, and if we all didn't come right out and say them, I'm sure we all felt like it, because on that particular night we couldn't possibly have seen anything wrong in Corporal McBurney. We were ready to trust him with our money and our virtue—those of us who had any—and our lives.

And he was enjoying it. He had probably never been such a center of attention before in his entire life as he had managed to become in one day and a half at this school. There was certainly no thought then in anyone's mind of turning him over to our troops or to his own troops either, even when he had recovered. In those few hours he had made himself such a welcome member of our little band that, if he had played his cards carefully and kept us all in the spirit of that night, Corporal McBurney could have stayed with us forever.

But that is getting into another part of the story. The end of this part was our prayers, which went very smoothly for a change and in which Mc-Burney participated as easily as though he had been born and raised a Protestant. When requests for blessings were invited by Miss Martha, he joined right in and asked for the Lord's protection of everyone in the school who had been so good to him and then to embroider it a bit, for the Lord's forgiveness of all the sinners in both armies, suggesting graciously that there probably were a lot more of them in his army than in ours. Well, it takes one to know one, as my father says.

Miss Martha responded generously with a request that the Lord watch over all the brave soldiers in both armies and that He especially guard and keep from harm our guest who was so far from home. To which we all added—oddly enough, it seems now—a very resounding Amen.

We were dismissed then in order that Miss Martha and Mattie might have a look at Corporal McBurney's leg and prepare him for the night. None of us were exactly willing to break up such a happy gathering but when McBurney, who wisely seldom disagreed with authority in public, declared that he was very tired, we all very cheerfully took our leave of him.

"Well, your treasured woods specimen seems to have won all hearts here," I remarked to my roommate, Amelia Dabney, as we went up the stairs. "I don't think you need to worry about him. He certainly doesn't lack for friends."

"It doesn't seem so, does it," said Amelia. "However we must remember that it is easy to be friendly to a person when you have no personal reason to feel otherwise. We must keep that in mind and stay on our guard so that we can help Corporal McBurney if he ever needs it."

"Corporal McBurney can help himself a great deal," I informed her, "if he minds his own business and doesn't give people personal reasons to dislike him."

And with that comment I went to bed. My last thought, I remember now, before I went to sleep was to wonder whether Miss Martha would remember to take her father's old pistol back to her room with her when she retired. As I recalled, she had put the pistol on the parlor table when the singing began. I wondered now if she would forget that it was there, although Miss Martha was not the kind of person to forget much of anything. Perhaps, I thought, she will leave it there deliberately as evidence of her trust in Corporal McBurney, or even more likely, she might leave it there, unloaded maybe, in order to test him. She might have taken the charge out of it secretly and might be watching him now from behind the partly closed door to see if he will take the pistol and try to conceal it. But then I thought, Corporal McBurney may be every bit as clever as Miss

Martha and will know that if the pistol is there, it is there for a reason and therefore he will not touch it.

With these speculations I fell asleep and by the next day I had forgotten all about the pistol myself.

Amelia Dabney

Corporal McBurney seemed to be improving rapidly from his severe wound and loss of blood. He grew stronger every day and before the week was out he was talking about getting up and trying to walk.

Miss Martha was opposed to this because she felt there had not been time for the splintered part of the bone to reknit and for the wound itself to heal properly. However, along about the sixth day, when it seemed he was determined to try it anyway, Miss Martha's permission or no, she allowed Miss Harriet to fetch an old family cane for him and then we all stood around the settee holding our breaths while she and Mattie helped him to his feet.

"Now lean on that cane and your good leg," Miss Martha instructed him. "Don't put any weight on the bad leg."

"He shouldn't be movin that leg at all," Mattie grumbled. "Even swingin it a little bit ain't gonna help it and if he bumps it on something all them stitches are gonna bust right out."

Miss Martha said that she agreed with Mattie but that the weight of public opinion seemed to be against them. None of the younger people in the house, she said, including her own sister, had learned the advisability of not rushing Nature but allowing her to take her own course. In any event, she said, if Corporal McBurney wanted to take the risk of reinjuring his leg, he was free to do so, but she wanted us all to know that she was not in any way responsible for the consequences.

While these statements were being made, the three of them were progressing very slowly across the parlor floor toward the garden door with Corporal McBurney in the middle leaning on the cane and half hopping on his good leg and Miss Martha and Mattie moving protectively beside him. Suddenly he slipped and would have fallen had not the two of them caught him.

"It was staged," my roommate, Marie Deveraux, remarked in my ear. "It was just a pretended slip to make the whole thing look more difficult."

"I'm sure that isn't so," I whispered back. "He could have hurt himself very badly if Miss Martha and Mattie hadn't been right there."

"But they were there and he knew it," said Marie who is just about the most cynical person I know of any age, no matter what her other virtues. "It's what acrobats and tumblers do all the time when they know they have nets below them. I've seen them take deliberate tumbles many times from tightropes and trapezes just to win a little audience sympathy at the Christmas entertainments at the Opera house in New Orleans. Oh my goodness, don't tell me he's going to try the same trick again!"

He didn't, if it was a trick and I still don't believe it was. He regained his own balance this time and made it to the garden door where he stood for a while, catching his breath and looking out at the garden.

"Your roses need pruning," he said after a moment. "And those hedges are in terrible shape. The whole flower garden needs a good goin over. I'll get to it tomorrow or the day after."

"You'll do nothing of the kind," Miss Martha told him. "It's kind of you to offer but that garden has been neglected for some time and it can remain that way for a while longer."

"It is most kind of you to offer, Mister McBurney," Miss Harriet said. "Have you had much gardening experience?"

"Oh yes," he replied. "I did a good bit of it at the big place back home. They said they'd make me head gardener some day if I wanted to stay, but I was eager for the higher things—such as getting myself blown up in the American war."

"Well if you really have a knack for gardening, you can make yourself most welcome later in your convalescence. That English box hedge has not been trimmed properly for three years or more. There's just no one around here capable of doing it."

"And I've tried a dozen times to put that rose arbor in order," said Miss Harriet, "and got nothing for my pains but wounded fingers."

"A flower garden like that needs a man all right," Mattie declared. "I sure can't do nothin with it. Anyway I was raised to work in the house and not in the yard."

"Mattie does very nicely with the kitchen garden," said Miss Martha, "but the flowers have defeated her as they have the rest of us."

That proved once again what an influence for good Corporal McBurney had become on the people here because it was very seldom that Miss Martha ever said a word of praise about Mattie's work in the vegetable garden, or anywhere else for that matter, and the dear soul does struggle awfully hard with her beans and peas and other plants, even though she does feel obliged to complain now and then about it not being her kind of work.

On the other hand Marie says that Mattie really does enjoy her outside duties and would be heartbroken if she ever had to give them up. Marie feels that since the kitchen garden is Mattie's special assignment, it is her one big chance to direct the whole school, even including Miss Martha who does her daily stint of hoeing along with the rest of us. According to Marie's reasoning, Mattie only complains about being unsuited for field or yard work in order that Miss Martha will not have the satisfaction of seeing she is happy with the arrangement. To be honest about it, I seldom bother to wonder about the reasons behind people's actions as much as my room-mate does.

"Well you can all quit worrying about your posies now," said Johnny McBurney. "You've got an expert to take care of them."

And he was telling the truth, as we soon found out. The very next morning he insisted on going out into the garden to see just exactly what needed to be done. I walked beside him while he hopped along on his good leg and the cane, inspecting the rose arbor and what Miss Martha calls her English box hedge surrounding it. It is really not an English hedge at all but a box huckleberry, *gaylussacia brachyeera*, a kind of evergreen shrub which is usually not raised successfully much farther north than Alabama or perhaps the Carolinas.

Well after that we had a look at the inner hedge of forsythia, which is named for the famous botanist, William Forsyth, and then at the rose arbor itself. Then after the arbor we went along examining the lavenders and lilacs and camelias which line the path all the way to the little Shrine of Eros, as Miss Harriet calls it and which is now just a mass of tangled jasmine and myrtle and honeysuckle and tall weeds some of whose proper names even I don't know.

Johnny even examined the lawn itself, sending me to step over the flower beds and pull specimen blades of grass here and there which he would take and squint at and roll in his fingers, in what I suppose was an expert's manner, and once or twice he even chewed meditatively on a blade as though he could tell just exactly what care it needed from the taste of it.

"Now this bit has an odd flavor to it," he said once.

"Perhaps Lucinda and Dolly have been out here."

"Who?"

"Our cow and Welsh pony. Miss Martha lets them graze out here."

"For pity's sake, dear girl," he said, spitting out the grass. "Why didn't you tell me?"

"You didn't ask me," I said. "It's how we keep the lawn trimmed. Of course someone is always sent out here with Lucinda and Dolly to make sure they don't eat any of the shrubs or flowers."

"No matter," said he. "A nice lawn like this hadn't ought to be used for pasture."

"I agree with you," I told him. "I don't see any value in trimming a lawn at all. It just takes away all the cover for little animals and birds and also, remember this: When you cut away the clover and dandelions you are depriving wild bees of a source of pollen. Have you thought much about that?"

"By golly, I haven't," Johnny replied, "but I'm certainly going to twirl it around in my mind a few times before this day is out. Now there's a week's work alone around that little open shed. It looks like you're cultivating weeds there instead of posies."

"Miss Harriet has thought about cutting them on several occasions," I said, "but that part of the garden is sort of Miss Martha's private domain so in the end Miss Harriet always decides to leave the weeds alone."

"What's that little house supposed to be?"

"It's a shrine of Eros—the Greek god of love."

"Fancy that. Were these people pagans in the old days then?"

"Oh no. It's just something that Miss Martha and her brother Robert built one summer when they were young. I guess there were some bricks left over from some building job or other and so they made those columns and roofed them over with some old boards and painted the whole thing white, as you see. It's supposed to look like the Acropolis in Athens but I guess the resemblance is rather slight. Then one of them—I don't know which one—got that old marble statue of Eros from a shop in Richmond and they put that in the middle of the house and planted these vines around the outside."

"That little naked fella is Eros?"

"Yes, or Cupid as the Romans called him."

"Fancy that. It's a strange thing for Miss Martha to be interested in. She just doesn't seem the type for it. And her brother, with all due respect to the gentleman, must've been an odd sort too."

"Well I never met him," I said, "and I wouldn't say anything about the shrine to Miss Martha if I were you. It's something that she doesn't like to talk about."

"Oh she'd be willing to discuss it with me," said Johnny. "I find people are quite often willing to discuss their most personal business with me. It's the disarming way I have."

"Why do you want to know so much about everyone's personal business?"

"Partly curiosity and partly for protection, dear Amelia. It's a cruel world we live in and a fella has to take precautions."

"Have you ever read any of the works of Mister Charles Darwin?" I asked him. "All nature is cruel, Mister Darwin says."

"Well thank God we're around civilized people here."

When Johnny had finished his estimate of the garden work he sent me to the tobacco barn for the necessary tools—the various spades and shears and trowels he required—all of which we found to be quite rusted now and in need of sharpening. So we spent the rest of the first outside morning at that task, buffing and honing the tools against a small slab of granite which I also found in the barn.

"This is good stone," Johnny said as he spat on it and applied the edge of a pruning knife to it. We were sitting on the bench in the arbor and I was watching the house, sort of hoping, I guess, that the others would sleep late and allow Johnny and me a bit more of the morning. Of course I knew that Miss Martha would be out at her usual time, fifteen minutes until eight, and Miss Harriet would follow with the girls soon after, but I couldn't help wishing anyway that things might change this morning.

Mattie was on her knees in the kitchen garden picking the weevils— *cylas formicarius*—off the sweet potatoes and I knew she would not bother us because she was already starting to worry about the possibility of Corporal McBurney's infringing on her vegetables. I had reassured her on this matter and had said that I was certain that Corporal McBurney, if he did volunteer to do kitchen garden work when he was able, would be very happy, I was sure, to do it under her supervision.

"That particular stone is called New England granite," I told Johnny now. "It's not native to this part of the country but I guess Miss Martha and Miss Harriet's father had a wagon load of it brought in here one time from the North."

"What did he want it for?"

"Most of it was used for paving in front of the house and the rest of the slabs were set by for grave markers in the cemetery in the woods. All the slabs have been used now except this one."

"Are the Farnsworths buried in the woods then?"

"Not the family. They're always buried in Saint Andrews Churchyard. It's the darky cemetery I'm talking about. Before Mister Farnsworth bought this granite their graves were either marked with boards or not at all. Now each grave has its own stone marker with whatever names and dates Mister Farnsworth could remember."

"Kept outside the walls even in death, are they? Well there's only need for one more marker. For old Mattie, eh?"

"I suppose. She's certainly counting on being buried out there. She's rather fond of the woods, like me—or at least in daylight she is—and also her husband is buried out there. He was owned by a farmer near here and when he died the farmer sent his body back to Mattie. I believe Mattie has said that Miss Martha paid the farmer ten dollars for the kindness."

"Well I'm not anxious to be buried anywhere myself," said Johnny, "but I guess if I had to choose, a woods might be better than a churchyard. Somehow I think a woods might not be quite so lonely."

"Do you believe in Heaven, Johnny?"

"To tell you the truth, I haven't thought much about it. Maybe there is a Heaven and maybe there isn't, but whatever way it is, I've never felt any need or desire to wonder about it. Maybe it's because I'm not yet convinced I'm ever going to die. That may seem strange to you, but that's the way I am. I've never even thought much about dying—even at the worst time in the battle I don't recall that I did. For some reason I just wasn't concerned about death—even with it happening all about me—but only of being hurt badly and disabled. During the battle, I remember, what I feared most was being blinded, and after that of losing a leg or an arm. I'll tell you a secret, Amelia. Do you know that I must have awakened fifty times during my first night in this place—I was never as unconscious as a lot of people thought, only in a kind of fog through which I could most times dimly see and hear but couldn't speak. Anyway I kept coming to my senses in a panic every little while . . . remembering the horror in the woods . . . the fire and the smoke and the screaming . . . and wondering now to myself, 'Is my leg gone? Will I ever walk again? Will I ever run and jump and dance again?' Then suddenly the pain would hit me and do you know, I'd bless it—I'd bless that pain—and after a while, I'd slip back down in the fog again."

"It's all right now, isn't it Johnny? You're not worried about your leg now, are you?"

"Lord no, I'm not worried about anything now. The leg is fine and I'm fine and I'm on my way to being a whole, live man again. I'll soon be ready and as fit as ever to take on all comers for a fight or a wrestle or a romp on the feathers, begging your little girl's pardon. That's my Heaven, dear Amelia. It's the only one I need. Do you believe in Heaven, darlin?"

"Well," I said, "it's a comfort, of course, to think that one's brothers are somewhere and that one will see them again some day, but there are times when I feel that such is not the case. There are also times when I feel that even if there is a Heaven I don't want to go there myself. Because my roommate,

Marie Deveraux, keeps telling me that, according to the best Christian theology, animals cannot possibly go to Heaven when they die because they have no souls."

"Ah well, I wouldn't worry too much about what that one says."

"Oh Marie is very bright even if she is young. Sometimes I think she deliberately avoids letting our teachers see how bright she really is. Anyway, I also asked Miss Martha and Miss Harriet if they thought animals would be allowed to enter Heaven and they both said they didn't think so. Miss Harriet said that possibly Heaven was already stocked with some eternally living animals but that it seemed to her very unlikely that any of our common earthly breeds would be admitted."

"Now let me tell you even Miss Martha and Miss Harriet don't know everything. Where've they been in this great world, will you inform me, that they're such experts on animal theology? What kind of a place would Heaven be if a man had to ride up to the gate and leave his horse outside? What about the donkey on which the Bible says, if I can recall my lessons, the Lord rode around Galilee? What about all these goats and cows and such like that were in the Bethlehem stable on that Christmas night? And while you're at it, consider all the birds and beasts that sailed around for forty days and nights with old Noah on the Ark. It would be mighty ungrateful of the powers that be, don't you think, to deny all those famous Biblical animals a bit of Heavenly reward."

"That's true, of course. I've never looked at it that way before."

"Well, keep thinking of it now. If there's any other world after this one, it stands to reason it'll be big enough to house all the animals this earth has known since time began to tick. They'll all be there . . . the good ones and the bad . . . all the dinosaurs and unicorns and dragons . . . the whale that swallowed Jonah . . . the lions that passed up the chance to eat Daniel . . . maybe even some of the other lions that ate the Christians in old Nero's day. A lion that has dined on a saint must take on a bit of saintliness himself, wouldn't you say, Amelia?"

"Yes," I said, giggling a little. "I'll tell you why I've been somewhat concerned about this problem, Johnny. It's because I have a pet snapping turtle who has been very sick."

"Don't worry about it. Turtles live to be very old."

"I know they do, or at least I know that some species do. I'm not so sure about snapping turtles. Anyway when you become attached to pets like that, you are quite apt to wonder what will become of them when they die."

"Well your turtle is still a long way from the pearly gates, I'll guarantee you, and that without even giving him a complete medical examination. I'll bet you that your snapping turtle outlives the both of us—or me, at least—and I've already told you that I'm not convinced I'm ever going to die."

That was about the end of my conversation with Johnny McBurney on that first outside morning because Miss Martha and the others began to come out then to work in the kitchen garden. I really think it was one of the best and most rewarding talks I ever had with Johnny. There were other talks on other mornings, of course, but the first was certainly one of the best. Also I think it may have been the longest talk I had with him all the while he was here because our opportunities for conversations lessened as Johnny grew stronger and able to attempt more work. Within a day or two, for instance, he was able to walk safely without someone standing by and a few days after that he was able to work a full morning in the garden.

He began with standing tasks such as pruning the roses and cutting away the dead vines at the back of the house. Then he progressed to bending and stooping tasks such as attending to the beds and shrubs and trimming and shaping the hedges, still favoring his wounded leg of course, but paying it less and less mind every day. His leg seemed to be improving as rapidly as the garden and that, Miss Harriet told us, was beginning to look as beautiful now as it had in the days when she and Miss Martha were young.

Miss Martha was not as enthusiastic about Johnny's work as her sister was, although I think she may have been secretly very happy about it. However she did at first refuse to allow him to cut the weeds around the Shrine of Eros. Johnny brought it up rather offhandedly on about the third or fourth outside morning when Miss Martha had come over from the kitchen garden to see how we were getting on.

"I'll be getting down to the end of the path here in a day or two," he said, "and I'll have that little Greek house down there fit to shelter old Homer himself if he should ever drop by of an afternoon."

"I don't think you need bother," Miss Martha said. "I plan to have that structure torn down one of these days. Meanwhile we'll let the weeds cover it."

"Why now," Johnny protested, "it's a nice little addition to this kind of garden. I'd only need to cut away the weeds and trim the vines and give the whole thing a good going over with a bit of whitewash."

"I said you needn't bother," Miss Martha told him sharply.

Johnny paused and studied her and then decided, wisely, not to press the point.

"Yes ma'am," he said, smiling faintly and giving her that little bow with which he always surrendered an argument and which some people later came to describe as mocking, but I don't think he ever intended it to be mocking at all. I think he was always only trying to be polite.

I decided then to offer an alternative. "Rather than destroy the little building entirely," I said, "you could just remove the statue and make the house a kind of feeding and resting place for birds and squirrels and rabbits and so forth. Why don't you consider that, Miss Martha?"

Miss Martha chose to ignore my suggestion. "Miss," she said coldly, "if Corporal McBurney has nothing more for you to do here today, you may return to your row in the other garden or else go inside and review your lessons."

"Oh Corporal McBurney has a lot of work for me, Miss Martha," I said. "Tell her all the things you want me to do, Johnny."

"Well her most important duties," said Johnny grinning, "are the guiding of my clumsy feet away from bird's nests and keeping my spade from decapitating friendly worms. That plus keeping me company and being nice to me."

"Are we not all being nice to you, Mister McBurney?" Miss Martha asked him.

"Yes ma'am, of course you are. I could ask for no nicer or more friendly treatment than what I've been given here. Even if I had been cared for behind my own lines, I could have asked for nothing better."

Miss Martha, pleased with this answer, went back to her own work then in the kitchen garden. When she was out of earshot, Johnny said, "I didn't tell her, but the main reason I like to have you helping me is because I consider you my best friend in this place."

Well those words affected me so much that for a moment I couldn't answer him. "Do you really mean it?" was the best I could finally manage.

"To be sure I mean it," he laughed. "Do I ever say anything I don't mean? Well of course I do, Amelia . . . hundreds of things . . . it's my nature. But not to you, Amelia. Remember that, my girl. I will never be anything but sincere with you. You saved my life, so the least I can do is be honest with you. Now then, no more wasting time on idle compliments. Let's get on with these hedges."

Which we did. I should say here that Miss Martha had very kindly granted me permission to work with Johnny for a while instead of in the kitchen garden, and I must also add that every other student in the school besieged Miss Martha immediately for permission to do likewise, but no more transfers from the kitchen garden to the flower garden were allowed. This caused some ill feeling toward me, I can tell you, even from such people as my own roommate who had boasted earlier that she would not volunteer to work with Corporal McBurney even if Miss Martha offered wages. But then, not surprisingly, she was the first one to try to join us in the flower garden on the morning right after my transfer was announced.

Furthermore, when Miss Martha told her to pick up her hoe and get back to her own row, Marie, in one of her terrible fits of temper, swung her hoe so hard that she chopped two whole stalks of corn right off at the roots and when Miss Harriet remonstrated with her about this, she just threw her hoe away and walked up and down several rows, kicking and hitting at corn and peas and sweet potato vines, until Mattie finally caught her by the ear and led her into the house where Miss Martha, following after, banished her to her room for the rest of the morning, and also sentenced her to three more days of going without her dinner, which, of course, is practically routine for Miss Marie Deveraux.

Anyway Marie was not the only one to become jealous over my new assignment, although none of the other girls protested as violently as she did—or at least they didn't in public. Both Alice and Emily, however, took to pinching me and pulling my hair whenever they caught me in a hallway or on the stairs, and Edwina told me in private that she considered me the most common kind of sneak who had arisen early on Corporal McBurney's first outside morning just to tell him a lot of lies about her. Truthfully, I had done nothing of the kind. In fact I almost never discussed Edwina with Johnny at all unless he asked about her and on those occasions I would try to answer him as briefly as possible.

Actually he did ask about her quite often because right from the beginning he was very interested in Edwina. And even when he wasn't inquiring about her, he was usually watching her as she worked on her row in the vegetable garden.

Edwina usually pretended to be unaware of this but in actual fact she wasn't. She always knew when he was staring because I noticed her glancing sideways at him now and then, although she never smiled or waved at him as Alice Simms was continually doing. And oddly enough, the more Johnny's interest in her increased, the more Edwina openly ignored him. During his first days with us, she had visited him in the parlor several times a day just like the rest of us, but once she sensed he was attracted to her she began to act—at least in public—as though he didn't exist at all. That, I think, is a very strange human reaction for which you can find no parallel in the animal kingdom.

Of course there still wasn't much time in the day for anyone to have a private meeting with Johnny. Classes always begin immediately after gardening period and once our books are open for the day it just seems that every single minute is occupied. Even when we did have a moment or two free from schoolwork it was always a case of everyone being free in a body and at those times each person's first thought was to go and see how Johnny McBurney was getting along.

As for Johnny himself, he was not restricted, as far as I know, once he was able to hobble around on his leg. It seemed that once Miss Martha had made up her mind that he could be trusted, she allowed him to have the run of the house, or at least the downstairs part of it.

By that time the battle had moved away from us, down around Spotsylvania and beyond, and if there were Union troops still in this vicinity they must have been avoiding the nearby roads. We never saw any more soldiers of any kind around the school and according to Emily Stevenson who had pondered the situation, it was quite likely that we never would because, as she explained it, there was nothing of any military importance in our neighborhood.

Well we were quite content to accept that. With the war gone away from us and likely to stay away, there was every day less reason to connect Johnny McBurney with it. It was becoming very easy for everyone to forget that he had ever been our enemy. I'm speaking now of those who may have felt that way in the beginning. As I have said already, I regarded him as a friend right from the start.

Also when he declared that I was his best friend at the school, I truly believed him, and that in spite of knowing of his interest in Edwina Morrow. Because I knew that the way he might have felt about her was entirely different from the way he felt about me.

I knew that when boys become a certain age they develop a biological interest in females which is very similar to the mating instincts of all animals. If Johnny McBurney had those kind of biological feelings about Edwina Morrow, I knew that he couldn't help it. From a scientific point of view it was only natural and maybe even proper for him to be that way.

Therefore there was no reason for me to be jealous about it. I wasn't old enough or pretty enough to stimulate the same kind of feelings in him, and I did have his friendship and his trust which to me was worth a whole lot more than just a common mating instinct.

Of course one thing that was troubling me even more than his biological urges was the worry over the coming time when his leg would be completely healed and he would have to go away. And I think this problem was on Johnny's mind too.

Even though his leg was much improved he was still residing in the parlor. A place could have been made for him upstairs, I suppose, but he knew that Miss Martha preferred that he remain on the first floor and so he never suggested any other arrangement. Also I think he felt that as long as he continued to occupy his original quarters he might still be thought of as our patient. Once he moved upstairs or elsewhere, he might be considered discharged as cured and there would seem to be no further reason for his staying on at the school.

In fact only a while ago Miss Martha reminded me of a brief conversation she had with Johnny which I think took place toward the middle of his third week here. It was late one afternoon after last class and I had managed by some miracle to have a moment alone with him. We were discussing our plans for the following day in the garden, although to tell the truth there wasn't a great deal left to be done. We had worked very hard for several mornings and, of course, Johnny was continuing by himself all day while I was occupied with my studies.

However I had noticed him dawdling a bit for a day or two especially in the afternoons. It might have been because his leg was bothering him but I suspected it was more because he was trying to make the work last longer. Apparently Miss Martha had noticed it too because on that afternoon she entered the parlor and came over to the settee where we were seated and in her usual direct fashion asked him about it.

"I was wondering," she said, not being at all unkind about it. "I saw you on the bench in the arbor this afternoon reading a book."

"This Shakespeare," said Johnny, producing it. "Is it all right?"

"Certainly, it's all right," declared Miss Martha. "I'm very glad to see you have a taste for books. You may feel free to browse in the library and take any book you please. My concern now is for your leg. I thought perhaps you were resting on the bench this afternoon because the leg was bothering you."

"It twinges a bit now and again," Johnny admitted.

"I would expect it to do so. You may recall that I was opposed to your walking on it as soon as you did." Miss Martha had stooped down and was unbandaging the leg as she spoke. "However I can appreciate your desire to be active. I suppose I would have rebelled myself at your age at the prospects of being confined to a bed. In any case, outside of a very dirty bandage, there doesn't seem to be too much wrong here. You haven't done the leg any fresh injury as far as I can see. The stitches seem to be holding properly and the wound is healing nicely. Perhaps we can take that thread out in a day or two."

"When do you think I will be entirely recovered?" Johnny asked her.

"I suppose it is a matter of opinion," Miss Martha said. "Although you are probably still a bit weak from the blood you lost, some people might say you are recovered now, as long as you can walk and stand for more than an hour on the leg."

"Oh but I favor it," said Johnny. "I don't put any weight on it. I could never do any marching for a good while yet, at least not any quick marching. Oh maybe I could do a slow hundred yards or so but I could never walk a mile on that leg yet."

"Nevertheless, I'm sure that if you were being attended by your own army surgeons they would pronounce you fit to return to duty. Very likely they would not have allowed you to walk at all with stitches in your leg, but once you were able to stand and get about on it. I don't think you would have remained hospitalized very long."

"So you'd like me to leave, would you?"

"I didn't say that."

"Surely not. You're too polite a lady, I guess, to be so blunt about it."

"I am as blunt as I need to be, Mister McBurney, as you should know by now. Since you bring it up yourself I will tell you that I think your leg is healed enough for you to leave here by the end of this week. Let us say by Saturday."

"That's four days from now."

"Yes, that is correct."

"Where would I go?"

"I'm afraid it is entirely your business where you go, Mister McBurney. However I should think you might find columns of your own troops on the Brock Road since that connects with the main road to Richmond."

"I don't know if I could walk as far as that Brock Road or not."

"I can take you in the pony cart."

"That's a deal of trouble for you, Miss Martha, which could all be avoided in another week or so. I certainly wouldn't mind the walking if I was only feeling up to it. Also there's the work in the flower garden. I'm not nearly finished out there yet."

"You've done enough. What's left I'm sure the girls can finish."

"That garden should have continual care. What you need is a full-time gardener here."

"Perhaps we need one but I expect we can do without one in these times."

"Could I please stay for only another week, Miss Martha," Johnny asked her then. He was so forlorn-looking and his lip was trembling so I thought he was about to burst into tears and I must admit I was very close to joining him.

"I'm sorry," Miss Martha said, "but I really don't see any reason for it. At the risk of seeming uncharitable, I just don't feel there is any more we can do for you."

"Maybe there is," Johnny said, "but it wouldn't come under the heading of charity, or nursing care either. I do sound ungrateful, don't I. Instead of begging to stay longer, I should be thanking you for keeping me this long."

"There's no need for thanks," she told him. "I've given you no more than I would have any helpless stranger."

"That's the rub, isn't it," he answered. "It's a pity, isn't it, that I couldn't have remained helpless."

Miss Martha made no reply to this, but only stared at him for a brief moment longer, then picked up her skirts and went out. Now the question is, what did Johnny McBurney mean by those last words? Miss Martha remembers the whole conversation about as well as I do, but she is now taking Johnny's last words on that occasion to mean that he really felt sorry that he wasn't still helpless. On the other hand I think I knew Johnny McBurney about as well as anyone in this house. I was sitting on the settee right beside him on that afternoon and I can recall the bitter tone in which he expressed those words. It was in the same way as unhappy people will sometimes say, "Oh I wish I were dead," or "I just wish I had never been born." They don't really mean those things and I don't think Johnny meant what he said either. I do know for an absolute certainty that the ability to walk and run and move about as he pleased was just about the most important thing in Johnny's life.

Well after Miss Martha had gone I remained with him for a few moments trying to think of something to say that might lift his spirits. However, since I was feeling as badly about the fact of his having to leave as he was, I guess I wasn't much comfort to him.

"It's very possible that Miss Martha will change her mind by the end of the week," was one thing that I told him.

"I doubt it very much," he answered. "And when you come right down to it she's probably right. I'm out of place here. I don't belong in this school and if I stay there's liable to be trouble."

"What sort of trouble?"

"The kind you might expect when a fella like myself is let loose in a flock of pretty girls."

"We're not all pretty."

"Yes, you are," he said, laughing suddenly, "every last one of you. And you're the prettiest of the lot, Amelia my darlin."

Well that was a very extravagant statement for anyone to make, even Johnny McBurney, but it was also a very nice one. Of course I knew that he didn't really believe it any more than I did, but I also knew that since there was nothing in the world he wanted from me—with the possible exception of my friendship, and he had that as a free gift without any necessity of purchasing it—it was a most kind and generous remark and yet, perversely, I didn't appreciate it at that time.

"If you really think you might get into difficulties here, Johnny," I said, "then perhaps it would be better if you leave in a few days." I didn't mean that at all but I said it anyway.

"The thing I don't like about it," he went on as though he hadn't heard me, "is the being asked to go. When I leave somewhere I prefer to make my exit at my own time and on my own terms."

"Then maybe you should leave before the week is up." I didn't mean that either but for some reason I just couldn't prevent myself from being spiteful.

And Johnny answered, taking me seriously, "I think you're right, Amelia. Maybe I should just take my leave of this place tomorrow or the day after before the time expires on the old lady's eviction notice. Just put on my cap, I will, and go out the door and down the road. I wouldn't want you to think I didn't appreciate how good you've all been to me, but I think it might be the best way to do it after all."

I can't deny I was rather angry at his sudden decision, even though I was aware that the decision had been forced on him. I'm sure he was not at all eager to leave us at that time, but it certainly did seem that he had gotten over being upset about the situation awfully quickly. Anyway I had no further opportunity to discuss it with him on that afternoon because Edwina Morrow entered just then and, of course, Johnny McBurney was of no mind to continue conversing with me.

"Oh, forgive me," said Edwina, pretending, I guess, that she had expected the room to be unoccupied. "I was only looking for the volume of Shakespeare," she said in a manner much shyer than her usual. "I noticed it wasn't on the library shelf and thought I might have left it in here."

"It's here all right," Johnny told her with great fervor.

"If you're reading it," said she, "I wouldn't dream of taking it. I can wait until you're finished."

"Not at all," Johnny declared. "You must take it. You probably need it for your studies."

"I can wait a day or two," she answered.

"Oh, don't be ridiculous," I said angrily. "You know you can't possibly wait one more instant, Edwina. Why don't you just sit down here on the settee with Johnny and you can both read the stupid book side by side to your heart's content!"

And with that I left the room and ran up the stairs. I don't think I have ever been in my life as angry as I was on that afternoon—angry at Edwina and Johnny and the entire world, I guess, and at the same time just disgusted with myself for being angry. I was all the way to my room before I realized that Johnny had not tried to call me back and, of course, that made me all the more furious.

I lay on my bed and wept for a spell while my roommate, who was serving out some punishment or other, sat propped up on her bed, silently watching me and eating a crab apple. When she had finished with the apple she threw the core out the window, which is a common practice of hers to get rid of the evidence.

"Very little in life is worth weeping about," she said finally, "unless some purpose is served by the weeping. I almost never weep unless I can gain something by it."

"I'm not crying out of unhappiness," I explained after a moment, "as much as I'm crying out of temper."

"Either reason is a waste of time," said Marie selecting another apple from a pile of them on her bed. It was evident that she had prepared herself for a long imprisonment this time.

I told her then about Johnny's having to go away and his willingness to accept it without protest and about Edwina and everything else that was on my mind. Marie made no comment until I had ended my story and she had devoured the second crab apple.

"We could think of a way to keep him here, if that's what you want," she said at last. "Frankly it doesn't make much difference to me. I'm kept in confinement so much here lately that I never see McBurney anyhow. I suppose we could get up a petition of some sort and all of us could sign it, but I rather doubt if that would have much effect on Miss Martha. On the other hand, since it is the condition of his leg which has made Miss Martha decide he is ready to leave, we might persuade him to have a relapse of some kind."

"Johnny won't go along with that," I declared. "He's not at all deceptive."

"Is that so? Apparently you don't know him as well as you think you do," said my roommate. "Anyway it probably would have to be a genuine relapse or none at all, because Miss Martha would very likely investigate it very carefully. He'd have to break a few stitches, or get an infection or something like that—maybe even develop a little blood poisoning, just to be on the safe side."

"I would never go along with that," I told her firmly. "I don't want Johnny to reinjure his leg in any way."

Emily Stevenson passed by our open door then on her way down to dinner, and she had to come back and find out what we were discussing. Since it seemed a matter which concerned her as well as Marie and I, we explained the problem to her. Then just about the time we had finished, Alice Simms came along and we had to repeat the story again to her.

"There isn't any unsurmountable problem here," said Alice. "Obviously all that needs to be done is to convince Corporal McBurney that he shouldn't leave."

"Miss Martha will have the last word on that subject," Emily remarked.

"Let her," Alice answered. "Let her have all the words she pleases. If Johnny refuses to go, there isn't much she can do about it—especially if all of us are on Johnny's side. After all, he is a man, isn't he—or so I've been told."

"I don't think it would be right for Corporal McBurney to disobey a direct order from Miss Martha," said Emily. "That sort of conduct doesn't sound very honorable to me."

"Why not, for Heaven's sake?" Alice wanted to know. "She isn't his commanding officer, is she? It might not be proper for students to disobey a direct order by their teacher, but I fail to see where Johnny is under any obligation to obey a person who, technically speaking, is his enemy. If you must drag your old honor in like some old cat—and if Johnny were the kind of person to be swayed by such old-fashioned ideas, which I doubt very much since he isn't one of your fancy plantation gentlemen—it could always be explained to him that it's more honorable to obey the will of a majority of ladies rather than a smaller number."

"I would appreciate your withholding your comments about plantation gentlemen since you obviously have never met anyone of that sort," said Emily huffily. "And now please tell me how we could prevent Miss Martha from raising a clamor and sending for outside assistance if McBurney were to attempt to resist her?"

"I would like you to know that I and my mother have had the most friendly relationships with the best plantation gentlemen from each and every state in this whole Confederacy," Alice shouted, "and only a very dull witted person could fail to realize that there is nowhere for Miss Martha to send for assistance against McBurney. There are none of our soldiers around here anymore and she would be very reluctant, I'm sure, to call any Union soldiers in to help her. We might have a hundred Yankee guests then instead of only one!"

"The prospect ought to be very pleasing to you," Emily retorted. "Anyway, the whole thing sounds like insurrection to me and I'm not at all certain I want to become involved in it."

"It wouldn't necessarily have to come to open hostilities between McBurney and Miss Martha," said Marie who had been eating her apples and listening to the discussion with half amusement and half irritation. Marie always hates to go along with any plan which she doesn't originate herself, although in this case—since she couldn't think of anything better—she had to be content with modifying it.

"What McBurney could do instead of openly refusing Miss Martha is just postpone his leaving for a while by saying he'd rather go next week or the week after instead of right now, and give some good excuse for it. For instance, he could say that he had learned that his own regiment would not be passing near here again for another month or so and he would have an easier time rejoining them at that time."

"Another thing he might do is decide that the time is not good for traveling just at present," Alice suggested. "He could have had a bad dream or seen some evil omen somewhere—an owl or a toad in the woods, perhaps."

"Owls and toads aren't evil," I informed her. "It's only superstitious people who believe things like that."

"And who is more superstitious than the Irish?" asked Alice. "My own mother, who is part Irish, is always reading terrible things in tea leaves."

"Well we have no tea," said Emily, "but on the other hand Mattie knows a great deal about evil omens. She could very likely give McBurney some good suggestions on the kind of omens to look for."

"But we still haven't solved the original problem," I told them. "You are all forgetting the fact that Johnny has already decided to leave."

"Then," said Alice, "we will just have to change his mind about that. We will have to make things so pleasant for him here that he won't even consider leaving us, until we decide, of course, that it's time for him to go."

"Do you have any definite suggestions to make in that regard, Alice?" Marie asked her.

Alice stared at her for a moment before she decided that Marie was not necessarily poking fun at her. "I have no specific proposals to make right now," she said finally. "I'll have to sit down and think about it."

"There is one thing we could do immediately, I suppose," said Emily. "We might suggest to Miss Martha and Miss Harriet that it would be nice if Corporal McBurney could join us at the table for dinner. He must get awfully lonely eating all his meals alone there in the parlor."

"That's a marvelous idea," Alice declared, forgetting her dispute with Emily. "That is an excellent beginning."

I agreed and Marie did too, although somewhat grudgingly since she hadn't thought of it.

Just then Edwina Morrow appeared at the bedroom door to inform us that Miss Martha and Miss Harriet were waiting for us in the dining room and, of course, we realized—or at least I did—that we had been making plans for Corporal McBurney without consulting the one person it seemed to me he was most interested in. I had been very angry at her only a short while before, but I did feel that this was her business as much as anyone else's and so, while Emily and Alice were hurrying downstairs—Marie, of course, was being confined again—I paused in the hallway to tell Edwina briefly what we had decided to do.

"You want Corporal McBurney to stay on here indefinitely?" she asked me.

"Yes, I do. Don't you?"

She backed me against the wall with her answer. "In some ways I want it very much—more, much more than you or anyone else in this place . . . and in some ways I wish he had never come at all."

"Why, Edwina?"

"Because I'm afraid. . . ."

"That something might happen to him?"

"Not necessarily to him. Maybe to me . . . or anybody. Why can't you idiotic girls stay out of other people's affairs!"

Without any doubt Edwina Morrow is the strangest person I have ever known. I would have expected her to be quite pleased at what we were doing but instead she was just as critical and nasty as she always is. However, I had no desire to argue with her. I merely stated that I felt Corporal McBurney's welfare was of concern to all of us, hoping she would let it go at that.

"His welfare, yes. But is that your main interest? Or do you want him to stay on here in order to keep you entertained—in your particular case maybe to tell you charming nature stories every morning in the garden—in between your gossiping about everyone in the house!"

"That's not true, Edwina," I protested as civily as I could. "I'm sure I don't gossip about anyone." I was determined to keep my temper this time.

"If you're planning to ask Miss Martha to allow Johnny to join us for dinner, you're too late anyway."

"Miss Martha's not sending Johnny away tonight?"

"You goose . . . you stupid little rabbit."

"Is she?"

"He's already in the dining room. Miss Martha was evidently fearful that she might have hurt his feelings a while ago, so she invited him to dine with us herself."

With that Edwina left me and continued on to her own room—to primp a bit more, I gathered, for this special occasion, although again in fairness I must admit that Edwina has always been more careful of her appearance than anyone else in this house. Emily is generally the best scrubbed person but Edwina, I think, would always take the prize for neatness and aptness of dress. Contrary to some opinions here I do admire neatness and cleanliness in other people even though I am sometimes a bit forgetful about such things myself.

Anyway I was not thinking about those things at that time but only of the fact that Johnny was dining with us. Indeed I was halfway down the stairs when my roommate, racing headlong, managed to catch up with me. "I heard what Edwina said," she whispered breathlessly, "and I thought I'd take a chance on coming down. I thought maybe in the excitement I wouldn't be noticed."

Well, if she was noticed no one objected to her presence. Everyone just had such a grand time that evening and we were all so jolly and cheerful and lighthearted that I firmly believe if Marie had not come downstairs on her own risk and initiative, Miss Martha would very likely have paroled her and invited her to join us anyway.

Because that's just the kind of festive dinner party it was. It really seemed that each one of the students and both members of the faculty were so happy to have Corporal McBurney with us that we were all agreeable automatically and it was simply not necessary for anyone to make a special effort to get into that frame of mind. The entire school was just in a pleasant mood, that's all, and, surprising as it might sound to anyone with any knowledge of the way our dinners customarily go, without Miss Martha suggesting it or any student consciously trying to achieve it.

Dear Mattie had very willingly gone to extra trouble and on short notice, too, in order to prepare a particularly nice meal for the occasion. It included all the things which we knew by that time Johnny liked—sweet potato pie, I remember, and black-eyed peas and beaten biscuits and, in his special honor, Irish potatoes which we have never grown successfully in our garden but which Miss Martha had apparently been able to obtain at Mister Potter's store.

Johnny seemed very satisfied and proclaimed it the best dinner he had attended since his arrival in America. "Both for food and for company," he added, which pleased everyone.

Actually, I think no better meal was prepared for him at this school, or at least some things about it were better, but I won't go into that matter now.

Anyway, from the atmosphere of cordiality which surrounded the table on the night of Corporal McBurney's first dinner with us you would have never dreamed there could be any question of his wanting to leave us or, on the other hand, of being asked to leave. As a matter of fact this thought occurred to me some time after the night of that first dinner: Supposing someone had just stood up on that night and said, "Miss Martha, it's obvious that we are all having a grand time this evening at table. We have had an excellent meal and Corporal McBurney has told us a number of very charming and witty stories about his travels and experiences. There have been no arguments or disagreements of any kind this evening. You have not had to reprimand Miss Marie Deveraux even once this evening, which is highly unusual as you must admit. Clearly, it is Corporal McBurney's presence here which has caused this evening to pass so pleasantly and I would like to propose that we guarantee many more such evenings at our school by deciding right now that Corporal McBurney must never leave us, or at least not for a good long time. I would like to suggest that everyone in favor of this proposal please signify their agreement by joining me in standing."

It has occurred to me that if I or someone had said those words, everyone at that table would have risen immediately, including Miss Harriet almost surely and maybe even including Miss Martha herself. And even if she hadn't joined us instantly I'm sure she would have been so impressed by the sight of the rest of us that she would have been very reluctant to bring up the subject of Corporal McBurney's leaving for a long while after that.

Because I believe that if Corporal McBurney could have known that everyone here wanted him to stay things might have turned out in a very different fashion. If he had realized that he was being given a unanimous invitation to stay here for a long while, I'm sure his conduct would have been completely different. Also, and equally important, is the fact that one gesture of unanimous friendship such as I have described might very well have prevented some people here from deciding later that they had to show Johnny McBurney some private kindnesses of their own.

Well there is no point in talking of any of that now. I did not rise to speak out for Johnny at that dinner. In fact I never even thought of such a thing on that night and I'm sure no one else did either. I guess maybe it is only in the light of evil consequences that we can think so readily of the good we might have done. Anyway after dinner we all went to the parlor and sang a few songs and said our prayers and then shortly after that we all went to bed. Other things happened on that night but I was not a part of them. That night Miss Alice Simms and Miss Edwina Morrow were the chief characters in the story of Corporal Johnny McBurney.

Edwina Morrow

I felt that he was attracted to me. If you want a detailed analysis of that attraction, I cannot give it. I'm not at all sure now that he even liked me and at one time I was convinced he didn't. We all know how people can be attracted by things they don't like, such as spiders on the ceiling and warts on the cheek. At any rate my knowledge of his interest in me was a collection of little and, perhaps to some people, inconsequential things: the way he stared at me in the garden and elsewhere, the way in which he undertook to stand near me every evening during prayers; the way in which, I'm sure, he tried to find out everything he could about me from anyone at this school who was willing to supply him with information, and that I can assure you would have included every person here.

I can't deny that I was flattered by it. I also can't deny that I was attracted to him. I will also admit that I liked him very much—at first—and that was one reason I tried to stay away from him. With very few exceptions I have never remained in mutual favor very long with people I have known well. They very quickly find things wrong with me, or I with them. And I suppose nowadays I anticipate the disillusionment of others by keeping free of any illusions myself.

Nevertheless I had enjoyed my first visit with Corporal McBurney, had very much wanted to make a good impression on him and thought right after our first long conversation that I had managed to do so. But then later I began to have some doubts about it. I should add doubts of that kind are very usual with me.

I felt at first that he had understood, as no one else around here ever had, the rather troubled and perhaps troublesome person that I am. I am not always the easiest person in the world to get along with, but I did feel that Corporal McBurney might possibly be someone who—even if he did not know all the reasons for my bitterness—would accept me the way I am with maybe the hope that affection might improve me. It might well have, you know. It really might have done so.

In any case, after he had been here for a day or two I began to wonder if "understanding" was the word he would have used himself in describing his appraisal of me. In a foolish outburst I had mentioned my regard for him to the other girls and I was in dread that one of them, Emily or Alice perhaps, might have gone back to him with a distorted or, bad enough, even true version of the incident, and that then McBurney and my fellow student might have had a great laugh over silly misunderstood Edwina. I began to think that "understanding" was not the way he would have put it at all. "Seeing through me," I thought, is more likely the way he would describe it—seeing through a shallow, prideless person who is so eager for friendship that she is willing to undergo the most personal questioning and accept the most flippant and direct comments about herself and then presume the whole thing has been complimentary.

And so I avoided him. I hadn't made up my mind to stay away from him permanently, but for the time being I felt that I couldn't afford to throw myself at someone who, seemingly, needed my company much less than I needed his. He had everyone in this house fawning on him and I made up my mind I was not going to stand in line and hope for crumbs of his attention.

Oddly, it began to seem that by ignoring him, I had aroused his interest in me. Although I had no conversation of any length with him for some time after the first one, I began to find him watching me and approaching me at every opportunity. I did not cut him or act unkindly to him on these occasions, or at least I never meant to do so, but I didn't encourage him either. When he spoke to me, I answered briefly but courteously, and when he stared at me, I smiled. However, because at that time I was afraid to trust him, I kept my distance from him.

Then on the afternoon of his first dinner with us, I was going over my lessons in the library when I noticed the volume of the collected works of Shakespeare was not in its customary shelf. We were not studying Shakespeare at that time in class but I am very fond of the plays and I quite often browse through them at odd moments of my own.

I remembered that I had left the book in the parlor some time before—on the very day, in fact, of Corporal McBurney's arrival—and so I assumed that it would still be there, since no one else here shares my interest in the Bard, with the possible exception of Miss Harriet. Therefore I came across the hallway to the parlor and had my hand on the door before I remembered who might very likely be inside. I entered anyway and found him on his settee engaged in profound discussion with our child of nature, Miss Amelia Dabney.

I told him what I wanted but Amelia decided at once that the book was only an excuse to enable me to visit with McBurney. Well, perhaps it was in part. He had been on my mind constantly, awake and asleep, and I can't deny that part of me—perhaps a very great part wanted very much to be near him.

And that side of me received its wish. After Amelia had fled the room in a tearful huff, I stood for a moment quite close to him as he attempted to press the book into my hands. We said nothing for a long time but only stared at each other. After a while we dropped the book and he kissed me. Very gently.

"I missed you," he said.

"Did you?" I asked him. "Very honestly, did you?"

"On my honor. On my life."

"I missed you, Johnny," I said. "I missed you very much."

Then he kissed me again, still gently, but for a much longer period this time. Then we sat on the settee and didn't speak again for quite a while.

"I'll be leaving here soon," was the next thing he said. "I've made up my mind. The old one has suggested that I'm fit and ready for travel and I'm sure she's right. I don't want to go away from you, and I don't suppose she'd throw me out if I offered her a stiff argument, but I've too much pride to stay on when I'm not welcome."

"I don't want you to leave, Johnny, but I don't blame you," I told him. "I'll go with you."

"To where? You couldn't go back to the regiment with me, though I'd be the envy of every man in the Army of the Potomac if you did. But I can't make a camp follower out of you, which is the name they'd give you, and I couldn't prevent it."

"I've had bad names put on me before now," I said. "I wouldn't care how they labeled me, as long as you thought well of me."

"I will always think well of you, Edwina Morrow. You'll be at the top of all my thoughts until my dying day. But it still would gall me to have others thinking ill of you, and I can't fight General Grant's whole army over it."

"No you can't," I said, smiling at that, "though I wouldn't require it of you. It would be like trying to carry water in a broken jug, as I have found out for myself. Everyone in this house thinks ill of me and I've never been able to prevent it by fighting with them, though I can't deny there may be better means. Anyway why do you need to go back to your Army? Couldn't we just go off together somewhere else?"

"Would you have me listed as a deserter?"

"Perhaps you're listed as one already. The armies exchange lists of prisoners, don't they? So your own people would know by now that you haven't been killed or captured."

"It might be too soon yet for any lists," said Johnny. "I might still be considered missing for a long time yet, like the honorable Robert Farnsworth, who, I understand, has not been heard from since the first battle in those woods. Anyway that whole area has been so burned over now, there must be thousands of fellas in there from both battles who'll never be identified."

"You could be missing forever then. You would never have to be found. You could go anywhere in the world you liked. You'd really never have to go back to your own army at all."

"If you must put it that way, I don't suppose I would."

"Don't tell me you haven't thought of it, Johnny. It's not dishonorable to think of it. In fact Emily Stevenson has said you mentioned that you might be willing to change your allegiance."

"Perhaps I did say that. I try to be agreeable you know."

"You must never be that way with me, Johnny. You must always tell me exactly what you think about everything . . . and me in particular."

"You know what I think about you."

"Tell me."

"I love you."

"Please, Johnny . . . you can take that back if you like. I'll pretend I didn't hear it. Please, Johnny, don't ever say that to me until you mean it."

"I mean it, my dearest. I swear it. I won't ever lie to you, Edwina. I know exactly how I felt about you from that first day I talked to you, but I was afraid to say anything then for fear you'd walk away from me and never let me near you again. I'm only telling you now because I have to leave here and there may be no better chance. I realize I'm not good enough for you, Edwina."

"That's not true. You don't know how untrue that is."

"Well I wasn't being humble about it. O' course I feel I'm as good as any man in the world, but if you're the sort who's concerned about family connections and past history, my ancestry for the past hundred years or so is not strictly royal blue. There's probably a few highwaymen and picklocks in there who ended their careers on the gallows or in the ditch, but on the other hand, if you want to go back a thousand years, I think I might produce a few kings. Course as all the world knows, every man in Ireland is descended from kings."

"Don't joke about it, Johnny. You don't really care about the past?"

"I couldn't care less, my sweet Edwina. I'll be honest about it. I don't want to go away from you, and I don't want to go back to the Union Army, or any other. I've had enough of war. It's not my quarrel and I want no more of it. Do you think any less of me for that, Edwina?"

"I think more of you, if that's possible," I answered, "because of your sincerity. I don't want you to go back to the war either. I think the whole thing is insane and at this point I don't much care who wins it. And I would die myself if anything more happened to you. You can say it again, if you like, Johnny."

"I love you, Edwina."

"I love you, Johnny," I said. "And I will never lie to you. I may not be able to bring myself to confess everything freely to you for a while yet, but I will answer any question. The last time I came to you I was unwilling to talk about my past life, but I am ready to do so now, if you ask me. Is there anything you'd like to ask me, Johnny?"

"No," he said. "I told you I wasn't interested in the past. I'm only concerned about the future . . . our future."

"All right, Johnny," I replied, accepting it. "Then you mustn't go back to your regiment. I forbid you to do so. You've done more than enough already for a cause that isn't your own. Now what you must do is go to Richmond. I'll give you a letter of introduction to my father, and he'll help you get out of the country . . . to England or Ireland or wherever you want."

"And what about you?"

"I'll follow you someday, if you still want it."

"Of course I'd want it. But how would I ever get to Richmond . . . alone and in uniform?"

"You needn't wear your uniform. I'm sure Miss Martha will let you keep those clothes of her brother's." Miss Martha had given him an old suit of Robert's a few days after his arrival.

"And the money to get me to Richmond?"

"I'll take care of that, too . . . somehow."

"You say your father can get me passage back across the water. How would he manage that? Is he in contraband?"

"Yes . . . I'm sorry to say."

"There's no reason to be sorry about. It's a respectable profession—to be supplying your country with the things they need and can't get otherwise."

"And making a big profit . . . and banking it abroad?"

"Nonetheless it's an honest kind of thievery and I say more power to him. But why are you sure he'd be willing to help me? He doesn't even know me."

"He knows me. And I think it would be of interest to him that I might be following you someday across the ocean."

"Does he want to be rid of you that badly?"

"Perhaps he does."

"He must be a great fool then, beggin your pardon."

"It's all right. You see he knows me much better than you do."

"He couldn't, if he doesn't prize you above all else on earth."

"Thank you, Johnny. If you never say one more nice thing to me, I am most grateful to you for that."

"I'll say so many nice things day and night for the rest of your life, that you'll go mad from the ring of my voice and will beg me to scold you or curse you just to break the monotony."

"Johnny . . . is it your intention . . . do you mean you'd want to marry me, Johnny?"

"To be sure. I was raised a good Christian. Do you think I'd propose to live with you in sin?"

"Hold me, Johnny," I said, shamelessly. "Hold me."

"There is one thing though," he said after a moment. "I'm not entirely sure I'd want to go back to the old land. I'd rather go someplace completely new—where a man might have half a chance of making a decent home for himself. I think I'd like to give your west here a try. I'd like to see what lies beyond them westward rivers. They say there's plenty of free land for the taking out there. Would you be willing to have a look at something like that with me, Edwina?"

"I'll go anywhere you go," I answered, "as long as you want me. If you want to go to the free territories, I'm sure my father can arrange that too."

"O' course I'll think about it very carefully," he said. "I won't come to any snap decisions. I'll study it for a while to find out what's best for you. That's the most important thing."

"What's best for both of us," I said.

"All right. Have it your way."

I think that was almost the end of our conversation that afternoon. Anyway we did no talking for a while although we didn't part immediately. That didn't happen until ten or fifteen minutes later, after old Mattie had come in to announce that "Corporal McBurney is being invited to dine with the ladies this evening." I gathered that Mattie didn't exactly approve of this decision of Miss Martha's.

Mattie, in fact, was never in favor of any unnecessary association between the Farnsworth household and Corporal McBurney. I think if she had been in charge of this place, Johnny would have had a very short convalescence here during which time the parlor door would have been kept securely locked against all unauthorized visitors.

Of course if she had her way, a similar policy would probably be adopted toward me. In a school operated by old Mattie, I should very likely be served my meals and lessons in a room apart from everyone else. As is evident to all, Mattie doesn't exactly approve of me either, but that is another story.

Well she left the room immediately, but even that brief encroachment on our privacy had put me in an evil mood—my usual mood some people would say. Anyway I began to have my customary doubts about the likelihood of anything good ever happening in my future.

"You can take back everything you said," I told Johnny. "I'm giving you another chance."

"I don't want to take anything back, my dearest," said he. "On my life I've meant every word. Don't you trust me, Edwina?"

"Yes . . . yes, I trust you," I said. "And that puts you in a very special category, Johnny McBurney, because for a long time I haven't been trusting anyone."

"Then if you do have faith in me, why the frown? Why mar those lovely features with a tight mouth and a wrinkled brow and a pair of squinty eyes, the way it'd be thought you were trying to stare into every dark corner of my mind to see if there wasn't one little bad thought about you tucked away there somewhere."

"I know there isn't any such thought, Johnny. It's not what you feel about me now. It's what you might feel about me in the future . . . when you know me better."

"I know you well enough now and my feelings about you will never change."

"You don't know everything about me. . . ."

"For pity's sake, what is there to know? I know you have a short temper, so have I. I know you have a sharp tongue, so have I. We'll murder each other very likely before the end of our first week together. Now for the love of the saints come away from it. I know all I need to know about you, all I want to know."

"If you're sure, Johnny," I whispered.

"I am absolutely sure, my sweet Edwina."

And that, I guess—if you can reduce such things to solitary moments— was the happiest moment of my life. It wasn't a very long moment, but it was a nice one while it lasted.

I realize, of course, that much of my misery has been my own doing because I have always been so suspicious of everyone around me, and so quick to take offense, sometimes with very little provocation. However when I left the parlor on that afternoon, I was determined to change my ways. My fortunes had turned from nothing to more than I could ever hope for. Nothing could hurt me now, I thought. I was sure at that moment that the terrors I have always suffered were gone and would never return.

And so I would make a great effort now to be nice to those around me.

Even if I was rebuffed, as I was sure I deserved to be, I wouldn't care. I had Johnny McBurney, I said to myself, and nothing could ever make me unhappy again.

My resolutions lasted me until I was halfway up the stairs. Then I met Alice and Emily coming down and with a very few words they sent me back to my accustomed state of mind.

"Good news, Edwina," Emily shouted. "We've decided that it's time for Corporal McBurney to become better acquainted with us."

"And for us to become better acquainted with him," yelled Alice as they went past.

"What do you mean?" I called after them. "What are you going to do?"

But they went on down the stairs and into the dining room without answering me. I continued up the stairs and met Amelia at the top. She had recovered from her fit of temper and was quite radiant as she informed me of the plan they had devised to keep Corporal McBurney with us. They had decided they would be so nice to him and shower such attentions on him that he would never agree to leave us, no matter what Miss Martha might have to say on the subject.

I knew this was ridiculous because if Miss Martha had really made up her mind to get rid of Johnny, she was certainly not going to be thwarted by the plotting of a lot of silly girls. If she had so desired, she could have made things so unpleasant for him and the rest of us that McBurney would have been on the road before sundown and, selfishly, I'll admit, I would have preferred that consequence than to run the risk of losing his affection in a competition with some of the others here.

Of course I am speaking now of the situation as it existed on that afternoon. The situation changed very much after that day and there came a time when McBurney himself stated that nothing anyone here could say or do would make him leave before he was ready to go. Whether that was true or not, I suppose, is open to argument.

Anyway I suggested to Amelia that it might be better for all if some idiots here could manage to mind their own business. Then I went to my room to tidy myself for dinner and in the course of those preparations began to think about what had just happened to me in the parlor and about the things Johnny had said to me and before long my fears and evil mood had passed away again. By the time I returned to the dining room, I was feeling almost cheerful and before we were ten minutes at the table, I was so gay and talkative that several people remarked about it.

"I don't think I have ever seen you so animated, Edwina," said Miss Martha.

"Nor I," said Miss Harriet, "and it is quite becoming to her, don't you agree, Corporal McBurney?"

"I couldn't agree more," he said. "In that black velvet dress and with her hair pinned up that way, and with that flush on those ivory cheeks, she's like some great lady at the court of some old Spanish king."

"Yes, Edwina does look rather Castilian, doesn't she," Emily said. I was watching her and I decided that she meant it only as a conversational remark.

Alice, however, was not so content with this turn in the talk and therefore felt obliged to state that she had heard there were usually a multitude of notorious ladies at the courts of the old European kings and, of course, as soon as the words were past her lips she realized that any discussion of notorious ladies could hardly prove a happy one for her. Therefore she took a new tack by making some comment about darker skinned girls always looking better by tallow candle light and then went on to declare that there were other people in the world with attractive shoulders and if gowns which exhibited shoulders were to be permitted at young ladies' schools, then the authorities should take steps to provide such dresses to all students so that no unfair advantages could be taken.

It was such a sad little thrust that instead of feeling angry, I felt very sorry for her. I did know that she was eager to win McBurney's attentions—just how eager I didn't realize—and because I thought then that there was little present chance of her succeeding—especially since at that moment he looked across the table and winked at me—I felt generous enough to say I would be glad to share my dresses with Alice or with anyone else who might be in need of one.

"I might borrow one some evening," said Marie causing some general tittering around the table which Marie did not appreciate.

"You would need stilts to keep from tripping on the skirt," Emily told her, "and a generous application of glue to hold it up on top."

"I cannot deny," Marie answered irritably, "that Edwina may be a bit taller and more fully grown than I. On the other hand there are certain persons here who could not fit into Edwina's dresses for other reasons. I am thinking specifically of a person who, in order to cram herself into one of those dresses, would have to submit to some pretty painful lacing. I am not mentioning any names, of course, but I might say that this person's initials are A.S."

"Girls, girls," said Miss Martha, rapping her glass with a spoon before Alice could reply to this. "This conversation is not a proper one for young ladies. And while on the subject of propriety I will add that I do not think

Edwina's costume is entirely suitable for a young ladies' school. However we know that Edwina has been accustomed to town society where different views on dress sometimes prevail. We also know that she has brought several such gowns with her to Farnsworth and has worn them on many evenings and not just this one. Therefore I will say nothing more about the matter now, except to suggest that Edwina might consider drawing her shawl over her shoulders in order to prevent any further speculation on the subject."

I did as she suggested, my face on fire, but keeping my temper by telling myself that I had been complimented. Also Johnny winked at me again and smiled and that made me think that it might not be too long before I need no longer worry about the provincial attitudes at Farnsworth.

The way I dress at Farnsworth is the way I dressed at Richmond where some of the very best Virginia gentlemen dined at our table. I know some Richmond people thought that such company was not the best kind for a solitary young lady but my father thought otherwise and so from my earliest days I was always invited to the table. These same Richmond people were of the opinion that my father had never permitted me to enjoy my childhood and that he had begun treating me as an adult too soon. However, after Johnny came to the school I began to see that my father had never really treated me as anything else but a child, no matter how he allowed me to dress or what company he permitted me to meet, and it was only when he realized that I could no longer be treated as a small, unhearing and uncaring toy that he sent me away to this school.

Of course it was not entirely his fault. I never lived in a house with other women, except for servants, until I came here and as a result my father put womanhood on me—if not adulthood—when he judged me fit for it—in the only way he could judge it, by my physical appearance. In that respect I became a woman very early in life, but I was never glad of it until Johnny came.

However I was not thinking of those things on that evening. At that time I was only thinking that I must guard my tongue in order not to make a bad impression on Johnny. I must prove to him, I thought, that I can accept correction from my elders and that I deserve to be considered a lady. And after all, I said to myself, the rebuke was mild enough and Miss Martha is certainly entitled to her own opinion about the way her students ought to dress. Perhaps, I decided after a moment, had I been in her position, I would have said the very same thing.

This self-control amazed my fellow students who apparently expected me to make a scene—as I might well have done at another time—and were watching me covertly. However I kept my eyes on my plate and said nothing and this forbearance eventually paid off because after a moment little Amelia Dabney said, "I don't think there is anything to argue about anyway. Edwina Morrow is the most beautiful girl in the school, no matter what she is wearing. Even if I don't like you sometimes, I must admit that, Edwina."

"Thank you," I said, embarrassed again but also very pleased this time.

"If we can't agree with that," said Miss Martha tactfully, "I think we can admit that it would be a very close competition between Miss Edwina and one or two others here, although beauty of form or feature does not necessarily indicate perfection of mind or soul. However I can say with no equivocation that Miss Edwina could be the brightest person here, if she applied herself with a bit more diligence."

"Thank you, Miss Martha," I said. "I will try to follow your advice." And felt my face go hot again because the last compliment meant much more to me than any of the others.

"My goodness," said Marie. "Is this Edwina Morrow at our table or some imposter?"

"I don't think that Edwina is showing us anything but her true nature this evening," said Miss Martha. "It is unfortunate that she has kept it hidden in the past, but perhaps now we can see more of it. On the other hand I do think that Miss Marie Deveraux must be represented by an imposter at our table because I believe the real Marie Deveraux has been confined to her room."

This remark caused a great deal of merriment at the table. Everyone, including Alice—who had been mollified by Miss Martha's allusion to competitive beauties—went into gales of laughter which only ended when Miss Martha rapped her glass again.

"It is obvious that you have a tonic effect on us, Mister McBurney," she said, "even when you do not enter directly into the conversation. We have not had such jollity at dinner for a long time. Now perhaps we can all be serious for a moment. Mister McBurney was reading from the works of Shakespeare this afternoon. I wonder if he will tell us whether he enjoyed what he read?"

"Yes, ma'am, I did . . . very much," said Johnny. It was obviously not a subject he was eager to discuss.

"Corporal McBurney is very familiar with the plays of Shakespeare," Miss Harriet put in. "He used to read them constantly at home."

"Then perhaps he could recite something for us," Emily suggested. "What is your favorite scene in the plays, Johnny?"

"Well o' course there are so many," he said. "It's hard to pick out any one favorite. For instance I was going over that old play today . . . the one about the fella . . . what was his name again . . . I think it began like mine."

"King John?" inquired Miss Harriet.

"No, his family name. Mack something or other."

"Macbeth," we all cried.

"That's the one. Well I was reviewing that old thing again, you know. But I'm sure you've all read it a hundred times."

"I haven't read it once," said Marie. "There's too much English poetry in it for me."

"And I began it but never finished it," Alice said. "The printing is too small in that old book."

"I've never read it either," said Amelia. "Why don't you tell us about it, Johnny?"

"By all means," said Miss Martha. "Even those of us who are familiar with the play can benefit, I'm sure, from hearing your interpretation of it, Corporal McBurney."

"That's possible," Johnny admitted. I'll try to tell it now as he did.

"Perhaps, being a man, I might look on the thing a bit differently than you. Well then to begin with, there's this young fella Macbeth who's an up-and-coming officer in the army of the old King of Scotland. The fella's rank isn't mentioned, as I recall, but I'd judge him in the beginning to be of junior field grade. A major, I'd say he was, or at the most a light colonel and that's about as high as he ever would've gone, except for a very queer set of circumstances that happened to him one day on a heath. You see that army was engaged in stamping out a combination invasion and rebellion—excuse the word, ladies—and the King had sent Macbeth with a small party of skirmishers to round up a few of these wayward lords. Well Macbeth and his chum Banquo were scouting along this heath when they came upon a very unusual thing indeed. Here was these three fierce old biddies stirring a foul-smelling broth in a pot and singing all the while they were in high, cracked voices, the way the Scotchmen knew at once the old girls were far from being mortal.

"'Hail there to ye, Macbeth,' says one. 'We've been waiting here for ye.' 'What on earth for?' says he. 'You're no friends of mine.' 'Well,' says another, 'we only wanted to salute ye. It might interest you to know that you're very shortly going to become King of Scotland.' 'You're mad,' says he. 'Are we?' says they. 'Here's proof that we know our business. Within the hour you'll be one step nearer the throne and before the day is out you'll be another, the way the old King'll be hurling the promotions at ye for your fine work in the battle.' 'Well I've my share I will admit,' says Macbeth, for he wasn't the most modest fella in the world. 'But I still say the old King is pretty healthy yet.' 'Have a peek in our pot then, Macbeth,' they told him. 'What's in the pot can't be denied.'

"Well he had a look in their dirty old pot but he could see nothing at all but a mess of boiled bats and toads and other such delicacies as witches are used to having for their dinner, for that's what these three old ladies were, no less, and as further proof of it they gave a horrible shriek and flew off on their broomsticks without another word.

"Well after a minute or two Macbeth and his friend weren't sure they had seen anything at all. They thought maybe the whole thing was caused by a touch o' the sun or maybe it was one jar too many on the night before. However they had no sooner got back to the main camp when the old King informed Macbeth that for his gallantry in action he was being promoted to a lord, and it wasn't more than an hour later the King decided a lord wasn't high enough so made Macbeth a thane, which I believe is even higher than a duke.

"So Macbeth went home and very foolishly told his wife the whole story. Now I think the man would've been satisfied then to take his winnings and drop out of the game, but his wife wouldn't hear of it. Oh the greatest old shrew in Scotland she was, with a block of ice where her heart should've been and a tongue on her that would've split an oak board. 'Now you've come this far,' she told Macbeth, 'why not try for the whole pot? The old King is our guest tonight. It needs only a sharp knife and a steady hand and the throne will be yours in the morning.' 'Oh God save us, I could never do that,' says Macbeth. 'Why not?' says the Missus. 'You've certainly thought of it.'

"It was true, o' course, but then all of us have terrible thoughts at times that we might never put into action if we didn't have people like Missus Macbeth behind us. And so with her urging him on Macbeth murdered the old King and won the throne for himself. It was a terrible thing to do and eventually Macbeth paid for it. The one crime led to more of the same, as they say very often happens when lads get hardened to the bad life. The old King was hardly cold before Macbeth and his Missus found they had to get rid of several other people, including his old chum, Banquo, in order to protect what they'd won.

"All the while o' course Macbeth was running off to the heath to see if the old crones could give him any consolation. They'd promised him the top prize in the land, now he wanted to know how long he was going to be able to keep it. 'Til all the trees in the woods move to the city,' the old hag said. Well Macbeth didn't see how that could happen but all the same he didn't feel too easy about it and it didn't help matters any when his wife decided that she still had some of the old King's blood on her hands and that no soap in Scotland would wash it off. Now whether she was really still stained with that blood or not or whether she was merely going daft, I can't honestly tell you. Whatever way it was, it only proved once again what my own mother always told me—no matter how fast you run, you can never get away from your past. It's like your shadow, she used to say. Some people like to think their shadows disappear with the darkness but my mother always claimed that's just the time the devil sets to work and your shadow catches up with you. 'If you've been good, Johnny,' she used to say, 'you've nothing to fear. But if you've been bad, watch out. All your evil deeds are strung out behind you wrapped in the folds of your shadow and some night the devil may creep up to your bed and snare you with it.'

"Well that's just about what happened to Macbeth and his wife. Their bad deeds caught up with them. Missus Macbeth went completely off her head eventually and finally died in a mad fit, I guess, and it wasn't long before her husband followed her. The woods did move on his castle and hiding behind each tree was an enemy soldier and they set upon poor Macbeth and cut his head off. And that's the end of the story."

"Does it have a moral, do you think, Mister McBurney?" Miss Harriet asked him.

"Certainly," said he with a grin. "The moral is—beware of women—especially if you're a weak mortal man. Like I said before, Macbeth could have lived his life out—with no great gain or fortune in it maybe, but very likely with no great evil in it either. Macbeth might've lived 'til his hair was white and with nothing worse on his conscience than a missed Mass on Sunday once or twice a year or so, and maybe a pint or so too many now and again on a Saturday night, and that only causing him to give the Missus an occasional crack on the gob to quiet her. And God knows she'd've deserved it the way she always went on. Yes, ladies—begging your pardon—it was women that did for poor old Macbeth—his own wife and three old biddies."

"Well I can see where Macbeth's wife had some motive for what she did, but I fail to see where the old witches had anything to gain," remarked Marie. "Why did they ever bother with Macbeth in the first place?"

"Witches don't have to have reasons for doing bad things," said Johnny. "Maybe it was only for the sport of it."

"Or maybe it was because they didn't realize that things would turn out as badly as they did," Amelia suggested. "It's possible, isn't it, that they could have foreseen that Macbeth was destined to become King without being aware of exactly how it would happen."

"But they put temptation in his path and that was very wrong," said Miss Harriet.

"Still if it was a definite fact that Macbeth was destined to become King," said Alice, "then it seems to me that whether he had advance information or not would have made very little difference."

"It might have made a difference in the way he conducted himself," Emily argued. "It might only have been necessary for Macbeth to wait a short while until King Duncan had died a natural death and then the people might have elected Macbeth King without any effort on his part at all. After all I believe he was a very popular military leader."

"It never does anyone any good to know the future," said old Mattie as she came in with more acorn coffee. "That's why the good Lord shields it from us. If we knew what was waitin for us just around the corner half the days of our lives, it seems to me we'd be too scared to get out of bed."

"I agree completely," I said. "I have no wish to ever know the future. It would be terrible if you were always certain of tomorrow, if you always knew that it could never be any better than you imagine it will be."

"Tomorrow and tomorrow and tomorrow," said Miss Harriet. "Do you remember that passage, Mister McBurney? Life itself is but a walking shadow . . . a momentary record of some wasted days."

"Do you speak from experience, sister?" Miss Martha asked her. "No day is wasted on which a lesson is taught and learned. As Corporal McBurney is wise enough to see in the play, most of the terrible things that happen to us are the results of our own bad conduct."

"Terrible things can happen as the result of mistakes, too, can't they Miss Martha?" Marie inquired innocently. "Sometimes people are punished when they never meant anyone any harm."

"I'm sure the law of averages takes care of people like that," replied Miss Martha dryly. "People who feel they have been punished unjustly should console themselves by applying the sentence to past misdeeds which have been committed but not found out."

"Or to future misdeeds, eh?" said Johnny cheerfully, "except o' course in cases of capital punishment."

And that cheerful note ended our table conversation for the evening. We said our grace and moved in a body to the parlor for songs, which had become a custom now, and evening prayers.

If I can recall my state of mind at that time, I'm sure I was happy again—perhaps nearly as much so as before. Johnny was walking beside me as we left the dining room and he took my hand and held me back from the others. No one noticed the action but old Mattie who had begun to clear the table and she frowned but said nothing. Whether she disapproved of me or of Johnny or of the two of us in combination I am still not entirely sure, although it may have been a little of all three possibilities.

Anyway I was not at all concerned with Mattie's opinions on that evening. I couldn't have cared less what anyone in the house thought of me as long as I was sure of Johnny's affection. I was in no way apprehensive—in fact you might have even thought me to be growing tolerant if you had seen me smiling and continuing an idle conversation with Miss Harriet even as I noticed Johnny move away from us to speak privately with Alice at the far end of the parlor. At that moment there seemed to me no reason why Johnny ought not to be permitted to speak privately to anyone he liked, and I told myself it was shameful of me to even think of becoming jealous over it.

All the same I was perhaps a little jealous and maybe I showed it because when the singing began, Johnny returned to my side and squeezed my arm reassuringly. He was still using his cane as he crossed the room, I remember, but limping rather less than usual. For Miss Martha's benefit, I wondered peevishly? I thought then and afterwards that his swaggering at that time and his activities a few moments later with me might have been entirely to show Miss Martha that he was no longer dependent on her. However when he stood near me, although I didn't look directly at him, I could see out of the corner of my eye how drawn and tired-looking he was. There were beads of perspiration on his lip which must have been caused by pain, since the room wasn't very warm that evening.

Well we sang a few of the old standbys—the good old *Bonnie Blue Flag* and so forth—and then Johnny sang an Irish song about a poor emigrant boy who is longing for fireside and mother, and then to take the company out of its sad mood, Miss Harriet began playing a gay polka on the harpsichord and almost immediately Johnny took hold of me and began dancing me around the room.

"Be careful of your leg," I told him. "You must be careful."

"Don't fret, dear Edwina," he laughed. "A good dance is the best thing for a stiff leg and you're the best possible partner."

"How do you know?" I asked. "You haven't tried anyone else here."

"There's no need," he answered. "None of them could possibly be as graceful and as light on their feet as you."

It was another nice compliment from Johnny although he didn't say it loud enough for anyone else to hear it over the music. Everyone was watching us, including Miss Martha, who didn't seem particularly annoyed, although she did call out a word of warning to Johnny as I had. I knew I should have stopped him instantly because there was a great danger of the wound reopening on his leg, but I didn't stop him. I was enjoying myself too much. All the girls, I knew, were unbearably envious, but that didn't bother me either.

"I'll tell you a secret," I said to Johnny, a bit out of breath now. "I have never danced with a man before—except my father. I haven't danced very much at all really, except here in class and all our dancing classes have been cancelled while you've been recovering."

"Well you must resume them again immediately," said my confident partner, "and I'll teach you everything I know." He was still smiling steadily, although he was much more out of breath now than I was. He was very pale too, and I knew his leg must be hurting him dreadfully.

"How will it be possible for you to teach us anything?" I inquired, trying to slow him down a bit. "I thought you were going away from us very shortly."

"Oh, that's right—it slipped my mind," he said. "Well there's one very important lesson that must be taught. I must teach you how much I love you, so that you'll never be able to forget me."

Those were Johnny's exact words and I have cause to remember them distinctly because it was nearly the last of the nice things he said to me. Anyway at that moment Miss Harriet saw that he was tiring and slowed the music to a waltz. He was as good at the waltz as he was at the polka. I told him so.

"Now I'll tell you a secret," he said. "I've never danced a waltz like this with anyone before. All I know about it is what I saw a few times through the window of the big house at home. O' course I knew from the start I could go at it as well as any of them fellas in the silk coats and red uniforms. Oh I've danced jigs and reels and the like at fairs and so forth, but this is the first time I've ever waltzed on a polished floor with a beautiful young lady like yourself in my arms."

We had moved to the far end of the parlor somewhat apart from the group around the harpsichord, but now Alice and Emily began to dance together and then Amelia and Marie moved awkwardly out on the floor. I knew it would not be long before one of them, Alice probably, decided to cut in on us and so I did my best to steer Johnny away from them. By that time he was perfectly willing to let me lead him. The back of his coat had become soaked with perspiration but he was still smiling grimly as he hopped rather than glided on his good leg.

"I think we'd better stop," I suggested.

"Not yet, not yet," he insisted.

"I believe some of the other girls would like to try a few steps with you—Alice Simms, for instance."

"I've noticed," said he. "Do you suppose I should be gentlemanly about it?"

"It's up to you," I told him. "It's none of my business."

"Oh, but it is, my dear one. I've made commitments to you, haven't I? We have an understanding, don't we?"

"If you say so, Johnny."

"Indeed I do say so. Oh this is the life for me. I'd rather dance than almost anything else I can think of . . . and I'd rather dance with you than with anyone else in this house . . . or the entire world for that matter. I'd like to spend my entire life . . . dancing . . . and making love to you, Edwina." He was so out of breath by now it was an effort for him to speak.

"You'd better begin to consider your words, Corporal McBurney," I answered. "I might just hold you to them."

He grinned and winked at me and squeezed my arm again but made no further comment. He was so exhausted that he was almost leaning on me. As I had expected Alice and Emily moved over to us then.

"May I share your partner?" Alice asked sweetly.

"You may," I said, "if you can carry him."

Miss Martha noticed his condition and halted the music. I helped him to a chair and he sank on it gratefully with the bad leg extended. He was half fainting from the pain but he was still grinning. He was so proud of his accomplishment. He was like a little boy sitting there—a little boy who has beaten all his playmates in a footrace or a game of toss.

"I knew it," he said happily. "I was sure I'd be as good as new again."

Miss Martha came over to have a look at his leg but he waved her away.

"It's all right," he said. "It's still in your good repair, ma'am. It's only a bit sore and stiff now but that will mend itself by morning. And I'm thinking I'll be leaving you then. If you'd be so kind, ma'am, maybe you'd take that bit o' thread out of the leg in the morning and then I'll be on my way."

"This *is* a change of heart, isn't it?" asked Miss Martha. "I understood you would rest here a while longer."

"If I need to rest I can do it by the side of the road. A man who can dance should be able to walk, isn't that right ma'am?"

"I suppose so, but you haven't danced for much more than five minutes and I don't think you'll be able to walk for much longer than that."

"Are you suggesting that I stay, ma'am?" he wanted to know.

"I'm suggesting that you do as you please," said Miss Martha angrily and she moved to the end of the room to begin the prayers.

Well, as you might imagine, a terrible gloom descended immediately upon the place. Miss Martha was angry, Miss Harriet and the girls looked as though they had just said farewell to their only friend and Johnny himself was no longer very cheerful now that he had announced his decision. I guess I was the only person in the house who was not completely upset by the news of his coming departure. I'm excluding Mattie, of course. I think Mattie was not displeased by the announcement.

My own feeling was one of relief. No matter how it may have seemed later, that was exactly how I felt at that time. I suppose it's true that a normal person doesn't want to be separated from someone to whom they are attached—and I did feel a deep and strong attachment to Johnny McBurney—but since I knew he had to leave us anyway sooner or later, I was just as satisfied to have him get on with it. It seemed better for both of us if Johnny could pick up his own life again as soon as possible somewhere away from here. If he truly felt about me as I believed now that he did there was no point in his wasting any more time here. The sooner he was gone from here, the sooner he could send for me and we could begin our lives together.

The evening prayers went more quickly than usual with none of the customary requests for private intercessions of the Lord that we usually have from some of the students. Miss Martha asked very briefly for the Lord's protection on the school and the brave members of our army and then, almost as an after-thought, she added that it would also be a favor to the students and faculty of Farnsworth if He would keep an eye on all travelers, North and South.

Now, encouraged, Miss Harriet very graciously asked for Heaven's blessing on Corporal McBurney, whom, as she put it, we had all grown to know and cherish as a friend during his few short weeks with us. She asked the Lord to allow Corporal McBurney to lead a long and useful life and to let him prosper in whatever good things he attempted, and finally she requested that the Lord see to it that Corporal McBurney never forgot us because we certainly would never forget him.

This naturally brought tears to the eyes of every member of the assembly—including Miss Martha and Johnny and, I suppose, myself. Miss Martha said that she, too, wished Corporal McBurney well and that he must not feel that he was under any obligation to us because his presence in the school had been of great value to us all. "Corporal McBurney's stay with us," said Miss Martha, "has taught us all a very important lesson—that the enemy as individuals are not necessarily wicked men."

That, too, I remember exactly. Those were Miss Martha's very words and she followed them with the customary call for silent meditation which always ended our evening prayers. A few moments later we were dismissed for the night.

I did not dawdle around Johnny as did the other girls, but took a lighted candle from Mattie and went directly upstairs. My plans were to arise very early and come downstairs for a private visit with him before he left the school. I was very sure that none of the others, with the possible exception of Amelia, would be able to awaken before dawn to bid anyone farewell, even if it was their own sweetheart.

And I was content that night to receive a smile and another squeeze of the arm from Johnny and a sweet something or other whispered in my ear—"my only love" or "my only darling" or something of that sort. He had walked to the parlor door with me and the words and gestures were accomplished very quickly and, I remembered later, were not observed by the others. At any rate I told him that I would see him in the morning and he smiled most lovingly and gratefully and humbly and I went upstairs to my room—most loving and most grateful and once again, and for the last time, most happy myself.

My room is at the back of this house near to the stairs which lead up to the garret. I formerly shared a room with Emily Stevenson but that didn't work out too well and since I was certain that Emily wanted to be rid of me and there was plenty of vacant space in the house anyway, I asked Miss Martha to assign me a room of my own.

Of course, on that night my head was filled with nothing but the nicest thoughts about Emily and everyone else in the house. I prepared for bed in my usual manner, rubbing myself all over with cold water—not just my face and hands, as do the others in this house—those of whom are not neglectful of even that most elementary bit of sanitation. I have always been something of a fanatic about personal cleanliness. At the house in Richmond I used to bathe and scrub myself several times a day which caused my father to remark one time that if I was not careful before long I would wash my skin away.

Well that never happened but at least I have always been certain that I am at least outwardly clean. And while on this subject I might mention that his neatness was one of the things that most attracted me to Corporal McBurney. Up until that time—except for the first day when Amelia brought him in all muddy from the woods—I had never seen him when he didn't look freshly washed and combed. As for his clothes, Miss Martha had also provided him with a change of linen from the stock which her brother and father left in the house and Johnny undertook to keep these items as clean as possible. As soon as he was able you could usually find him once a day in the wash house scrubbing his stockings or shirts or undergarments. Mattie would have been willing to take care of these chores, I'm sure, as she does for the rest of us, but then I am seldom willing to let Mattie launder my personal things and I guess Johnny felt the same. Of course I must repeat that when I speak of his neatness of appearance, I am referring to him as he was prior to this particular night.

And so after bathing, I brushed my teeth and hair and put on my Parisian lace night dress which was another parting present from my father. If you ask me how he came by it, I cannot tell you, although I am sure he didn't purchase it especially for me. It might have been a gift for someone who didn't appreciate it, or perhaps it was just something that was left behind one time in his room. I didn't want it and I don't know why I ever brought it here to Farnsworth, except possibly to have something else with which to torment myself. Anyway I had never worn that nightdress before that night and I never wore it after.

Why did I wear it on that night? And why did I brush my hair two hundred strokes instead of the customary fifty, which made it shine quite dazzlingly although it didn't make it any lighter. And why did I rub myself in several places with my French perfume—another one of my father's leftovers—and why did I leave my door ajar slightly?

Because I thought he might come to me. I knew it was very wrong of me to think of such things and even worse, to desire them, but that is how I felt and I don't apologize for it. I don't suppose I would ever have asked him to come but with all my heart I wanted him to come.

And so I didn't sleep. I lay propped up in bed with my candle near me on the stand and my book of the poems of William Blake on my lap and I listened. I listened to the sounds of the rest of the house retiring—Emily doing her breathing exercises at her window, which are supposed to be good for one's complexion, Amelia and Marie conversing and giggling, Miss Harriet whining and Miss Martha reprimanding her for it—and then the sounds of the night outside—the owls in the old tobacco barn, the nightingales in the laurels out back, the locusts in the hedges and the frogs in the woods, the wind passing softly through the eaves and the oak tree rubbing the roof edge above me—and then once more the sounds inside— the parlor clock ticking, Miss Harriet weeping, several beds creaking, a window rattling—and then Johnny coming.

He was in his stockings but I could hear him all the same from the bottom of the stairs. There is one loose tread on that stairs and he stepped on that and confirmed his presence and then waited, evidently frightened, for a moment. And I waited, trembling, in fear that the pounding of my heart would be heard. Then after I had counted to more than a hundred, he came on again, more slowly this time but still steadily, up the stairs and down the hall toward my room.

I sank down in the bed and closed my eyes and held my breath and bit my lip to stop it quivering and heard him no more because I didn't need to hear, because I knew he was there and that in a moment he would pull the covers away from me and bend down and kiss me and say, as he had said before, "My darling Edwina. . . ."

But he didn't. I would have sworn I had heard him breathing, but it must have been the blood rushing in my own head because when I opened my eyes he wasn't there. Had he entered and been afraid and gone out again? Had he only looked in at the door and thought me asleep and gone back downstairs? Or was he still waiting out there in the darkness of the hall—waiting for me perhaps to summon him?

"Johnny. . . ." I whispered very softly, and paused. There wasn't any answer. I held my breath again and listened. There was no sound of anyone breathing in the hall. I was almost certain he was no longer out there, or at least not anywhere near my door.

After a moment, however, there was another sound—the creaking of a tread on the stairs which leads to the garret. He was going upstairs and not down. There is nothing up there but some old furniture and our trunks and other things in storage—and Alice Simm's bedroom.

I blew out my candle and pulled the covers over my head and held my ears against any more sounds and did my best to make my mind a complete blank and tried to go to sleep, but I couldn't. I don't know how long I tried, but I couldn't. Then I began telling myself that she had invited him upstairs on some pretext or other—maybe to show him something or maybe just to say goodbye to him—and when he discovered that she had nothing of any consequence to say to him he would come right back down again. Maybe, I thought, she had even seen Johnny in the hall outside. Maybe she had been coming down from the third floor herself and she saw him near my door and then she made him go back upstairs with her by threatening him— beckoning him silently, very likely, with her finger, and pretending that if he didn't come she would call out and awaken Miss Martha.

On the other hand maybe it hadn't been Johnny coming up from downstairs at all. It could just as easily have been someone else, possibly even Alice herself, walking very softly in order not to disturb any of us and going past my door on her way up to her own room. But what would Alice have been doing downstairs after everyone had retired? It wasn't very hard to think of an answer to that—pestering Johnny, without any doubt. But would Miss Martha have allowed it? She certainly would not have granted any such permission, but on the other hand, Miss Martha needn't have known anything about it. Alice, I decided now, had most likely gone into the dining room or the library until everyone else was safely upstairs and then she had slipped back into the parlor for a private conversation with Johnny. Well, if this was the case—and it seemed now that it must be—she hadn't managed to stay down with him there alone for very long.

But hadn't I heard Alice go upstairs a while ago? Hadn't there been some goodnights exchanged in the hall between Emily and Alice or Amelia and Alice? I racked my brain but I just couldn't remember now. And of course even if Alice had made a pretense of going to bed there was no reason why she couldn't have slipped back down to the parlor again after the others were in their rooms.

That certainly must be the case. There was no earthly reason, except my own penchant for self torture, for imagining anything else. And anyway, whether Alice had remained downstairs after everyone else had gone to bed or had gone back downstairs later, she was certainly upstairs now—and almost as certainly alone—and I was determined not to allow myself to think of any other possibility.

I sat up in bed again and tried to read my William Blake by moonlight but it wasn't any use. The moon was soon clouded over and I couldn't keep my mind on the poems anyway. Then I tried to think of how wonderful it would be sometime soon when Johnny and I met again somewhere far away from this school—far away from anywhere I had ever been miserable. I tried to picture Johnny and me as man and wife living in a nice house somewhere—in New York or Philadelphia maybe, or some other city in the North where I believe people are sometimes valued more for who they are and what they can do rather than what they are and where they come from—because in some ways I hate the South more and more every day. Sometimes I just hope we lose this war and are utterly destroyed by the Yankees—just ground down under all their heels so that there will never be any more trace of us, or our mothers or our children. I hate Richmond and Savannah and this school and all the rest of it. I hate it now but I hated it more on that night, because with the expectation of something better in store for me, there was no reason to hold back my hate. I just hated the whole world, except Johnny, on that night. And I loved him, I knew then. I had said the words to him in the afternoon and meant them but now I knew for certain that I loved only him.

And loving him, I must trust him. And feeling thus, I decided, it was

ridiculous to stay at this school any longer. I might just as well go away with
Johnny in the morning rather than stay behind and regret it as soon as he
was out of sight. Downstairs I had convinced myself that it was best for him
to go away from Farnsworth, and now it seemed that without any question
leaving would be the best course for both of us. We had only to go to Richmond together and see my father and tell him of our plans to marry and my
father would be so overjoyed at the news he would arrange our passages to
England or California or anywhere we liked. It was all so obvious once the
missing part of the picture was in place—once I was completely committed
to McBurney.

It needn't be a difficult undertaking at all, I decided. I would need only
to pack my small handbag with a few necessary things and everything else
I would leave behind to be distributed among the girls. Even Alice might
have some of my clothes, I thought. In fact I decided I would give Alice my
black velvet dress, the one that had caused all the comment at the dinner
just past. And my red silk brocade, Alice could have that too if she liked.
And all my afternoon dresses I would give to Emily, since those would suit
her better. And all my perfume and soap and silk kerchiefs could be shared
by Marie and Amelia and perhaps Miss Martha and Miss Harriet could
find some use for the several shawls and scarves I would leave with them.
Of course Miss Martha and Miss Harriet might have any of the things they
liked, although I would be very mannerly and careful not to give offense
when I made the offer.

As for money, all of my gold pieces were gone, but I still had five Yankee silver dollars and ten more in paper which ought to be more than
enough for the fare on the Richmond and Fredericksburg Railroad. The
problem was the Yankee army which was between us and Fredericksburg
now, driving southeast out of Spotsylvania Courthouse the last we had
heard and encamped now supposedly somewhere down around the North
Anna River. There seemed no doubt that the Yankees had taken complete
charge of the Fredericksburg road to Richmond if they had not ripped up
the tracks entirely. On the other hand there was still the Virginia Central
Railroad which stopped at Gordonsville about twenty miles to the southwest of us. I seemed to remember that the Virginia Central ran east to
Hanover Junction before it turned south for Richmond, but it was very possible that the Yankees hadn't reached Hanover Junction yet and that the
railroad was still in operation.

Therefore the plan was simple. Johnny, wearing the old suit of Robert
Farnsworth's, and I, in my brown satin traveling dress and blue bonnet,
would walk to Gordonsville in the morning and take the Virginia Central

Railroad to Richmond. Miss Martha would know if fifteen Yankee dollars was sufficient fare for two of us, and if it wasn't, I was sure she would lend me the necessary balance. As for that, if I presented all my excess belongings to Amelia and Emily and Marie, without a doubt one of them would be glad to give me some money. They all come from wealthy families and are very generous girls too—I thought then—even if they do have other faults.

And so the only thing left to do now was to tell Johnny about it. I didn't anticipate any difficulty in getting his agreement because he had convinced me of his affection for me and I had arguments for all the rest of it. Johnny would see immediately, I was sure, that it would be to both our advantages if we set off together. Even apart from our feelings for each other, there was the fact that I wanted to leave the school anyway and that he would have a better chance of traveling unmolested if a person of the opposite sex were with him.

And so filled with these thoughts I arose and put on my blue silk dressing gown over the Parisian nightdress and went to the door. At that moment I became aware of the noise in the room above me—Alice's room. I think now that the sounds must have been occurring for some time but I had managed to shut my mind to them. There were sounds of movement and of furniture bumping and when I came outside to the hall I heard a voice—Alice giggling, I was sure—but still only one voice. I waited by my door and listened but no other person was joining in her merriment.

Was she laughing to herself—reading a book perhaps and laughing? Hardly likely, considering Alice's distaste for the printed page. Could it be just some private joke of her own? Or maybe—I forced myself to face it—there was someone else up there with her—Amelia, perhaps or more likely, Marie. True, Alice and Marie were not the best of friends but Marie was in the habit of wandering around the house at night, especially on those occasions when she had been ordered to remain in her room. She had been sentenced to some such punishment that very day, I remembered, and although she had apparently been paroled later because of Johnny's dinner, she might still be feeling truculent about the punishment and be flaunting her disregard for authority by prowling the house.

If Alice had company at all up there, it must be Marie, I was certain—so certain that I even started for the other stairs, but then Alice laughed again and I wondered suddenly if she were laughing at me. Was Johnny up there after all—telling her about me—repeating all the stupid things I'd said to him that afternoon? Was Alice telling him all the school gossip about me—mimicking my precise way of speaking—making fun of me—mocking me?

Anything was possible, I knew, where Alice was concerned, but I would still have bet my life that if Johnny was up there, he would have a perfectly legitimate explanation which I would accept instantly and without question. And in any case, if he is up there, I told myself, he is certainly not discussing me with Alice. I know him better than that, I said. I may not be the greatest judge of character in the world, but I certainly know Johnny better than that. How could Johnny or anyone else in the world deceive a person who all her life has been only waiting and watching for the words and glances that don't match, for the raised brow and the turned back, for the scorn behind the smile?

Still, I thought, before going down to the parlor it might be just as well to walk softly up to Alice's door and listen very briefly, just to set my mind at ease. Whether he is in there or not, I thought, it will be better to know. If he isn't in Alice's room, then I can go straight down to the parlor and tell him of my plan for tomorrow. If he is in there, I won't feel at all unhappy about it, but will just accept it as some private personal business that he has with Alice and I'll come straightway back to my own room and wait until morning to tell him that I am traveling with him.

Thinking those things I went up the stairs. Halfway up I decided against walking softly because it seemed unnecessarily sly and deceitful. I made up my mind now that if I heard his voice inside her room, I would rap and say, "Sorry to disturb you, Johnny, but there is something I would like to tell you, if you will be so good as to stop by my room on your way downstairs," or, "If Alice would not mind my interrupting your conversation, there is a matter of some interest to you which I will tell you about if you will only step out here in the hall for just one moment."

There was a light shining under her door, but no sound of any conversation now within. Perhaps Alice was alone after all. Perhaps she had been laughing in her sleep before—or even crying since they sound much the same. Apparently I have cried in my sleep on one or two occasions—although I denied it when Emily told me—and Miss Harriet quite often weeps at night. Certainly there was no reason why Alice couldn't have troubled dreams as well as any of the rest of us. As to her candle being lit, perhaps she was afraid of the dark. If I had to sleep on the third floor by myself, I thought, probably I would be reluctant to blow out my candle, too.

Glad to grasp at this explanation, I turned to go back down again, but wasn't quick enough. Alice laughed again, and then Johnny laughed. And then he said . . . quite clearly . . . "I love you."

I opened the door. He was in bed with her. I yelled . . . or screamed . . . or called out something. He jumped up . . . and took his trousers from a chair . . . all the while smiling and nodding at me as though nothing was wrong and he could explain everything. He came toward me then . . . and reached for me. I backed away . . . still screaming, I think. He said, "Dear Edwina" . . . and I pushed him away. I struck at him . . . at his face . . . and shoved him. He fell . . . backwards . . . down the stairs. . . .

Emily Stevenson

Well, as you can imagine, there was a great deal of consternation at this school after Edwina Morrow awakened the whole house with her screaming and shouting that night—and I must say she used some pretty horrible language. I don't know where Edwina ever learned all those terrible words—the meaning of some of which I didn't even know myself. Marie Deveraux, who is quite a precocious child—and in much the wrong way, if you ask me—assured us that the words and expressions Edwina used were very common among New Orleans riverboaters, and slave traders, and trashy people of that sort. Anyway we all decided that it would be mighty ridiculous for Edwina ever to put on any more airs around here or ever again try to play the Richmond lady after a shocking performance like that.

McBurney was unconscious—from hitting his head on the stairs, I suppose—and in addition his leg wound had reopened and was gushing blood all over the hall floor. We had thought at first he might be dead but after Mattie brought a light from the kitchen, Miss Martha inspected him quickly and decided his heart was still beating but would not continue to do so for very long unless the flow of blood was halted.

On Miss Martha's orders Edwina had stopped her screaming but was still standing at the top of the stairs gazing with no expression on the scene below. As for Alice, as far as I know, she had not yet come out of her room at all, unless she may have peeked around the corner of her door momentarily and then retreated again. Consequently, except for what we could gather from Edwina's angry tirade, we had very little knowledge then of what was going on. And Edwina refused to answer when Miss Martha asked her for an explanation.

"Well, sister, are you satisfied now or do you still think this is a virtuous young man?" said Miss Martha, turning her wrath in another direction.

"I don't know that he is guilty of anything," said Miss Harriet.

"You see him here and you say that?"

"I see him lying on the floor. I don't see any evidence that he has committed wrong. Will you let him bleed to death, sister, before you've even charged him with anything?"

"Move aside, girls, for pity's sake," said Miss Martha sharply then. "Don't stand there gawking. Harriet, or one of you, get strips of cloth of some kind—anything!"

Now Edwina deigned to come downstairs. "Wait," she said, descending slowly and holding back the skirts of her dressing gown.

When she reached us she removed the dressing gown, revealing the most indecent night dress I have ever seen. It was made of lace and the thinnest possible material, which little Marie remarked would have served as window glass. We didn't get a chance to examine it very carefully, however, since Edwina dropped it off her shoulders immediately and then stepped out of it, baring herself completely. Then she took it from the floor and tore it savagely into strips.

"There," she said, handing the results to Miss Martha. "That may do you for the moment."

"Cover yourself, Miss," said Miss Martha. "There's a chill in this hall." Then without further comment or even another glance at Edwina, she set to wrapping the strips around McBurney's leg.

I don't know whether Edwina expected to be thanked for the donation or not, but if so she was disappointed. She put on her dressing gown again and tied it carefully and smoothed out the wrinkles in it and then without another word to any of us, she went into her own room and closed the door.

By this time Mattie had returned with a basin of cold water and was bathing the bump on the back of McBurney's head, and then Miss Harriet joined in with her smelling salts, attempting to revive him. However he was in such a state of total insensibility that I doubt that anything could have brought him out of it—even the Angel of Doom with his silver trumpet. On the other hand, as I reflected later, it was just possible that McBurney was shamming all the time in order to avoid embarrassing explanations. Of course, if this was the case, he was a better actor than I ever thought him because he gave no sign of feeling any pain as Miss Martha applied the tourniquet.

"Couldn't that possibly be done more gently, Miss Martha?" Amelia enquired anxiously.

"If it's going to be done at all, it must be done quickly," said Miss Martha without bothering to reprimand her.

"Your prize doesn't feel anything just now anyway," I told her. "Though in my opinion he deserves a twinge or two for his conduct, don't you agree, Miss Martha?"

Miss Martha made no answer but I believe she fully agreed with me because it was true that she was not being nearly so careful in attending to McBurney's leg as she had been the first time. Oh she was being thorough enough, I suppose, as she is with every task she sets herself, but I must say I would not want my leg attended to quite that roughly even if I were unconscious. Anyway Miss Martha completed the tourniquet and then began to rip away McBurney's trouser leg.

"That's the second pair of trousers Johnny McBurney has ruined," said Marie. "First his own and now this pair that Miss Martha gave him."

"Perhaps these can be repaired later," Miss Harriet suggested.

"There may be no need of that," said her sister. "It's quite possible your Mister McBurney will never need two trouser legs again."

From the appearance of his leg that was an understatement. The wound had not only reopened but the bone which had been splintered before seemed now to be completely broken from the way the leg was bent below the knee.

"We can do nothing more for him up here," said Miss Martha. "He will have to be taken back downstairs again."

"Why couldn't we just put him in one of the bedrooms up here?" asked Miss Harriet. "The room opposite Edwina's is empty."

"Are you looking for a repetition of tonight's incident?" Miss Martha wanted to know.

"In Heaven's name, Martha!" Miss Harriet practically shouted, "the boy is helpless."

"At the moment perhaps," our headmistress retorted, "but he isn't dead yet. Besides I have another reason for wanting him downstairs. We may need to put him on the dining room table in order to take care of that leg. Now we can use the assistance of all of you for this. Take his arm, Harriet, and you, Emily, take the other. Mattie may grasp him by his good leg and I'll hold up the injured one. Amelia and Marie, get behind his shoulders."

Somehow we managed to lift him off the floor and then we struggled down the hall with him toward the first floor stairs. Those of us who were walking backwards had the worst time of all because there always was the danger of our tripping on the skirts of our night dresses. Well, just at that moment, Miss Alice Simms came shyly out of her room on to the third floor landing.

"Is there anything at all I can do to help?" she called down.

Miss Martha and the rest of us ignored her. We were so out of breath from our burden that I doubt we could have answered her anyway, even if we had wanted to. Taking courage now, Alice came down her stairs and trailed along behind us.

"I was just so shocked and shaken by my experience," she said, "that I could hardly bring myself to leave my room."

"Is that so, Miss?" Miss Martha panted.

"Yes. I was asleep, you see, when he came upstairs."

"Were you indeed?"

"Oh yes," said wide-eyed Alice. "It was terrible the way he rushed in there. I was just about frightened half to death when I saw him, and then Edwina came up there and began fighting with him. Edwina pushed him down the stairs."

"We didn't suppose he had jumped," said Miss Martha.

"What in the world do you suppose Johnny wanted up there in your room, Alice?" Marie asked her.

"How should I know?" answered the innocent one.

"I thought maybe he had told you," said Marie. "I thought perhaps some moments might have elapsed between the time he rushed into your room and terrified you like that, and Edwina's coming upstairs to get rid of him for you."

"Be quiet, all of you," Miss Martha ordered. "Attend to your business here."

We finally managed to reach the stairway to the first floor with our precious package and we just dropped him there for a moment while we all took our well-earned rest.

"I don't see how we're ever going to carry him all the way down those stairs, sister," fretted Miss Harriet.

"It will be difficult," Miss Martha admitted. "And we can't afford to drop him. I don't think your friend could tolerate another fall."

"He doesn't have to be carried, does he? Why couldn't he be lowered on a rope or something," I suggested.

"Now that isn't a bad idea of Emily's," said Marie. "What we could do is tie him up and slide him down very slowly on his back. We wouldn't hurt him much if we were careful."

"Where would we get the rope?" Miss Harriet wondered.

"There's old rope in the barn, ain't there?" said Mattie. "And a lot of old harness too. Harness might be better for what you want."

"Go and fetch it," Miss Martha instructed her. "But be quick about it—otherwise we won't have any need of it."

"Still, we'll have to get him downstairs some way, even if he does die," reflected Alice as Mattie went off as speedily as she could on her old bare feet.

"But he's not going to die," Amelia cried. "That's a fine way for Alice to talk anyway, after the way she and Edwina have been lolly-gogging around him and pestering him and encouraging him to do the Lord only knows what all!"

"That's exactly right," her roommate Marie shouted. "It's Alice and Edwina who always cause all the trouble here and other people get blamed for it. I say Alice and Edwina should be confined in their rooms without dinner for one month each!"

"Be silent, all of you," commanded Miss Martha. "I'll set the punishments here. I will only say now that no matter what happens to Mister McBurney, there will be no more episodes like tonight's. And I intend to find out the truth about that as soon as possible."

"Nothing happened," Alice said beginning to sob. "I swear to the Lord nothing very much happened, Miss Martha, or nothing very bad anyway. Just like I said, he came to my room and right after that Edwina threw him down the stairs."

"All the same, it might be interesting to hear McBurney's version of it," I said. "Of course, if he dies, we'll just have to depend on Alice's and Edwina's word, won't we?"

"But I don't want him to die," Alice protested tearfully. "Miss Martha make these girls stop saying I want Johnny to die!"

"Be quiet . . . be quiet, all of you, or go to your rooms," Miss Martha ordered. "It's like bedlam here!"

But the weeping continued unabated. I believe everyone present was weeping with the exception of Miss Martha and myself and possibly Marie, who seemed to be yelling more than sobbing, and, of course, McBurney, who was doing nothing at all but lying there, limp as an old rag and pale as parchment. Reconsidering it, he really mustn't have been shamming after all because not even the greatest charlatan in the world could have lain there quietly through all that racket unless he was unconscious.

After a bit Mattie returned with an armload of carriage harnesses and we tied the longest pieces of these securely under McBurney's arms and around his waist, and then with Marie carrying the lamp and going before to guide the parcel and Amelia holding his leg steady, the rest of us hung on to the straps from above and thus we lowered McBurney, sliding on his back, as carefully as we could down to the first floor.

"Thank you, Emily," said Miss Martha after she had caught her breath. "That really was a very clever notion."

"It was only a simple problem in logistics," I said. "Any good quarter-master could have supplied you with the same answer."

Then we pulled McBurney, still in his harness, into the parlor and lifted him on to his settee.

"There you are, Johnny old thing," said Marie. "If you had only re-mained there like a good boy earlier this evening, you'd have saved us all a lot of trouble."

Mattie was applying cold water to his head again and Miss Harriet was still waving the smelling salts under his nose. Whether it was the result of these remedies or of the jolting he had received on his journey I cannot say, but in any event shortly thereafter he opened his eyes and stared at us in apparent bewilderment. It seemed almost as though he had forgotten where he was. Then in a moment he got his bearings and managed a weak grin.

"The top o' the mornin to yez all," he said, and then he must have real-ized that none of us were smiling because his own look of cheerfulness soon faded. He tried to get up but couldn't quite make it.

"Be still, sir," said Miss Martha, who was having another look at his leg.

"Have I banged up the old stem again?" he asked anxiously.

"Yes, you have, Johnny," Amelia told him. "But don't worry about it. Miss Martha is going to fix it for you again."

"O' course she is," he said. "There's none better for patchin up a leg than dear Miss Martha." He closed his eyes and was silent for a long mo-ment. Then he said, "I'm sorry to have caused any trouble here tonight. But I won't make any more. If you can just cover that leg a bit to keep the dirt out of it, I'll still be leaving you in the morning."

"Your leg is broken—badly this time," Miss Martha informed him, "And I am incapable of setting it."

"Just push it all together like you did before, and wrap a bit of rag around it. It'll be all right. It don't feel any worse than it did before." He was trying to raise himself on his elbows all the while to see how bad it really was.

"I'm afraid it may give you some discomfort later, Mister McBurney," Miss Harriet put in. "You're still in a state of shock right now. But don't fret. We'll do our best for you."

"Just what do you think that might include, sister?" asked Miss Mar-tha. "I can't do anything at all to repair that injury. I'm not a surgeon—although I doubt that even a surgeon would attempt it. However, we can try to find someone qualified, if you feel that we should. I can go to the Brock crossroads in the morning and ask one of the Union officers to send a doc-tor here."

"I thought you didn't want to bring any more Yankees in here," said Miss Harriet.

"I don't. But it occurs to me now that it may be unavoidable. I should have reported him to our own troops on that first night. It would have been better for him and for us all."

"But he wanted to stay," I told her. "You can't blame yourself, Miss Martha."

"There ain't no need of fetchin a doctor here anyway," declared Mattie. "We can just put him in the cart and take him down to the crossroads. His own will come along and attend to him."

"All right," said Miss Martha. "We can do it that way, if Miss Harriet agrees. Either way, whichever she prefers."

"Why do you ask me, sister? Why do you leave it up to me?" said Miss Harriet, wringing her hands.

He had managed to get a look at it now and saw how it was twisted and gashed again. "What do you suppose the army surgeons will most likely do with that leg?" he asked in a small voice.

"Amputate it," said Miss Martha flatly.

"That's about the way I figure it too. They don't like to waste much time, them fellas. They haven't got the patience of you ladies." He sank back again and closed his eyes. "If it's all the same to you, I'd rather you didn't notify anybody. I don't fancy myself with one leg. It'd ruin my dancing style."

"Also they'll very probably charge you with desertion," I told him.

"You may be right at that, Miss," he said. "That's very possible too. . . ."

However that seemed the least of his worries at that moment. His voice had faded away and he seemed to have lost consciousness again. Miss Martha watched him for a moment and then pulled his blanket over him.

"All right," she said. "Back up to bed with all of you."

"Aren't you even going to attempt to sew it up again?" Miss Harriet asked.

"If I can't set the bone, I can't stitch the flesh above it," Miss Martha said.

"You could straighten it a bit, couldn't you?" Miss Harriet persisted. "Put splints on it like you did before. So neatly, too. . . . I watched you closely."

"Then you do it this time," Miss Martha suggested angrily. "I've told you that it is impossible, but if you want to try it anyway, you have my permission!"

"I'll try it," said Amelia as Miss Harriet hesitated.

"You'll do nothing of the sort," Miss Martha informed her. "You'll return to your room immediately as you have been instructed."

"Corporal McBurney will be all right, dear," said Miss Harriet, who was trying to convince herself. "The bleeding has stopped so he is in no immediate danger. Tomorrow morning, when the light is better, Miss Martha will have a look at his leg again . . . won't you, sister?"

"Yes," said Miss Martha noncommittally. "I imagine I will look at it. All right, young ladies. . . ."

She moved to the door, holding the lamp, and waited while we all went past her and up the stairs. Amelia was the last and she paused to tuck McBurney's blanket around his feet before she trailed after us staring very hard and defiantly at Miss Martha, I noticed, as she went by. Of course, Miss Martha, very properly, ignored her. Amelia, who used to be a very sweet little thing, is becoming a bit of a problem in this house and I believe her difficulties can be traced to her association with the one who shares her room. Marie Deveraux, I'm sure, would be enough to demoralize a whole regiment of girls like Amelia.

Well I went back to bed but naturally I couldn't fall asleep immediately after all that excitement. Also there was still so much noise in the house a stone deaf person would have been kept awake by just the buzzing and muttering alone. Amelia and Marie, who are right across the hall from me, just chattered away like two old magpies about the situation until finally Miss Martha herself could stand no more of it and had to go to their door and threaten them with the most dire consequences if they didn't immediately shut their mouths. Perhaps she was a bit more ladylike in her choice of expression, but that was certainly the content of her message. Anyway that quieted Marie and Amelia, but now our rest was interrupted by Edwina, sobbing behind her closed door, or maybe she had been sobbing all the time and it was just now noticeable.

Finally—and this is one of the last disturbances I can remember from that night—I heard Miss Harriet slipping quietly down the stairs. It is easy to recognize Miss Harriet's steps because they are such quick little nervous ones. Then almost immediately there was the more purposeful tread of Miss Martha going down the stairs in pursuit, I supposed, of her sister, but by that time I was frankly so tired that I could hardly bring myself to speculate on what commotion might be taking place. However we have our little people at this school who must wonder about everything, no matter how late at night it occurs.

"Miss Harriet has gone to the cellar for wine," hissed Marie opening my door, "and Miss Martha has gone after her!"

"How do you know?" I managed to ask.

"I guessed. I also predict that the wine is really for herself but she'll say it's for Corporal McBurney in case the pain in his leg awakens him."

"Go to bed . . . you're keeping me awake."

"Do you think Miss Martha would really let the Yankee army know McBurney is here?"

"I haven't the faintest idea . . . go to bed."

"I'm almost sure she wouldn't," said my little visitor, or at least I think that's what she said. "Miss Martha would be afraid they'd shoot us all for harboring a deserter."

"Please . . . please go to bed!"

"Isn't it all terribly interesting? What do you think is going to happen next, Emily?"

"This!" I yelled. And threw a shoe at her. She ducked and it hit the wall outside.

"Oh Emily," she chortled. "You'll never make the artillery." And then she skipped away.

I had half a notion to go after her and box her ears, but while I was in the process of considering this, I fell asleep—and remained asleep for the rest of the night, thankfully. If there were any more disturbances in the house on that night, I didn't hear them.

The next morning we were forbidden to enter the parlor. Only those with urgent business would be allowed to visit that part of the house until further notice, said Miss Martha, and that would not include any students without special permission from her.

This announcement came at breakfast and I personally thought it was a very good idea. To be sure there were some vociferous objections to it—from Amelia and Marie mostly. Amelia was always the last to admit the existence of any flaw in the character of her dear McBurney, and as for Marie, she just naturally would complain about any restriction on her movements, no matter what the cause. If Marie had never even considered entering the parlor before for any reason, and you told her she was forbidden to do so, why then naturally she would want to spend all her time in there.

However Miss Martha had apparently changed her mind about not trying to repair the damage to McBurney's leg, because as soon as we arose from the table she sent all the students into the library to study while she and Miss Harriet and Mattie went into the parlor, carrying with them Miss Harriet's sewing basket, some pieces of wood bark, which could be used as splints, and some strips of a bedsheet, which, we guessed, Miss Harriet must have sacrificed from her own bed.

"Miss Martha also donated another bottle of wine to the cause," Marie reported from the library door. "Either Johnny or Miss Harriet must have drained the last dregs out of the one that Miss Harriet gave him last night."

"I wonder if Johnny is angry with me," said Alice.

"But why on earth would he be angry with you?" inquired Marie quite sober-faced. "I should think it would be the other way around, after the way he forced himself into your room and overpowered you and mistreated you."

"I don't believe I used those exact words," said Alice, watching us all very carefully.

"Well then use some exact words now, Alice. Tell us all the horrible things that did happen. You must've had a simply dreadful ten or fifteen minutes or was it longer than that? Did you scream for help or were you too paralyzed to even open your mouth? Do you have any scars or bruises you could show us from your brutal treatment?"

"I didn't say I was brutally treated," cried Alice nervously. "I said I was frightened."

"Why were you frightened?" Amelia inquired. "Johnny told me a while ago that you invited him up there."

"Did he say that? Oh I guess I might have mentioned that he could drop up there some time when he had nothing else to do. He's certainly no gentleman talking that way behind a girl's back."

"He wasn't talking behind your back," said Amelia angrily. "I merely asked him a question and he answered it. He said that you had told him you had a map in your room that he could take with him when he left here, and that's all he said."

"And Miss Martha asked him the same question a few moments ago before breakfast, while I happened to be standing by the parlor door," said Marie, "and he gave Miss Martha very much the same answer. And then Miss Martha remarked that it must be an awfully heavy map if you couldn't carry it down to him yourself. She also said that she intends to have a look at that map herself before the day is out."

"She's entirely welcome to if she can only tell me where it is," declared Alice. "Do you know I have been searching for that particular map for a solid week now and I just haven't been able to find it. It's a very good map of this area too. A Mississippi captain gave it to my mother during our journey here but I just don't know what I did with it."

"Well you had better search harder for it," Marie informed her, "because I'm afraid there may be some people in this house who will refuse to believe that particular map ever existed."

"Stop your bickering, both of you, and get busy with your English grammar," I commanded them. Since I am the oldest at this school—with the exception of Edwina, who was still in her room, having ignored all rappings, poundings and loud calls to breakfast—I am usually put in charge when Miss Martha and Miss Harriet are absent. Of course, Edwina is so moody and wrapped up in her own affairs that she really isn't qualified for leadership, although you can bet your next year's crop of cotton it doesn't make her happy to see me given the responsibility.

Well, close to the time on our midday meal, Miss Harriet came into the library, looking very haggard and more than usually subdued. However her tone was cheerful enough as she told us that Miss Martha had set McBurney's leg and was now engaged in stitching it up again. Miss Harriet added that, although Miss Martha was not as yet overly optimistic about the thing, she herself felt that the leg would be better again very shortly. She also predicted that once our visitor was on his feet again we would find him a different person.

"This accident may have taught him a much needed lesson," said Miss Harriet. "In the future I think he may prove himself a much more trustworthy young man."

"You know it's possible what he says is true, Miss Harriet," Alice remarked. "It's possible he came to my room looking for the map. My goodness . . . if he had only told me at once what he wanted. . . ."

"By golly, do you remember that time I saw the two of you on the parlor settee, Alice?" Marie asked. "I'll bet McBurney was searching for that map then, wasn't he? I'll bet he thought you had it hidden somewhere on your person."

"Please, girls . . ." said Miss Harriet, stepping in between Marie and the murderous-looking Alice. "This is no time for personal quarrels. Miss Martha is depending on you to attend to your own lessons today. You know how I tell her that you are diligent young ladies—that we have nothing but virtuous and studious young ladies at this school."

"And no matter how often you tell her," remarked Marie, "I'll bet she still doesn't believe it, eh, Miss Harriet?"

"Miss Harriet, is Johnny in any pain?" Amelia asked.

"No more than he has suffered in the past, I think. We have given him a little wine and that has deadened it."

"Will you please tell him that we are being kept away from him." Amelia persisted. "I wouldn't want him to think that I didn't care to visit him."

"Yes, I will tell him," Miss Harriet promised. "And perhaps we can have that order modified in a day or two—when we have all proven to Miss Martha—and this includes Corporal McBurney—that we are as good as she would like us to be."

"That's a physical impossibility," Marie stated.

"Nevertheless I am sure we will all strive for perfection," our executive headmistress continued sweetly. Of course if Marie had made a remark like that to Miss Martha she would have received one week's confinement to her room without dinner, but Miss Harriet just acts as though half the time she doesn't even hear what goes on in this house. Anyway she went on to tell us now that she had to return to the parlor and help Miss Martha, but that she needed some willing girl to take a tray of food to Edwina. I volunteered. Surprisingly enough, everyone else did too.

"Miss Edwina must be more popular than we thought," said Miss Harriet with her little smile.

"It's not popularity," Marie informed her. "It's curiosity, and I'm the only one honest enough to admit it."

That was not exactly true in my own case. I did sort of wonder, naturally, what Edwina might have to say about the events of the night before, but I also had some sympathetic feelings about her, too. I have always felt rather sorry for Edwina and I will not hesitate to admit this to anyone.

Anyway Miss Harriet must have recognized my true motives—or again perhaps it was only because she considered me the most reliable—because she immediately selected me to be the Good Samaritan. She then returned to the parlor and I went to the kitchen to prepare the tray, leaving the study group temporarily in Alice's charge. There was no help for that. Someone older, if not wiser, must always be delegated to keep an eye on Amelia and Marie.

"Emily . . . oh, Emily," our problem child shouted after me. "Alice forgot to salute when she relieved you!"

Naturally, I ignored this and continued on to the kitchen. Well I guess the tray I fixed for Miss Edwina might not have seemed too appetizing to the diners at the Exchange Hotel or the Oriental Saloon in Richmond but it was good nourishing food all the same. There was still a little barley porridge in the pot and I filled a bowl with some of that—although I didn't reheat it since that would have meant rekindling the fire and we were keeping our cooking fires down to a minimum while the Yankees were still in the general area. Not that we were trying to conceal our presence, but we weren't advertising it either by sending up unnecessary smoke during the daylight hours.

So I took the porridge and some leftover corn cakes and a cup of acorn coffee—admittedly cold too, but still invigorating—and went up to Edwina's room. We two roomed together at one time, but we didn't get along. She was constantly accusing me of prying into her affairs, even to the point of spying on her and searching her belongings. I'll admit I did question her rather closely at first, but it was only in an effort to learn if there was anything we shared in common—likes and dislikes and so forth—on which at least a temporary friendship might be built. It was a waste of time, of course. Even if she had been willing to tell me anything about herself—which she wasn't—it wouldn't have been for the purposes of friendship. Edwina Morrow doesn't want any friends.

I didn't expect her to answer my rapping and she didn't. However, since I had been instructed to deliver breakfast to her, with no mention of any asking whether she wanted it or not, I considered it within the limits of my orders to open the door and walk in. Which I did. Miss Martha has never permitted us to lock our bedroom doors—in fact we have no keys—just in anticipation, I suppose, of such emergencies.

Miss Morrow, still wearing her blue silk dressing gown, was sitting by her window which overlooks the woods and a part of the garden. There was an open book on her lap but she wasn't reading it. In fact, she didn't seem to be doing anything but sitting there in a kind of trance, awake but seemingly unaware of anything around her.

"Here's your breakfast," I informed her. "You're getting headquarters service this morning."

Not a flicker of an eyelid, so I tried again. "Corporal McBurney's leg may be all right, Miss Harriet says. It may not have been permanently injured after all." No answer, but definitely quickened breathing. I decided to push farther in this direction.

"The general feeling seems to be that what happened last night was just an unfortunate accident and that it would be well to forget it as soon as possible."

"Who thinks that?" asked Edwina in a low voice but without turning to me.

"Well, Miss Harriet for one. And possibly McBurney himself for another. He certainly hasn't been accusing anyone of causing him to fall. As for myself, I can't imagine anyone being interested enough in McBurney to bother harming him. Of course, we all gathered from your rather angry words last night that you and McBurney had been having some kind of argument."

"I pushed him," she said, still in the same soft tone. "I shoved him down the stairs."

"Why?" I asked quickly.

"Because I hate him."

"Because of his uniform? Or because he was up there visiting Alice? Alice claims he only came up to borrow a map from her. Of course we all have our doubts about that, but I must say she doesn't seem very concerned about him at the moment."

"When will he go away?"

"As soon as he's able, I suppose."

"I don't want to have to look at him again."

"It shouldn't be necessary," I told her. "He's confined to the parlor and we're forbidden to enter."

I put the tray on a table near her. She had begun to weep again and her book fell from her lap. The tears were running down her face and she was making no attempt to halt them or even wipe them away. This sort of thing—or indeed, I suppose, any such sign of unopposed weakness—always makes me a bit impatient and that was just the way I felt as I turned away from her and went to her chest of drawers in search of a clean handkerchief.

Now, I assure you, finding that handkerchief was my sole intention at that moment. I had not the least desire to pry and I'm sure my curiosity was hardly stirred as I opened the top drawer, which seemed the logical place to find the piece of goods I wanted.

The handkerchiefs were there all right—a good number of all kinds and colors, probably more than were owned by all the other students combined. And atop the pile of handkerchiefs was a small toilet mirror with an ivory handle and next to that a pocket-size, cheaply framed tin picture, somewhat bent and faded.

It was a picture of a young, light-complexioned Negress in a frilly summer dress and with a parasol in her hand—both dress and parasol, I assumed, having been borrowed from her lenient mistress for the occasion or else from the photographer himself, whose establishment, I noted from the label on the frame, was located in Savannah. The girl was of at least half mixed blood and strikingly pretty too and was, I supposed, some nurse or house servant Edwina had become attached to as a child, although it is difficult to think of Edwina's being attached to anyone. However I had turned my attention from the picture and was examining the mirror—which was of very intricate, though somewhat mawkish design, with cupids and rosebuds and the like carved on the handle and frame—when a rather disagreeable little incident occurred.

I must explain that I hadn't picked up the mirror—or the picture, for that matter—but was looking at it in the drawer so that I suppose Edwina had no idea which of her hidden treasures I had found. Anyway when I turned back to her with the handkerchief I found her staring at me with a look of absolute terror on her face.

"Your gold and jewels are quite safe," I told her. "I haven't taken a thing."

"You didn't . . . ?"

"I didn't touch a thing," I said, quite angrily. "I'm sure I don't care a fig for any of your possessions!"

"I'm sorry, Emily. I didn't mean anything by it."

"You should be sorry," I informed her. "Your manners are atrocious. Now dry your eyes and compose yourself. You look absolutely hideous."

As a matter of fact her tears had stopped, I noticed, as I handed her the handkerchief. Evidently greed can sometimes take precedence over worthier emotions. Anyway, vexed as I was, I continued my work of charity by putting her dressing gown in order, as it had opened, exposing a good deal of her natural self. She was dressed exactly as she had been when she left us on the night before and therefore it seemed evident that she had never gone to bed. Well, realization of the misery that must have kept her from sleep cooled my temper a bit.

"I'm sure Miss Martha and Miss Harriet would understand if you decided to rest here until dinner time," I said. "With the McBurney situation as it is, we are likely to have no classes anyway for the remainder of the day."

As one more good-will gesture I picked up her fallen book. It was *The Works of William Blake* and it was open to a poem of few words but much gushy sentiment.

"Never seek to tell thy love," I read aloud. "Love that never told can be. For the gentle wind does move . . . silently, invisibly."

"Please, Emily," said my former roommate biting her knuckles.

"I told my love, I told my love, I told her all my heart . . . trembling, cold, in ghastly fears—ah, she doth depart."

"Please, Emily . . . don't read any more!"

"It's mighty foolish stuff, don't you agree?"

"Yes, Emily. Emily . . . ?"

"What, what? Speak up."

"Do you like me, Emily?"

"Not particularly, at the moment, no. However, under ordinary circumstances I think I can safely say that I like anyone with gumption. You are free to keep that in mind and conduct yourself accordingly. Now compose yourself and try to act like a grown lady."

"All right, Emily."

"There is enough trouble in the world today without anyone making a spectacle of herself over a trifle like this. However Corporal McBurney may have offended you. You are a Southern woman and have more worthy things to weep about, if weep you must."

"Yes, Emily."

"All right then. Eat your breakfast and let's have no more of this nonsense."

"Yes, Emily." Obediently, she picked up her spoon and set to work on the barley porridge.

Feeling that I had accomplished a little something, I left the room then and went back downstairs. "Girls!" I remember thinking impatiently. "Idiotic girls who can lose all their control and dignity over a worthless vagabond like McBurney." In my mind I had begun to disassociate him from the Yankees because his being a member of even an enemy army made the whole war seem less noble and the Yankees much less worthy to be our opponents. As a matter of fact in my disgust, I think I was even beginning to disassociate myself from the entire female sex.

Well there was no studying but much enthusiastic discussion taking place in the library when I returned there. You cannot trust those young students to carry out your orders for five consecutive minutes unless you are standing right over them.

"For pity's sake, what is it now?" I asked them.

"It's poor Johnny's leg, not that you're at all interested in that subject," Alice informed me impertinently.

"There are indeed more important things in life at the moment," I replied. "Anyway I thought Miss Harriet said McBurney's leg was getting better."

"Miss Harriet was wrong about that as she is about so many things," said Marie with her customary disrespect. "Miss Martha just came in here a moment ago with some official and exact news about McBurney. And, Emily, I'm so sorry that she didn't ask whether you were present or not before she made the announcement."

"You will get a good ear boxing before this day is out, Miss," I told her. "Now either one of you will tell me what Miss Martha said or you will all get back to your books immediately. It doesn't make a particle of difference to me which you choose."

It did slightly, of course. I am as interested as the next person in whatever goes on in this house. And that was about as severe a punishment as was in my power to inflict on them. And as I expected, it worked.

"It's terrible," said Amelia, whom I noticed now wasn't sharing the enthusiasm of the others but in fact was weeping. I should have expected that, of course, because in those days in this house some one person was nearly always weeping.

"What is terrible, you poor thing?" I inquired.

"Johnny's leg," said our nature girl. "Miss Martha is going to cut Johnny's leg entirely off!"

Martha Farnsworth

I knew he was guilty, no matter what secondary responsibility might have been charged to any of our students. No matter what actually happened on the third floor that night or what his provocation, I knew what had been in his mind and in my rage at this betrayal of my hospitality I would have dragged him down to the Brock road and left him there had not my sister stayed my hand. Then later it occurred to me that such an action on my part might scandalize the younger students who presumably would have no idea of what McBurney had intended.

At any rate the certainty of his guilt did not prevent me from giving him all the immediate comfort I could. I stopped the bleeding and got him back to his downstairs bed and then the following morning, egged on by the entire household, I made quite a lengthy attempt to repair the damage Mister McBurney's folly had caused him.

"It would take a magician to restore this leg to its former usefulness," I said as I stitched it for the second time.

"And you're the lady with the old magic wand," said my patient cheerfully. "Now don't trouble to deny it, ma'am, for there's not a soul here will believe your story."

"It looks as neatly done as before, sister," said Harriet bravely. She had been feeling faint a few moments before and so I had sent her across to the library to check on the activities of the students. However she had then obviously tarried in the hall as long as she could because when she returned I was almost finished.

"It may look neat but it certainly doesn't look healthy," I remarked. "Notice how swollen and discolored the calf is."

"Good God, if the calf is discolored I wonder what state the cow is in." Mister McBurney shouted merrily. "Ah to hell with all calf cuddling and general leg coddling anyway. Excuse me dear ladies, but that old stem needs only a cold cloth and a good rub down with the lily white hands of Miss Martha Farnsworth and 'twill be as sound and sturdy as the day I walked into the world with it. Them's my opinions and the Pope, President Lincoln and good Queen Victoria won't change them!"

"Notice also the complete lack of any feeling in it."

"How dare you, Miss, how dare you! I'll have you know that particular leg is the most sensitive part of my entire body. That leg blushes to the bone in bad company. I've used that leg for years like a weather glass to keep me always in the state o' grace!"

"He does feel some pain, I'm sure," Harriet insisted. "It's only the wine and his braggadocio that won't permit him to flinch when you apply the needle."

It was true that the wine—whether it had any pain killing effect or not—had given him the courage to put on a show of complete indifference. Moreover the wine, which my sister had been pouring for him in most generous quantities, had loosened his tongue considerably. He had begun to use the worst kind of blasphemous language, following each curse and vulgar expression with a mocking apology to my sister and me.

"God flog the rich—my apologies, ladies," he said now. I am reporting his exact words. "There's nothin like havin two fine Southern ladies playin with your leg of a warm spring mornin. Get in there won't you, Miss Harriet dear, and give it a pat or two. Don't be shy, dear. D'ye see how your sister works away at it? She's had a man's leg in her lap a time or two before—you can tell that from one glance at her. Oh carry my leg back to old Virginny! And give me a pair o' bonnie lasses to polish it . . . and pinch it . . . and knead it a bit on the sly. Oh the bonnie lasses o' the three B's. Well born, well bred and well bosomed too, eh? None o' yer tavern types or country types o' bosoms, by any means, but the genuine, registered, first class regal kind. The real landed gentry, touch me if you dare, small but never insignificant, more for viewing than for using, dainty, lofty, lady-like, kind of perky little perty. . . ."

"Stand erect there, sister, or move away," I told Harriet.

"Move away, Miss Harriet. Your dress is too low cut for the operating room."

"Pay no attention to it, Harriet, do you hear me?"

"I'm not, sister, I'm not." But she was as flushed as a ripe apple and she was even smiling faintly which, of course, only encouraged him.

"Don't be jealous, Miss Martha. I was referrin to both of you in my last remarks."

"One more word out of you, my man," I informed him, "and you're going to get a cold cloth to chew on. Do you understand me?"

"Oh yes, ma'am. No offense, ma'am. How could a poor country hulk like meself ever dare to displease the lovely likes of you . . . the tall and stately, poised and perfect, seldom smilin, never laughin, mostly kind but sometimes cruel . . . always dreamin, never darin. . . ."

"Enough!"

"Right you are, ma'am. Bend over a bit and I'll chew on your lips a little."

With that I could take no more and so I did what I had threatened to do—threw the cold cloth across his face. He continued to giggle happily underneath it, but made no move to take it away.

"I would like to know which one of us has been dreaming but not daring," my sister suggested softly, "and also what that dream has been."

"You shall not hear it," I declared. "We will have no more of this vulgar prattle." I tied a knot in my stitch and cut the thread, then stood there for a moment, studying my handiwork.

"Do you want me to bandage it, Miss Martha?" said Mattie who was waiting nearby.

"You can if you like. Frankly I don't think it will make much difference."

"What do you mean, sister?" Harriet asked.

"Whether it be kind or cruel, there is nevertheless a time for stating the truth. This man's leg is becoming morbid. It will have to be removed."

Well you might have expected the giggling beneath the cloth to cease right then, but such was not the case. The sounds of merriment continued as though the listener was finding my remarks extremely comical.

Miss Harriet was more alarmed. "You're not serious, sister!"

"Am I not?"

"But you haven't given his leg a chance to reheal."

"It won't heal again. I knew it was useless to attempt anything. I only tried to keep you satisfied."

"Do you mean you'll turn him over to the Yankee surgeons now after all the time you've spent with him this morning? Will you take him to the crossroads or let one of them come here?"

There was a silence now beneath the cloth. It was evident that Mister McBurney was much more afraid of the consequences of being discovered by his own people than he was of anything I might do to him.

"I will do neither," I said. "I spent a sleepless night considering the matter against this very contingency. I have decided it wouldn't be at all prudent to bring any more soldiers here. Also Corporal McBurney states he doesn't want to see any of his own surgeons either. Therefore, with all other possibilities eliminated, it seems we shall have to amputate the leg ourselves."

At this there was a great burst of laughter from our guest. He threw the cloth aside and roared with unrestrained glee.

"Go ahead, Miss Martha, chop away," he cried. "You have my permission!"

"All right," I said quietly. "That makes it easier—although I intended to ask for it in any case."

"You have it and gladly," said he. "Saw away with a will, my dear, while sweet Miss Harriet holds my hand to comfort me."

"It will take some time to prepare for it," said I. "We may not get to it until later in the day. However I think it should be this afternoon, since I would hesitate to attempt it by lamplight."

"He thinks you're joking, Martha," said my sister.

"Does he?"

"He thinks you're only trying to frighten him."

"Why would I want to do that?"

"To punish me, dear heart," McBurney grinned. "And the Lord knows I deserve it—the shameful way I've treated you two darlings, abusin your hospitality and all. But I'll remedy that very soon, I promise you. Before I leave you, I'm going to give you both a great hug and a kiss for being so nice to me. I'll do that, I will, as soon as the fumes o' the wine is faded . . . so's I wouldn't be offendin you with my barroom breath. . . ." Still chuckling he lay back and closed his eyes.

"He is very intoxicated, Martha," my sister said.

"Of course he is. I wonder that he can speak at all. You've given him enough to paralyze two men."

"But he doesn't realize what you're saying!"

"Because he thinks you're playing a game with him, you know that, Martha. And even if he realized you meant it, you couldn't accept his permission anyway. You can't rely on the judgment of a drunken man!"

"It's not his judgment I'm relying on, it's my own. It's quite possible, I suppose, that sober, he'd refuse to let me do it, but I think my evaluation of the situation is more to be trusted than his own. I happen to think this admittedly drastic step is necessary to save his life."

"It's his life, Martha."

"Not his alone. We are all responsible for each other. Each of us belong to his brethren . . . and to God."

I think McBurney had gone to sleep because he gave no sign of having heard these last remarks. He was still grinning slightly with his mouth agape. He didn't stir even when I put my hand on his brow.

"He's got a fever all right, there's no arguin that," commented Mattie as she wrapped a strip of cloth around the much debated leg. The cloth—the last piece of something donated by Miss Edwina Morrow might better have been saved, in my opinion, for later use, but I kept this thought to myself. "Yes ma'am, he's got a misery somewhere in his body that's causin his heat to rise."

"You do agree with me then that the leg is infected?"

"You askin my opinion? I think his leg is some worse than it was before, yes. It's gettin black all right and it's swolled up like you say. Course part of that might be due to the fact that no blood is getting down there. I think maybe you got that blood-stoppin bandage tied too tight."

"Couldn't that tourniquet be removed now, sister?" Harriet asked. "Perhaps it should have been loosened before this."

"It was necessary to keep the lower veins pinched off to prevent his bleeding to death during the night," I told her sharply. "If you feel you have a more expert knowledge of this business than I do, I wish you would take over here and allow me to get some rest."

Harriet made no answer to this but only smiled faintly in her foolish way and lowered her eyes. I turned to Mattie but she only shrugged and said nothing either. Then—rather peevishly, I suppose. I satisfied them both by taking my scissors and cutting the tourniquet. The leg jerked and McBurney frowned and moaned a bit. Mercifully, however, the stitches held and the leg did not begin to bleed again.

"He certainly felt something then," said my obstinate sister.

"It's possible that it will begin to twinge him now and then," I admitted. "I assume the presence of gangrene doesn't necessarily mean the total absence of feeling in the affected member. Therefore I'll assign you a task you ought to welcome. You may go down to the cellar and fetch another bottle of wine—two bottles, if you like. Then for the next few hours you may continue to dose him with it. I want him to be absolutely stupefied before we begin this thing."

"You won't wait and discuss it with him when he's rational?" Harriet persisted.

"It wouldn't make any difference," I told her with great patience. "No matter what he might say. And we just don't have that much more time."

"You sure he's that sick, Miss Martha?" Mattie wanted to know.

"Yes, I am entirely sure."

And I was. I went across the hall then to inform the students of my decision. My motive here was to give them enough time to consider it and become adjusted to it, since some of them had become very attached to Mister McBurney. I explained to them as briefly as possible that the step was absolutely necessary in order to preserve McBurney's life and that the operation most certainly would have been performed long ago if he had been in the care of the medical departments of either army.

"That's because they wouldn't have the time to trouble with him," said Miss Amelia with a touch of impudence.

"We have taken a great deal of trouble with him already, Miss," I said, "and I can assure you I would take more if I thought it for the best."

"Best for who, Miss Martha?" asked Marie.

"It needs to be done because that is best for Corporal McBurney. We will do it ourselves—and as well, I'm sure, as any army surgeons—because that is best for us."

Then I went upstairs to my room and prayed that I would continue to be as confident in the hours ahead. I prayed that my hand would be steady and unwavering and that I would never doubt that I had done the right thing.

I sat on my chair by the window overlooking the arbor which the young man had restored to the state of order and beauty I remembered from my childhood. The boy had a knack for gardening, there was no doubt of that. Even the small circular plot at the far end of the garden where our little imitation temple stands had been cleared, I noticed now, although I remembered distinctly having forbade him to work in that area.

He had cut away the underbrush around the little building and then evidently had applied a coat of whitewash to the exterior, because in the midday sun it looked as clean and new as it had that summer day long ago when my brother and I first built it. I assumed McBurney must have done all the work on the previous afternoon and it had escaped everyone's attention because, with all the excitement, there had been no chores in the vegetable garden this morning.

Well I would certainly speak to him about it, I thought, just as soon as he recovered. Perhaps it would be well to assign him the task of demolishing the little building before we sent him away. I had been thinking of having that done for some time anyway and it might be a good lesson for McBurney to set him doing it. Then I remembered what I was planning and that it would be a long time, if ever, before he could work at any such arduous tasks again.

Well that wouldn't matter. The little temple could wait, or someone else could tear it down. Or perhaps it would be just as well to leave it as it was in its shining restoration—as a monument to all those things in a lifetime that don't turn out the way they are planned.

But the venture this afternoon would be successful, I was certain. McBurney would recover from it quickly and go away and then order would return to the school as it had to the garden. McBurney could go anywhere he liked. To expedite his leaving I might even provide him with some money for the railroad fare to Richmond or Charleston or wherever he chose. It was obvious he had no desire to go back North, and incapacitated, as he would now become for military service, the Northern authorities would very likely have no further interest in him. In that sense we might even be doing him a favor. He would see that, I was sure, as soon as the thing was over. He would realize the necessity for it and adapt to it and make the best of it. As we all must do, all our days.

He would know we had done nothing which wasn't necessary to save his life. We weren't deliberately punishing him or crippling him in order to restrict his movements, but only trying to help him. He was—if nothing else—a clever boy, I thought, and he would not fail to apprehend that the whole business had been no pleasure for any of us here, and certainly not for me who would have to bear the burden of not only the physical task itself but the responsibility for it as well.

I slept then for about an hour and awakened when Mattie entered bringing me a cup of mint tea. That is one thing we do not lack in this house. We are well supplied with mint leaves and herbs of all kinds by our little Amelia Dabney who brings back a supply—most of them, I fear, indigestible—whenever she is permitted to go to the woods.

"The young ladies have had their noon meal," Mattie reported now, "and Miss Harriet says the Yankee is as stupefied as he's ever gonna be. What you want us to do now?"

"A number of things," I said, "and each of them must be done carefully but without wasting any time. First you must collect all our sharp kitchen knives. I'm not sure which ones I'll need so you had better prepare them all. Hone them to a fine edge and then boil them in hot water."

I went to the large chest of drawers where I keep some of the personal belonging of my brother and my father and brought out two ivory handled razors of the finest Sheffield steel which my father had bought in England many years ago.

"I think these are clean," I told Mattie, "but boil them in the pot with the rest. You might also get the large meat saw from the smoke house and clean that up as best you can. Then take up the dining room carpet and scrub the table well."

"You want to ruin that good wood?"

"It can't be helped," I said. "It's the only large table we have. And even if it isn't scrubbed now we would have to do it afterwards anyway. Perhaps it can be varnished again someday, but we have no time to discuss that now. Next you must gather a good supply of all the clean cloth you can find. Bed sheets, table cloths, excess pillow cases. . . ."

"We ain't had any excess pillow cases since the first year of the war," Mattie informed him. "And there ain't no sheets now on your bed or Miss Harriet's. There ain't but four or five sheets in this whole house."

"Take those and we'll use what we need. Take all the pillow cases too. The girls will be glad to donate them, I'm sure. And you might also ask them if they are willing to follow Miss Edwina's example and give us any shifts or night dresses they don't need—linen, preferably, if they can spare them. I want a good supply of it in readiness and then we'll tear it to suit our purposes as we need it. Now you may tell any of the students you wish to help you. Inform them that I have given you permission."

"Only one that's any good at all is my poor little Miss Amelia and she's too broke up about the whole thing to help anybody. Miss Amelia's the only one round here that's good for anything. Miss Emily's too bossy and Miss Marie is too devilish and Miss Alice is good for nothin but standin in front of a mirror to see if she growed any in the chest overnight. Then that other one who's shut up in her room . . . I don't know what a body could say about her. She ain't good for one solitary thing at all includin herself."

"I agree that Miss Edwina is a very difficult young woman. She has never shown any signs of fitting in at all. Perhaps when this business of Corporal McBurney is over I may write to her father and ask him to take her away from here."

"I'll bet you all my meals for a month her Daddy never answers your letter. I'll bet he don't want her any more than you do."

"She may have to leave us anyway. We may have to send her home whether her father wishes it or not."

"You figure her money is all gone?"

"Enough of that!"

"I was just wonderin why you hadn't sent her home a long time ago."

"Because I thought possibly I could do something for her. Because in a way she's been a challenge to me. I've never yet admitted failure in the case of a student, but perhaps there has to be a first time. And perhaps, while I'm at it, it would be well to admit two failures. Yes, I think at the end of this summer Miss Edwina, and Miss Alice too, may have to be sent away. The war should be over by that time—no matter who wins it—and the school will soon be crowded once again with more worthy students."

"I feel sorry for those two," said Mattie. "They can't help what they are. Miss Alice can't help what her Mama made her. And the same for the other one."

"I feel sorry for them too," I replied, "but you can't operate an institution like this on pity—or any other emotional feelings for that matter. Just as I can't let my emotions interfere with my decision to amputate Corporal McBurney's leg."

"You sure you ain't doin exactly that?"

I repeat this exactly as it was said. If I am ever accused of having unworthy motives in this affair or if it is ever stated that I was warned against performing an unnecessary operation, it can be affirmed that Miss Martha Farnsworth has never refused to discuss the matter freely and openly and completely and has never attempted to conceal any part of it. She certainly doesn't feel guilty about anything now and she didn't then, unless it might have been the fact that she was penalizing her students by spending the entire day on the trouble of an outsider.

And this was Miss Martha's reply to her servant. "You are a presumptuous and uncivil wretch and you are becoming more sinfully vexatious with each passing day. Sometimes I think I offend the Lord myself by keeping you here to plague me!"

"I just asked a question," declared Mattie boldly.

"It was a highly improper question," I informed her, "as you know well enough. It certainly deserves no answer but in order to prevent your speculating on the subject in the presence of others, I will assure you that my decision is entirely an objective one. I am not going to cut off the Yankee's leg out of fear or anger or pity or any provocation other than common sense and cold logic. I am going to do it because I have decided it is the only reasonable thing to do."

"Reasonable for him?"

"Yes!" I almost shouted, "for him!"

"All right," she answered coyly. "There ain't no need to get upset about it. I just wanted to make sure that you were sure, that's all. Drink your tea now before it gets cold. You want me to bring you up some nice turnip soup and some greens and maybe a little of that bacon we got left?"

"No, I don't want anything," I told her.

"You got to get something in your stomach before you start workin on that boy. You got to be strong and steady and not the least speck lightheaded. It ain't gonna be a very pleasant thing and you wouldn't want to go faintin in the middle of it the way Miss Harriet almost did this mornin. I'll have some soup ready for you when you come downstairs and I'm gonna stand right over you until you swallow all of it."

She left the room then, having once again demonstrated her sly ability to move from outright defiance and arrogance to the most persuasive and—if you didn't know her—endearing solicitude. Well I do know her and I am not taken in by these abrupt changes of face. However my anger had abated by that time with the realization that the problem of Mattie was not a new one, nor was it anything which could be solved in the way such problems were dealt with in the days before the war. You cannot sell off your vexations any more, if there is no one to buy them. You must put up with them, and wear them like the proverbial millstone, until the times get better—which they are bound to do, I think, since they can hardly get any worse.

Meditating thus I drank my herb tea, then changed into an old but clean gingham dress and pinned my hair securely so that it would not come loose and interfere with my vision, and finally scrubbed my hands and arms well with soap and water and a hard brush, and then, assured that I had done all I could to prepare myself, came downstairs to see how my hospital arrangements were coming on.

And indeed the dining room had taken on the appearance of a make-shift hospital when I arrived there. Mattie and the girls had taken up the carpet and removed the chairs; Emily now was applying tallow soap and steaming hot water to my beloved walnut table; Alice and Marie were racing excitedly about the house gathering the stock of cloth I had requested and this, I noted with approval, was being piled on a stand adjacent to the table. In an excess of enthusiasm one of the workers had even decided to collect all the medication in the house and these bottles and jars were piled on another stand. I anticipated no need for stomach sweeteners or rheumatism salves or any of my sister's headache remedies, but not wishing to discourage zeal, I smiled privately and said nothing.

Mattie I found in the kitchen, boiling and scouring the cutting instruments as I had requested. My good humor was all but restored now and I was satisfied that the arrangements were proceeding satisfactorily. Therefore I accepted the bowl of turnip soup which my erstwhile antagonist silently ladled out for me and sat down to eat a few spoonfuls of it.

"Where is Miss Harriet?" I asked her.

"She's across the hall keepin watch on the Yankee. I don't think she's goin to be much help to you when you get down to the business."

"I'm not counting on her for much help," I said civily. "Where is young Amelia?"

"She run off somewhere. She ain't in favor of what you're gonna do either."

"That's too bad," I answered, ignoring the "either." "I'm sorry we can't run an Athenian democracy here which would permit us to be guided by Amelia Dabney and everyone else. I'm afraid of Miss Amelia becoming as headstrong as Marie Deveraux. Very likely it's a result of too much association with Marie. Perhaps it would be wise to put them in separate bedrooms."

"I don't think you're right in punishin the child just because she's ten-derhearted."

"Three items for you to ponder, Mattie," I said, irritated again. "First,

I'm not thinking of punishing her. Second, tenderness of heart is not necessarily a virtue—indeed, under some circumstances, it may be a folly. Third, when I want your advice, I'll ask for it."

"Finish your soup before it gets cold," said she imperturbed.

I did so quickly, no longer enjoying it, and then went across the hall to have a look at my patient. He was, as Mattie had reported, quite unconscious now. My sister was seated beside him treating herself to a glass of wine.

"This is the last of it," she explained. "I thought I might as well finish it off."

"It may be the last of that particular bottle," said I, "which only means that if he wakes up again during the proceedings we shall have to open a new bottle."

"It might be better to do that anyway, sister. It might be wise to have a fresh bottle ready, mightn't it, just to be on the safe side?"

Here, of course, was another eternal thorn in my side and this one— war or no war—I could do absolutely nothing about.

"Corks can be pulled instantly," I reminded her, "and Madeira spoils after it has been exposed to air."

"Yes, that's true," said Harriet with a sigh. "Isn't it a shame we don't have any more of the plum brandy Marie's father sent to us? Brandy would be an even better narcotic than wine."

"Yes, it would be," I agreed. "It is too bad we don't have any more brandy and it is also too bad we didn't save what we had."

My sister made no reply to this beyond another sigh—or perhaps it was an eructation. I didn't attempt to distinguish, but instead returned to the door and summoned Mattie and the girls from across the hall.

"We're going to move Corporal McBurney to the dining room now," I explained when they arrived, "and you'll all have to lend a hand."

"Are you going to use my method again?" asked Emily. "Shall we pull him over as we pulled him downstairs last night?"

"I don't think so," I said. "For one thing I don't want to awaken him if I can help it. Also there would still be the problem of lifting him up on to the table which is much higher than the settee."

"Why not make a sling of some kind," my sister suggested. "Fold a bed sheet and sew it to a pair of broomsticks, or maybe two vine poles would be better. I presume we would need something of that sort anyway to move him . . . when you're finished with him. . . ."

"That is an excellent idea, sister," I said. "It shows your mind is still productive when you use it properly. Vine poles would be better, I think— they're stronger. Go out of the barn and select two sturdy ones, Emily. And you get one of the sheets from the supply in the dining room, Alice, and Marie, fetch my sewing basket from my room."

"No, fetch my sewing basket," said my sister. "Let me do it, Martha . . . I thought of it."

"All right," I consented without rancour. "I suppose you might as well try something useful. But be quick about it. I want to have the best of the afternoon's sunlight for this task. Meanwhile the rest of us will continue with the other preparations. The girls and Mattie will return to their work in the kitchen and dining room while I do a little medical browsing in the library. You call out, Harriet, as soon as you're finished with the sling."

She did so and in comparatively short order too. It took her no longer than fifteen minutes to sew the cloth securely to the poles—and with neat, straight stitches, too, notwithstanding the nervous state she was in. I took the time to compliment her on the work and she managed to smile a bit, though still biting her lip.

"I wanted to make it strong enough so that Corporal McBurney wouldn't fall again and be injured even more seriously," she said. "Do you think it will suit your needs otherwise? You see I've left a good space on either end of the cloth so that four people can carry the poles."

"It's very nice, Harriet," I said. "You are a good seamstress. No one will ever deny that. Now if you will help us carry Mister McBurney across the hall, I will not insist that you take any further part in the proceedings. I know you have an unusually weak nature and I think it might be better not to bring you into this at all, rather than be charged for your reluctant assistance by a fainting spell or some other kind of disturbing commotion. Therefore, I won't hold it against you if you leave the project to the rest of us, while you retire to your room and pray for our success."

"Do you know . . . I think I might prefer to be present," she answered. "I may be of little physical value, as you say, but I promise not to cause you any trouble. As long as you say the thing is necessary . . . and must be done today . . . then I feel it is my duty . . . not to leave you here alone . . . with these children. . . ."

"Bravo, Miss Harriet," said Emily. "That's the spirit. That's the very thing our brave boys always say to themselves before they go into battle. Even though they don't want to do it, they go ahead anyway, without complaining, because that's the only way we're ever going to win this war."

"Bosh," said Marie. "They go ahead because there's a great line of generals behind them ready to prick them with swords and bayonets if they don't go."

"Miss Martha," Emily cried, "are you going to permit this treasonable talk in your school?"

"I'm not going to permit any more talk at all—on any subject," I announced. "We have work to do. Now, Harriet, you and Mattie each take an end of the sling while Emily and I lift his shoulders on to it. Then Emily will join you at the front end, Harriet, while I lift his feet on to the other. Finally, I will join Mattie on the other pole at the foot end. Is that clear to all?"

"It's very clear, but isn't there something I can do?" Alice wanted to know.

"You can walk beside and steady him so that he won't be jostled too much."

"What about me?" Marie demanded indignantly. "Am I to be left completely out of it?"

"You can walk on the other side and make sure he doesn't fall off. Also, you can carry this anatomy book and Miss Harriet's sewing basket. Are we all ready now?"

"I'm doing this for his sake," my sister muttered. "I know it's for the best. I would never sleep again if I wasn't there . . . and something happened to him. . . ."

"All right, Emily," I said. "Let us lift together."

And we did so. We raised him and moved him on to the carrying sling even more quickly and smoothly than I had anticipated. The whole movement was accomplished so efficiently that Corporal McBurney never blinked an eye or ceased his open-mouth snoring.

We carried him, as gently and securely as we might have a crate of new eggs, across the hall to the dining room and then with a concerted effort—assisted this time by Marie Deveraux who was small enough to get beneath the sling and push upward—we lifted our patient on to the scrubbed and spotless dining-room table and then slid the sling out from beneath him.

"There we are," said I. "The parcel wrapped and delivered safe and sound. Well done, all of you."

"Had you thought of awakening him now, sister?" Harriet asked softly.

"Awakening him! For pity's sake, we've used three bottles of wine to put him to sleep."

"I know," she persisted, "but I was thinking perhaps you wanted to ask him . . . you know . . . just ask him if he is certain he wants this thing done. We have more wine . . . we could put him to sleep again."

"Harriet," I said, trying to suppress my annoyance, "you just stated that you knew what we're going to do was for the best. I know it to be for the best, as do Mattie and these young ladies. We can see and judge the condition of this boy's leg, much more capably than he can. Will it serve any purpose to arouse him now and ask him once again for his permission? He has given it once—and I realize he was somewhat intoxicated then. He would still be intoxicated, if we were to awaken him now, and whether or not he gave us his permission this time. I'd still vote to go ahead with it. Now I am getting a little tired of continually having to convince people of what is correct and proper and justifiable in this case. I get a bit weighted down with responsibility sometimes too, you know, and therefore I am now willing to pass this present load on to whomever is able to shoulder it. Now what do you say, Harriet? Shall we awaken him and chance subjecting him to pain?"

"No . . . no."

"Perhaps I've been too hasty here. Perhaps I'll leave the decision up to you. What about it, Harriet? Shall we take his leg off now, or let him die from the poison in it?"

"Please, Martha!"

"Answer me, Harriet."

I waited. She opened her mouth to speak, but could not. I folded my arms and watched her steadily as did the rest of the company. Finally, after quite a long while, she said, "Do whatever you think is right. Martha. I will share your responsibility but don't make it all mine."

"We may proceed then?"

"Yes, damn you, go ahead," she shouted. "Cut off both his legs if that will satisfy you!"

"Harriet," I said quietly, "you are not in a normal state of mind."

"I'm not drunk," she said, staring defiantly at me, "if that's what you mean."

"Whatever you are, there are students present. I must ask you to withdraw."

"And I must tell you I refuse to go! I've accepted half the responsibility, I have an investment in this and so I intend to remain and be a spectator, if nothing else. You needn't be alarmed, Martha. I won't make any more disturbance. I can't afford to upset you, can I, and cause your hand to tremble maybe . . . if half the guilt is going to be mine. . . ."

She was ashen and seemed on the verge of collapse and so I decided it best not to debate the matter with her—especially since the students were gathered around us, wide eyed and obviously enjoying our discomfort. The only sensible course now, I decided, was to have done with the business as quickly as possible. My differences with Harriet could wait until later.

"As you wish," I said. "Marie, you may leave the room."

"Why?" that young person yelled. "I'm sure I can be of as much service here as Alice or Emily!"

"Alice and Emily are both some years older than you. I am appreciative of your desire to help, but there is nothing you can do here."

"Go find Amelia, dear," Harriet told her in a voice more calm than her appearance might have indicated. "Find your roommate and try to comfort her. That will be a most useful task for which Miss Martha and I will be very grateful."

Marie's little Latin temper was not to be soothed that easily, but she obeyed me anyway—leaving the room and slamming the door so hard that every window in the house was shaken. I made a mental note, adding Marie to my list of problems awaiting later solution.

For the present I made no comment on her outrageous conduct, but instead closed my eyes and waited there at the foot of the table, until the sound of her footsteps pounding up the stairs had ceased. Then I said, "Ladies, we shall begin this work in the way all righteous things should begin—with prayer. We will all bow our heads now and ask Almighty God to bless our efforts and grant us success. We will ask Him also to grant Mister McBurney a speedy return to vitality and health. Finally we will ask that Mister McBurney be granted the gift of understanding, so that he may know the necessity for what may seem in the beginning to be an undue hardship. Until he can overcome this hardship, may he accept it with resignation as part of Thy divine plan for him."

We all meditated for a moment on this and then I said, "All right, ladies—to work. Bring the cutting instruments in from the kitchen, Mattie, and place them on a stand near my hand. Emily, you may tear one of these cloths into strips and then wait beside me in case I need a tourniquet. Alice, give me the scissors from Miss Harriet's basket."

"Is there anything you wish me to do?" asked the last-mentioned lady, quite meekly now.

"Nothing."

"I will do whatever you wish."

I turned and studied her briefly. If she was going to insist on staying, it might be just as well, I decided, to keep her occupied.

"All right, sister, you may read to us. Take this book and open it to the place where I have put the mark. Glance over the checked pages quickly. In a moment I will ask you to read the passages I have underlined."

The book was *Gray's Anatomy of the Human Body*, which I had purchased in Richmond some years previously, intending to use it as a text in practical science. We have never established that course as part of our regular curriculum and so the book had had little use until this time—beyond an occasional nervous thumbing by some young lady who wanted to acquire some surreptitious knowledge of male physiology.

I took the scissors now and cut away McBurney's right trouser leg above the knee. The trousers were an old dress pair of my brother's and I suppose I might have rolled the material up again as I had just a while before when I bandaged the wound, but it might have slipped down and interfered with my work. And in any case McBurney would never need that trouser leg again.

"He's so pale now—how like Robert he looks," I thought. I had noticed that resemblance before, on McBurney's second day in our house. It caused me then to feel a great pity for him and it caused me now to hesitate briefly before going on to cut the bandages I had wrapped and tied so carefully only a short time before.

The leg was exposed now and I noted that my stitches were still holding nicely though, of course, there had been no strain on them. The calf was still discolored, although the swelling might have been reduced somewhat since my last inspection.

"It looks a mite better, don't it?" said Mattie.

"No, it does not," said I. "It's still as morbid looking as before. Also remember we are only gazing at the surface now. We are not even considering the splintered bone inside. Now, one final admonition. If there is anyone here who does not feel capable of viewing this, let her leave us now. Alice? Emily?"

This time I didn't even glance at my sister. There was no indication of retreat on the part of either Alice or Emily.

"Very well then." I turned to the stand on which Mattie had placed the instruments, examined them carefully and finally selected one of my father's ivory handled razors as the tool with which to begin. I opened it and tested its keen edge on my thumb as I had seen my father do many times. "Now then . . . above the knee or below . . . that is the question."

"Whatever may be the state of his leg below the knee, there is absolutely nothing wrong with it above the kneecap," said my sister flatly. "That seems obvious to me."

"It may seem obvious because again you are only looking at the surface. You have no way of knowing how far the infection has spread beneath the skin."

"Cut it off at the hip then, and be done with it."

"Harriet," I said sharply. "I will not tolerate this."

She stared at me for a moment with an expression which a stranger, not knowing our relationship, could only have interpreted as absolute hatred. Then she lowered her gaze. "I'm sorry," she said. "I apologize. I will make no more comments."

"Very well. Then I will admit that I am inclined to agree that there is not enough evidence of spreading infection to justify amputating above the knee. The wound begins approximately three inches below the knee cap on the side of the leg and the discoloration begins about two inches below the cap on the front and back of the leg. Therefore let us cut just above the discoloration. Now, Harriet, what does it say in your text about the bones of the lower leg?"

Harriet peered at the book. "The calf bones are the *tibia* and the *fibula*. The *tibia* is situated at the medial side of the leg and, excepting the *femur*, it is the longest bone of the skeleton. The *fibula* is placed on the lateral side of the *tibia*, with which it is connected above and below."

"The *tibia* is on the inside I believe, and the *fibula* on the outside—is that not correct, sister? And they are separated, I think, by cartilege—or something of the sort. Do you have a diagram there?"

Harriet found one for me and I studied it quickly and compared it with McBurney's leg, identifying the area of bone through which I would have to cut.

"In the male," Harriet continued, "the direction of the *tibia* is vertical and parallel with the bone on the opposite side, but in the female it has a slightly oblique direction, downward and lateral-ward, to compensate for the greater obliquity of the femur."

"Fancy that," marveled Alice.

"The *femur* is the thigh bone," announced Emily.

"And that information is not at all important," I stated, "nor is the oblique angle of the bone of any consequence to me. Now get on with what it says about the muscles. How many muscles will we have to sever?"

"The main muscles seem to be the *gastrocnemus* and the *soleus* which unite to form the tendon at the heel. Then there are the *tibialis anterior* and the *digitorum longus* in the front of the calf and the *peronaeus longus* and the *peronaeus brevis* at the sides of the calf and the *biceps femoris* at the back of the knee which from the diagram seem to be connected with some larger muscles above."

"That is what I wanted to hear about," said I. "Let me have a look at that diagram. Now do you understand the importance of finding the exact location of these muscles? Perhaps we ought to risk cutting a bit lower than our first mark in order not to take any chances on injuring the muscles of his upper leg and possibly giving him a stiff knee."

"What difference will that make as long as the knee isn't attached to anything?" asked Alice.

"That shows what you know about miltiary surgery," said Emily "We can always make a wooden leg for him and it will be that much easier if he has the knee to manipulate it."

"Be quiet, you girls," I commanded. "Now Harriet, what about the veins and arteries?"

"Well it seems the main artery in the back of the calf is the *popliteal*. It is the continuation of the *femoral* artery which arises somewhere in the trunk of the body."

"We are not interested in that."

"Then the *popliteal* divides—apparently just below the knee—into the *anterior* and *posterior tibial* arteries."

"How far below?"

"It doesn't say, but on the diagram it doesn't appear to be very far."

"You will have to be more accurate than that. Let me see that drawing. It would help, I suppose, if we could cut above the *popliteal* division rather than below. That would give us less individual arteries to contend with."

"Would you like to hear about the veins? The veins of the lower extremity of the leg are subdivided into two sets—the super filial veins and the deep veins. Then there are the sub-arteries, such as the branches of the *popliteal* which are the *muscular* sural and the *muscular superior*, the *cutaneous*, the *medial superior genicular*, the *lateral superior genicular*. . . ."

"Enough," I said, "my head is whirling."

"It seems you will have plenty of blood vessels to contend with no matter where you cut. If you want my advice, I'd say bind the tourniquet around his upper leg again and forget about the book. Tie each artery with a thread or something as you come to it."

"I intended to do just that anyway, Miss," I informed her, "but I thank you all the same for reminding me." I took some of the strips of cloth from Emily then and bound them as tightly as I could above his knee. "And as for the book," I added as I worked, "I think it has been of great help to us. We know now what to expect anyway. We're aware now that our task will be a very complex one."

"I wish you would stop saying 'we.' You are performing the task even though I've agreed the responsibility is partly mine."

"As you wish, sister. I will say 'I,' then. I am ready. Is everyone else?"

"We been ready for fifteen minutes," said Mattie.

"Be silent, you!" I half shouted.

"Yes'm. My feet's gettin sore is all, standin here."

"Your back will be sorer than your feet, I guarantee you."

"For God's sake, Martha, begin," cried my sister. "If you're going to do it, then go ahead with it."

"Very well." I marked the new place on his leg with my forefinger and laid the edge of the razor on it. Then—a mistake—I looked up again to make sure he was still unconscious. He was, but that momentary glance cracked the edges of the detachment I had maintained until then. McBurney looked suddenly, not like a problem to be solved, but like a person about whom I had some feelings—not always liking, perhaps, and probably on some occasions even disliking, but always something, some very personal interest. I couldn't ignore him as a person any longer—especially now that I had remembered a resemblance to someone else.

"Take one of those sheets, Mattie, and put it over him," I said.

"He ain't cold."

"Do as I say. Cover him down to the knees. Put it over his face, too, but fold it up a bit around his head to let the air in."

"There is some frailty in you, after all, isn't there," observed my sister as Mattie took the sheet and put it over him.

"I have never denied it," I told Harriet. "I do deny myself the pleasure of giving in to my weaknesses. What I have done now is not to spare myself, but to prevent a possibly dangerous distraction." And I began to cut Corporal McBurney's leg.

I will not describe the following half hour in detail beyond saying that it was the worst such period in my life. There were later unfortunate and unpleasant events in this house, which to the participants may have seemed like worse times than the thirty or so minutes it took to amputate McBurney's leg, but to me those moments were the most agonizing I have ever experienced.

And yet, they seem so only in retrospect. I recall them vividly, I dream about them constantly—and yet while they were occurring, the urgency and physical effort involved permitted me to think of little else but getting the job finished. Even when he awakened and screamed, I was still able to concentrate on the task itself. I even remember what I was thinking about at that moment. It was . . . "Mattie can hold him . . . what a mess we're making . . . is the tourniquet tight enough . . . it is a pity Mattie couldn't find a better saw."

Alice crumpled to the floor and was left there. Emily walked rigidly out to the kitchen and didn't come back. Mattie earned her keep that day, as she always does in any such emergencies. My sister comported herself remarkably well throughout the entire ordeal. When McBurney awakened, for example, she pulled the cork on another bottle of wine and held his head up and poured half the bottle into him, whispering words of comfort to him all the while.

He wasn't awake long, thank God. The wine or the shock and loss of blood soon rendered him unconscious again, and then my sister took a drink out of the bottle herself and afterwards extended it to me. I looked up and nodded my acceptance and she held it to my lips while I took a good draught of it. Then she passed the bottle on to Mattie who finished it.

Mattie at one point in the proceedings had gone out to the kitchen and obtained a garden basket. She waited with this now and when the blade cut through to the table she took the separated portion of McBurney and put it in the basket, then covered it with a cloth—gently. I noted, and neatly too. Two more irrelevancies crossed my mind. One was . . . "I've gashed the walnut table" . . . and the other . . . "I might have thought to remove his stocking."

My own work was neat enough, too. I think if a surgeon inspected it, he would have agreed that I had made a very tidy job of it. I tied all the major blood vessels off with some of Harriet's silk thread and then, having left a sufficient flap of skin all around the stump, I folded this together and sewed it as tight as a drum against the bone.

"There," I said, backing off. "There we are."

"Yes, there we are," said my sister.

"What do you want me to do with this?" asked Mattie.

"Bury it somewhere. Get a spade and dig a decent place for it. But first you'd better see to Miss Alice here."

"What are you going to do with him?" asked Harriet.

"Take him back to the settee, when I've caught my breath."

"I mean later . . . if he lives."

"He'll live."

"I'm told that in the armies, it is seldom that the men recover from this kind of surgery."

"You didn't mention that before."

"I thought you knew it."

"Well, it doesn't matter. He'll live—I know he'll live. And then he can stay here, if he likes. He'll always have a home here for as long as he likes."

I don't know why I said that, but I did. I think I must have been half out of my mind from the strain at that moment and capable of saying anything. I was in a state, it seems now, of something close to exultation. I felt a sense of triumph—of having won a great victory against overwhelming odds. I have said that I know those thirty minutes now to have been the worst ones of my life, but I also know I didn't feel that way then. Then, if you had asked me, I might have called those moments my best.

"All right," I said then. "Let us take him back to bed. Raise him gently . . . so . . . and slide the sling under him. Now, Harriet and Mattie, take the head poles, while I carry the bottom."

"It's too heavy for you alone," said Mattie.

"Nonsense," said I as we moved out. "I could carry twice this weight, if necessary."

In the hall we found the sullen Marie Deveraux sitting on the bottom step of the stairs. When Harriet called to her she arose and took one of the poles from me. Then we continued across into the living room and put Mister McBurney back on his settee.

Marie Deveraux

I wonder if when Miss Martha thinks about the afternoon when she cut McBurney's leg off, she ever remembers the pretty vile way I was treated on that occasion. I'm talking about being sent out of the room like a leper or a person with the pox without even being given the opportunity to explain that I had no intention of interfering with the business of the operation or distracting the lady surgeon in any way. I was not even permitted to tell how I had spent one entire afternoon at home, when I was only seven, watching Doctor Bonnard probe for a bullet in my uncle Georges' chest which my uncle, who was normally a very expert duelist, had obtained as the result of an unfortunate slip on early morning grass. Admittedly, I was trying to hide behind a certain but Doctor Bonnard knew I was there because at one point when he had paused to come over to the window for a breath of air and a sip of brandy, he turned and winked at me. Also, to return to the present case, there is always the question of why, if I was old enough and sensible enough to watch the repair work on McBurney's leg, I couldn't be allowed to watch the cutting off of it.

Well I bear no grudges. McBurney's leg is past history now. I have been subjected to a thousand fresh indignities since that time but I have learned to live with them. It's all a matter of deciding what you want and then making the little necessary adjustments which will enable you to get your wish. What I wanted very much that day was to see McBurney's amputation and naturally I did. Through the keyhole. Or rather, at first through the keyhole and then later around the edge of the door, which I opened very quietly.

And, not to brag about it but only to be accurate, I was the only student here who did see the whole thing from start to finish, because Miss Emily

Stevenson ran off, sick to her stomach, and Miss Alice Simms gave one heave of her marvelous bosom and fainted dead away. Of course Edwina Morrow and Amelia Dabney were not present for any part of the proceedings.

I might add that I helped carry him back into the parlor. Miss Martha didn't need me to assist with the surgery but when those two shining example of beauty and intelligence turned out to be complete failures, why then Miss Harriet was very glad to call on your obedient servant to assist in getting Johnny back to bed.

Well after we had unloaded him, Miss Martha felt his brow and his pulse and put her head on his chest and listened to his breathing—all in the best medical manner, I assure you. For a while there, as I later told my roommate, I was very much afraid this surgery idea would become over popular and we might be faced with a regular epidemic of cutting people's legs off. "We had better sleep with our legs tucked under us in future," I jokingly told Amelia sometime later, "or else we may wake up some morning and find we have sacrificed them to Miss Martha's new enthusiasm." Of course Amelia didn't think this was very funny because she took a very personal exception to Johnny's operation and she was terribly upset for a very long time after it.

As Miss Martha was too, I can tell you. She didn't reveal any emotion in the dining room but once she had McBurney tucked in bed, she just became absolutely hysterical, and ranted and raved and went on in the wildest fashion 'til she just about drove us all right out of the room.

I think Miss Harriet started her off by making some innocent remark about Johnny's not looking much like her and Miss Martha's brother any more. As I recall Miss Harriet said that she had considered Johnny's resemblance to her dead brother quite striking at one time, but that this resemblance seemed to be gone now.

"I suppose you think I cut off his leg to change his appearance," Miss Martha practically shrieked.

"No, no . . . of course not," Miss Harriet said, trying to calm her. "I wasn't referring to his leg at all. I just meant that his face seems changed now. It seems more drawn and older looking than before. But I suppose that's only a natural reaction to the shock and all."

"Of course. That's been your reaction too, Harriet. You look years older than you did this morning."

"I imagine I do," Miss Harriet answered. "I certainly feel that way."

"And what about me?" Miss Martha persisted. "Or has the ordeal left me unchanged. Do you think it was just another day's work to me—or maybe you're under the impression that I did it for enjoyment."

"Not for enjoyment, Martha, but possibly for something else . . . satis-faction."

"Of course I'm satisfied," Miss Martha shouted. "I admit it. I'm satis-fied that I have done my best to save a boy's life! Is there something wrong in that?"

"Nothing, sister. If you can honestly take pride in this accomplish-ment, then I envy you. I envy you your peace of mind."

"Do you really, sister? Wouldn't it make you just a trifle happier if you thought I was feeling some remorse?"

"This talk is foolish, Martha. It doesn't make any difference now what either of us feels. The thing is over now and whether you are sorry or glad about it won't change anything. Your remorse wouldn't restore this boy's leg any more than it brought Robert back after you drove him away."

Well whatever the meaning of that remark it evidently had great signifi-cance for Miss Martha because I think she was about to attack Miss Harriet physically then—if she didn't perish from apoplexy first—because she turned in her tracks and started for Miss Harriet with her hands upraised and clawed, ready to scratch Miss Harriet's eyes or pull her hair out. And Miss Harriet just stood there, not even preparing to defend herself, but just waiting calmly as though the onslaught was something she had been expecting for a long time and now that it was finally coming, she rather welcomed it. Or at least that was my impression of her attitude when I thought about it later.

Anyway at that moment good old Mattie stepped quickly forward and grabbed Miss Martha around the waist and held her tightly. Miss Martha tried frantically to escape for a moment but naturally Mattie was too strong for her. Then after maybe a half minute or so Miss Martha stopped strug-gling, and her face turned from fire red to the color of McBurney's, or maybe even paler, and then she just sighed and went all limp in Mattie's arms. Then Mattie eased her to the floor very gently and unbuttoned her and loosened her stays.

"Miss Harriet, pour me a little water here. Miss Marie, fetch me a good size onion from the kitchen," Mattie instructed us.

Well I was so fascinated by all these happenings that I just hated to leave the scene. I waited for a moment to see if the water alone might restore our headmistress, but when it didn't and Mattie continued to yell for the onion, I left the room, pausing only briefly in the hall outside in the hope that Miss Harriet might be going to offer some kind of explanation to Mat-tie. It was really very interesting to observe Miss Harriet's attitude on that day. I had just never seen her speak or act with such confidence before, and I don't think anyone else around here has ever seen anything like it either.

"That was mean of you, Miss Harriet," I heard Mattie tell her. "It was just downright shameful of you to say those things."

"I know," said Miss Harriet, but she didn't sound at all ashamed. "Nevertheless they needed to be said. It's time Martha was notified that she can't run the world to suit herself. Well never mind, she's finished now. She's done her worst with this boy. She's not going to treat him the way she treated Robert. She isn't God and it's time she realized it."

"You ain't God either, Miss Harriet."

"I don't care to be. I don't want to change him. I don't want to make anything out of him. I just want him to be happy."

"You talking about this boy or Mister Robert?"

"Both of them."

Now that was certainly a strange coupling since Robert Farnsworth is dead and buried, or so the students here have always been led to believe. If there was any more to this conversation I didn't hear it because Mattie caught sight of me at the door then and shouted that I'd better get the onion quickly or she was going to tan me. Naturally I am not at all upset by such talk from Mattie who is just like all the house darkies I have ever seen. They will threaten you with the most horrible punishments imaginable without the faintest hope of ever being able to carry them out. I suppose it is one of the few ways the poor dears have of expressing their dissatisfaction with the white world. Anyway, even though I have not been alarmed by such threats since the age of seven or eight or possibly even younger, I generally play along with them to give Mattie a little pleasure.

On this occasion I opened my eyes wide, clapped my hand to my mouth and began to tremble violently for a moment and then rushed off to the kitchen as fast as I could calling out things like, "Yes, Mattie . . . right away, Mattie . . . please don't be angry, Mattie" and so forth. I think my performance as a frightened child gets better every time I play it. I can hardly wait to get back home and try it on Betsy and Cleo and the rest of the house people at our place. I might even give my mother a taste of it, but only if my acting seems to be getting superlatively good because my mother is probably the hardest person in the world to fool—as my father keeps learning to his great sorrow.

Also there was something else besides fooling which hurried me to the kitchen on that day. It was the sudden thought that Miss Alice might not yet be recovered from her faint and consequently might be available for a good whiff of the onion before I took it to Miss Martha. I knew that Mattie had been instructed to see to Alice after McBurney was taken back to bed, but with teachers fainting Mattie had no time to worry about students and so I had great hopes of finding our golden-haired temptress still stretched out on the dining room floor.

Unfortunately my hopes were in vain. Alice apparently had managed to come to her senses without any help because she was nowhere in sight when I reached the dining room and she wasn't in the kitchen either. However after I had obtained my onion from the larder I stepped out the back door for a short glance around the garden and there was Miss Alice seated on the bench in the arbor beside her fellow deserter, Miss Emily Stevenson.

Well, I thought, now that I've come this far, I might as well take a moment longer to find out how my fellow students are feeling.

"Girls, if your stomachs have settled you can come back in the house now," I called to them as I approached. "The operation is all completed, although the dining room is still somewhat unpresentable, in case that sort of thing is distressing to you."

It evidently was. They were sitting there, the two of them, as pale as bedsheets and as rigid as a pair of scarecrows, as though the slightest word or breath escaping them would bring the past hour back again and make what could just possibly have been a bad dream a thing which had really happened.

Thinking to cheer them, I added, "I believe Mattie will have our dinner ready shortly—just as soon as she has the dining room tidied up a bit."

"Get away from here, you little monster," hissed Alice between her teeth.

"I'm not staying," said I. "I'm on my way to revive Miss Martha who just fainted, but much more gracefully than you did, Alice."

"Then get on with it," Emily said, "and leave us alone."

"Now, Emily," I said soothingly. "I rather expected Alice to be upset since she obviously is a girl of very delicate feelings. However, I didn't think a person like you who has so much knowledge and experience of military affairs would be overcome by a little thing like this."

"I wasn't overcome by the operation," Emily replied. "It was just that the dining room had turned so stifling and I've had a headache anyway since early this morning."

"I was certain it must be something like that."

"How is Johnny now?" asked Alice hesitantly.

"I guess he's as well as might be expected. He's still asleep."

"I think it was a terrible thing to do to him," Alice said.

"You didn't mention that before."

"I didn't realize what it would be like."

"These things are naturally a bit upsetting for people who aren't familiar with them," Emily agreed. "But it's just something soldiers have to get used to and put up with. I expect Corporal McBurney has been in the army long enough to accept it philosophically. The really unfortunate thing about it is the fact that it probably means the end of his military career. And the poor fellow has been after me for weeks, too, just wanting me to write my father about Johnny joining his regiment."

"Well, I think if Johnny puts his mind to it he may be able to get over that disappointment," I remarked.

"Probably we ought to be extra nice to him from now on," said Alice.

"I was under the impression that you had adopted that policy already," said I. "I'm afraid if your being nice to him is going to result in someone knocking him down the stairs again, you had better think twice about it, for Johnny's own sake."

"I don't exactly mean a romantic kind of niceness," Alice said, although she didn't state that she was excluding that kind either. "What I had in mind was that maybe we ought to be kinder and more considerate toward him. We ought to make a great effort now to show him that he's really welcome here."

"I think I know what you mean, Alice," Emily assured her. "What we must do now is spend as much time with him as possible and help him get his mind off this affliction. We can read to him and tell him stories and just generally talk to him about our homes and families, and keep him abreast of how the war is going, and all sorts of comforting things like that. In fact we may be able to improve his mind and character a great deal that way."

"And before you know it," said I, "Corporal McBurney will be so improved he will be thanking us for cutting off his leg."

"Will you get away from here, you nasty little thing!" yelled Emily.

Of course I wouldn't have paid the slightest attention to that order had not Miss Harriet at that moment opened the parlor windows and stepped out on the lawn. This caused me to remember the onion I was carrying and poor Miss Martha prostrate on the parlor floor, and so I hurried over to the house as rapidly as I could.

"I'm sorry to have been so long about this," I explained to Miss Harriet, handing her the remedy. "I just felt I ought to stop for a moment and see if I could do anything for Alice and Emily. Those two girls are not feeling at all well. I do trust Miss Martha is somewhat improved."

"Miss Martha has recovered from her faint and gone to her room," Miss Harriet answered rather waspishly. "I hope I am never in such a spell and have to depend on you for assistance. Now there is something else you can do and I want you to set about it more quickly than the last. Did you manage to find Amelia as I asked you to do earlier?"

"I haven't had time to track her down," said I, "but from past experience I'm sure I know where she is. She's sitting in a special hiding place she has in the woods. She likes to be alone out there sometimes when things aren't going too well for her."

"Then I want you to go after her and bring her back. I don't like to have her in that woods by herself, especially with night coming on. Also she may be able to do something for Corporal McBurney."

"What?"

"I hope she may be able to calm him. He opened his eyes a moment ago and said something which sounded like he was asking for water. But when I took the water to him, he stared at me in fright . . . and shrank away from me. I came away from him then, and he went back to sleep . . . but he continues to moan softly."

I was rather pleasantly surprised to be taken into Miss Harriet's confidence that way. "Don't worry about it," I told her. "There's no reason for him to be afraid of you. He's probably delirious or something and confusing you with Miss Martha."

"Nevertheless little Amelia has always been the most loyal to him and I think he knows that and would trust her. If he asks for water again, I'd like her to be here to give it to him."

So I started for the woods, reflecting that I wouldn't blame Amelia in the least if she never came back. What had happened to McBurney was in some respects an unpleasant thing for all of us, but it was especially hard on that poor girl who had found him and brought him here in the first place.

As I crossed the lawn it occurred to me that there was one other person in the house who had missed the operation—Miss Edwina Morrow. She supposedly spent the entire day in her room and it was therefore quite likely that she didn't know anything about what had happened.

Thinking of Edwina, I turned and looked up at her room and there she was standing at her window, staring back at me. It gave me quite a shivery feeling to consider that she may have been there watching me the whole time I had been in the garden—just standing there staring coldly at me and thinking the Lord knows what kind of nasty thoughts about me.

Anyway I decided I might as well do her the kindness of bringing her up to date on the happenings in the house. I didn't want to shout the news and have Miss Harriet and possibly even Miss Martha at my throat again, and so I did my best to pantomime it. I pointed to the parlor, assuming that Edwina would grasp that as a reference to McBurney, and then I pointed to my own leg and finally made a snipping movement with my fingers. To climax the presentation I gave a grimace of horrible pain and then lowered my cheek on to my folded hands to indicate unconsciousness. Edwina however was singularly unimpressed and if it made any sense to her at all she gave no sign of it.

In fact she turned her head to look beyond me, and, following her gaze, I saw that Mattie had come out of the kitchen carrying the garden basket containing Corporal McBurney's leg. The basket was now covered quite tastefully and appropriately with some clean Irish linen napkins, and Mattie was bearing it reverently and slowly as she headed for the shed where the spades and other digging tools are kept. I noticed also that Emily and Alice, who had not moved from their bench, were keeping their eyes on Mattie, too.

Well I realized with a start that if I was going to be back in time for the burial ceremony, I had better be on my way to the woods and Amelia. Therefore I set off, running at my best speed for the distance, across the lawn and the corn field and then over the old logging road and the high ditch, and up into the woods itself, where my pace was lessened somewhat by the thickness of the brush and the uneven ground.

The smouldering from the battle of a few weeks before had ended by that time, although when the wind was right there was still an unpleasant odor from the burned-over area to the east. Anyway it wasn't any smell of old battles that bothered me on that journey but simply the natural hazards of the woods—the creeper vines and twisted roots which block the trail, the swarms of bees and June flies and other insects, the slippery log you have to travel in order to get over the branch of the creek and worst of all, of course, as in any woods, are not those things that can be seen but the invisible dangers—the snakes and spiders which may be hanging from the next branch, the wolves and wildcats which might suddenly appear from behind the next tree, the leaf covered boggy places that just possibly might be quicksand into which one false step will send you swooshing down forever, leaving not a single bubble on the mud to mark your grave. Well, those were the kind of terrible thoughts which occupied my mind on that particular expedition.

However I did know exactly where I was going and the shortest way to get there. Until quite recently I was the only student here who had ever been permitted to visit this hiding place of Amelia's—and those who know Amelia very well realize how much of an honor it is when she trusts you enough to share any of her secrets with you. Anyway, this place of hers is in a little glade in the center of a ring of oak trees which have grown very close together and whose trunks are covered by a lot of underbrush and tangled vines. There is only one way to get inside this glade—a very low and narrow tunnel in the brush through which you practically have to crawl on your hands and knees. When you finally come to the end of the tunnel—most likely with your face and arms and legs all scratched and your dress ripped to shreds from the thorns—you emerge into a very tiny but high-walled room whose carpet is of moss and whose ceiling is of lighter green with a small patch of blue in the center of it. Except at noonday, this room is very cool and shadowy—a very pleasant place indeed in which to lie on your back and listen to the birds rustling in the walls and watch the clouds float across the opening overhead.

And that is exactly what Amelia was doing when I came out of the tunnel—just lying there as I had predicted, and beside her in my teak wood jewel box was a dozing turtle—that smelly, ailing, snapping turtle which she was carrying with her constantly at that time.

"I really don't know if it's worth all this discomfort or not," I said, sitting down beside her and beginning to pick the leaves and branches out of my hair. "Although I must say you always seem able to float through that tunnel very easily without tearing yourself half to pieces."

"You disturb all the plants when you come in," she said softly, still staring at the sky. "That's your trouble. You can't just fight your way through them. You have to push them aside gently the way they want to go. That's the way animals do it and they seldom get scratched. Be careful how you move around there, please."

"How is your pet feeling anyway?" I asked, not really caring but only to be sociable.

"Much better. He's much better today."

"I understand Corporal McBurney isn't feeling too well."

"I don't want to talk about anyone of that name," she said, still not looking at me. "I don't know anyone of that name."

"You found him."

"No, I didn't. I never met any such person in my life."

You can't argue with Amelia when she decides to act like that. She just shuts everything that bothers her out of her mind and the Lord Himself with an iron drill couldn't bore the truth back into her.

"Well," I said, "suit yourself. But whether you know him or not, if you stay out here much longer you're going to miss a very unusual funeral ceremony. We're all going to get together in a little bit and bury Corporal McBurney's leg."

I thought that might arouse her interest but it didn't seem to have much effect. I was trying desperately to think of something which might bring her to her senses, because the afternoon was getting on and I was in severe danger of missing the burial myself. On the other hand, I was reluctant to return to Miss Harriet and admit defeat. When I set out on a task I like to finish it—even if on some occasions I'm in no particular hurry about it.

"Even if you don't know Corporal McBurney, perhaps you'd enjoy meeting him now," I told her. "I'd be glad to introduce you just as soon as he wakes up."

"I don't believe I care to know him."

"But he's such an interesting person. I'm sure you would enjoy his company. Also dinner will be ready very shortly anyway."

"I have plenty to eat right here. I have some nuts and berries and mushrooms."

"You're going to eat the wrong kind of mushroom one of these days and that will be the end of Amelia Dabney."

"That might be all right, too—except that I don't think it could happen since the inedible ones are so easy to identify."

"When do you think you might condescend to return to good old Farnsworth school?"

"Maybe never—maybe I'll never go back."

"Don't you know those people either—Miss Martha and Miss Harriet and the girls?"

"I'm beginning to think maybe I don't know them."

"Well you know me, don't you, for pity's sake!"

"Yes, I think I will always know you, Marie."

I didn't say anything for a long while after that. To tell the truth I couldn't think of anything to say after that very nice remark Amelia had made about me—and in response to my shouting at her, too. Finally I told her, "I'm sure I will always know you, too, Amelia. I think you're the nicest person at the school, even if you probably are the strangest too. Now just stay here in this hiding place for as long as you like. I'll go back and tell Miss Harriet that you won't be dining with us, and that possibly you won't ever be returning to the school at all. I'll say that if Corporal McBurney asks for you again, she had better give him that message, too."

"Did he ask for me?"

"It seems to me Miss Harriet said he did. You see he apparently knows you, even if you don't know him. That's why Miss Harriet sent me to find you. Johnny McBurney is very hurt and afraid and she thinks you are the only one who can help him."

"You never tell lies to me do you, Marie?"

"Not in important matters."

She arose then and closed my jewel box with her turtle in it.

"Tuck up your skirt and follow right on my heels in the tunnel," she said, "and you won't get scratched again."

And I didn't. With Amelia leading we just glided through that tunnel and came out into the sunlight without hardly ever touching a branch or thorn on the way. That girl just seems to have a way with everything that lives in the woods. The normal person may be bitten and stung and torn and bruised whenever she sets foot out of the civilized world, but not Amelia. The thorns don't scratch her, the gnats never bite her and I believe she could sit down to a dish of poison ivy pie without it ever raising a rash on her tongue.

"I'm really convinced you are some kind of woodland creature who was turned into human form by a witch," I said as we trotted along at the pace Amelia says was always used by Indians when they were roaming around here years ago. "I am mortally certain I am going to awaken some morning and find a giant lizard or a huge toad in the bed across from me, and then you will stare at me sadly with your beady eyes filled with tears and you will say, 'Goodbye forever, Marie. I'm sorry I've been so mean to you.' And then you will hop or scuttle, as your form permits, through the window and out of sight."

"How am I mean to you?" she wanted to know, without denying my charges of bewitchment. As a matter of fact I think she would be very happy if such were the case. It would suit Amelia wonderfully well to be anything but a human being.

"You are not really mean, I suppose," I told her. "In fact, now that I think on it, you are probably the unmeanest person I know."

Shortly after that very sincere statement of mine we came out of the woods and crossed the road to the field. I could see some people now huddled in the garden and I was praying that at least a part of the burial service would be left by the time we got back there.

Well it had not yet begun, thank the Lord, but I didn't make it with much to spare. Mattie had just finished digging the little grave under the arbor and she was standing next to it holding her garden basket. Beside her were Alice and Emily looking very solemn, with their hands folded demurely and their heads bowed.

Without breaking her stride Amelia continued on to the parlor door, bearing her turtle box carefully clutched to her breast, while I joined the little group in the arbor.

"Lord," Mattie was beginning, "let us be buryin all this poor boy's troubles along with his leg. Let us be buryin all the future pain and misery and grief you might have had in mind for him if this thing hadn't happened.

Let him lead a long and happy life on the one leg he's got left, and when you come to take him up to Heaven with you on the Judgment Day, just remember where his right leg is and glue it back on him so's he'll be restored to his full and handsome manhood for all the days of eternity. Let us here be good and kind to him from now on while he's with us and put up with him if he complains and grumbles a bit, cause he's got a lot to grumble about. Give him his health back now and make him ready to be on his way again soon. And let him remember all of us . . . or anyway most of us as his friends. All this for your great glory . . . and our salvation . . . amen."

"Amen," we all said.

Then Mattie put the napkin-covered garden basket in the hole and tossed a clod of dirt after it, and then each of us picked up a handful of dirt and followed suit.

"Now you young ladies go in and wash your hands and get yourselves ready for dinner," Mattie said, as she took the spade and began filling the hole. "The services are over. There ain't no more for you to do here."

"We ought to put some flowers on the grave," said Alice. "Roses would be nice, or hyacinth."

"Hollyhocks or iris are more manly flowers," said Emily, "and either of those would make a nice contrast with the rest of the arbor."

"If we're starting a campaign of friendliness toward McBurney," said I, "it might be a nice beginning gesture to leave the flower choosing to him. After all, it's his leg."

The others nodded, whether in agreement or only in acknowledgment of having heard me, I cannot say. Anyway on that note we left the arbor and returned to the house via the kitchen door to prepare for dinner.

Amelia Dabney

On the day of Corporal McBurney's disfigurement I went out to the woods and stayed there for a long time until Marie Deveraux came about four o'clock or a little after to tell me that Johnny needed me. Then I returned to help him however I could.

I was afraid to look at him at first, thinking that he would be completely changed by what had happened and that I really wouldn't know him—as I had been telling myself all day would be the case. Finally I reproached myself for my cowardice and stole a quick glance at him, and then I saw he was really no different than before. Of course the lower and most changed part of his body was covered by a blanket, but his face was the same—only a bit gaunter maybe, but certainly no paler than the day he first came.

Miss Harriet was, like Johnny, asleep. She was seated in a chair near him with a half filled glass of wine in her hand. She was shivering and twitching as though from a bad dream, causing the wine to spill on her dress, so I took it from her as gently as I could and put it on the stand beside the bottle. Then I pulled another chair up beside the settee and sat down to wait for Johnny to awaken and tell me what I could do for him.

Right then I would have done anything he asked. I felt very bad, you see, because I had brought him to the school and told him that he would be safe and happy here, and now this terrible thing had been done to him. I didn't know whether it needed to be done or not, but I was sure it needn't have been done so quickly. And, of course, whatever the necessity, I felt the responsibility was mostly mine. I could have left him in the woods and his own people might have found him and given him much better care than we had been able to offer him. I could have left him lying on the leaves and gone away and he might have recovered by himself as wounded animals sometimes do, or else have died very quietly, without fear of pain, as is the case I think with animals.

Well I just felt at that time as though I had reached the absolute depths of misery. I felt worse I believe than I did on the day I learned my brothers had been killed at Chickamauga. This doesn't necessarily mean that I thought more of Johnny than I did of Dick or Billy—although it may be possible that I did—but what I'm trying to say is that I have always been more distressed by the thought of suffering than I have been by the thought of death. Death is a natural biological event but there is no rule in nature which demands our suffering. Perhaps this is a law of religion—as my roommate once tried to tell me—but I am certain there is nothing of the sort in the world of nature.

Of course I have no way of knowing whether Dick and Billy's deaths were painless or not, but Johnny McBurney's suffering was very plain to see. It couldn't be denied. Even by remaining in the woods, I realized now, I was only comforting myself. I wasn't making his pain go away.

As I was thinking these things he opened his eyes and looked at me, and whispered, "Mum. . . ."

I went over to him. "What's that, Johnny?"

"Mum . . . where's Mum?"

"It's Amelia. There's no one here but Amelia . . . and Miss Harriet."

"Amelia?"

"Yes . . . your friend."

"My leg hurts, Amelia."

"I'm sorry, Johnny," I told him, and didn't know what else to say. After another while he opened his eyes again and asked for water. I poured a glass for him and held it to his lips while he swallowed a bit of it.

Then he stared directly at me. "Did they cut it off, Amelia?" he asked very clearly.

I thought of lying to him about it, but then realized it would only be a temporary comfort. "Yes," I said, "they did." There seemed no way of softening it, so I didn't try.

"I'll fix them," he said distinctly. "I'll bloody well fix them."

Then his lip began to quiver and his eyes filled with tears. "I was the best damn runner in the county," he said, "and the highest jumper. . . ."

"And you can still be both those things, Johnny," I told him. "We'll make another leg for you out of wood and after you've practiced on it for a while, you'll be able to run and jump and leap as well as you ever did."

I wasn't awfully confident of that, of course, but I wasn't sure it would be entirely impossible either. In fact the more I began to turn it over in my mind, the more reasonable it seemed that we could make a nice wooden leg on which he ought to be able to get around very nicely, even if at no great speed.

It was something to occupy my mind and it was what he needed too. And so I began to tell him of the fine new leg we would make for him. "You can choose your own wood, Johnny," I said. "I know where there are some fine new logs . . . oak and cedar and beech wood, too . . . from trees knocked down by cannon fire. Pine is the easiest wood to work, of course, but I think for hard use you'll want something more sturdy than Virginia pine. Now walnut is a good dependable wood and I believe I can locate one fallen walnut tree, but perhaps, for good long wear, hickory would be your best choice. It's a bit hard to cut, of course, but we could take our time with it and in the end you'll have a leg that will last forever. I'm going to start right out tomorrow, Johnny, and look for the best hickory tree in these parts. I'll go clear to the Rapidan, if I have to, in order to find that tree . . . and if the guns haven't knocked it down, then you and I will get axes and saws and cut it down. What do you think of that plan, Johnny?"

"All right," he whispered. "Whatever you say. . . ."

"Everything is going to be all right, Johnny. You just have to believe that."

"I believe you, Amelia. I trust you. . . ."

"Well I'm glad you do. . . . I want you to keep right on trusting me. And when this pain gets better, I promise you that no one in this house will cause you any more pain. I'll take you away from here myself if I have to, in order to prevent that. Do you hear that, Johnny?"

"Yes, I hear. The leg hurts awful bad, Amelia. Are you sure it isn't there?"

"Yes, I'm sure."

"Would you ever take a look, Amelia. Maybe it's a joke they're playing!"

So I took a deep breath and made myself lift the edge of the blanket. There hadn't been any jokes played on him.

"It's gone all right, Johnny," I said. "Therefore it will definitely have to stop hurting after a while. It will stop hurting soon and won't hurt you ever again."

"I'll fix them," he murmured again. "By God in Heaven I'll fix them. . . ."

"You mustn't talk that way, Johnny," I said. "It's not a nice way to talk. And who would you fix anyway? I'm sure Miss Martha and everyone else thought they were doing the right thing. And although it must seem pretty bad now, at least you know that nothing worse can happen. They can't do any more harm to you now. As a matter of fact I'll bet that everyone here will try to make it up to you now in every way they can. From now on I'll bet you're going to be the Lord of the manor around here. You'll get such attention from now on that it won't be any time at all before you've forgotten about that old leg."

Then I opened a box which I happened to have with me and showed him what was inside. "Do you see this little snapping turtle in this box, Johnny? Well this little turtle was so sick and defeated a few weeks ago he just didn't care whether he lived or died. But just look at him now. He's recovered completely and barring an accident, he'll probably live to be a hundred. And do you know what did it, Johnny? Do you know what cured this little turtle?"

"What?"

"Love. Love and tender care. And that's what you're going to get. And not only from me. I'll bet my last dollar you'll get it from everybody else too."

"I don't want anything from them. They may have done their worst to me . . . but I haven't done my worst to them."

Well that kind of talk was very disturbing to me, of course. But he did seem to be taking a kind of comfort from it, and right then, I thought, he deserved all the comfort he could get. I expect if he hadn't been able to cling to those revengeful thoughts, he might have gone ahead and died right then.

"Johnny," I said, thinking to change the subject. "Johnny, do you know what I saw a while ago in the woods? Do you remember the bird you were telling me about on the morning after you came—the bird which you said is almost always on the wing and has no real home? Well I saw that very bird today. It was very small and brightly colored—something like a humming bird but not quite the same. For one thing its beak wasn't quite as long and also it didn't beat the air with its wings in the fashion of a humming bird, but instead hovered very gracefully and without effort as gulls and other sea birds do. It descended toward me and then rose again and went off and came back several times as though it was trying to tell me something. I couldn't imagine what possible message that little bird might have for me and then all at once it came to me. That bird was trying to say, 'Amelia, look at me. See how fast I can fly out of the shadows up into the sunshine. Why don't you do the same, Amelia? Whatever your troubles are, they can't be any greater than mine. You know I happen to be one of the last of my kind and maybe I won't ever be able to find a mate to perpetuate my line, but I'm not worrying about it. I just keep thinking that summer is here and the sun is shining and I have the whole wide sky to fly in. Why don't you think that way yourself, Amelia? Why don't you forget your gloomy thoughts and fly up with me into the shining sky?'

"And at that moment the little bird flew off at the great speed you described, Johnny—right up into the sun. I watched him as long as I could and then, when he was only a small speck in the light, I covered my eyes and imagined I was climbing up into the brightness with the little bird and leaving all my troubles behind me. It really works, Johnny, and you can do the same. You can forget all your troubles and fly up into the sunshine. You can forget all about Miss Martha and the others and just concentrate on all the good days that are to come. Just keep all the pain and fear . . . and all the worry and all the gloom . . . out of your mind. Just keep thinking how nice things will be for you from now on. You don't ever have to go back to the war for one thing. Even if your people find out where you are, they can't ever make you go back now. They'll have to give you an honorable discharge from the army and maybe they'll even give you a citation of some kind to go along with it . . . in remembrance of the wound you've suffered . . . like the one that General Bragg sent to my mother when Dick and Billy were killed. I don't set much store by such things myself but my mother does and perhaps your mother would too, if you sent the citation home to her."

His eyes were closed again now. "I'll fix them . . . I'll fix them," he was still muttering faintly.

"All right, Johnny," I said. "You fix them. You fix them by just forgetting that they ever existed."

I had drawn my chair back a bit so that Johnny might have full benefit of the afternoon breeze which was sifting gently through the curtains on the garden door. My chair was in the shadowed part of the room and since it was the chair with the high back and was turned away from the settee, I suppose it was very easy for visitors to overlook me. I wasn't attempting to spy or to listen to the remarks of the people who came in, but on the other hand I didn't advertise my presence either because I didn't want to be sent away from Johnny or to be drawn into some useless conversation about him with some other student. I didn't want to discuss Johnny's condition or to hear any more about the operation than what Marie had already told me. I wasn't at all interested—or only very slightly interested—in what any of the visitors had to say, beyond hoping that none of them would awaken Johnny, who now seemed to be sleeping quietly.

He was awakened after a while, but not by the first visitor. The first one who came in was Miss Martha herself and she entered very quietly. She crossed the room on tiptoe, glanced quickly at Miss Harriet, who was also still sleeping, and then just stood there for a long while by Johnny's side, studying him quietly.

Then she said softly, "You don't look like him at all. You don't now and you didn't before." And then after another long pause, "I'm sorry. I didn't intend you any harm."

She stared at him for a while longer and then felt his brow and the heart-beat in his wrist, and then she came back and picked up the wine bottle from the table beside Miss Harriet and left the room, taking the bottle with her.

The second visitor was Mattie who entered after a few more minutes and came over also to have a look at Johnny and a feel of his brow.

"Poor boy," said Mattie. "You had to come all the way from some foreign country just to have this happen to you."

Then she turned and noticed me. She was the only one of all those who came in to see Johnny on that afternoon who did notice me.

"Get on out of there, Miss Amelia," she said. "Get outside to the well and fetch yourself some water and then march upstairs to your room and get yourself ready for dinner. I declare you're gettin to be most as untidy as Miss Marie—and that's a ways to go."

"Limbs never grow again on people the way severed tails sometimes do on lizards, do they, Mattie?" I asked her.

"I never heard of such a thing happenin," she said.

"Neither have I. I was pretty sure it was impossible, but I thought maybe you might have heard of something like that happening in Africa, or wherever your people came from."

"My Daddy came from right here in Virginia and that's where I come from."

"What about your Daddy's father?"

"I never seen him. He might have come from some foreign land but I was never told about it if he did."

"But didn't any of your people way back come from strange places where they had magic cures and medicines which could accomplish all sorts of wonderful things which are never possible here? Mattie, I'm sure I've heard the people on our own place at home talk about things like that."

"Maybe you did hear your Daddy's people talk about them, but you ain't heard me talk about them and you ain't gonna hear me! That's Devil talk and it ain't nothin for a little Christian child to be foolin with."

"Mattie, could the Devil restore Johnny's leg to him?"

"I expect he could. The Devil can do most anything he sets his mind to—'cept get into Heaven."

"How would one go about arranging that kind of thing for Johnny?"

"You crazy, child?"

"I was just wondering."

"Well stop wonderin. It ain't nothin for anybody to be speculatin about, specially a little girl like you. I said the Devil prob'ly could restore this boy's leg if he wanted to, but he sure ain't gonna do it for nothin. The Devil don't run his business that way. If he does you a favor, he expects a favor from you in return. And in this case—which would be a mighty tough case, since it wouldn't be no child's play to fasten a person's leg back on, specially after it's buried under a yard or more of dirt—in this case the Devil wouldn't take the job for anything less than the guaranteed payment of a first class human soul. That means you'd have to sell your soul to the Devil in exchange for the restoration of this Yankee's leg. Now do you think that one little Southern lady's pure white soul would be a fair exchange for the leg of one no-account Yankee soldier?"

"But he isn't no-account, Mattie."

"Well, let's say . . . somewhat no-account. And even if he was of great account . . . even if he was a Yankee general or the King of France . . . or the Mayor of New Orleans . . . it wouldn't be a good bargain. A human soul is a precious thing, honey, specially an uncontaminated hardly-used little soul like yours."

"But why would it have to be my soul which was offered in return for Johnny's leg? Why couldn't Johnny bargain with his own soul?"

"Cause he ain't that foolish, that's why. He knows when he comes to die he ain't ever gonna get into Heaven without a soul. And for a second good reason, there ain't no comparin your soul and the soul of this Yankee who's been bummin all over creation ever since he growed up gettin into the Lord only knows what kind of mischief. Your soul is a hundred times as valuable as this boy's and the Devil, who ain't no fool, knows that as well as I do. The Devil wouldn't be at all interested in this McBurney's soul if there was any chance at all of gettin yours instead. Now let's have no more of this talk. Fix yourself for dinner like I said and stop all this foolishness."

"I don't feel much like eating, Mattie," I said.

"What you don't feel like don't matter in the least. You got to learn to be strong and to carry your troubles without bein weighed down by them. Everybody who was ever born has got some misery in their life. If you got a big load of it today, and you carry it without complainin, moren' likely the good Lord will send you a lighter load tomorrow. Least that's always been my way of lookin at it."

"It's not my misery that's bothering me," I said, "it's Johnny's. And I'm afraid he may not be so willing to put up with it."

"Oh, he'll come around all right in a day or two," said Mattie. "It ain't the end of the world to lose one leg. There's plenty more like him who'll come out of this war with one leg gone, and maybe some with two, and they'll likely live just as long and get just as rich and be just as ornery to their neighbors as anybody else. Now if you're gonna stay in here for a while, be quiet. I'm gonna let poor Miss Harriet catch a little extra rest in here too."

Miss Harriet showed signs of awakening now shortly after Mattie had left the room. She stretched a bit and sighed and glanced drowsily at the table and must have realized then, I guess, even in her state of half consciousness, that the wine bottle had disappeared. She came fully awake with a jerk and leaned over and examined the table carefully but, of course, to no avail. Then she sighed again, more heavily this time, and settled back and closed her eyes once more, maybe thinking it might be possible to dream about some wine even if she didn't really have any. Then after another short while she evidently remembered about Johnny, which caused her, with what seemed like some annoyance, to shake herself and sit erect in her chair. She rubbed her eyes and leaned forward for a good hard look at him.

"Mister McBurney?" she asked rather tentatively. "Are you awake?"

Miss Harriet doesn't see as well as most people and she couldn't at first determine whether or not Johnny was still unconscious. Obviously she couldn't see me farther over in the shadows and a bit later I began to wish I had identified myself but by that time it was too late to do it without embarrassing her.

Because the things Miss Harriet began to talk about were very personal matters which I'm sure she would never have mentioned if she had realized there was a conscious person within sound of her voice. It seemed as if she was taking advantage of Johnny's being asleep on the settee to talk about matters which she had kept to herself for a long time. I think maybe she needed the presence of another person to whom she could direct her words, but at the same time that person had to be incapable of listening, if you know what I mean. Well it's no disgrace to talk to yourself that way, in my opinion. I do it myself all the time in the woods. I talk to birds and animals whom I know can't understand me either—although they most certainly do listen to me, sometimes very attentively.

Now I imagine Miss Harriet had been waiting a long time for this opportunity and she made good use of it. She began by referring to the missing wine and saying that she had known it would be gone when she awakened.

"Martha was just waiting for the chance," she said. "She no doubt walked by the door here a dozen times, just waiting for me to close my eyes so she could steal in here and take the wine away. It's too bad it won't be here if your pain gets worse and you need it, but you can blame my sister if that happens. It was for you I was saving it, but naturally Martha would never be convinced of that. You might have been thinking me to be the weaker of the two sisters, but I'm not, you know. I'm much the stronger, much more self-sufficient than Martha . . . and I'll always be that way. I have an ultimate strength, you see, which guarantees my position in this house. Until now I've been reluctant to use my power, but it's there if I need it. I know certain things, Mister McBurney, and because of that my sister fears me. Oh she can mock me before the students, and she can ignore me at the table, and she can subject me to a thousand small indignities such as hiding the key to the wine cellar when I need a remedy for a chill or an aching back, but there are limits to all this, Mister McBurney. There are bounds beyond which I will not tolerate my sister. She can wait outside in the hall until I am asleep and then sneak in here like a thief and snatch almost-empty bottles of wine from me, but she dares not face me directly with an order which I do not wish to carry out. She cannot bid me go or stay or sit or stand . . . or do anything contrary to my own desires . . . because I have this strength, Mister McBurney . . . I have the power to destroy her.

"I do believe my sister was honestly appalled at the realization of what she had done to you, Mister McBurney," Miss Harriet continued, "just as she was completely broken up when she realized what she had done to my brother. Of course she got over her grief for Robert very quickly—just as she may recover in a day or two from the shock of knowing that she has performed an unnecessary amputation."

Miss Harriet was speaking softly now though much more urgently and perhaps even more viciously than she does at normal times. In fact her whole manner was completely unlike that meek and hesitant person who generally always yields in any disagreement, even with students like Edwina and Emily and sometimes even with Marie.

"It's a pity you didn't come to visit us a long time ago, Mister McBurney," was the next thing she said. "You would have enjoyed yourself then at Farnsworth. In the old days, when Father was alive, this was a nice house . . . and a nice home. Everything was different then. We had company all the time, or most of the time. We had parties of all kinds . . . barbecues and balls and galas . . . oh nothing of the magnitude that is put on in Richmond, perhaps, but very pleasant occasions all the same. I think I may safely say that the Farnsworth parties were quite the best ones in this part of the county. And people from all over came to them. We had guests here from Fredericksburg and Culpepper and Warrenton . . . and from the Courthouse and from Richmond, too, on many occasions . . . and a few times people who knew our family from the old times came here—people from around our old place down on the James. And, of course, the year Robert was at the University he brought many of his friends here for the holidays. And that included people from all over. That Christmas, I remember, there were boys here from Augusta and Biloxi, and one from the capital—the Yankee capital, I mean—and another very pale and shy boy from the city of New York, who was very friendly with me—not with anyone else—only with me. And of course Howard Winslow was here too . . . he was always / here in those days. Well we had parties or entertainments of some kind every day and evening for a solid week. Martha and I were attending Miss Monroe's Seminary in Fredericksburg at that time too, and three of those girls came home with us for Christmas . . . Mary Bradley, as I recall, and Elizabeth Colby and a gawky girl from Boston whose name I can't for the life of me remember but I do know she had the most terrible complexion of anyone at Miss Monroe's. Of course Elizabeth and Mary were nothing to brag about in the beauty line either which, naturally, was the reason Martha invited them. She wouldn't have wanted Robert to be subjected to any undue temptations.

"Yes, Martha and I were away at school that year. Prior to that time we had been taught by a succession of middle aged and impoverished immigrants, mostly Germans and Austrians, none of whom were ever very happy out here in the hinterlands where they had Martha's continual attitude of superiority to add to their discomfort. So since we had no tutor at the moment and since Robert was going to be away at the University, my sister persuaded Father to send us off to Miss Monroe's. I recall she had wanted him to enroll both Robert and herself at a university in France where it seems females are admitted, but Father was never very enthusiastic about education of any kind for women and in Martha's case he realized— quite properly—that an experience of that sort would just make her more insufferable than she already was.

"Of course I'm not suggesting that Martha isn't bright. She always did have it over Robert and me in that respect. I'm sure if she had been born a man, she might have made a fine career for herself in education or politics, or maybe even in medicine. You've had a taste, haven't you, Mister McBurney, of my sister's eagerness to practice medicine. And it's possible she might have talked Father into the Paris scheme, as she had talked him into everything else she ever wanted, except it turned out Robert wasn't very eager to go to Europe himself and that, needless to say, caused Martha's interest to dwindle. I believe Robert was making an honest effort at that time to escape Martha's influence and that's why he decided to go to the University of Virginia.

"Well, Martha is a strange woman. She is my closet kin but sometimes I feel no affinity with her at all. Sometimes I think she is a person who is not only incapable of natural love herself, but also lacks whatever kind of spiritual magnetism is necessary to attract it. She can command respect of sorts, but not love. She just seems compelled to rule and possess everything and everyone about her, and obviously a person with those qualities is neither going to be liked nor loved.

"And so I can tell you truthfully that I'm sure my brother never loved her. In fact he may well have hated her toward the end, the way she treated him. It was like he wasn't her brother at all or wasn't even related to her— the way she went on, if you know what I mean. Maybe she thought that no one here was aware of the situation, but she couldn't fool me. I saw the way she petted him and fondled him and followed after him wherever he went around this place. He couldn't go ten steps toward the stables or the fields or the woods without her trailing after him. And, Mister McBurney, there were times when she even followed him to his room at night. Most often his door was locked but my sister had great patience. She would wait there in the hall, smiling to herself, and rapping softly and calling to him. 'Just for a moment, Robbie,' she would say. And after a while she would win him over. She would always win out in the end. He would open his door and stand there, pale and trembling, in the light of her candle, and then he would step aside and she'd enter . . . smiling . . . smiling. And the door would be closed, perhaps for hours, perhaps until dawn. And bad things would happen inside.

Sometime I'll tell you about everything that happened on those nights, Mister McBurney, if you'd be interested in hearing it.

"And the next day she would act as though nothing unusual had occurred. Indeed if her manner changed at all it would be for the better and she might seem happier and more contented with what she might have described on the previous day as our dull life here at Farnsworth. Robert on the other hand might stay in his room all that following day, never coming out at all, even for meals . . . waiting perhaps until after dark and then slipping down to the stables and saddling his horse and racing off to the Courthouse . . . or maybe even to Fredericksburg, where he'd be drunk in some tavern or worse place for the better part of a week.

"Father never knew what was going on upstairs, of course. He saw the result in the eyes of his wastrel son but he never knew the guilt that caused it. He always kept to himself a good bit anyway, Father did, in his later years. He took to spending most of his time on the porch or in the library, when we didn't have company, since he couldn't seem to find much in common with his children. He even slept on the settee in the library many nights when his gout was troubling him and that, of course, made it all the easier for Martha.

"Well she got her payment in the end, Mister McBurney. Robert went away and never came back. My sister was in despair, I can tell you. For many months he'd been trying to get away from her but she managed to keep him here on the pretext that Father needed him, but then Father died and she had no excuses any more. He went away for the last time and she never saw him again. Oh she tried desperately to find him. She traveled many miles in search of him and wrote him hundreds of letters and sent them to places where she'd heard he had been or was expected to be. She even continued to write letters when she had no address to which she could mail them because she had things on her mind and she wanted to get them put down and she kept hoping soon . . . maybe tomorrow or the day after or next week at the latest . . . she'd hear from him . . . or from someone who had seen him and could tell her where he was. I have secured some of those letters and I have them upstairs in my room, Mister McBurney. Sometime . . . if you are interested . . . I'll show them to you. They're very revealing letters, I can tell you. I think your opinion of my sister will change considerably after you've read them. In some of the letters she says she is sorry for the way she treated Robert and for her feelings about him, which she sometimes thinks now may have been wrong. She says in one letter that if he will only come back he'd need never fear her because she promises to remain at a distance from him and not even to speak to him unless he wishes it. Well you can't believe any of that. If Robert returned tomorrow things would still be the same between them as far as she's concerned. Of course she's claiming now that he's dead but you mustn't believe that either. She buried something in the woods one night which she said was Robert, but it wasn't, Mister McBurney, don't you ever believe that it was. It was a bundle of rags is all that she picked from a hundred other bundles. It wasn't Robert any more than you are Robert.

"She realizes what she did, you see, that's what's causing her to suffer, and you can make her suffer, too, Mister McBurney, for what she did to you. Your pain will be her pain every time she looks at you. . . . The nights you lie awake in misery will be sleepless ones for her too. And even if you die from this, Mister McBurney, she won't forget you. She'll remember what she did to you. I'll see that she remembers this day, too."

Miss Harriet paused again now and sighed and looked once more at the table and at the floor beneath it to see if she might possibly have misplaced the wine bottle. But it was definitely gone and this caused her to mutter a brief sentence which wasn't entirely audible to me except that I know it included Miss Martha's name and some words of profanity I had never heard Miss Harriet use before. Then she arose and without another glance at Johnny she left the room, walking slowly and stumbling a bit against the furniture. In a moment I heard her proceeding in the same unsteady fashion up the stairs.

Naturally I was somewhat disturbed by what Miss Harriet had said, but I thought that since it was not at all like her, it simply must have been due to one glass too many of the wine. I think if a person is generally kind and gentle and soft-spoken in all of her dealings with those around her, as Miss Harriet certainly is, then it is not at all fair to judge that person by words or actions which are the results of unusual circumstances. It is true that there came a time when I might have applied that principle to an action of Johnny McBurney's, and I failed to do it. The explanation for this, I suppose, lies in the fact that that particular action of Johnny's affected me deeply and the affairs of the Farnsworth family don't and never have. My final thought about Miss Harriet's remarks on that afternoon, I remember, was that actually she was no worse than I. I myself had often said hateful things about people in the privacy of the woods and it wasn't Miss Harriet's fault if the parlor on that afternoon was not as private as she thought.

After that I was alone with Johnny for a while. I heard Miss Martha and Mattie conversing in the kitchen garden as they gathered some herbs and vegetables for dinner. I heard Emily and Marie come down the stairs shouting insults at each other every step of the way. It seemed that Emily was accusing Marie of stealing some soap—which was an unusual thing for Marie to covet, unless it might have been scented soap. Then Miss Martha came into the hall and told them to be quiet and not disturb Corporal McBurney, and to insure this, ordered them both to the kitchen to help Mattie with the dinner.

I remember reflecting then that in most instances of missing soap at this school, Alice Simms is generally the first person to be accused. This is because Alice is extraordinary proud of her milky complexion and although she doesn't seem to make any great attempt to keep the rest of her person particularly clean, she does spend a good deal of time bathing her face. My own feeling is that dirt is as much a part of nature as the sky and air and, although I will admit that certain occasions are best served by neatness, the whole notion of continous washing can become a dreadful nuisance, especially at a modern school like this one. I might add here an opinion of my roommate. Marie says it seems to her that one of the few blessings this war has brought is the universal shortage of soap, which proves to her that there is always some good to be found in the very worst situations.

Just then one of the very people in question walked into the room— Alice Simms. She halted just inside the door and looked around very carefully—to see if Johnny had any other visitors, I suppose. Like Miss Harriet before her, she didn't observe me and so she came over to the settee.

She was wearing one of the several brightly colored dresses which it is supposed were originally the property of her mother and were donated to Alice as fashions changed or her mother's position improved. The dress she wore on this day was her pink taffeta with the black silk ribbon in the bodice. Unfortunately it is much too large a garment for Alice who is rather small of stature, though she is undeniably well developed. The dress could easily be shortened, of course, but Alice is not much of a seamstress, and also she says she prefers to grow into all of these costumes rather than risk destroying them by alteration.

"Johnny," she said now, hitching up her skirt, "are you feeling better? Don't wake up on my account if you're asleep, Johnny, because you need all the rest you can get. You'll be up and around again in no time if you just eat plenty of food and get your proper rest. Well I just came in to tell you that I don't hate you any more, Johnny, but if you're really asleep I can tell it to you another time. I'm trying to say I'm sorry about what happened to you— Edwina pushing you down the stairs and everything. Of course I was very angry when you acted so concerned about her and rushed out to the hall to explain to her, as though she meant more to you than I did. But then later I started to worry about you . . . to wonder if maybe you had been seriously hurt . . . and, Johnny, I didn't hardly sleep a wink all night over it. And this morning I was even more worried for fear you might have died down here alone without my ever having a chance to even talk with you again. Because you know I really do think a lot of you, Johnny. You are honestly the most exciting boy I've ever met and I like you such a great deal . . . and sometimes I even think I love you. Now wrap that up and put it under your pillow if it pleases you, Sir Johnny. Oh you just make me feel so glorious when you hold me and kiss me, dear sweet sweet Johnny. You're a wicked boy but so nice all the same. . . . I've looked forward to every day since you came. Now can't you see how miserable I would be if you were to up and die on me now, Johnny, just when we were beginning to get on so well together."

Well there was more of that kind of talk but that's the general sub-stance of it. I didn't put much stock in it, of course. Any getting on between Johnny and Alice must have been mostly in her imagination, because for one thing they had had very little opportunity to be by themselves—which is the first step in "getting on" together, or so I'm told. With the exception of the previous night I was pretty certain they had never been alone for any lengthy period. You see I was keeping a pretty close watch on Johnny at that time because I was fearful that someone like Alice would try to take advan-tage of him. And sure enough that's what happened.

Now I didn't know exactly what took place in Alice's room on the pre-vious night and I didn't want to know. Whatever went on I was sure Alice was entirely responsible for it. However as it turned out she didn't go into any details about the past but instead began to speculate about how she and Johnny might get on together in the future. "The fact that you've lost one leg shouldn't hinder you romantically, it seems to me," she said. "I'm sure a one legged man or even a no legged man can enjoy himself in that way and probably father just as many children, if that is his intention, as any other member of the male race. And probably he could give just as much pleasure to the young lady, too, despite his amputated condition. I've been thinking this whole thing over very carefully, Johnny, and I'm almost convinced that your missing leg won't make any difference to me, as far as romance is concerned—once I get used to it. Oh it might disturb me a trifle at first, but I'm sure I'll get over any little squeamishness like that in no time at all.

"In fact I'll be honest with you, Johnny," she continued. "It was the thought of how the loss of your leg might change you as a man which upset me more than anything else earlier this afternoon in the dining room. I believe that was the main reason that I fainted—if you happened to notice me do that—but of course you couldn't have seen it because you were unconscious then. Now I probably should also explain why I was in the dining room in the first place, Johnny, during the time your leg was being cut off—just in case that seems rather cold-blooded of me. It never occurred to me that anyone would think that, but Marie Deveraux informed me a while ago that such was exactly her opinion. Marie said it seemed extremely hard-hearted of me to take such an interest in your amputation within twenty-four hours of having entertained you in my room. Well of course as we both know, the entertainment had hardly begun when that savage Edwina burst in on us, but it did strike me that Marie might have a point.

"And so," Alice went on, "after thinking about it I have decided that perhaps I should explain to you what my feelings were as I watched Miss Martha cut off your leg—apart from worrying about your possible loss of manhood, which I've already mentioned. I'll tell you the honest truth, Johnny. The primary reason I went to the dining room and watched that horrible event was because I wanted to ease Miss Martha's suspicions about the two of us. I'm sure Miss Martha and probably Miss Harriet, too, were wondering if you and I had been having an *amour* as Marie calls it, and it dawned on me that my presence right beside the operating table was the best possible way of setting their minds at rest. Because naturally, Johnny, if those in charge here are going to be continually watching us, we are not going to be able to have much of a romance for ourselves, are we, dear?

"Therefore," said Miss Kindhearted Alice, "I determined to stand there and observe the whole bloody business if it made me sick to my stomach for a solid week. I resolved to act as though I hardly even knew you, Johnny. I thought to myself, if that won't fool Miss Martha and Miss Harriet, nothing will. Of course I will admit that I didn't expect it to be quite as horrible as it turned out to be. I don't believe I'd care to go through that experience again, Johnny. Once was enough for me, thank you. However I do think I succeeded in my plan for misguiding our dear teachers. I'll bet if some stranger were to walk in this school right now and inquire whether Miss Alicia Simms had any strong feeling of attachment toward Mister Johnny McBurney, I'm sure our teachers would answer emphatically in the negative. And we both know that nothing could be further from the truth, don't we, dear? At least I know it, and I surely to goodness hope you do too. Oh you and I are going to have some wonderfully romantic times together, Johnny, just as soon as it's ever possible for you. Of course I realize that you are in a very weakened condition now and it may take a while for you to get your strength back. You just take your time about it, dear, and let your poor stump heal properly, and then when you feel you're strong enough for romance again, you just beckon to me and I'll come to you. Meanwhile I may try to keep up a little of the same sort of pretense with our teachers—just to make it easier for us later, Johnny. So don't be disappointed if I seem to ignore you during the next few days, or if I say things that might seem to be unfeeling about you in the presence of others. You and I both know how I really feel about you, don't we, and that's the only important thing."

Alice bent over him now and kissed him lightly on the forehead. "I have to go to dinner now, Johnny. I suppose you haven't heard a word I said, have you? But that's all right. I'll watch for a good chance tomorrow or the next day, and then maybe I'll come in and tell you the whole thing again." She giggled a bit at this. "If I can remember it all, I mean."

Then she kissed him again and backed off, waving a shy little goodbye to him, which was even sillier than her remarks. I suppose there was some possibility that a few of the things she said might have sunk into his head, since there was no way of telling just how deeply unconscious he was, but his eyes had definitely remained closed all the while Alice was with him, so there was no chance at all that he could have seen her waving her farewell.

Well the ways of some girls are strange and if Alice Simms is not the best example of this then perhaps Edwina Morrow may fill the bill. Alice was scarcely out of the parlor and across the hall when Edwina came in. She must have been waiting at the top of the stairs—or perhaps she was watching from the library—until Alice's exit and then she hurried into the parlor and over to Johnny's side, almost as though she had decided if she didn't do it quickly she wouldn't do it at all.

And there she stood for a moment, breathing heavily and biting her lip as she stared at him in a way which I don't think could be described as friendly. But then again it is hard to be exact about Edwina's mood on any given occasion, since her every day manner is usually not a very warm one. Well she waited for so long without saying anything that I thought she never would begin. It was my impression however that her feelings about Johnny changed while she stood there. I think maybe she might have entered assuming that Johnny and Alice had been having a tender conversation in here, but then when she saw him and realized how sick he was, her anger lessened and she even began to feel a little pity for him.

Because at last she whispered very softly, "I'm sorry for what happened to you. I never wanted anything like this to happen . . . although I don't think I regret what I did. I'd probably do it again, if the situation were repeated . . . not that it ever will be. I can never feel about you again as I did before last night. But that's not important now . . . to you or me. What is important now is your will to get better and I think you have it, Johnny. I think you have a great determination in you for doing almost anything you set your mind to . . . a great strength for hanging on when other people might let go and die. You lived and almost recovered from your first wound, and I think you're capable of doing it again . . . if you want to do it. And I'll guess you'll want to do it, if only to show us that you can't be defeated by a lot of women and girls.

"I do want you to get better, Johnny," Edwina went on. "I want you to recover and go away from here forever . . . and I'll admit my reasons for desiring that aren't entirely unselfish. Maybe I want you out of sight in the hope that will eventually put you out of my mind, too, and then I can begin to recover from you myself. I'm sure I don't have feelings of love for you anymore, you understand, Johnny . . . but I am disturbed by you and I suppose I will continue to be disturbed as long as you are here.

"And therefore I'm willing to help you leave here. You can go ahead with the same plans you said you had in mind for both of us. If you want to start from Richmond, I'll write to my father and ask him to do everything he can to send you wherever in the world you want to go . . . or to help you find a position somewhere, if that's what you'd like instead. I'll tell him that I would regard this as a very special favor to me, and that if he will do so, I will promise to stay away from him myself . . . and never ask him for anything again. I will also say that I am requesting this favor for a special friend of mine . . . someone who has been very close to me. . . ."

Edwina paused then and turned away and covered her mouth with her hand. After a moment she got control of herself and was able to look at him again.

"That's all I had to tell you, Johnny," she said, her voice quivering a little. "I thought maybe you could hear me. If you didn't, it's all right too. I'll write my father anyway and ask him to help you."

Then she moved away from him and started slowly for the door. Now while she was saying her last words I happened to notice a slight movement of Johnny's lips. His mouth had curled just a tiny bit at the edges into what might have been a smile.

And then he opened his eyes and said softly but distinctly, "Edwina. . . ."

She came back hesitantly. "How are you, Johnny?" she asked.

"Grand . . . considering the circumstances."

"Did I wake you?"

"If you did, I thank you. I'd've hated to have you here without my knowing it."

"Did you hear what I said before?"

"No, what was it?"

"I'll tell you another time."

"My apologies for what happened, Edwina . . . the last time I saw you. When was that anyway?"

"It was last night."

"Only last night? It seems years ago. Well anyway, I'm sorry I hurt you, Edwina. It was never my intention to do so. I wouldn't hurt you . . . for all the Alices in the world . . ."

"Johnny, while you were asleep I said I was sorry too . . . for what happened to your leg. I'll say more now. I'm sorry that I followed you last night, Johnny . . . and that I struck you. But believe me, Johnny, I never meant for you to fall."

"I know that, sweetheart," he said. "I had no doubts about that. It was an accident, that's all."

"Johnny . . . I was glad though . . . when you fell."

"That's all right too. I deserved what I got, Edwina. . . ."

"You didn't deserve to be so badly injured as to bring about . . . what happened today. I was never glad about that, Johnny . . . and now I'm sorry about all of it. What I did was unjustifiable. You probably had a perfectly good reason for going to see Alice. You wanted to say goodbye to her probably."

"Maybe that's so."

"And you were exhausted, probably, from the climb up the stairs, and you were just resting for a moment on her bed."

"Yes . . . that's it."

"Oh, Johnny, I'm sorry I ever thought anything else. Is the pain bad, Johnny?"

"Bad enough."

"It will get better after a while."

"Maybe some of it will."

"Why did you go to her room, Johnny?"

"You said it before. I wanted to tell her goodbye."

"You could've told her downstairs."

"I guess I must've forgot it."

"All right, Johnny, we'll leave it that way."

"You're not interested in the way I said goodbye to her? You don't want to hear how I went about it?"

"Please, Johnny. . . ."

"I kissed her . . . and squeezed her . . . and all sorts o' things like that."

"Please . . . please. . . ."

"You saw it anyway. You knew I was doin more than restin."

"My God, Johnny . . . I beg you, please. . . ."

"Don't beg me, dearie. You'll never get anything outa me by beggin."

"You pig . . . you filthy pig . . . I hope you die!"

Johnny chuckled. "Ah now, you don't mean that, sweetheart."

"I never meant anything more," Edwina said. She was clenching her hands so tightly she must have torn her palms with her nails.

"I was teasin you, Edwina," Johnny told, grinning weakly. "Teasin you and testin you I was. You were right the first time. You didn't see anything because there was nothin to see. Now if I had said somethin like that to Alice, she would've laughed, wouldn't she? Ain't I right about that? She would've split her pudgy little sides with glee, wouldn't she, all the while she was tellin me what a shockin nasty fella I was. But you didn't laugh, Edwina. I knew you wouldn't laugh . . . because you're a lady. . . . Don't you want to know why I had my pants off, Edwina?"

"Go to hell . . . go to hell," Edwina moaned.

"It was only to save the wrinklin of them . . . while I was restin there on her bed and all. . . ."

She started to leave then but he grabbed her hand and held her in a tight grip when she tried to pull away. "I wouldn't've gone to your room, dear. I wouldn't've even asked to go . . . because you're a nice girl . . . and I love you. . . ."

"You lie . . . you lie," Edwina cried softly.

"I'll make you believe me. I'll make you see I'm tellin the truth. Tomorrow . . . or the day after . . . just as soon as I can get about again . . . I'll show you, Edwina, how much you mean to me . . . and how I plan to repay you . . . for all you've done for me. . . ."

His grip on her hand relaxed then and he closed his eyes.

"Johnny," she whispered. "Johnny, I will try to believe you. I'll try to have more faith in you from now on."

But he was asleep. She waited there for a moment longer, holding his hands now in her own. Then she released him gently and pulled the blanket higher on him since the room was getting a bit chilly now. Finally she smoothed his hair with her fingertips and wiped the perspiration from his forehead and upper lip with her handkerchief. And then wiping her own eyes with the damp handkerchief she left the room.

Well, I said to myself, there certainly seems to be a lot of unsuspected trouble in this house. Johnny McBurney, I thought, you really have managed to cause a wagonload of commotion and consternation in this school in the few short weeks that you've been here.

But I still didn't think any the less of him despite the various things I had heard on that afternoon. After turning the more recent things over in my mind, I wasn't any more disturbed by Edwina's remarks than I had been by Alice's or Miss Harriet's. And what was more important, I wasn't hardly bothered at all by what Johnny had said to Edwina.

I know his remarks were probably rather vulgar, but that sort of thing never upsets me. I've heard it all before. I've overheard enough conversations between overseers and field hands on our place at home which included a number of remarks which were less refined than Johnny's.

And as for the rest of it, I didn't know whether he was being sincere with Edwina or not and I didn't much care. I was almost always certain that he was entirely sincere in anything he ever said to me, and that was all that counted. The others, I decided, could look out for themselves.

While I was pondering these things in the growing darkness, Mattie came to the doorway.

"You still in there, child?" she demanded.

"Yes, I'm still here," said I.

"The others are all at the table," Mattie grumbled. "You gonna force me to feed you in here? Miss Martha and Miss Harriet are gettin too easy with you chil'ren. They ought not to put up with all this nonsense, makin all this extra work for me."

"What table are you serving at tonight, Mattie?"

"The kitchen table! Is that what's botherin you?"

"Is Edwina there . . . and Alice?"

"Yes, they're all there but you . . . and Miss Harriet who's sick again. None of the other young ladies is as foolish as you. They know they gotta eat their meals at the proper time and place, no matter if all the Yankees in the world gets their legs cut off."

"All right," I said, rising. "I'll come out and join the rest. I'm still not very hungry, but I am satisfied now that Johnny is in no danger at least for the time being."

"You think he's a mite stronger then?" Mattie came over and inspected him.

"I don't know whether he's any stronger physically or not," I said, "but I believe he has more vitality now than he seemed to have a while ago. I think now Johnny may have found something to live for."

"And what would that be?" Mattie asked.

"I think maybe he has a goal now," I said. "I think he's planning to show certain people here that they were very wrong in treating him as they did."

"More power to him then," said Mattie. "There's a few folks here that need to be took down a peg or two."

Then she left the parlor and I followed her and joined the other girls at dinner in the kitchen.

Alicia Simms

Before I begin to say anything about Johnny McBurney as I knew him after his operation, I want to state emphatically that I thought the entire thing was horrible. It seems to me that cutting off a human leg is a terribly cruel thing to do to anyone, especially without a person's permission, unless that person is absolutely at death's door and unable to speak or consider things sanely. Also I think you can hardly blame the victim of such an operation for being very mean and nasty about it afterwards. Well that's the way Johnny was and I never held it against him hardly at all—except that I did think he was rather unfair in the direction of his meanness sometimes, since he turned it indiscriminately on some people who didn't deserve it. I happened to be one of those people.

Anyway it was several mornings later before I managed to have a private conversation with him. This, I might say, was no mean accomplishment at that time when the awakening thought of everyone here was always, "Is Johnny McBurney still alive or not? Or if he hasn't died, has he become reconciled to his crippled condition?" With thoughts like these in mind all the students usually rushed downstairs in the morning and crowded around the parlor door, but they were always refused admittance by Miss Martha or Miss Harriet who would post themselves there before any of the girls arrived. However on this particular morning I didn't rush down with the others. I adopted the tactics of some of the slyer girls here—girls like Marie and Amelia who astonished me by not thinking of it themselves—and I waited, upstairs until Miss Martha had shooed them all into the dining room for breakfast and then I slipped down the stairs very quietly and went straight into the parlor.

Surprisingly enough, he was sitting, bolstered up with pillows on his settee. "Surprisingly" is probably not even a strong enough word to use in these circumstances, because I think anyone would reasonably expect a person who had just undergone a serious leg amputation to be knocking on death's door, or mighty near to it, for a good many days subsequently, and not be sitting calmly propped up, staring intently at a girl as she entered his room, hardly three days later.

Well I tell you when I left that boy after visiting him briefly on the day of his operation I really never expected to see him alive again, but there he was, as cool as you please, nibbling on one of Mattie's beaten biscuits and sipping at a cup of acorn coffee. However, I did observe that he was still extremely pale and drawn looking, and I expect he was experiencing a lot of pain, although he was not about to admit anything like that. I guess by that time, he had made up his mind that he was not going to be defeated by a flock of women. I guess he was just bound and determined to recover from his operation, just out of spite, if for no other reason.

"Fine, I feel just fine," he said in answer to my question. "I believe I'll recommend to everyone the job that was done on me. It's a great thing for tonin up the constitution."

"You seem to be doing so well already, no doubt you'll be up and around again in a few days," I told him.

"I will, I promise you," he agreed. "Maybe 'twill be before that even. I have a lot to do here, and I must be gettin on to it."

"What exactly must you do?" I inquired.

"Various things," said he with a nasty grin. And with that he put down his coffee cup and reached over and pinched me very hard and, I can almost certainly say, viciously, on the tender part of my back body. It was really done so meanly that it just brought tears to my eyes, but that devil, Johnny, just continued to grin.

"That's nothin," he told me, "nothin at all compared to what you'll get if you don't pay attention to me. From now on you must do just exactly as I tell you, or you may wish you'd never been born."

"But what's wrong, Johnny?" I asked him in great surprise. "What have I done that displeases you?"

"You haven't jumped fast enough when I've snapped my fingers, dearie, that's the whole trouble. You've acted so pert and snappy with me sometimes that I've been thinkin lately you might take it into your head to disobey me entirely, and o' course I won't have any of that. I've a couple of little tasks in mind for you now, and they've got to be accomplished very quickly."

"I'll do anything I can for you, Johnny," I told him. "You can believe that."

"I hope I can believe it. I think at heart you're a willing girl and maybe you'll improve a bit now that your mistakes have been pointed out to you. If you do you'll be rewarded, and if you don't, you'll be punished, like I told you. If you're good, you'll get this." And he patted me gently in the same region as before. "But if not, you'll get this." And once again he pinched me, even more cruelly than the first time. I would have cried out with the pain, had he not pulled me down to him and clapped his hand to my mouth.

"Now, now," he said, "no tears, there's my brave girl. It was only the one more lesson you needed. You won't get any more like that if you're a good girl. Now then, are you ready for your first instructions?"

I had to nod my agreement, because I couldn't even speak with the way he was practically smothering me with his big hand. I suppose I should have pulled away from him right then and walked right out of that room and never had anything more to do with Johnny McBurney, but I guess I was just simply afraid to do it. He couldn't have leaped up and caught me right then, of course, but I had to think of the future—of the time when he had recovered his health and strength as it seemed right then he was surely going to do.

And also I must admit I had liked him in the past and I was hopeful that I might like him again at sometime in the future. I won't deny that I had been very attracted to him for several reasons, one of which had been his kind and gracious manner with me, and so I began hoping that this strange meanness of Johnny's would pass and that he would become the dear person he had been before.

"All right then, sweetheart," he said, "here's the first task I'm assignin to you. It's a very important job, and you must handle it carefully. Are you up to it, do you think?"

"Yes, yes," I said, not wanting to be hurt again.

"Very well. Here's what you must do. You must fetch me Miss Martha's key ring."

"But she won't give it to me." I really thought he must be joking.

"I'm not suggesting that you ask her for it."

"You mean you want me to steal it?"

"Oh that's a terrible word, an awful word to use. And it ain't even appropriate. When you steal something, it usually means you want to keep it, don't it, or else sell it. I don't want to keep the key ring. I just want to borrow it for a little while, and then I'll return it to dear old Miss Martha."

Well, as you can imagine I was very shocked. The key ring to which he was referring is the one Miss Martha generally wears attached to a sash around her waist, and whether he intended to return it eventually or not, taking it without Miss Martha's permission seemed to me to be a very serious matter—one which Miss Martha would regard as a very grave offense—an offense for which a person might well be discharged from this school.

And more than that, it was impossible. I told him so. "Miss Martha has those keys with her practically all the time," I said.

"But not constantly," said Johnny McBurney. "I believe I've seen her without them. In fact I have the impression she doesn't always wear her key ring at dinner."

I had to agree with that. Miss Martha kept the keys at hand most of the day to open the bookcases and various locked closets and cupboards with which this house abounds, but when she came to the dinner table—especially when she had changed into her good black velvet dress—she seldom brought the key ring with her.

"And so," Johnny continued, "you could slip up to Miss Martha's room tonight during dinner, couldn't you, and whisk that key ring down to me in an instant with no one being the wiser. Couldn't you do that for me, dearie?" And he made as though to pinch me again.

"I suppose I could," I admitted, "but I would surely be caught at it. If the keys were missing and I was absent from the table for even an instant after Miss Martha came downstairs, I would surely be accused of taking them. You don't seem to be acquainted with the rules of this school yet, Mister McBurney. It just so happens that all students are supposed to be at table when Miss Martha enters the dining room and they are supposed to remain there until after she leaves the room."

"Well, she does walk around without those keys on some other occasions, doesn't she?"

"I suppose she does," said I, "but it doesn't happen very often. What do you want with those keys anyway?"

"Nothin, nothin much at all. I only want to play a joke on Miss Martha."

"She won't think it's very funny. She'll raise a terrible fuss if she ever finds that key ring missing."

"I'm sure she will," he grinned. "That's the joke of it. And she won't blame you for taking it, don't worry about that. I'll bet you a dozen kisses that she accuses her sister of makin off with it. She'll think Miss Harriet has grabbed the keys in order to get at the wine downstairs."

"Miss Harriet seems able to get the wine without the keys whenever she wants it," I said, "but even if Miss Martha was misled, Miss Harriet has always been most kind to me and I'd hate to get her into trouble."

"Ah, it won't be anything serious," said Johnny. "Her sister can't drive her out of the house, can she? In fact we'll probably be doin Miss Harriet a favor with this joke, because if she's falsely accused of somethin like this, she may just rear back and assert herself and tell the old bat off for the first time in her life."

It didn't seem awfully likely, but I supposed it might be possible. "But how will you get the keys back to Miss Martha when you're finished with your joke?" I asked him.

"I'll just throw them somewhere and let her find them. Maybe I'll toss 'em over behind that chair there, or over by the window, and she'll come in and think she dropped them and that they've been there all the time. Now, darlin girl, don't you see how simple the whole thing is?"

Well I still didn't want to do it. If he had to begin playing jokes, I told him, he'd be better off to get himself a partner who liked that sort of thing—someone like Marie Deveraux, for instance.

"I don't want a child," said he. "I want a quick and clever girl like yourself who knows what she's doing. Marie Deveraux might agree to grab the keys all right, but she also might decide to improve the joke and drop the keys in the well and then where'd we be? You see, dearie, I think I can make you toe the line more easily than I can Marie."

"I'm not that much afraid of you hurting me," I said, more bravely than I felt. "I can always stay away from you."

"No, you couldn't sweetie. I'd catch you sooner or later, even with my one poor leg. And even if you could avoid my hand, you could never get away from the sound of my voice—my rich tenor voice that'd be continually singin out, accusin you of all sorts of sly and fancy deeds with me in your room that night the black-haired bitch pushed me down the stairs."

I'm just repeating his own words now, I certainly wouldn't use that kind of language myself. And also I really hadn't done anything wrong that night, but naturally I realized at once that I could never prevent him from saying that I had, and of course, I'm in such a precarious position here, what with my mother never bothering to send Miss Martha any money for my education and keep, or for that matter never even writing occasionally to say that she intends to send some money at some time in the future when she is more able to do so, and also what with the way that some girls are somewhat jealous of me—or of my appearance, I mean, and my hair especially—which sometimes causes some trouble to arise here, that sometimes I think it wouldn't take much provocation at all to cause Miss Martha to send me away from here, war or no war.

One other little thought did occur to me at that time, which, in order to be completely honest, I will report now. Although it was a terribly nasty and vicious word to use in describing her, it did give me some comfort to realize that Johnny had at last recognized Edwina Morrow for what she was.

Anyway I finally did consent to try and get Miss Martha's key ring for Johnny. He had never given me any reason to doubt him in the past, was the way I argued it to myself, and therefore if he insisted it would only be a joke there was no good reason for me not to at least try to believe him. The final and winning argument was, of course, when I decided that I had more to fear from Johnny right then than I did from Miss Martha or anyone else in the house.

Well, once I had consented, his disposition changed and he became the Johnny of old. He was tender and soft-spoken with me once again, and before I left him I permitted him to kiss me once, which he did in a most gentle manner. As I departed he was starting on his breakfast again, and singing to himself as though he hadn't a single care in the world and was as healthy and complete as any man alive. Of course, I suspect the act was put on because he was very pale, I noticed, and stuffing the food in his mouth and not really enjoying it, and also he certainly wasn't singing as well as he had sung in his better days. Therefore, as a little further test, I bumped his right leg—or what remained of it—accidentally as I departed, and I can tell you he practically bit through his lower lip from the pain.

In any event, I had no opportunity for several days to accomplish the thing he desired of me. Miss Martha seemed to be wearing her key ring on her sash every time I caught sight of her, and on those occasions when she did remove it, she handed it immediately to someone else, such as Miss Harriet or Mattie, and then saw to it that the borrower returned the keys as soon as she had finished with them. As I told Johnny, Miss Martha has always been very reluctant to part with those keys for any great length of time.

Meanwhile, to everyone's surprise, Corporal McBurney really was improving rapidly. By about the fifth day after his operation he was trying to sit up on his settee and swing his good leg over the edge. Marie, in fact, reported that she had seen Johnny with his left foot on the floor looking very much as though he was going to try to balance himself on it. Marie had rushed off to Miss Martha with this news, and Miss Martha had gone immediately to the parlor and very firmly insisted that Johnny, for his own good, must remain in at least a semiprone position for a while longer.

Of course, Miss Martha was very happy, along with everyone else, at his speedy recovery, and in addition, I believe Miss Martha was a little proud of her own accomplishment. As I mentioned, I never expected Johnny to get better and I'm sure she really didn't either. Therefore, when he astonished her by starting to seem almost normal immediately, she evidently made up her mind she would do all in her power to keep him that way. In one afternoon, she had become a successful surgeon, and she wasn't going to have her glory taken away from her now.

Well, I can tell you, that boy fared better in this house after he lost his leg than he or any of the rest of us did before. He was given meat and broth and all kinds of fresh greens at just about every meal. He was fed salt pork and bacon and dried beef stew—and that I can tell you was the cause of plenty of eyebrow-raising among the students here who were not aware that Miss Martha had any more dried beef locked up in her larder.

Marie spoke for all of us when she remarked, "Some more people here may soon feel like sacrificing a leg if it means this kind of improvement in our menu."

One day about a week after the operation, Mattie came up with a real treat for him—and to some extent for all of us, with the exception of Miss Amelia Dabney. Old Mattie happened to be browsing around in the far tobacco field near the logging road—looking for herbs and dandelions, I guess—when she suddenly spied something fluttering out of the woods into the ditch which separates the woods from the road. She went out to investigate and found to her great joy it was a young wild turkey.

He had evidently broken his wing in some way, so it was not any trick for Mattie to grab him and dispatch Master Tom with a nearby rock. Then she brought him home in triumph, swinging him around her head and shrieking and yelling and looking, as Emily said, like some old African Amazon returning from a successful war.

Well, naturally, Johnny got the lion's share of the turkey, which Mattie roasted that same night. The rest of us had to be content with little nibbles of it. I had a portion of the neck and gizzard, as I recall, which was about as much as any student managed to get. And strangely enough, no one begrudged Johnny's having the best of it, because at that time everyone here really did want him to get well. However, it wasn't long until some people began to change their minds on that subject.

As you might suspect, there was one person here who refused to end any of that turkey. That was Miss Amelia Dabney, who protested violently during the plucking and cleaning of the bird and then marched upstairs when it went on the spit, and stayed in her room and refused to join us that night for dinner. Of course, I think she might have been sentenced to that exile anyway, as a result of her noisy demonstration. That strange little girl has evidently got it into her head that everything that walks or flies or crawls in that woods is her personal property, and even though this turkey had plainly strayed outside the limits of the trees—as Miss Harriet did very kindly try to explain to her—Miss Amelia would have had Mattie carry it back to its mother's nest, or else bring it home to Amelia for repair of its broken wing.

Anyway, you can be sure Corporal McBurney was not suffering for lack of attention at that time. Every student here, including Edwina, did her best to be unceasingly civil to him, and Miss Martha even began to cooperate a little in this respect by gradually permitting us to visit him just as often as we pleased.

Well, when others were present he played the proper gentleman, but when

I was alone with him, he frequently reverted to his tricks of pinching me and squeezing my hand painfully hard, and one time when I innocently leaned over to give him the friendly kiss he requested, he pulled my hair so savagely that I almost screamed with the agony of it.

"The key ring, darlin," he hissed. "Fetch me that key ring as you promised, or I'll pull every strand from your lovely head."

Of course that threat didn't bother me as much as the one I've already mentioned. I would have risked the pain or the possible loss of great clumps of my hair—which everyone seems to agree is one of my most attractive endowments—but the thought that he might start a false scandal about my friendship with him really troubled me. Consequently, I was very thankful that same afternoon, when I noticed Miss Martha picking bugs off the greens in the kitchen garden and seemingly not wearing the precious key ring. She had come downstairs on Mattie's summons and she and Mattie were working with great concentration, hunting some new kind of weevil Mattie had discovered.

Classes were finished for the day, and there was still an hour until dinner. Miss Harriet was resting in her room, which adjoins Miss Martha's and all my fellow students, presumably, were engaged in various activities downstairs or in the garden. It seemed the perfect opportunity to slip upstairs and see whether Miss Martha had happened to leave the key ring in her room.

The upstairs hall was empty and the doors to both our teacher's rooms were closed. I paused briefly and listened at Miss Harriet's door until I heard the sound of her snoring. Her head was evidently buried well beneath the bed covers, I decided, because ordinarily the sounds of Miss Harriet sleeping can be heard as far as the front gate.

That poor thing is the most uneasy sleeper I have ever come across. She takes each breath as though it is bound to be her last and, moreover, as though she is in mortal terror of the life to come. Well, I feel sorry for anyone like that who cannot rest easily at night, since all my dreams are always pleasant ones and, I believe, I am descended from people of the same conscience. At any rate, my mother has always taught me that a lady's bed is not the place to bring her troubles and she follows this principle by always sleeping like an absolutely petrified log herself. Or at least she was in the habit of doing so the last time I shared a bed with her.

Anyway I moved on to Miss Martha's room, assured that Miss Harriet would cause me no distress. Her sister's door wasn't locked, I found when I tried it gently, good evidence that the key ring might be somewhere inside. The door squeaked a bit as I opened it, and so I waited for a moment until I could hear Miss Harriet's snoring once again. Then I entered the room on tiptoe to begin my search.

Now I must admit I had not been overly alarmed about the project until that time. It had been merely something to accomplish whenever I could in order to satisfy McBurney, and then my intention was to forget the whole matter immediately. In addition, I had promised myself that I would never become a participant in any such risky venture again. As a matter of fact, I think I was seriously considering staying away from McBurney entirely after the business was finished.

But now, standing in the middle of the enemy camp, I suddenly realized how risky the business really was. It dawned on me that if Miss Martha were to walk in and trap me, I might as well start at once to pack my bag, because I would very likely be ordered out of the house before morning. I knew well enough that Miss Martha was not going to believe me, or even listen to me for one instant if I tried to explain to her that the undertaking was just a prank. No ma'am and no sir, thank you very much. I had come into her room without asking her permission, and that is all the evidence she would need to convince herself that Alicia Simms was a trashy thief.

Well, I guess I just stood there for a minute or more, shivering and trembling, and then I got hold of myself and decided that the best thing was to get the business over with as quickly as possible. The problem was how to discover in a hurry where Miss Martha had put the keys, there being no sign of them in the obvious places such as the top of her bed stand or her dressing table, and without moving further I could see they weren't on the table or the chest of drawers in Miss Martha's adjoining sewing room either.

Well, I thought, if those pesky keys aren't on top of some article of furniture, they must be inside or underneath—always provided they haven't been left or given to someone downstairs. If I cannot find those keys within a very few minutes, I told myself, I will have to conclude they're not in this room at all, and then I'm going to give up on the entire undertaking and Mister Corporal McBurney can go hang himself. Already I had made a very honest effort to help him and if he had any decency at all he couldn't possibly hold it against me that I had failed.

And so I began searching the drawers in the dressing table and bed stand. Miss Martha had apparently gone downstairs in such a rush she left every drawer in the place unlocked, which was fortunate for me in one sense, but in another sense unfortunate because it caused me a number of distractions.

For example, there was a very handsome jewelry box—locked—in the top drawer of the bed stand, along with a lot of legal papers, which seemed to relate to this property here as well as other Farnsworth properties else-where in Virginia. Most of these papers were receipts for the sale of land, which my mother always says is a sure sign a family is on the decline.

Then in the middle right-side drawer of the dressing table was a supply of lead balls for Miss Martha's father's pistol—although not the pistol itself—and also a packet of old letters tied with a red ribbon. The top letter—and all the rest of them too, I think—was from the Farnsworth boy, Robert, who had signed his name on the envelope together with his address at the University of Virginia. All of the letters had obviously been written many years ago, and I had neither the time nor the inclination at that moment to read any of them. For one thing, I doubted whether I could get the same perfect bow on the ribbon if I untied it.

Anyway the amazing find was in the bottom drawer on the left side of the table. Now you could rack your brains for a hundred years and never guess what was in that drawer concealed beneath a lace shawl and a pile of handkerchiefs. As a matter of fact, I believe I am discreet enough and lady enough not to expose this secret to any outside acquaintance of Miss Martha and as far as that goes I did not disclose it to more than two other people at this school. One person was McBurney himself, to whom I merely related it in passing, and that disclosure certainly doesn't matter now. And the second person was a student to whom I mentioned it—as will soon be evident—before I really had a chance to think about it.

Now let me reveal the secret in this way, by asking what is our Miss Martha's most attractive feature? Well I think everyone will agree that our headmistress is not the most beautiful woman in the world. She is tall and well proportioned and has a graceful carriage, but she is undeniably rather plain of face and also there is something slightly unfeminine about her, if you know what I mean. She is too much the farmer, there is too much of the field and stable about her for my taste, and this is why the discovery was even more surprising. It was something that in my wildest dreams I would never have connected with Miss Martha.

Because there was one possession of Miss Martha's of which I always thought she need never be ashamed. Even if she were thrust into the most civilized Washington or Richmond society, she had at least one acceptable and redeeming feature, I thought, and that feature was her hair. As anyone can observe by looking at her today, Miss Martha Farnsworth has a very lovely head of jet back hair. And it is not her own!

That is what I found in that dressing table drawer—another wig exactly like the one she was wearing at that same moment in the garden!

Well, I guess I was so stunned I must have remained kneeling there by that drawer for several moments, forgetting completely the dangerous situation I was in. And I was brought to my senses in a hurry when I heard a voice behind me say triumphantly, "Ah ha, the criminal is caught in the act!"

Now as you can imagine, I just about went through the ceiling from shock, and then I turned very slowly and fearfully and found Miss Edwina Morrow, standing in the doorway with her arms folded, smiling at me. I had not closed the door completely in order that I might hear any footsteps on the stairs, but I had forgotten there are people in this house who can move like cats and Edwina is one of them.

"Why, Edwina," I said, trying to be civil, "I thought you were downstairs in the library."

"How unlucky for you. As it happens, I was in my own room, which I suppose is very lucky for me—otherwise you might have been in *there* trying to steal something."

"That's not so," I protested, half on the verge of tears. "I didn't come in here for that reason at all."

"Then what is your reason, pray tell, for being in this room snooping through Miss Martha's possessions?"

"I'm not snooping," I almost shouted. "I'm only looking for something which Corporal McBurney would like to borrow from Miss Martha."

"Would you like me to believe that Miss Martha sent you to do this?"

"Of course not! Actually it's only a trick—a trick which Johnny is playing on Miss Martha, that's all it is."

"Is that so. Well, Johnny must be in a very lighthearted mood then, and right after his serious operation, too. It's nice to know he's feeling so jolly once again."

"Especially nice for you," I retorted, feeling braver. "It must be a comfort to you, since you were the cause of the operation."

"Let's not go into those matters, shall we?" She wasn't smiling at all now, just staring at me with such a cold expression that I really was very afraid of her for the first time in my life.

"What is this secret thing you're looking for then?" she asked after a moment. "Is it something out of Miss Martha's jewel case?"

"It's her key ring," I said. I really wouldn't have admitted that if I hadn't been afraid of Edwina.

"I might've guessed it," Edwina said. "Johnny will be playing tricks in the wine cellar and in every cabinet and cupboard in the house."

"Well I didn't ask him why he wanted the keys," I said. "However, I don't see how he can rush about the house opening cupboards in his present condition."

"Oh he'll be moving around again shortly, I fancy," said Edwina. "Emily and Amelia are making a pair of crutches for him right now. Tell me, what do you find so fascinating in that drawer?"

"Nothing," I said, trying to close the drawer casually. I honestly didn't want to tell her about the wig, because I didn't think she was the kind of person who ought to be entrusted with information like that.

"Get up out of there and let me see."

"It's nothing at all," I said again, "only someone's old hair piece is all it is." If the information about the wig was going to be spread throughout the school, I was determined I would be the one to tell it and not Edwina Morrow. Little enough attention is paid to me around here to pass up an opportunity like that without a struggle.

However, the unmannerly Miss Morrow pushed me aside and jerked the drawer open. She had a brief look at the contents and then stood back as though disappointed. "That must be her dress-up one," she commented. "I think it's a bit glossier than the other."

"Do you mean to stand there and tell me that you knew about this before, Edwina?"

"Certainly. A blind person could tell Miss Martha's hair is not her own."

"And you've never told anyone here?"

"To whom would I tell it—you, for instance?"

"No, I suppose not," I admitted. Edwina has no friends here to whom she might naturally confide a secret like that. Of course, as far as that goes, neither do I.

"Do you think Miss Martha is completely bald then?" I inquired.

"I don't know and I don't care," was her ungraceful answer. "During your snooping you didn't happen to notice Miss Martha's jewel box, did you?"

Well I'm sure I would have told her that I hadn't but after a pause she continued, "If you tell me where the jewel box is, I might locate the key ring for you."

"Where is it?"

"There, you ninny." She pointed to Miss Martha's wardrobe closet, and there, through the half open door, the key ring was plainly visible, hanging on a hook. Edwina went over, took it down and tossed it to me. "Now where's the jewel box?"

"In the second drawer," I told her, feeling obligated to do so now. "It's locked though," I added.

"You've tried it, have you?" Edwina opened the drawer and brought out the box. "Well, perhaps the key to it is among the dozen or more on here."

She grabbed the key ring from me and sitting down on the floor with the box on her lap she began trying the keys, finally succeeding in springing the lid, on the tenth try. Then she lifted out the inner tray with its contents which included a very few objects of jewelry—some rings with very modest stones, an inexpensive looking coral necklace and a few tarnished pins and brooches—and quite a number of gold coins.

"There we are," said Edwina with satisfaction. "There's my money."

"How do you mean—your money?"

"I've given it to her, all of this, in the years I've been here. What the rest of you have contributed may be in the bottom of the box." She indicated a rather meager-sized bundle of Yankee paper money which was in the second compartment along with a man's gold watch and a pair of gold cuff links.

"There doesn't seem to be a great deal of money here," I remarked. "I rather thought Miss Martha had more than this. Although perhaps she keeps it hidden elsewhere. She must have batches of Richmond money tucked away somewhere in the house."

"Possibly so," said Edwina, "but I would guess Miss Martha is smart enough to realize Richmond money isn't worth hiding. Anyway I'm only interested in gold pieces like these and I believe I'll just take a few of them back."

"That's stealing," I told her. "That really is stealing!"

"I don't consider it so," she said. "I feel I've been greatly overcharged at this place. I've paid Miss Martha more than any other student during my time here—a great deal more, I'm sure than what you've paid. Anyway I'm not planning to take it all, just a little of it." She removed about ten double eagles from the fifty or more in the tray, taking only the shiniest ones, I noticed.

"If I had the nerve to take any," I said, "I'd surely take it all."

"Oh, I don't want it all," said Edwina, "I won't keep these for very long. Miss Martha will get them back again eventually. I just want to hang on to these few pieces for a while longer, as a sort of safeguard. As long as I have money, I can't be discharged from here, can I?"

Well I had no way of knowing the answer to that. I suggested that if Miss Martha really wanted to be rid of a person, she wouldn't let money stand in the way. She might be strongly influenced by money, but I don't hold with those here who feel that she is interested in nothing else.

Anyway during this conversation I had taken a little gold and enamel locket from the tray and was toying with it. It happened to be the kind of locket which opens to reveal a tiny portrait and the portrait in this locket was a miniature version of Robert as he appears in the painting of the three Farnsworth children which hangs in the library. Well none of this is important, except that as I was examining the locket, Edwina replaced the tray, closed and locked the box and put it back in the drawer, apparently without realizing that I still held the locket. Or perhaps she did realize it and wanted to see if I would make her open the box again.

Well I felt it was not worth starting a fuss over it, and so I slipped the locket in my bosom, intending to show it to Johnny and to replace it some time later. I certainly felt that it was nothing which would be missed immediately by Miss Martha.

"Here are your keys," said Edwina, handing me the ring. "I'll say nothing about the keys, if you'll agree to do the same about the gold pieces."

"All right," I said. "After all neither of us is stealing anything, are we?"

"I'm not, certainly," Edwina said.

"I intend to keep quiet about Miss Martha's wig also," said I.

"You can do as you please about that matter." Then as we came out into the hall she added, "The hair she had made is rather like my own natural hair, don't you think?'

"Yes, something like it."

"The color and texture are much the same. My hair is very straight too, like the kind Miss Martha chose, can you notice?"

I noticed and agreed. Anything to keep Edwina satisfied. And amazingly enough, it won a smile for me—a friendly smile this time.

"Will you give the keys to Johnny now?" she asked.

"As well now as later," said I.

"Tell me truthfully, Alicia," she said then, "are you very fond of him?"

"Not as much now as before," I admitted. She had used my proper name for the first time and I appreciated that. "How do you feel about him now?"

"I feel nothing for him," she said, and her smile was gone. "I think more of you, much more, than I do of McBurney. You and I have many things in common, Alicia. It might be well if you kept that in mind."

She put her hand gently on the back of my neck and squeezed one of my curls a few times between her fingers as you might do with a piece of goods. That girl apparently has a positive obsession about hair, although in all honesty it is not unusual for people to admire mine, since it is so naturally blond and silken. Anyway Edwina made no comment and I made none and then she smiled again and, jingling the gold coins in her hand, went off to her room.

Well, of course, I had no desire to become a chum of Edwina Morrow. I have been around this school long enough to know that it is far better to remain friendless yourself, than to become involved with someone like Edwina, who seemingly needs friendship so badly. It was something I had not suspected about her before, thinking that she kept apart from the rest of us through choice and not for want of an invitation. Anyway I don't lack for companionship here, and as for something more enduring, I'm sure there will always be members of the other sex to supply me with affection when I have need of it. I'm speaking now of the time when this ridiculous war is over and I can get away from here.

So I traveled back downstairs to the parlor with my gift for McBurney. He was sleeping when I entered the room, but I overcame that by tickling the sole of his remaining foot.

"Mum," he said drowsily. "Stop that, Mum. I'll get up in a wink . . . so I will. . . ."

"It's not your mother, it's me," I told him, "and here's your key ring." I threw it on his chest. "Now I don't want to hear any more about it."

He opened his blue eyes then and stared at me for a rather long time. "You are a dear girl," he finally said, "a sweet lovely girl and to reward you I might even make you my wife."

"No, thank you," said I.

"What's wrong with the notion? Is it my lack of a leg?"

"It's your lack of money," I informed him. "When I marry I'll pick a wealthy man."

"You've decided that already, have you, little girl?" Johnny grinned, still in good humor. "Well you've changed your tune since a while ago then, though I can't say I blame you for it. You're startin to realize it's a hard tough life and the devil take the last in line. Anyway I intend to be rich someday, my dear, and then you may wish you'd been nicer to me."

"I'll always be nice to you, Johnny, as long as you're nice to me."

"That's my girl. We'll be nice to each other then, shall we?"

"All right, Johnny."

And so I spent some time with him there on the settee and just to show you how completely his mood could change from one day—or even one hour—to the next, I believe Johnny was nicer and gentler with me on that afternoon than he had ever been before, or for that matter, ever was again.

We really didn't accomplish much in the romantic way, of course, be-cause he just wasn't in any physical condition for it. We mostly joked and giggled and talked about our past and speculated about our future. For in-stance, Johnny said he wasn't at all concerned about his missing leg any more because he'd been totaling up all the advantages which a one legged man could enjoy, such as the savings on stockings and shoe leather, to say nothing of reduced corn and bunion problems, as well as much less time wasted trimming toe nails. Well we both laughed uproariously over that and then I told him about Edwina's gold pieces and the other things we had discovered and even about Miss Martha's wig, because right then I didn't see any need to keep anything from him.

Then I showed him the little locket, which I had concealed in my bosom. He didn't seem much interested in that—just glanced at it for a moment and then wanted to put it back in its hiding place, but naturally I wouldn't permit anything like that, especially in broad daylight in the parlor. Finally he shoved the locket and the key ring behind the settee cushions and then we just went on talking, and kissing once in a while too, I guess, until it was nearly time for dinner, when we were interrupted by Miss Amelia Dabney, who came in the room and made a very savage remark.

"You are thought to be upstairs readying yourself for dinner, Miss Alice," she said bitterly, "along with all the others who went up some time ago. Whether or not you are planning to come unwashed to table is of ab-solutely no consequence to me. However, I think Corporal McBurney might be interested in knowing that Mattie is about ready to bring his din-ner in here, and she may be a bit surprised to find two people instead of one lying on this rather narrow settee."

"I was only resting a little, Miss," I shouted at her. "And if anyone comes to table with dirty hands more often than you, I certainly don't know who that person could be. Kindly mind your own business, Miss!"

"I always do so, Alice," she said, more cheerfully now that she had made me angry. "One other announcement for Corporal McBurney. Emily and I have finished his crutches. They may not look the kind you'd get in Richmond or New York City, but they're the best we could do with the ma-terials on hand."

"I'm sure they're very nice, Dolly," Johnny told her. "And Alice really was only restin a bit here. She sat down for a moment to chat with me and then she went into a sudden doze like and just toppled over. Where are the crutches, Amelia, dear?"

"You're to get them tonight. We're having what Emily chooses to call a 'Crutch Presentation Ceremony,' which will take place immediately after dinner. Really, Johnny," Amelia went on, "I don't give two figs for your bio-logical affairs, but I should think your companion might have the grace to arise from her extremely unladylike position, especially after comments have been made about it."

"Who are you, who are you?" I yelled after her as she left the room. "Is Amelia Dabney, who carries bugs around in her dress pockets, supposed to be some kind of authority on ladylike behavior!" Oh I was really angry then, you can believe me, especially since I was just about ready to get up from that settee anyway, if the nasty little thing had given me half a chance. And Johnny's attitude didn't make me feel any better about it.

"Oh Lord God," he cried, whooping with laughter. "You girls will be the death of me yet!"

"I don't see anything funny about it at all," I told him as I arose abruptly.

"Look out there now, dammit. . . . You've bumped that leg!"

"Oh, Johnny, I am sorry," I said, even though I wasn't really. "Do you think I injured anything?"

"I don't know. I can tell you it hurts like the old Nick."

"Take a look."

"I can't look. . . ."

"Haven't you ever looked at it yet?"

"No, and I don't intend to until I have a first class wooden one strapped on there."

"That may not be for quite a while yet."

"Maybe not so long. Amelia says she can show me where to get some good stout timber, once I'm on the crutches. Then I'll get started carvin myself the new one."

"How do you avoid looking at your stump when Miss Martha comes in to change the bandages?"

"I close my eyes and keep them closed. And I do the same when Mattie comes in to help me with my private needs, since I'm sure that would be your next question, you shameless thing. Well, I won't need the bandages much longer, according to the old lady, since it's almost healed she says. And I won't need Mattie's services either, thank God, since I can fend for myself once I get the crutches."

"You're feeling better about the whole thing now, I guess."

"Maybe I am. I've been thinkin it's hardly more than my foot and a bit above I've lost. It'll be no trouble to replace that with a piece of good wood, and then in a month or so I'll be hoppin about on it as good as new. Don't you believe that, Alice?"

"Oh sure I do," I said, although I didn't. His leg had been severed very close to the knee and Emily Stevenson had told us a few days earlier that, based on conversations she had had with her father about these matters, she doubted very much if McBurney could ever get a good fit with a wooden leg, because of the lop-sided way the bones had been cut.

Well Johnny would find all that out later. There was certainly no point in my spoiling things for him. I gave him a very sisterly kiss then—because of his condition—and took my leave of him. In all honesty I must say that we had enjoyed a very pleasant hour together, and I was feeling very sorry for him as I went up the stairs. He had been very mean to me only a short while before and, if I had only known it, very soon he would be extremely mean again, but on that afternoon I was willing to forget his nasty side. In fact, I believe that afternoon was the closet I ever came to loving him.

Emily Stevenson

Amelia would have had me go out to the woods and chop down a tree to make the supports for McBurney—or perhaps it was a tree already fallen she wanted me to saw into boards, since she is so loath to destroy any living thing in that forest. However I had neither the time nor the training for that kind of labor, and so I finally convinced my assistant we must make do with the boards and sticks on hand.

Miss Martha had assigned me to the task and commended me to be hasty with it when she saw how rapidly McBurney was beginning to recover. I suppose Amelia would say that making the crutches was her idea, and that may be true, but nevertheless it was I who was put in charge of the project, no doubt due to Miss Martha's feeling that it needed a person of some responsibility at the helm.

And so I began by gathering all the wood I could find and putting it in one great pile and then when it was all assembled I set to studying it. I might say I tried my level best to get some of the other students to help me in this preliminary task but not one of them was willing—with the exception of Amelia and, of course, she was only participating because of her great fondness for McBurney. Anyway some of the others—Marie Deveraux especially—took great pleasure in standing by and making nasty comments as I labored.

"Those crutches may not be the finest ever made," was how one such Marie Deveraux remark began, I remember. "Those crutches may not be the best in the world, but they will certainly be the funniest. I expect a person would have to travel far to find another pair of crutches made out of table legs and bed posts."

"Clear out of here, you little imp," I shouted at her. "These crutches are not being designed for beauty but for service!" And in my wrath I banged my thumb with the hammer and then tore my skirt on a projecting nail when I reached down to find a chunk of wood to hurl at my tormentor.

"Amelia," Marie yelled from a safe distance, "you'd better prepare to make some crutches for Emily. I think she'll need them before she's through with her carpentry work."

"It's best to ignore her," Amelia advised me, and of course I knew that already. If Marie ever finds she is managing to irritate you, she will go without food or rest for a solid week in order to continue it.

Well, as I said, the crutches were no works of art but I did hope they would serve their purpose. Admittedly, I was using the legs of an old dining table as the main upright supports and to the tops of these I had nailed what might have been bed posts and slats, and also some stair dowels which were apparently left over from the building of the Farnsworth house. The crutches may have looked a trifle odd but they also seemed to me to be very sturdy. Anyway, as I told McBurney, soldiers cannot afford to be choosy during times like these.

He agreed, although rather listlessly. I had gone in to measure him for the crutches, and I was trying to accomplish this by stretching a piece of thread from his armpit to the sole of his remaining foot. McBurney didn't cooperate at all but instead, when I lifted the blanket which covered the lower part of him, he shut his eyes tightly and turned to the back of the settee which meant that he was lying on his good leg, thereby making it awfully difficult for me to measure.

He feared to look at his stump, you understand, even though it was still heavily bandaged. I might also add that he was still wearing an old night shirt which had belonged to Robert Farnsworth, and which Mattie had put on him during his period of unconsciousness, and it was therefore not at all improper of me to raise his blanket.

"If you're going to act this way," I told him," you will never be allowed to serve with my father's brigade. A Southern soldier has to learn to bear misfortunes without whining."

"Is there a chance yet of my being taken on there?" he asked, still facing the settee.

I didn't think there was any chance, of course, but I didn't want to discourage him by telling him so. Even were he able to overcome the physical handicap, I had begun to develop serious doubts that he had the courage to be of any use in our Southern cause.

"One thing I can tell you," I said, "is that General Joseph Johnson was wounded twice at Seven Pines, but lived to fight again. General Jubal Early was wounded very badly at Williamsburg two years ago but recovered and took the field again."

Then I also mentioned a few other such incidents which had happened in my father's own brigade. Many of his officers and men had suffered severe wounds, during their three years of service, including the loss of one entire right arm by one brave fellow, and they had all returned to duty just as soon as they were able.

"Godalmighty, wouldn't they even let a fella out of it after he'd donated an arm to the cause," was McBurney's muffled comment.

"Not now," said I. "We need all the experienced help we can get right now. Besides that particular man I mentioned is an officer, Lieutenant Stewart Meadows of Mobile, who had his arm blown off at the shoulder at Sharpsburg, and officers can't be spared right now if they're able to get about at all."

"The more I hear about your Pa's brigade, the more I think a fella'd be wise to think twice before he joined it," said McBurney.

"Anyone who felt that way about it wouldn't be welcome anyway," was my rejoinder.

"Now, now," he said, turning around now and grinning. McBurney was like Marie in that way. It always seemed to put a spark of life in him if he thought he was annoying someone. "I was only foolin a bit, Emily dear, but tell me, can't they ever find replacements for wounded men in your Pa's army?"

"It's very difficult nowadays," I admitted. "My father's own regiment is now less than half the size it was before Gettysburg." And immediately I was sorry I had said that. It was not the sort of information to be entrusted to someone like McBurney. But then I also thought, what difference does it make? Our boys will always compensate in spirit for what they lack in numbers. And McBurney isn't going to leave us in the near future anyway, I thought—because that's the way it seemed then—and when he does go, he isn't going to be eager to return to his army. Also by that time the tide will very likely have turned in our direction.

And so, foolishly, I told him more. It was partly to take his mind off his own troubles, I guess, and partly to show him that we could be completely realistic about our problems, facing them squarely and surmounting them so that we were bound to win in spite of them.

When I was home last Christmas, my Daddy explained the whole situation to me. Since my brothers have been gone my mother is upset by any talk of war, so Daddy really has no one else but me at home to discuss his troubles with and since I was a most willing listener I really learned a lot last Christmas about our military situation.

For example Daddy made me understand how important it was that our armies remain intact and mobile. Even though the Yankees do outnumber us now, they will never defeat us, according to Daddy, if they can't pin us down. And if we can just hold out a while longer, Daddy says, the Yankees will exhaust themselves. Also, it's well known how much dissension there is in the North. Very many of the natives up there are sick and tired of this war which that insane Mister Lincoln forced on them. Even the Yankee troops are becoming disgusted and, well fed and well armed though they may be, hundreds of them are deserting every day. Therefore, says Daddy, all we need to do is hang together, never let them get us into a corner, conserve our strength and wait for just the right moment. Then bang! Up through Maryland and Pennsylvania we'll go again and this time they'll never stop us.

"When does your Pa think this will likely happen?" Johnny asked after I had explained it to him.

"Soon now, very soon. In fact," I said, "Daddy has a plan all worked out for such a venture and he may be presenting it to General Lee very shortly, if he hasn't done so already."

"Will he dig a tunnel from the Potomac to the Hudson or what?"

Well I told him all I knew about my father's plan. It was very imprudent, I realize now, and I don't believe I ever would have gone so far had not Johnny been exhibiting such a sneering and sarcastic attitude, even though at that time there seemed no harm in telling him.

I explained that the success of the plan would depend on General Grant's being kept occupied in front of Richmond while a small striking force led by my father, General Stevenson, would slip in behind them, cross the Potomac quickly—avoiding the enemy strongpoints—and then rush up through Maryland to the Yankee capital where they would proceed to burn it before any force could be organized to stop them. My Daddy's feeling is that the Yankee civilian population would be so demoralized by such a catastrophe that the whole country would just rise up and demand an immediate end to this war which they have started.

And the more I talked the more I told. Maybe for bragging as much as any other reason, I went ahead and reported to McBurney everything my father had told me . . . the route of march he was suggesting, the places where they could safely cross the Rappahannock and the Potomac, even the identities and locations of some reliable people on the way whom my father thought could be relied upon to supply information and possibly even food and shelter for his band. Of course, Daddy didn't tell even me the exact addresses of these people. It was more like . . . a farmer he'd heard about who lived near a Rappahannock ford and had lost two sons to the Yankees at Malvern Hill . . . or a man in Alexandria whose brother the Yankees had hanged for spying. Not exact names and descriptions of those people, you see, but still close enough so that a determined enemy could certainly find them.

Well I must say McBurney listened to it all with little show of enthusiasm. "It's been thought of before," said he when I finished. "I'll bet a bob there ain't an officer in the rebel army above the rank of major who hasn't at one time or another dreamed of makin himself famous by burning Washington."

"My father isn't out for personal glory," I answered him hotly.

"Oh I'm sure not. I wasn't referrin to him, only to the common run of rebel officers. Well your father can burn the whole shebang, from the Potomac to the Hudson, for all o' me. Just tell him to leave one boat in the Bay of New York so's I can get back home, if he doesn't mind."

"The difference between Daddy's plan and the others—if there have been others—is that his is very carefully worked out. He has these contacts I've mentioned, people behind the Union lines who're ready to help him."

"How'd he hear about these people?"

"I don't know. Possibly the information was given him by some disgruntled prisoners he captured—boys like yourself, who may have been very dissatisfied with the state of things in the North."

"You can't always trust fellas like that, you know," Johnny said and looked away from me again. I've been thinking lately that was the most honest statement he made while he was here, and perhaps the only one.

Anyway I left him then, thinking no more at that time of the potentially dangerous news I had disclosed to him. I went back out to the stable with my measurements and continued to work on the crutches, hoping to have them finished by the time he was ready to use them—or rather when Miss Martha was ready to let him risk using them.

And I just about managed to meet that deadline, notwithstanding an ever-increasing number of saw and nail scratches and an uncountable amount of bruised fingers I suffered, many of which were inflicted on me by

Miss Amelia on those occasions when I gave in to her entreaties and let her use the hammer while I held the nail. It is my belief—unprovable unfortunately—that several and perhaps all of her misdirected blows did not happen accidentally. Amelia is too agile a little creature, it seems to me, to ever do anything like that without intention.

At any rate the crutches were finished and brought to Miss Martha for inspection. Miss Martha was rather doubtful about them, I must admit, but I tried to calm her fears.

"I believe they may prove a deal sturdier than they appear, Miss Martha," I said. "Just look here." And I demonstrated their strength by hopping about the room on them, rather awkwardly, of course, since they were too large for me.

"Well I guess I have no objections," Miss Martha finally said, "as long as they satisfy Mister McBurney. I suppose he can always improve them if he likes."

I thought privately that McBurney ought to be very thankful to be getting such a nice gift and went quietly ahead with a little plan I had devised for presenting the crutches to him.

Now I know the event has been labeled The Great Crutch Presentation Ceremony by some people here who chose to mock it, but actually there was very little formal ceremony attached to it. In brief what I did was recruit all the students after dinner for a few moments' instruction—one person in particular whose first name like my own begins with E was a very unwilling participant I can tell you—and then together with our teachers and old Mattie we proceeded to the parlor and stood in formation in front of Corporal McBurney's settee—or rather the others did. I sent the others in advance, you see—Mattie first, and then the students in descending order of their age and then our teachers by rank—while I waited in the hall until they were all in a row and then I entered, bearing the crutches, to a place midway between the group and Corporal McBurney.

There was some childish and uncalled for snickering in the line as I came in and out of the corner of my eye I noted Marie Deveraux, who with Mattie stood at one end, with her right leg drawn back a bit—all ready. I was certain, to throw it out in an attempt to trip me as I went past. Unfortunately for this dirty scheme, however, I halted before I reached her and wheeled around and stood in silence for a moment until I had a reasonable amount of attention—all you could ever get in this place—before beginning to make a few remarks I had prepared.

Well I won't go into those remarks—I can't remember half of them now anyway—except to say that they were on the general subject of patriotism and self-sacrifice, with a few allusions to great military heroes of history, especially those who had been wounded in combat. The whole thing was ruined anyway by the tittering and giggling in the ranks behind me.

"Present crutches," whispered Marie. "Right shoulder crutch—left shoulder crutch!" And she went on with other such annoying and disgusting comments like that. Miss Martha and Miss Harriet did try to shush her but of course their shushing was as much an interruption as Marie's nasty comments.

"I think we had better end the speech, Miss Emily," said Miss Martha before I was scarcely into it, when order became increasingly difficult to maintain. "Give Mister McBurney his crutches and let him try them, if he is willing."

"Oh I'm willing enough, ma'am," McBurney said. He had been sitting there very solemnly watching and listening, with his blanket over his lap. Mattie had helped him dress himself in another shirt and pair of trousers which had belonged to Mister Robert Farnsworth and which Mattie had pressed very neatly, even tucking up the right trousers leg and fastening it with a pin so that it would not dangle loosely when he attempted to walk.

"I thank all you ladies, young and otherwise, for your kindness," he said now as I placed the crutches atop the blanket on his lap. "Maybe I'll give them a try a bit later."

"I'd prefer you'd do it now if you don't mind, while we're here to help you," Miss Martha told him.

"But I don't need any help," he insisted.

"All the same, it would be a comfort to us if you'd try them now, Mister McBurney," said Miss Harriet. "That way we'll know whether the crutches are suitable or not."

"Also," said I, very disappointed at his stubbornness, "it was part of my plan to have you walk down the row in front of us. I was planning to join the others in the line and then you were to pass in front of us and then we would all follow you out to the dining room where Mattie has prepared a little celebration treat for us."

"Yes, for pity's sake, Johnny," snickered Marie, "review the troops here as Emily has planned. Otherwise she'll keep us standing here at attention all night and we never will get to eat any of those delicious corn meal cakes with blackberry jam which dear sweet Mattie has fixed for us."

"You ain't gonna get but one," Mattie retorted, "no matter how much or how often you dear sweet me."

"The cakes couldn't be brought in here, I suppose," McBurney persisted.

"No they couldn't, sir," Miss Martha said firmly. "I will not have crumbs and jam scattered all over my parlor. Now, sir, will you get up and try your crutches . . . or are you afraid to do so?"

"No, ma'am," said he, very pale now. "I'm not afraid, never think that." And he pushed himself erect on his one leg, trying to tuck the blanket in the waist of his trousers.

"You're not going to begin wearing a skirt are you, Johnny?" Alice laughed. "It's not at all becoming."

"Perhaps there are holes in his trousers which he wants to cover," said Marie.

The blanket dropped to the floor anyway when he reached for the crutches. He refused to look down at all at the pinned up trousers leg but stared straight ahead, his forehead beaded and his lips trembling, while Amelia and I set the crutches beneath his arms.

"Now then," I said, stepping back, "off you go, Corporal."

"Forward march, Johnny," yelled Marie. "Show them how the Catholics do it."

Well it was a complete disaster. Whether his fear and uncertainty were the cause of it, or the floor was too highly polished, or the crutches had been tampered with—which I am not really suggesting but only mentioning as a possibility, because I did think the crutches were strong enough if he had managed them properly—whatever the reason, he had no sooner taken more than two or three hesitating steps on his left leg before the crutches went flying and McBurney landed with a terrible thud on the parlor floor.

"Are you hurt, Johnny?" screamed Amelia, rushing to him. Well I suppose we all rushed to him, including Miss Martha who inspected him quickly and, thankfully, found him undamaged, except for his borrowed trousers which were split on the bottom where he had landed. His right leg stump wasn't hurt at all and in fact the bandage wasn't even torn.

But he just sat there, searching all our faces—quite pitiously I thought at first—and then, unbelievable as it seems, he began to weep as though he had lost his last friend.

"You've made a fool of me," he cried. "You came to laugh at me!"

"No, we didn't, dear," Miss Harriet told him. "No one's laughing at you."

"You fixed those miserable old crutches so's they'd break on me!"

"Not at all," I put in, a bit annoyed at that. "That's quite untrue and unfair, Corporal McBurney. In the first place only one crutch is broken and that one might have cracked when you fell on it."

"I didn't fall on it," he shouted tearfully. "Goddamit it snapped when I leaned on it!"

"Please consider your language, Mister McBurney," Miss Martha requested him.

"To hell with my language," he yelled, "and to hell with all of you!" He pushed back on the floor to the settee and then attempted to rise by pulling himself up on it. This was very difficult for him to do so because the settee is fairly high and he was in a rather awkward position, so as a result he became even more angry and tried to hurl himself up, thereby catching the torn part of his trousers in some way and tearing them even more, all the way down the right side, ripping even Miss Martha's carefully tied bandage so that it all came away revealing the bruised and only partly healed stump beneath.

"Oh Jesus, Jesus," he moaned. Apparently it was the first time he had seen it.

"Now, now, dear," said Miss Harriet, weeping herself, "everything will be all right." She went to him again as did Amelia and some others—Edwina and Mattie, I believe, but not me because I was just too exasperated by his entire behavior—and tried to help him up but he wouldn't permit it.

"Get away," he shouted. "Get away from me, all of you! A bunch o'bloody old hags is what you are! Look what you've done to me . . . Jaysus God just look at me!"

And he reached for the crutches and flung them at us, the splintered halves of the broken one and the good one too. It was just a wonder someone wasn't badly hurt with the vicious way he hurled them, but fortunately he didn't aim well and no one was struck.

"Now get away," he shouted again. "I want no more of you, any of you . . . clear out of here!"

"All of us, Johnny?" asked Amelia, somewhat shocked.

"That's what I said . . . all of you!"

"Young ladies," said Miss Martha with most admirable calmness. "Go to your rooms this instant."

So we did and with hardly any hesitation. Amelia and Marie, of course, wanted to hang back a bit to see what sort of terrible punishment Miss Martha was going to levy on McBurney for his outrageous conduct but Miss Harriet hurried them along. Some of the girls were rather dumbfounded at his outburst but I personally was surprised that it hadn't happened sooner, considering what a really uncourageous fellow he was.

I think it's possible he had been lying there on the settee all those past days, pretending that we were all just fooling him and that his leg really wasn't gone. I think maybe that he tried to deceive himself like that for as long as he possibly could—maybe until the very moment he found himself on the floor, staring at that vacant space below his knee.

At any rate I let Miss Harriet lead them out and then fell in as the last in line—acting as rear guard for the party, so to speak, since there seemed no end to what McBurney might do in his maddened condition. From this rear position I could hear Miss Martha say to our still weeping guest, using her most cold and commanding voice, "Sir, this is still my home and I am still in charge of it. Do not think for one moment, sir, that you are dispossessing me from this room. I have sent the young ladies away to spare them your vulgar temper and I will take myself away now for the same reason."

"Hurry along, hurry along, you bald-headed old goat," I thought I heard McBurney shout, or maybe it was some other descriptive word he coupled with goat, such as "bone headed" or "gall headed" since the adjective "bald" would not seem to be of any significance when applied to Miss Martha who has as much hair as anyone here.

Anyway there was a pause and then Miss Martha continued as before and with no change in her voice, "Mister McBurney, I cannot ask you to walk out of here in your present condition, but I can have you taken away from us. In the morning I shall go and inform the first Union soldiers I can find of the presence of a deserter in my house."

A roar of laughter greeted this remark, almost insane laughter, I think you could call it. In the midst of it, Miss Martha, bayonet still and deadly pale, shot out of the parlor holding her skirt in her two fists in front of her, like the prow of some man o' war.

"If you are not otherwise occupied, Miss Emily," she said as she swept past, "I suggest you obey my order."

"I'm coming, Miss Martha," I called to her as she went up the stairs. "I'm only waiting here to see that Marie comes along."

And that was true. Marie Deveraux had dropped out of line and rushed into the dining room to sample the corn cakes with blackberry jam. Finally she did return, nibbling one messy looking cake and carrying two or three others in her other hand.

"Will you kindly step more lively, Miss?" I requested. "You've kept me waiting here and irritated Miss Martha no end."

Marie just winked at me and started up the stairs with her mouth full, dropping crumbs and jam at every step. I was so put out at her contrariness that I just felt I had to rebuke her by grabbing her skirt, pulling her back and taking one and a half of the cakes away from her. I'd've taken them all away had she not struck and kicked at me and spit crumbs in my face in the most unladylike way you can imagine. Then I let her continue up the stairs, yelling savage threats at me—as only Marie can do—while I disposed of the corn cakes by eating them.

Then I went back to the parlor for a last quick glance at McBurney. He was still sitting on the floor leaning back against the settee, not laughing any more but weeping again, this time as though his heart was about to crack in two. I slipped away again before he noticed me and went upstairs to my room.

"No sir," I remember saying to myself, "there is absolutely no place for anyone like Johnny McBurney in my father's brigade. Johnny McBurney may be good for something but I'm convinced that something is not soldiering for our cause."

And so, thinking that Farnsworth School had experienced quite enough excitement for one evening, I retired to my bed, hoping to be able to fall asleep immediately.

However my descent into the grasp of the well-known Morpheus was interrupted before it had scarcely begun. Not ten minutes after I had drawn up my blanket there was a terrible uproar from the vicinity of Miss Martha's room. Miss Martha was shouting and Miss Harriet was screaming and for a moment I thought the Yankees must have arrived in force and were besieging the school.

I went into the hall to investigate and found my fellow students doing the same. Marie was there with the others—which cancelled out my second thought, that she might have been apprehended in a raid on the dining room for more corn cakes and jam. It never entered my head that McBurney might have caused the trouble, since I had left him, seemingly helpless, only moments before.

But that was where I was wrong. It developed later that McBurney was behind this second disturbance of the evening also, although his complicity was not discovered immediately. At first it seemed that Miss Harriet was the guilty party. Miss Martha was very plainly accusing Miss Harriet of having broken into her room and stolen several valuable items. Money, I gathered, was missing and also Miss Martha's key ring and possibly other things.

"I don't see why poor Miss Harriet has to be charged with everything," said Amelia from her doorway, sticking her nose into what was obviously none of her business. "Maybe some robber from outside the house came in here and took the things."

"Maybe nothing much at all is missing," suggested Alice Simms who had come down from her garret room. "Possibly Miss Martha only misplaced those things she's shouting about."

"That's not likely either," said Edwina with her customary nasty smile. "Miss Martha never misplaces anything. She is a paragon for keeping things in their proper place."

"Then that leaves only two possibilities," remarked Marie. "If Miss Harriet didn't take the keys to get at the wine—which I gather Miss Martha is implying—then one of us must be the culprit . . . or else it's dear old Corporal McBurney."

"That's a terrible thing to suggest," said Alice sharply.

"About one of us?" asked Edwina.

"Well it certainly is a thousand times worse than awful to say about Johnny who can't even walk," Amelia shouted.

This started a small private commotion led by the two roommates and they and the others made so much noise in the hall that it caused Miss Martha and Miss Harriet to interrupt their argument in Miss Martha's room and come out to investigate the cause of this new disturbance.

And when Miss Martha learned the cause of it she was very indignant that we young people had been listening to what she said was a very private disagreement. However the mention of McBurney's name did cause her to stop and think about the possibility of his having been involved in the robbery of her room. Apparently she had not considered it before but now I guess she began to realize that it would not have been impossible for the fellow to have dragged himself up the stairs, one leg and all, at a time when her room was unguarded.

Well what happened next convinced Miss Martha and the rest of us that McBurney must have been the culprit. Now would you say that two very loud commotions were more than enough to expect on one evening in what was at one time a fairly fashionable young ladies' school—and even now is not one of the worst such places in the country. Then you may be astounded to learn that we had still another disorder on that evening, and this third one was far louder and more alarming than both of those that had gone before.

It began with a loud crashing noise downstairs, resulting in the immediate end of the controversy upstairs as all students and teachers froze in their tracks. The crashing noise—which seemed to include the sounds of wood splintering and glass shattering—was followed by a terrible banging and thumping and then more crashing.

"Dear Lord," whispered Miss Harriet, "is he smashing all the furniture in the house?"

"He must be breaking all the china and the crystalware too," said Miss Martha, very pale.

"Maybe he fell down again," suggested Amelia nervously, loyal to her hero to the bitter end. "Maybe he fell against a window or something, and possibly even cut himself."

Did anyone whisper "good" in answer to that? I don't remember actually hearing anyone utter the word but I believe I can state that from the expressions around me it seemed evident that one or two people were thinking it. One of the people might have been Edwina Morrow and another, Alice Simms. A third person who didn't seem overly concerned about McBurney's health at that moment was Miss Martha Farnsworth herself.

"It's quite apparent what he's doing now," said that lady as she listened at the top of the stairs. "He's just opened the door to the wine cellar. That door has a peculiar squeak like no other in the house."

"Mattie's down there," I said. "Why doesn't she stop him?"

"Why don't *you* go down and stop him," Marie retorted sarcastically. "Old Mattie knows what's good for her all right. She's not about to fool around with a white man on a rampage. She probably ran out of the kitchen and off to her old place in the quarters as soon as Johnny started acting up."

"In any event it's quite plain now where my keys are, if not my money," said Miss Martha, "although I don't understand how he could have come up here without someone seeing or hearing him."

"Perhaps you dropped the keys downstairs and he found them," Alice suggested.

"No, I did not," replied Miss Martha. "I remember hanging them on a hook in my closet and anyway, even if I had left them downstairs, that wouldn't explain the money which is also missing."

"Was all your money stolen, ma'am?" Edwina inquired.

"No, Miss, but a very substantial part of it was."

"Maybe you've miscounted," persisted Edwina. "Count it again, carefully, and perhaps you'll find it's all there after all."

"If you please, Miss," said Miss Martha, exasperated. "I know what has taken place. My room is in disorder and some jewelry is missing besides the keys and money."

"All the same it doesn't seem to me the kind of stealing a man would do," said Amelia, still defending him. "If Johnny wanted to rob you why wouldn't he take all your money and jewelry and not just some of it?"

"Oh be quiet now," commanded Miss Martha, tilting her ear down the stairs again. "I've had quite enough comments and advice from the lot of you. Go to your rooms, all of you, and remain there."

"But aren't we going to do anything about him?" I asked, quite baffled. "I think we should all go down there together and subdue him and tie him up or something."

"Do you, Miss?" Miss Martha answered. "Perhaps when you are made headmistress of a young ladies' seminary you will find opportunity to risk the minds and bodies of your charges in such activities, but nothing of the sort will take place at this institution. Now at this time I will issue an order that must be obeyed under penalty of my severe displeasure. From henceforth no student in this school is to have any communication or contact with this man as long as he is in the house. And that will not be long, I promise you."

"We are safe enough up here, girls," said Miss Harriet, trembling. "Miss Martha has Father's loaded pistol in her room."

"Miss Martha does not have Father's loaded pistol," her sister snapped. "The pistol is in the library cabinet and the key to that cabinet is among the others on the ring."

"Well maybe Johnny doesn't know that," said Marie. "So all we'll have to do is rush downstairs, smash open the cabinet, take the pistol and capture him."

"We wouldn't even have to do that," Amelia interjected. "I could go down alone and ask him for the keys and if he has them—which I'm not sure of at all—but if he has, I'll bet he'd give them to me."

"Will you people go to your room as you've been instructed," Miss Martha hissed, really annoyed now, though mostly at the younger students I believe.

"Move along, move along," I told them, taking a hand in clearing the hall. "There's nothing to see here. Obey your superiors and vacate this area."

I managed to shove Amelia and Marie back into their rooms without much trouble although the latter little person did aim another kick at me, which did no serious damage fortunately. Edwina and Alice were greater problems because the former refused to move at all at my command and just stood there glaring at me and the second, when I nudged her, clenched her fist and indicated that she was prepared to resist me with extreme violence. However to prevent any further complications, Miss Martha stepped in and shoved all of us along—me included, in order not to seem to be showing any favoritism—and in that manner Alice returned to her garret and Edwina and I went back to our rooms.

I left my door open a trifle in order to be able to hear any student who might attempt to sneak out of her room again. Then it occurred to me I ought to take some precautions in case McBurney decided to invade the upstairs while I was asleep. I was certainly not afraid of him but I realized that my value to the school as a leader of the students would be greatly diminished if I were to become injured or incapacitated as a result of a conflict with McBurney. Therefore I determined to reduce the chances of something like that happening by moving some of my furniture in front of the door. What I did was wedge my door in place with my open Bible and then I shoved my chest of drawers and my two chairs in front of the opening. Then I went to bed.

Well there was no more turmoil on that night, as far as I know. After I had been in bed for a quarter of an hour or so, I heard Miss Martha leave her room again and start down the stairs, whereupon I sat up and called, "Miss Martha, is there anything I can do?" but she evidently didn't hear me. Then a moment later Miss Harriet came out of her room and to my door and said, "Thank you, Miss Emily, but Miss Martha and I can take care of everything." Then she followed her sister down the stairs.

And so I retired under my blanket again, feeling that I had done my duty to the best of my ability. I always try to be in this frame of mind before I relax in slumber. I had volunteered my help, it had not been accepted, and so quite satisfied, I went to sleep.

Harriet Farnsworth

I was not particularly alarmed by Corporal McBurney's first outbursts on that night. I appreciated the young man's feelings about having been badly treated here. I think I would have felt the same had my leg been amputated as quickly, and seemingly recklessly, as Corporal's McBurney's. Even though, in the days since the operation, my sister had just about convinced me that her action was justified, I still believe I would have felt very rebellious had I been in Mister McBurney's shoes. Or in his case, shoe—to make an unfunny joke.

Anyway he did cause another disturbance later that night, frightening the students and causing my sister to return downstairs to investigate. After she had been gone for a few moments, I decided that Mister McBurney could be in such an overly anxious state of mind that she might need help in quieting him. I wasn't thinking of any physical restraint, of course. I'm afraid I'd be the last person in this house to whom such a notion would occur. All I planned to do was offer him a few soothing words which I was sure was the only remedy needed to calm him.

But, unfortunately, he was beyond that kind of placating. When I found him and my sister in that corner of the cellar where my father used to store his small stock of wine, Mister McBurney was sitting on the floor, his back against the open wine cupboard, drinking wine from a broken bottle. There were several other empty bottles with their necks smashed around him on the floor. He was just sitting there, glaring at my sister by the light of her candle, and trying to see how fast he could gulp that good Madeira wine.

As I may have mentioned before, I enjoy a tiny glass of wine myself on occasion. Therefore, I certainly did not object to Mister McBurney's enjoyment of it. What did offend me was the manner and amount of his consumption. At the rate he was going, I was certain the small remaining supply would be completely exhausted before morning.

I had paused in the shadows on the stairs so that neither my sister nor McBurney was aware of my presence. I assumed that he had reached the cellar by lowering himself a step at a time on his haunches, although he had his one good crutch with him and he was holding this like a lance in his free hand, keeping my sister at bay. He was getting very drunk but there were signs of fear in his eyes, too. That is something which should be remembered about McBurney. Although he may have seemed to have the upper hand here for awhile—indeed did have it—he never really lost his fear of my sister.

He finished the bottle now and threw it against the far wall. It didn't miss my sister's cheek by much before crashing behind her, but she wouldn't give him the satisfaction of flinching. It was he who finally lowered his eyes, wiped his lips with the back of his hand and reached behind him in the cupboard for another precious bottle.

"You might at least try to remove the cork," my sister told him in a steady voice.

"No time for that," said he, and he rapped the bottle sharply against the cupboard door, snapping off the neck and splashing half the contents on the floor.

"You're going to cut yourself severely on that glass," Martha told him.

"Ah wouldn't that be the luck, dearie? You're hopin I'll cut my throat, aren't you, old thing? Wouldn't that solve all your problems now? Well, run along to bed now like a nice old sweet and say your prayers and maybe when you come back in the light o' dawn, you'll find me bled to death down here . . . and then you can just sweep me away with the other mess I've made. I think it's the mess that bothers you more than the wine, isn't that right, Miss Martha dearie? Now if it was your sister, it might be the other way around, eh?"

I'm not really sure what he meant by this—assuming that at this point he was capable of any coherent meaning. If it was a criticism of my house-keeping, it was unjustified, since I am no less tidy than my sister.

"I'll ask you again," was the next thing my sister said to McBurney. "How did you obtain my keys?"

"And I'll answer you again, dearie," he smirked. "A little bird brought them to me . . . a little white bird flew in the parlor window with the key ring in his beak. He circled around the room a few times, dropped them in my lap and then flew away."

"Did you go upstairs to my room this afternoon?"

"Maybe. I came downstairs to your wine cellar tonight, didn't I?"

"Then if you admit taking the keys from my room, I assume you will also admit taking the money."

"Money? Is there money missing, too?"

"Don't add poor acting to your list of failings. You know there is two hundred dollars in Federal gold coins missing from my jewel box and a piece of valuable jewelry, too."

"This?" grinned he, taking something from his shirt and revealing it to her.

"Yes, that," she answered not quite so steadily.

I came down another step or two and could see the object now as it caught the light. It was a small gold locket which had belonged to our mother.

"I opened this a while ago," McBurney said, "and saw a picture inside. Is it your sweetheart?"

"It's my brother," Martha told him. "Give me the locket please."

"Not so fast, ma'am," he said, lifting his crutch as she started to approach him. "If I stole the thing from you, why would I want to give it back?"

"Because it's of no value to you. I'll make a bargain with you. You may keep the money and drink as much of the wine as you like . . . providing you return the locket . . . and agree to leave here in the morning."

"Bag and baggage as they say?"

"Whatever possessions you brought with you . . . whatever we've given you . . . you may take when you leave."

"Everything I brought?"

"Yes, of course."

"What about my right leg? Can I take my right leg or must I leave that behind?"

"There's no point in discussing that."

"Maybe for you there isn't, lady." He hurled his still half-filled bottle and this time my sister was splashed with wine as the bottle burst against the wall.

"Not for you either," said Martha, as evenly as she could. "It's over and done."

"The thing is over but not the consequences. They'll be with me and you for the rest of our lives."

"How with me?"

"You'll see, dear lady. You'll find out. But to go back to the first condition. No, I won't give you back your locket—at least for the present I won't. I want to hang on to it for a bit in order to remind myself of what you really are."

"What do you mean by that remark?"

"I think you're an unnatural woman," said McBurney, reaching for another bottle and opening it in his usual fashion. "I think you had unnatural feelings for your brother."

He seemed about to say more, but then changed his mind. Perhaps he was shocked at his own drunken words. My sister was certainly shocked. She seemed as close to fainting as I have ever seen her. Of course, at that point I was not very steady on my feet myself.

"You beast . . ." Martha said finally in a very low voice, the candle trembling in her hand.

"I'm sorry," said McBurney, trying to grin now. "I didn't mean to upset you. It was just the picture in the locket and all."

"That locket belonged to my mother."

"But you had it in your drawer . . . along with all those letters from him. . . ."

"Tell me what you read in those letters."

"You know . . . you know," he said, "all about you two."

He took a long swallow of wine, cutting his lip on the jagged glass and then wiping the wine and blood on his sleeve. He was very intoxicated by this time and I suppose not really responsible for anything he said. I kept wishing Martha would realize that and pay no attention to him. In fact, I was almost tempted to speak out and tell her that, but then I decided she might feel embarrassed at my having overheard McBurney's terrible accusation.

"I demand to know what you read in those letters," Martha told him. "Those letters are the innocent account of my brother's experiences at his University. If you've found something else in them, I demand to know what it is."

"Never mind," he said, grinning wildly now. "I take it all back. I was just jokin is all, just teasin you. Here, you can have your locket."

He tossed it to her. She made no attempt to catch it but let it land at her feet.

"I'd give you back the money, too, if I had it," McBurney said. "Here, I'll give you something else. You want this?"

He fumbled in the darkness beside him and brought up my father's huge military pistol. "You can have this, too," he said, extending it—but whether by the barrel or by the grip, I can't remember now. In fact, I might have closed my eyes, I was so frightened by my first glimpse of it.

"You keep it," my sister said. "You may have need of it."

Now, I think this is what she said, but again I suppose I was not really paying very close attention. Anyway, I do remember her next action very clearly and the words which followed. She raised her foot and brought the heel of her shoe down deliberately on the locket and smashed and ground it into the floor of the cellar.

"You may keep that, too," she said, and holding her candle before her in her right hand, she drew back her skirts with the other and moved without haste toward the stairs and the place where I was hidden.

I know now I should have revealed my presence as soon as I entered the cellar, but having failed to do so, I could not dream of doing it then and embarrassing her. Or for that matter, embarrassing McBurney. I was still in an uncertain mood about him, you see, still somewhat inclined to put his actions down to the understandable anger of a hurt and lonely boy.

Anyway, I hurried up and out of the cellar before Martha reached the bottom of the stairs. I do not think she said anything more to Corporal McBurney on that night.

His parting words to her—or at least the last I heard—were, "Please, ma'am, don't be sore at me. You've treated me first rate here . . . most of the time . . . and I didn't mean to offend you."

When she didn't answer that, his tone grew rougher again and he shouted something which to me was quite unforgivable, even considering his state of intoxication. What he called out was, "All right, you old biddy, go along! But be careful you don't trip and lose your hair!"

I shall have to explain this remark, although I have always tried to be discreet about the matter, particularly as far as the students here are concerned. The plain fact is Martha lost all her hair as a result of a fever many years ago and she has worn artificial hair ever since.

It was the great tragedy of my sister's life. I think she was perhaps twenty at the time it happened and it probably contributed more than a little to her withdrawal from society. Pursuing that line I suppose you could say it was the primary cause of her spinsterhood, and similarly by extension, the main reason, too, for mine. However, all that would require a long time to explain properly and I suppose it is not really relevant to the matter at hand.

Anyway, when Martha had recovered from her fever, Father took her, turbaned and veiled, to a private and secluded place in Richmond—the establishment of a famous and skillful French wigmaker—and when they returned several weeks later, Martha was wearing the hair which can be observed on her now.

I believe she brought one or two spare wigs with her, although we have never discussed it. In fact, I have never spoken to her about the matter at all. Robert and I were not even here during the summer of her illness, having been sent away to cousins in Roanoke in order to avoid contagion. When we came home that Christmas, Father took us aside and warned us never to mention Martha's hair.

Even now sometimes it escapes me that her hair is not as real as mine. It is certainly a very cleverly made wig and without doubt more convenient than natural hair like mine which must be brushed and otherwise attended to constantly if the gloss is to be retained. Although I suppose wigs need a certain amount of attention, too—cleaning, mending and the like—which I presume Martha takes care of in the privacy of her room.

Well how McBurney found out about my sister's unfortunate condition I did not know, but I did hope that when his head cleared in the morning, he would be gentleman enough to keep the information to himself. Indeed, I resolved to pledge him to silence at the first opportunity, telling him, perhaps, that I had noticed him staring at my sister and surmised that he had detected her secret.

I do have my troubles with Martha, as must be obvious to everyone, and I do get very annoyed with her sometimes, but in this matter she has my complete sympathy and I would never be heartless enough to use such information against her, even in my moments of greatest rage at her.

As my father said that day to Robert and me, "A lady's appearance is her only weapon and we must never reveal that we know this weapon has no edge." Of course, I know now that my sister has other swords at her disposal, but Father's point was valid enough.

At any rate I was beginning to agree with Martha that McBurney could not stay here much longer. However, the problem I was trying to solve on that night was how to talk her into letting him stay just a few more days until his leg was completely healed and he could move about fairly well on his crutches. I was hoping that Martha would not set out at once to inform his army about him, as she had declared she would do. I was trusting that when her temper had cooled, her charitable nature would take over, persuading her to grant McBurney a few days' grace.

And in the morning it seemed at first that she must have decided to do just that. When the young ladies and I came downstairs—I might add that none of the students were tardy on that morning, nor were they ever on any morning after a McBurney episode, which is one thing, at least, that might be credited in McBurney's favor—we found my sister at the dining room table, drinking a cup of Mattie's excellent acorn coffee and giving no outward evidence that she had spent anything but a restful night.

I had peered into the living room for a moment prior to this, but saw no sign of McBurney. The room was a shambles of overturned and broken furniture, some of which—I told myself—could have been caused accidentally by his stumbling around after consuming all that wine. But then, on second glance, some of the chairs and one small table looked as though they had been picked up and hurled some distance from their customary positions. The nicks and scratches are still visible on that furniture, all the result of Mister McBurney's activities that night.

As I say, I peered in but did not enter and, obeying my sister's order that we must all avoid having contact with the young man, I refused to allow any of the girls to enter. Young Marie and Amelia were very eager to do so, of course, even though I had reported he was nowhere in sight.

"Possibly he's behind the corner cupboard," Miss Marie suggested, "or curled up between the harpsichord and the wall."

"There isn't enough space there," said Miss Amelia, "but he might be behind the curtains. Although I don't think he'd ever hide from me that way."

"It is of no consequence to any of you where he is," I informed them, "since you are not permitted any conversation with him." And I hurried them all along to the dining room, where as I mentioned, my sister was having her morning coffee.

"The young ladies may proceed to their chores in the garden," Martha announced. "There is no reason to interrupt our routine."

"Where is Mister McBurney, sister?" I inquired.

"I have no idea," she said without change of expression.

"He isn't in the parlor," said I.

"Then he must be elsewhere, mustn't he?"

"Perhaps he is still in the cellar."

"What do you mean 'still'?"

"Well, he was there last night, wasn't he?"

"Was he?"

"Well, we heard him making a loud noise, didn't we, and then you stated that you believed he had gone to the cellar." I was in a most awkward position, since I didn't want to admit that I had seen both of them down there.

"Was he in the cellar when you came down last night, Martha?" I ventured now.

"How do you know I came down?"

"I heard you, sister. Was it wrong of me to hear you?"

"I really don't care to continue this discussion," she said, and looked away.

Well, I kept my peace for the moment. The girls had gone to the garden as ordered and I joined Martha at the table where we sat in silence for some moments. After awhile Mattie brought me a cup of acorn coffee and I just remained there quietly, provoking no quarrels, just sipping the coffee.

Mattie was very subdued on that morning, too, and of course she had good reason to be. She had left the house at the first sign of trouble from McBurney and I assumed she'd spent the night in her old cabin in the quarters instead of on her cot in the kitchen. She still keeps a bed in the old place to which she repairs whenever she's in trouble with my sister. Anyway, I expected she was ready to plead ignorance of the whole disturbance on the previous night.

"Mattie, do you happen to know anything of Mister McBurney's whereabouts?" I inquired of her.

She said nothing, but looked more frightened than before.

"Where is Mister McBurney, Mattie?" I asked more sternly.

She still made no answer, but looked back over her shoulder at the kitchen doorway. I followed her glance and there he was, resting on his two homemade crutches and smiling shyly. He was neatly shaven, too, and his long and rather ragged hair was plastered down with water.

"Good morning, ladies," he said. "How are you both this fine summer morning?"

"I'm well enough," said I. "And you?"

"Very well, thank you," said he. "Do you see here now how grand I can get about on these fence posts?" He demonstrated by swinging himself a bit farther into the room.

"You are doing excellently," I told him. I was not prepared to forgive him entirely at that moment, of course, but I saw no harm in being civil to him.

"I got up early this morning," he reported in his best small boy manner, "and went out to the barn and repaired the one crutch that was broken, and then made a few small alterations in the other. There wasn't a great lot that needed to be fixed, you know. Miss Emily did a fine job in making them. It was very nice of her and all of you."

He glanced sideways at Martha as he said this, but she ignored him and continued drinking her coffee.

"Ladies, I want to say I'm sorry about last night," he went on. "I know apologies aren't enough to cover all of it and I don't expect them to, but if you'd only try to think of it as a very low point in my life—which is over now, thank God—and from now on I'm ready to accept whatever fortunes or misfortunes each day brings without complaining. If you could only manage to look at the whole thing that way, I'd be eternally grateful."

There was still no reply from my sister, not even an acknowledgment of his presence.

Well, I decided suddenly to follow the dictates of my feelings and so I said firmly, "I'm willing to accept your explanation and apology."

"Oh, God bless you, Miss Harriet," he said, "thank you very much, ma'am." He and I both looked at Martha now but she kept her gaze directed at the opposite wall.

"Now if you'll just give me another couple of days to get used to these sticks," he continued, "I'll be on my way up the road and be no more trouble to you."

"That seems a reasonable request," I told him, "although in fairness I must admit that most of the time you have been of very little trouble to us. Won't you agree with that, Martha?"

But now she refused to answer me as well as him.

"It's very nice of you to take that attitude ma'am," McBurney remarked. "A lot wouldn't," flicking his eyes toward his foe. "Anyway, I know I've been a great bother to all here, yourselves and the young ones included. I must apologize to all of them, too. I've stayed out of their way so far this morning . . . thinking to pay my respects to you ladies first . . . but now, with your permission, I'll just skip outside and see the girls."

"You don't have that permission," said my sister evenly, still staring at the wall. "I have instructed the young ladies to have no communication with you."

He paused and watched her for a moment before replying. "All right, ma'am, if that's the way it has to be. Perhaps you'll pass my apologies on to them."

"I will give them no messages from you on any subject."

"All right, ma'am," he said, smiling ruefully. "Have it your way."

"Furthermore, my sister has been disregarding my instructions. I intended that she be included in my order. From now on she will have no more to say to you."

"Anything to keep you happy, ma'am," said he grimly. "Even if she speaks to me then, I'll try not to listen."

"Also," said Martha, "I want you out of here by noon today. It is now eight o'clock. That gives you four hours in which to practice on your crutches."

"And if I don't leave by noon?"

"Then I shall set out and bring back the first men I can find—Yankee soldiers or Confederates. I imagine either side can be persuaded to shoot you on one charge or another."

"Oh I don't doubt that. They'll believe whatever you tell them about me, you being a lady and all. Well maybe I hadn't oughta waste as much as four hours on the crutch practice. Maybe I oughta cut the practice to an hour or two, so's I could get a good head start down the road ahead of you in your pony cart. Now then will you permit me a bite o' breakfast to give me the strength to begin this concentrated practice?"

"Mattie will fix you something in the kitchen," said Martha.

"I'd prefer it in here," he said. He was smiling again but there was no humor in it. "I'd love to be served in here in the company of you fine ladies."

"And I say you'll have it in the kitchen or you'll have nothing."

"Oh Miss Martha," he said in a sad voice but with the same expression. "That's not very hospitable . . . to treat a poor lad like that on the last morning of his stay."

"I have no more to say to you, Mister McBurney," my sister said, staring at the wall again as she lifted her cup of acorn coffee.

At that moment, still smiling rigidly, he tossed his right crutch in the air and caught it by the lower end. Then he raised the crutch high and swung it down with all his might, smashing the Limoges china cup in her hand and spattering the coffee all over her dress and the tablecloth.

"There, ma'am," he said softly. "Do you still have nothing to say to me? Or do you need another little tap to loosen your tongue. Now, on second thought, maybe I will go out to the kitchen and eat with the darky. Come to think of it, maybe I'd rather be in her company than yours. Of course, Miss Harriet, I'm not including you in this. You and I are still friends."

He swung around on his crutches and moved toward the kitchen door. Then when he reached the door, he paused and turned to us again. "Just one more thing," he said. "I won't be leaving here at noon today. In fact I won't be leaving at all until I'm ready to go. And I can't say right now just when that will be. It might not be for quite a spell yet." And he gave us that same humorless smile again, bowed slightly and entered the kitchen.

Mattie, who had been standing to one side—petrified at his outburst—came forward now with a napkin and shakingly began to mop the table. "Miss Martha, what you want me to do 'bout him?" she quavered.

"Give him his breakfast," my sister replied, "and bring me another cup of coffee." She gave Mattie the handle of the broken cup which she was still holding in her fingers.

"Pretty soon we're all gonna be livin in the barn and eatin outa the same one pot, if that boy is gonna be allowed to keep breakin up this house," Mattie mumbled as she went off.

Well, I just had to marvel at my sister's calmness. I am frightened half to death of any violence, particularly when it occurs unexpectedly, but I think the whole ceiling could collapse on the dining room table and it would not ruffle my sister's breakfast composure—unless, of course, she wanted to appear disturbed. I have never seen another person so able to control her emotions as my sister, which might lead a stranger to think she is totally without feelings, but of course that is not at all the case. At this particular time, in fact, she was very likely raging inside but she refused to betray it by more than a slight trembling of her hand on the table and a bit tighter than usual compression of her lips.

"That boy is not well," I said, when I could manage to say anything. "A temper like that is far from normal."

"You think he is insane?" asked Martha. "I don't agree. He is as responsible for his actions as any of us. He will not find refuge in that excuse."

"Will you go out and look for soldiers now as you said you would?" I wanted to know.

"Not just yet. I'd be afraid to leave all of you alone with him. He probably has Father's pistol, and all of the knives in the house."

I knew perfectly well about Father's pistol, of course, having seen it the night before, but I didn't mention that to Martha.

What I did say was, "I don't really think he'll bother us, if we leave him alone."

"How would you describe his actions just now?" Martha demanded. "Do you mean you wouldn't consider swinging a club at my fingers as an act intended to bother us? And even if he did leave us in peace if we ignored him, how long do you think we could continue that policy? Can we operate a safe and successful school here with that fellow in our midst?"

"No, I suppose not, sister," I said. "And so what will you do then?"

"I don't know. I need to think about it . . . I need to think a lot about it."

"Perhaps if we wait a few more days another squad of our soldiers will come along like the group which stopped here a few weeks ago."

"There's small likelihood of that. According to Mister Potter, there are no more of our soldiers in this vicinity. He says he hasn't even seen any cavalry for more than a week."

"You've never told Mister Potter about McBurney, have you, sister?"

"No, and I regret it now. If anyone outside the place knew about his presence here, an investigation might be started, particularly if no word was received from us for several days."

"My goodness," I exclaimed, "things may not be that bad, Martha. We're not trapped inside this place yet, are we? McBurney has merely said that he isn't leaving, he hasn't said he'll try to prevent any of us from going out."

"But his defiance of me came after I had threatened to send for help, didn't it? That would seem to prove, wouldn't it, that he doesn't plan to let me carry out my threat."

"Well, sister," said I, "you'll never know until you try it. Put on your going-to-store dress and I'll hitch Dolly to the cart, and then we'll both drive down to the end of the lane and just see if he'll try to stop us."

"No," she said, "I won't today."

"Then I'll stay here and reason with him while you're gone. I'll be friendly and reasonable with him—I'm not afraid—and I'll bet he won't pay any attention at all to your leaving."

And I really wasn't afraid of him then. In fact, even though I deplored his terrible conduct, my intention then—had I been able to get Martha out of the house—was to persuade him to leave immediately. I would have tried to send him back into the woods the way he came, so that he could avoid whatever soldiers Martha might send after him. Then I thought, when the pursuit was over, Mister McBurney could make his own way back to the Union lines. But that solution was not to be.

"No," declared Martha, "I won't take a chance on letting you stay here alone with the girls, not now anyway."

"I don't really think he'd harm any of us, Martha."

"Perhaps not, but it's too much of a risk. I know you too well, Harriet.

You wouldn't stand up to him in a critical situation. You'd likely shut yourself in your room with one of your headaches if he got violent, and then the Lord only knows what might happen."

"Please, Martha . . . you could trust me in this."

"I said 'no,'" my sister half shouted, and then after a moment added, "Perhaps you'd like to leave right now and look for help yourself. If you'd like to do that, it's agreeable to me. I'm sure you could get into the cart, give Dolly a few slaps with the reins and be off down the road before McBurney could fire a shot at you. I don't think Father's pistol was ever a very accurate weapon anyway, not at any distance. Now, would you like to go for assistance, Harriet? You have my permission to do so."

Of course she knew I wouldn't go. She knew I was opposed—at that time anyway—to the whole idea of denouncing him to either his military people or our own. But naturally Martha didn't choose to interpret my refusal that way. She chose to see it only as another indication of my weak character.

"I really think everything will be all right, Martha," I said, "if we just remain calm and try to reason with him."

"You're a fool," my dear sister informed me, "and you become a greater fool with every passing day."

"Perhaps you're right, Martha," I answered. "I know sometimes it's much easier to be foolish than to be wise. As long as you insist, I'm quite willing now to relinquish all responsibility in this matter."

"You've never had any responsibility to relinquish."

"Just as you say, Martha. Perhaps it is a mark of your courage that you're deciding now to wait and do nothing. Perhaps the situation will improve if you just sit a while and think about it."

"Be quiet, be quiet!" she screamed, and brought her closed hand down with such force that she smashed the second Limoges cup which Mattie had just brought her.

"Yes, sister," I replied very patiently. "As always I will do whatever you say."

And in all truthfulness, I was hoping that the situation would get better, if we did nothing to worsen it. If only McBurney and my sister could learn to keep their tempers in check, I thought, we might be able to return to a semblance of harmony once again. I didn't think at that time that McBurney was an evil man, I really didn't. I thought he was evil tempered and impulsive, but if we were all to merit damnation for such personality defects, my sister would have been consigned to the flames long ago.

Anyway after a moment I did begin to feel a bit sorry for the burden she seemed obliged to bear alone. "Sister, I hope you didn't think I was siding with him against you," I told her. "I don't want you to get that impression from his last remark about he and I being fast friends."

"What he thinks of you is not important," she said. "It's what you think of him."

"Well naturally I couldn't think very highly of him after what he just did."

"And he is capable of much worse than that," she said in a somewhat warmer tone. "You will see, sister, you will see."

And she was right. That was the beginning of what someone has described as our "Reign of Terror." I don't remember who put that name on it—possibly Emily or Edwina or maybe it was Martha herself, although I am certain none of those people was as terror-stricken as I was during the period. The odd thing, as Martha has since remarked, was that strangers coming into the house at that time might have noticed nothing out of the ordinary at all in McBurney's conduct—or perhaps even in the conduct of the rest of us, at least in public and particularly during the first few days after he declared war on us.

His first thrust in that war was the decision to, in all possible ways, circumvent my sister's order about the students associating with him. He began by seeking out the students and engaging them in conversation at every opportunity and, although some of them did try at first to avoid him—albeit not very strenuously—it soon proved impossible in the fairly close confines of this place.

At first we conducted our classes as usual and he did not try to interrupt them. I think he spent most of that first day rebuilding and improving his crutches, although later in the morning, between classes, I heard him laughing and joking with students in the kitchen garden. One time it was with Alice and later with Marie and Amelia. In the afternoon Martha called the girls together and reprimanded them, but I'm sure even she had begun to realize by then that her words were wasted. It is just impossible to legislate against the natural inclinations—the friendliness and curiosity—of young girls. If McBurney insisted on joking with them, they would laugh and if he teased them, they would retort and no law of Martha's was going to prevent it.

McBurney's second tactical maneuver was making up his mind on that same day that from henceforth he was going to dine with us and again it seemed we were powerless to prevent it. He waited until everyone else was seated that evening and then swung himself into the dining room on his crutches, freshly scrubbed and combed as he had been in the morning, pulled up a chair and sat down, smiling and nodding cheerfully at us all. If you are going to continue having your meals in a group, he seemed to be saying, you will have to include me because there is no way you can keep me out.

Martha realized this as quickly as the rest of us, but naturally she was not going to admit it, especially in front of him. Likewise she was not going to give him another opportunity to defy her in the presence of the students. Therefore when he asked Mattie—politely enough—for a table setting, Martha lowered her gaze to her own plate and refused to look at Mattie who had turned to her for a decision.

"Yes, you may serve him, Mattie," I said finally. It seemed to me that if the situation was hopeless we might as well accept it as gracefully as we could, although I half expected my sister to leap up in a violent rage. But she didn't. She just devoted all her attention to her food and took no part in any of the conversation which followed.

Well McBurney had very little to say on that evening. As I have mentioned, he was then, and, in general company, continued to be extremely courteous with us—perhaps just a trifle overly, mockingly so. Anyway he didn't press his advantage very heavily on that evening and the students, thankfully, did not respond to any great degree to his casual overtures about the pleasantness of the weather (it had rained intermittently on that day) or the deliciousness of the meal (Mattie had burned the biscuits, as I remember, on that evening).

But from that time on he made little attempt to play the gentleman in his individual and private dealings with us. I have very good and personal evidence of this change in his conduct which I will mention in a moment, and there are other people here—students and adults—who can offer similar testimony. I'm not even referring now to the incident which I have just described as happening in the wine cellar—when he said those drunken, nasty things to my sister. That sort of conduct might possibly be excused because of his condition, but as you will soon realize, he said and did plenty of other brutal things when he was stone cold sober.

Also he later on one or two occasions did state publicly that he would not permit any of us to leave the boundaries of the school. He said nothing like that on the first day of his opposition to us, I will admit, but he definitely did say it later. On one occasion I think Alice and Emily were present and on another Emily and Marie.

Now as to whether he actually threatened anyone with bodily harm on those occasions, I cannot recall right now. If such threats were uttered they were undoubtedly reported at the little investigation we conducted here a fortnight ago and they will be found noted in the record which I kept of those proceedings. Anyway I am certain that verbal threats of violence were made at some time if not at those exact times.

Also on two occasions when I was present he made an unmistakable silent threat by exhibiting, if not actually flourishing, my father's pistol. One time he did this at the dinner table and the second time it occurred during a French language class which I was conducting.

On the first occasion he entered the dining room carrying the pistol at his waist and then made a pretense at apology, explaining that he had been cleaning the weapon on the bench in the rose arbor and hadn't wanted to leave the gun out there for fear the evening dew might make it rusty. "Or where one of your enemies might find it," remarked Marie Deveraux slyly, at which he only grinned and made no further comment.

On the second occasion which was a day or so later, he passed by the library door holding the pistol in his right hand along with his crutch. He paused there and shouted, "Oui, oui, my pretty mademoiselles . . . keep studyin them parley vous, but don't forget the poor downtrodden Irish." Then he added something about having finished cleaning the pistol which I did not hear in its entirety because I closed the library door.

Now perhaps it may be said that on both these occasions he was carrying the pistol as a joke and meant no harm by it, and perhaps this is so. I was always one of McBurney's staunchest defenders and I am ready to believe that he might have been teasing us at those times. Again it may be stated that the pistol was not loaded either time, or that he was drunk both times. Again, both of these statements may be true. However neither of these defenses can mitigate the shock and fear which was felt by all present during these exhibitions. No such defenses can excuse the daily disruption and disorganization of our lives at this school, caused either by the incidents themselves or the apprehension that more serious incidents might occur at any time.

In any case, McBurney continued to drink very heavily and although I did at first feel some sympathy toward him in this regard, after a while my patience began to wear thin. At first I thought the wine supply would soon be exhausted and, although that irritated me, at least I hoped it would lessen the McBurney problem and perhaps solve it altogether. If his intransigence was caused by the wine, perhaps it would disappear with the last bottle. As it turned out, however, there was either more wine downstairs than I had known about or else McBurney was a very inexperienced drinker.

But now I will come to my personal difficulties with Mister McBurney which led to my losing all of my sympathy for him.

The first difficulties occurred three or four days after his initial defiance of Martha. During that time she had done nothing to try to enforce her authority, but continued to tell me privately that she was still afraid to leave us alone with him for the length of time it would take her to find help outside. For my part, I was still inclined to minimize our danger as I tried to assure her I felt quite capable of coping with him. My courage, however, was soon to be put to the test and my feelings about our guest were soon to change very radically.

Well on the afternoon of this incident I was alone in my bedroom on the second floor. Martha was conducting her class in the history of England in the library—or perhaps she was in the parlor, since that is where that class is customarily convened and with McBurney wandering all over the house anyway we had returned many of the classes to their regular locations. Anyway I was lying on my bed, having retired there with a slight headache, when I heard the measured thump of his crutches as he lifted himself slowly up the stairs. I sat up, realizing instantly who was coming and where he was coming, since I was the only person upstairs. My heart just froze in my breast as I sat there waiting for him to reach my door.

At his first knock I couldn't bring myself to answer. He knocked again and called softly, "Miss Harriet, are you in there? May I speak with you for one moment, ma'am?"

His tone was as gentle as it had always been with me. It seemed an appeal and not a demand, I thought, and in any case the rest of the household was surely within immediate call. And so I forced myself to arise and walk to the door. I had neglected to bolt it when I entered which was another thing impelling me to action.

"What do you want?" I asked as steadily as I could.

"It's just a small private matter, Miss Harriet," he whispered against his side of the door. "Won't you listen to me? You're the only one can help me." He paused and then added, "You're the only friend I have here, Miss Harriet."

I couldn't accept that, of course—that I was his only friend, or for that matter, that I was his friend at all—but at any rate it didn't seem the statement of a person bent on violence and so I opened the door an inch or two.

"This is my bedroom," I stated.

"Yes ma'am," said he, "I realize that. But you have a sitting room in there too, don't you?"

"That is adjoining," I told him. "You may come to the next door."

I crossed to my sitting room, opened that door and waited for him to proceed down the hall. When he arrived on his crutches I stood aside and permitted him to enter.

"Thank you, Miss Harriet," he said smiling. "I knew I could count on you."

"I'm not sure that's so," I replied. "It depends on what you want of me."

"Just your good will, ma'am, that's all," he said. "Not that you wouldn't prob'ly give me that without my askin."

He paused, apparently waiting for me to sit down but I was reluctant to oblige him since I was hoping to keep the interview as short as possible.

"The entire world has my good will," I told him. "I feel no hatred—or even strong dislike—for any creature, even those who are supposedly my enemies. Though I will admit I lack the courage to make that statement in every company."

"Oh you have plenty of courage, ma'am," he said. "You've got a good strong heart, I'm sure, inside that delicate little body."

"If you don't mind," I said, "I'd rather not discuss my physical qualities—or my spiritual either, for that matter."

"Oh I wasn't intendin to discuss them," he smiled, "only statin them is all. What I mean is I think you've got a good strong will inside you that lets you carry out anything you set your heart to do. Some people might be deceived by the timid look of you, but not me. I know you for what you are, Miss Harriet, and I admire you for it. Help me, Miss Harriet."

"Help you to do what?"

"To stay here. That's all. I'd like to stay here for a while."

"You seem to be doing that without anyone's help."

"But I know I can't keep on like this for very long. Without the permission of her royal highness—no offense, intended, ma'am—I can't stay on here much longer. I don't mind admitting that to you, Miss Harriet. I was never one to stay any place where I wasn't wanted. Anyway all I want from you, ma'am, is to put in a good word or two for me with your sister so's she'll change her mind about me. I'm really not a bad fella at heart you know, Miss Harriet."

"I'm sure that's true," I answered, "and I'm equally sure my sister knows that too, but none the less she's angry with you and I'm afraid she won't be quick to forgive you."

"But maybe if you asked her. If you kept after her you maybe could convince her that I was truly sorry and that I never intended her or any of you any harm. Then maybe things here could go back to the way they were before. I could be of great use to you around here, you know. I could more than pay for what I eat by the work I'd be doin around the place. I've got two good arms and a strong back and I'm learnin to get around very well now on these two old pegs. I'm very quick to learn anything I put my mind to, Miss Harriet. All you need to do is tell me once or show me and then you can forget about it, whatever it is—choppin wood or trimmin hedges or plantin corn or paintin fences—anything like that I can do, anything at all. You want a loose board nailed down or a clock repaired or a well dug? I can handle all them jobs for you. Now I won't say I'd want to stay on here forever—just a year or so, maybe, and then we could take another look at the situation and see how well it had turned out, if I had done everything expected of me, if I had paid my way. Maybe just till the war was over I could stay and then we could examine the thing again, how does that strike you, Miss Harriet? Will you help me, Miss Harriet, will you ask her to let me stay?"

"She seems to be doing that."

"I mean I'd like for her to say to me that I'm welcome. I'd like her to be friendly to me again and talk to me and let the girls talk to me. Would you ask her if she'd do that, ma'am?"

"I'm afraid she won't listen to any such request, from me or anyone else."

"If you told her it's what you want . . . that you'd like me to stay."

"I'm not sure that would be true, at least not any more," I told him steadily.

"Ah Miss Harriet," he said, putting on a very shocked expression. "You can't mean that. I've been countin on you. You're the one I was sure would always stand by me."

"Whatever made you think that?"

"Why because we're so much alike, I guess. You said that yourself one time."

"Did I? When did I say that?"

"Well maybe it was I that said it, but I'm certain you agreed. We're alike because we like the same things, we decided, don't you remember . . . good poems and fine wine and all kinds of nice things like that."

"Whoever told you I had a liking for wine, Mister McBurney?"

"Why you did . . . didn't you?"

"If I did, I must have been temporarily out of my senses. It's hardly something that a lady would say, now is it—that she had a craving for wine."

"Oh come on now, Miss Harriet," said my visitor. "That isn't what I meant at all. I only meant that you appreciated good wine, that you had a knack of knowin the good stuff from the bad."

"And I suppose I have become an expert by consuming a lot of it?"

"No, no. . . ."

"You protest too feebly, Mister McBurney. Now what about this other interest you say we share. Have you such a passion for poetry, Mister McBurney?"

"Oh, yes, I told you that before . . . Shakespeare and all that."

"That's right, I remember now. You recited sonnet number one hundred sixteen and you told me that you had read the works of Shakespeare many times when you were a boy. Then one evening at dinner you told us the story of Macbeth and very amusingly too."

"Thank you, Miss Harriet. It's one of my favorites."

"And what's another, Mister McBurney?"

"Another what, ma'am?"

"You used the plural. What's another play of Shakespeare's that you like?"

"Oh I like them all I guess. It's hard to choose sometimes, don't you know?"

"Name just one other than Macbeth."

"Let's see now . . . there's so many of them. . . ."

"Volpone, perhaps . . . or Doctor Faustus?"

"Yes, those are good ones."

"The first was written by Ben Johnson and the second by Christopher Marlowe. Well if you can't name another Shakespeare play, perhaps you can recite another sonnet for me."

"It's only the one that sticks in my memory."

"Then recite that one again."

"Let's see now . . . how does it go?"

"Those lines that I have writ before do lie . . . even those that said I could not love you dearer."

"That's it."

"Yet then my judgment knew no reason why my most full flame should afterwards burn clearer."

"Keep it up, ma'am, you're doin fine."

"Thank you. Of course that's sonnet one hundred fifteen and not sixteen. I'm afraid you're a charlatan, Mister McBurney. I think you came upon a copy of the works of Shakespeare in our parlor—I've been told by one of the students that it was missing from the library shelf for a time—and I think you read Macbeth and memorized the one sonnet and retained it for a day or two and now you've forgotten it."

"But why would I want to do a thing like that, Miss Harriet?"

"You tell me, Mister McBurney. You're the only one who knows. I might guess it was to portray yourself in a way which you thought might be attractive to us, particularly to me."

"Why particularly to you, ma'am?" He just stood there, smiling, not at all abashed. In fact it was I who now began to grow embarrassed.

"Well perhaps you weren't trying to win me over then," I said, "any more than you were trying to win the others."

"Ah God, to tell you the truth I was, Miss Harriet. The whole thing was done specially for you. You were quite right, ma'am. Before I landed in your parlor, I'da prob'ly told you Shakespeare was a nervous Indian if you'd've asked me to identify the gentleman. The fact that he was English would be enough to bar him from bein read at Irish firesides and besides we got better poets of our own. But anyway I did try to make you think I had some learning. I found the book and I read that play and several of the poems and I picked out the one and studied it. Because I did so want you to like me."

"I'd be much more apt to like you if you hadn't tried to deceive me," I informed him.

"I realize that now," he said solemnly, "and I swear I'll never do anything like that again. In fact, I'll read all those plays and poems of Shakespeare's now and all the other good books you've got in the house besides. Just give me a month or two at it and you'll see what a polished fella I'll become. Maybe you could even spare an hour or so now and then to give me a bit o' help on the side, just so's I know the books to study the hardest, don't you see. I can memorize anything at all, o' course, but it's true I don't always understand it. That's where you could help me most, by explainin it all to me. Oh I'll be your prize pupil, Miss Harriet. You'll be awful proud of me."

"Why is it so important to you that I like you and be proud of you?" I asked.

"Because I have a great affection for you. I'm in love with you is the way I suppose I ought to put it."

He stared at me unblinking as he said this, without any trace of hesitancy and as matter of factly as though he were discussing the weather or the condition of the garden. Needless to say, my reaction was not as calm as his statement.

"I think you had better go back downstairs now, Mister McBurney," were the first words I could manage.

"Have I offended you?" he wanted to know.

"You've disturbed me greatly," I said.

"Oh that's not so bad then," said he with great confidence. "It was to be expected that you'd be shocked a bit at the news, since I've been around here all this time and never mentioned it before. I don't mind you feelin a bit nervous about it, as long as you're not insulted."

"I'm not insulted," I said, "but please go."

"You wouldn't be feelin the same way about me, I suppose. Though I suppose you wouldn't want to admit it if you did—on such short notice and all."

"Mister McBurney," said I more heatedly, "I happen to be very close to a generation older than you are."

"You don't look it at all," he persisted. "And that don't matter anyway. You're as young in heart as any of your girls here and a lot more attractive than the whole pack of them."

"Mister McBurney," I said, close to anger now, "I simply cannot continue this conversation."

"It's because of the side I been on maybe that you don't want to declare yourself, is that it, ma'am? Because it might be thought you were consortin with the enemy. You're a bit nervous, maybe, about revealin your true feelings right now."

"Mister McBurney, if you please," I half shouted.

He grinned now. "That's another good reason for me to wait around here 'til the war is over. Then we can bring the whole thing out into the open, without any worry about the social consequences, eh?"

"Why do you persist in this, Mister McBurney?" I cried. "I have never said. . . ."

"You've never said nothin, ma'am. I'd never tell a soul you've said anything at all about me. We'll just keep it a secret between ourselves, if that's the way you want it."

"Please, Mister McBurney, I beg you. . . ."

"Sit down, won't you, ma'am. Sit right down there, why don't you?"

He advanced toward me on his crutches and I retreated to the small settee behind me. "You must go . . . we both must go downstairs," I told him even as I obeyed him and sat down. I was very frightened, I remember, but I was acting as though I was hypnotized. My wisest course would have been to scream for help right then, I suppose, but two things prevented it—one the fear of him and the other the thought that he had really done nothing worse than compliment me in a silly, boyish fashion and ridiculous though that was, to raise an alarm now about it would make it seem even more ridiculous, and moreover put him in a worse position in my sister's eyes than the one he already held.

"There now," said he as he stacked his crutches and sat down beside me, "that's much better. Now stop your tremblin, Miss Harriet. Nobody's gonna hurt you. As I told you before, all I want of you right now is your good regard. I'm sure something better will come in time if we start with that much now."

"Mister McBurney, you're a very young man—just a boy in fact," I told him, "while I'm a woman of near middle age. What do you think could possibly come of this?"

"Is that all that bothers you?" he wanted to know. "My age?"

"No, it's not all," I answered as gently as I could. "Even if we were of the same age, difficulties would still exist. The biggest difficulty of all is the fact that I don't feel about you as you apparently do about me."

"You will," he said with great confidence. "Just give me time. I'm going to repay you in full for the generous way you've treated me. Oh, Miss Harriet, if you ever knew how grateful I was for your comin to me on that first morning here and puttin your hand on my forehead the way you did and then speakin to me that way in your soft little voice. Do you recall that day at all, Miss Harriet, and the things you said to me? It was then you told me—or at least I thought you told me—of the things we had in common. Course maybe I was only dreamin your words from the wantin you to say them and also the terrible weak state I was in. For instance one thing I seem to remember is you tellin me about the Chinese statues and the old-Spanish lace you have. Now was it that first morning you told me about those things or was it some other time or was it imagination altogether? Do you have those things, Miss Harriet? Could you show them to me if you do?"

"Yes, I have them but I'd prefer to show them to you at another time."

"All right, ma'am, as long as I know I wasn't dreamin entirely about our conversations. We'll spend our time today on other matters then, shall we—namely you and me, eh?"

He took my hand then and squeezed it—not brutally, I think, but then I was so paralyzed with fright by that time that I probably would have felt no pain in the hand had he crushed it.

"Do you remember one other thing that happened that first morning, Miss Harriet?" he went on. "Do you recall my tellin you how the landlord's daughter came to see me when I was a small boy and sick that time at home and she took care of me like you did and I kissed her. And I showed you how I did it. Does that come back to you?"

It had never escaped my mind but I didn't say so. I couldn't even move as he put his arms around me and demonstrated the act again. It was done very gently—expertly, I suppose—and it was over before I could pull away.

"Mister McBurney," I said when I could speak, "you must never do a thing like that again."

"You told me that the other time," he grinned. "It didn't hurt, did it . . . it wasn't painful, was it? Ah Miss Harriet, you're a handsome little lady and I don't care if you're twenty five or fifty, but I see you're gonna take some trainin. Tell me, Miss Harriet, was there ever anybody who could kiss you and make you like it?"

"There may have been once," I admitted. I would have agreed to anything in the hope of getting rid of him.

"Who is the person?" he persisted. "Where is he now?"

"I don't know," I said.

"Is he dead? Was he killed in the war?"

"He's gone," I said. "I don't know where he is. Now please . . . leave me, Mister McBurney."

"Wait a bit. I have to explain something else to you. Why do you think I came here in the first place, Miss Harriet?"

"You were lost in the woods, weren't you, and Amelia Dabney found you," I said without interest.

"That's what she and everybody else thinks. I wasn't really lost at all. I knew exactly where I was going. Oh it's true I was wounded in the battle and I had stopped to rest a while when Amelia came along but I'd've been on my feet again in a moment without her help and I'd've been on my way to . . . where do you think, Miss Harriet?"

"I haven't any idea."

"Here, right here. This is where I was headed for—this very house," he said triumphantly. "And do you know why? Can you guess at all why I was comin here?"

"No," I said wearily.

"To see you. I was comin here to Farnsworth for no other reason but to see you."

"But why? You didn't even know me."

"Oh but I had heard about you, my darlin. I knew what you looked like and what a dear sweet person you were and as a consequence I was half gone on you before I met you."

"Who told you about me?" I demanded. "Who described me to you?"

"That's the most astoundin part of all. It was someone who knew you very well—someone who felt very close to you even as I do now. It was nobody other than your intended."

"My intended?"

"That's right," he asserted, "the fella you were gonna marry. Let's see, what name did he give me now? Was it Harry Wilson? No, Howard Wilson. No, that's not quite it. Howard Winslow it was . . . yes I'm sure that's the name."

"And where did you meet this Howard Winslow," I inquired.

"On the field of battle, ma'am," said he gazing at me steadily. "It was back there beyond the woods the morning after we had crossed that river called the Rapidan. The battle had just begun and I was moving forward through the brush alongside my pals. The smoke was so thick you couldn't see the nose of your bayonet or your own legs from the knees down, and if you were separated by as much as an arm's length from the fella next to you, you were lost in a little chokin blisterin world of your own. O' course you had the comfort of knowin there was still civilization outside the smoke because the grape and cannister and minié balls kept whizzin and there was plenty of bangin and shoutin and screamin goin on all over the place. Well we had been advancin like that for maybe five minutes—though it seemed more like five years—when I began to wonder if I was the only one of our company still on his feet. They could all be dead and lyin fifty yards back, I was startin to think, and here's this poor Irish boy strollin along all by himself and maybe it won't be twenty more paces before he bumps into General Lee havin his breakfast. 'Good mornin to you, General,' I decided I'd say. 'Greetin's to ye from the old sod and how's the war goin for ye this fine summer mornin? It's not goin at all well for me so with your permission I'll just draw up a chair and join ye in a plate of rashers.'

"And so," McBurney went on, "I went along like that, talkin to myself, don't you see, mainly to keep my teeth from chatterin to bits with the terrible fright I was in every time one of those chunks of iron flew past my ear. Then all at once I stumbled and I thought for a second I'd been hit, but it was only somethin on the ground that tripped me. I went headlong over it down into the smoke and I must have knocked my head against the ground or maybe it was the side of a tree because I was dazed for a moment or two, just long enough for the rest of my pals—or what there was left of them—to move along without me.

"Then I heard an awful groanin behind me and so I crawled back and found what had tripped me. It was a reb soldier—an officer—and he was stretched out there on his back, moanin and callin out for water. Well I unslung my canteen and held it for him while he drank, takin a quick look at him meanwhile. He wasn't far from the end of his road, I could see, from the terrible shrapnel wound he had in his chest.

"There was only a few drops left in the canteen, but I let him have it all. 'Thank you kindly, friend,' he says to me, his voice very weak. 'I wish there was some ways I could repay your kindness.'

"'Don't fret about that,' says I. 'It's no hardship at all for me to rest down here on the ground a while away from all that metal that's whinin overhead.'

"His eyes closed then and I thought it was all over, but he wasn't quite dead, for after a moment he spoke again, but very faintly now, so's I had to bend over very close to hear him. 'If you're ever in need yourself and can't get help elsewhere, I'll tell you where to find it. Just follow this woods the way you were headed until you come to a creek. Cross it and then turn left on the other side and pretty soon you'll come to a farm with a big white house and inside the house will be a beautiful lady who'll help you. Her name is Miss Harriet Farnsworth and when you see her you can do me one more favor. You can kiss her and tell her Captain Howard Winslow was awful sorry he never got back to her.'"

McBurney paused in his very sad story while he squeezed my hand again and stared at me soulfully. I tell you, for the moment I forgot my fear of him and just wanted to laugh right in his face.

"The gentleman was a captain, was he?" I inquired.

"Yes ma'am, near as I could tell. His coat was stained with the blood and dirt and all but I think he wore the marks of a captain."

"My stars," I said, "I would have expected Howard Winslow to be a general or at least a colonel before he died. He did die, I expect?"

"Yes ma'am . . . just then while I was with him. Those words were the last he ever said in this life."

"Just think . . . poor Howard Winslow and he died right there in your arms."

"That's right, ma'am."

"Would you describe him to me, Mister McBurney? Not that I doubt your word, of course, but it could've been someone posing as Howard Winslow, couldn't it, using poor Howard's identity for some unscrupulous purpose of his own? Just tell me briefly what this poor fellow looked like, if you please, Mister McBurney?"

"Let's see," McBurney said, seeming a bit disconcerted now. "You must keep in mind how smoky it was there and also how dirty and bloody this man was. I'd be hard put to describe my own father to you, if I come across him under conditions like that. Anyway to begin with he seemed a rather tallish fella."

"Oh I'm sorry," I said, trying to conceal my smile. "The Howard Winslow I knew was of small stature—not much taller than I."

"There you see. I musta mistook his gauntness and the way he was stretched out there."

"He was gaunt, you say? The man I knew was broad shouldered and stocky."

"But don't forget that a few months on army rations will take weight off any man," said McBurney smoothly. "Come to think of it this fella did have wide shoulders. It was mainly his face that was thin and sunken."

"What color was his hair?"

"Ah . . . sorta brownish I think."

"And his eyes?"

"Blue . . . or gray . . . something like that."

"Did he have any scars of any sort?"

"Ah . . . none that I could see."

"And was his hair straight or curly?"

"Ah . . . curly . . . somethin like mine."

"Mister McBurney," said I, "you are the world's greatest liar. The Howard Winslow who used to visit here had brown eyes and black, Indian-straight hair."

"Well don't forget," said McBurney quickly, "that this fella was wearing a hat and I could only see a bit of his hair . . . and come to think of it his eyes coulda been brown. There was so much gray smoke around there, you see. . . ."

"Moreover," I interjected, "Howard Winslow had a pronounced white scar on his forehead—the result of a riding accident—and if you had really seen him, the scar would have been the first thing you noticed."

"Please, Miss Harriet," he said, "don't call me a liar. Maybe you were right before. Maybe, if this wasn't Howard Winslow, it was some other fella posin as him. Maybe Howard Winslow was in the army with this fella and had been killed already, let's say, and then this fella, for reasons of his own, decided to take Howard Winslow's name. Anyway whoever he was, he knew you and Howard Winslow had been engaged to marry and that's why he knew enough to send me here."

"There is only one thing wrong with that theory," said I. "Like the rest of your story it is not based on fact. The Howard Winslow who used to come here occasionally to visit my brother was not my fiancé or my lover or even my friend. He was an idler and a wastrel of no family who trailed around after Robert, doing Robert no good, I might add. Mister Winslow had few means and no talents of any kind, as far as I know. He was not even a good horseman as his scar could testify, and if he ever did join the army it must have been his first employment of any kind. He was not handsome, clever or personable . . . in short, Howard Winslow had absolutely nothing to recommend him for any position, least of all marriage."

"But," said McBurney wide eyed, "I was told. . . ."

"Exactly. You were told—but hardly, I'm sure you will admit, could you have been told by Howard Winslow—who, I might also add, thought about as little of me as I did of him. I believe you were told something all right, Mister McBurney, that is the one part of your story I do believe. You were told something by my sister—who is liable to say anything about me—or by

Mattie—who has decided that matrimony is the only happy state for females and that I therefore must want desperately to be married and consequently, since Howard Winslow spent more idle time around this place
than any other young man with the exception of my brother, that I must
have wanted and intended to marry Howard Winslow. Or possibly your
information came from one of the students who, having heard Mister Winslow's name mentioned as a former visitor here, decided out of malicious-
ness or ignorance, or maybe both, to couple his name with mine!"

I finished my tirade—for that's exactly what is was, I admit it—and sat
there glaring at him.

"Oh I love to see you when you're like that," he said grinning again,
"with some color in your cheeks and your hair beginning to come un-
pinned and your little snow white bosom throbbin like a frightened dove."

He took hold of me again and pressed his lips on mine, but forcefully
this time. I tore myself away and screamed.

"Please, please," he said, still grinning foolishly. "I love you, I love you,
Miss Harriet."

He grabbed the back of my neck with his left hand and clamped his
right hand against my mouth. I couldn't breathe and the room began to go
dark. I remember thinking, "Please, Mister McBurney, please don't hurt
me," but I don't know whether that was one of the things I managed to yell
or not before I fainted.

When I recovered consciousness he was gone but everyone else in the
house was there. I was lying on the floor and Mattie was loosening my stays
and my sister was rubbing my wrists and Alice was holding an onion underneath my nose and Emily was applying wet cloths to my forehead, while the
other girls were hovering over watching in various stages of pleased
excitement—and in some cases possibly regretting my fairly quick recovery.

For it was quick, Mattie said later, considering the shock I'd had. Of
course Mattie always measures such things by the standards of the old
Tidewater society where a lady never recovered from a faint in less than a
quarter of an hour, unless she was having an attack of what Mattie calls the
"galloping faints," which is a condition wherein you regain your senses for
brief intervals and then—preferably with a little shriek—sink back into
your stupor again.

Anyway, although these remarks may seem rather lighthearted, considering the events I've just related, I must explain that I was not feeling all
that distressed when I awakened and as long as there seemed no likelihood
of any immediate reoccurrence of the disagreeable business, I was quite
prepared to forget the whole matter.

However my sister refused to take it that lightly. "He was trying to kill you," she said.

"No, no," I told her. "You're mistaken."

"He was, Miss Harriet," stated Emily. "I saw him too. He had both his hands on your throat and he was trying to strangle you. Then he ran away as soon as we came in."

"He didn't exactly run," remarked Amelia, always the first to defend him. "He merely backed away when we all came in. And he wasn't strangling Miss Harriet at all when I first saw him. He was bending over her on the floor, lifting her head and asking her if she was all right."

"I believe Edwina was the first one on the scene," said Marie Deveraux. "At least she was standing here in the doorway watching everything that was going on when I arrived. And I believe I was the first up the stairs after Miss Harriet started to yell, even though Alice did grab the back of my dress and practically rip it off my back in an effort to beat me up here. Anyway when I arrived I found Edwina here already. I gathered she came here directly from her room, is that correct, Edwina?"

"I don't think I'm required to stand here and be interrogated by you," Edwina told her, and started to leave.

"You may be under no obligation to answer Marie," my sister informed her, "but you certainly have a duty toward the school. If you saw the man McBurney attempting to harm Miss Harriet, you are definitely bound to so state."

"He wasn't harming her," Edwina said sullenly. "She isn't harmed, is she?"

"But he intended to harm her," Martha persisted.

"How should I know what his intentions were?"

"Don't fence with me, Miss," said Martha sharply, "Just tell me what you saw."

"I saw him trying to quiet Miss Harriet."

"By choking her?"

"He was covering her mouth with his hand, if that's what you mean by choking. It was my impression that he was only trying to prevent her screaming—and not doing a very good job of it, I might add—since I'm sure the armies could have heard Miss Harriet at Spotsylvania or wherever they are."

"I'm sorry," said I, rather weakly, I guess, for the room was still spinning and I was still trying to catch my breath. "I'm very sorry to have disturbed you, Miss."

"For shame, for shame, Edwina," I believe several of the girls shouted.

"It's certainly a great pity if the person who is second in command at our school cannot be allowed to protest vocally when she is under attack by the enemy," said Emily.

"Oh bosh," yelled Amelia. "Miss Harriet was no more under attack than you are."

"Oh but I am. That's just the point," Emily replied. "We're all under attack here and it's time we realized it."

"Girls, girls," I said. "I wish you would try to forget this incident. Perhaps Amelia is right. Maybe Mister McBurney didn't mean any harm."

"Perhaps he didn't," said my sister, "but we cannot be sure of that. I hope this has been a lesson to everyone here. No one must permit herself to be alone with McBurney for a single instant. Once again let me repeat my previous order. No person here is to have any further communication whatsoever with McBurney. If my sister had remembered that order and obeyed it, she might have avoided this danger this afternoon."

"Are you so sure of the danger, Miss Martha?" yelled Amelia impertinently.

"Be quiet, Miss, this instant," commanded Martha, "or you will be sent to your room."

I was able to arise from the floor by that time and Mattie helped me to a chair. "I don't see how we can continue to live in a house with a person without communicating with him," I said when I was able to speak. "Perhaps you will explain that to us, sister."

"We can't continue living here with him," Martha answered. "As Emily said, that's just the point. We shall have to do something and quickly about McBurney. I'm very much afraid of what might happen here next."

"Do you intend to set out for help immediately?" I asked her.

"I don't know. I'm even more afraid now to leave you in charge here. Anyway I know I must come to some decision about him very soon."

"If he was really convinced that you wanted to be rid of him that badly, I'm sure he'd leave without any more argument," said Amelia. "In fact I'll tell him that he's no longer welcome around certain people here, if you like."

"You'll do nothing of the sort, Miss," Martha informed her. "You've been warned against associating with him and if we are to have much more of your insolence you may be asked to leave this school along with Mister McBurney."

"Amelia Dabney is a total idiot if she imagines that McBurney is going to take any suggestions from her anyway," Emily remarked. "He won't listen to her any more than he'll listen to any of the rest of us. McBurney is our sworn foe and it's time we all realized it. Instead of finding ways to ignore him, we ought to be thinking about how to defend ourselves against him, if I may say so, Miss Martha."

"You may not say so, Miss," snapped my sister.

"If we all had bolts or locks on our bedroom doors we might feel safer at night," declared Alice. Miss Alice is, of course, a charity student but sometimes she forgets herself.

"Yes, perhaps Alice should have a lock on her door," Marie observed. "If she had locked her door against Johnny McBurney in the first place—as I'm sure she would have done had it been possible—we might have escaped these difficulties with Johnny now. As I recall Johnny was about ready to leave here under his own power and with no one urging him to do so on the night he had his unfortunate accident—which, it is obvious now, was a direct result of Miss Alice's not being able to bolt her door."

Whereupon Alice grabbed Marie's curls and gave them a good tug and then the entire household forgot about my fainting spell in a general effort to separate the angry Alice and the kicking and yelling Marie. Martha finally solved the problem by repeatedly boxing the ears of the two of them, voluntarily assisted by Emily—which naturally only made matters worse since it caused Amelia to defend her roommate Marie by setting upon Emily fang and claw.

The thing was not ended until old Mattie joined forces with my sister and I myself arose—still feeling light-headed—and offered what remonstrance I could and in that way the three of us managed to tear apart the four struggling girls, all of whom were ordered without further ado to their rooms.

"You wretched creatures!" my sister shouted. "You'll all go without your dinners and possibly without your breakfasts too!"

"But Miss Martha, I was only trying to help," Emily protested.

"Be quiet, Miss," my sister commanded. "You've begun to take on too much authority here. No one asked you for any help. I was quite capable of chastising Miss Alice and Miss Marie by myself. Now get to your rooms, all of you, and remain there with your books until you're given permission to come out."

They all left my room then without further argument, although Emily was as red and angry as I've ever seen her. Edwina Morrow who had taken no part in the disturbance was standing by the door wearing a very self-satisfied little smile.

"You may follow the others, Miss," my sister told her and Edwina gave her customary little mocking bow and started out.

"Stay, Edwina," I said. "Will you tell me the truth? Do you really think McBurney meant me no harm?"

"Why don't you ask him?" was her reply. "I'm sure he'd tell you if you asked, since you've always been so friendly with him."

That nettled me and caused me to make a remark for which I was rather regretful later.

"Perhaps I will ask him," I said, "and perhaps he will tell me too, since he's always been free with other information. For example, he's told me many things about you, Edwina."

At that she went white—or perhaps gray would be a better way of describing it since her skin normally is so dark.

"What things did he tell you?" she demanded.

"Oh all sorts of things. We had quite a little discussion about your background. It seems you were guilty of the same offense of which you accused me—being overly friendly with McBurney."

"Move along now, Miss," Martha told her. "Let this be a warning to both you and Miss Harriet. This must be the end of any friendship with McBurney."

Edwina left then, still quite pale, and my sister turned to me. "What was all that business about McBurney having talked to you about Edwina?"

"Well he did one time," I answered truthfully. "He told me that he liked her very much. It was one day when he was working in the garden and I had a brief conversation with him about her. I remember that he told me he thought Edwina was the most sincere young person here."

"What else did he say about her?"

"That was about the substance of it."

"It hardly constitutes a long discussion of her background."

"Did I say a long discussion? I really didn't mean that, if I did," I explained. "And I certainly didn't intend to disturb Edwina as I apparently have."

That was true. I never wanted to cause the girl any grief. As I have said many times, even though she can be awfully difficult, I do feel very sorry for her. I have never wished anything but the best for that poor child.

Well my head had begun to ache terribly by then and so I begged my sister and Mattie to excuse me. When they left I retired to my bed and after quite a long period of painful suffering I finally managed to fall asleep and remained asleep until Mattie summoned me for dinner.

I had a terrible dream, I remember. That is I remember that the dream was unpleasant although I can't relate very much about it beyond stating that it included memories of my past but in misshapen form. I think at one point I dreamed that I was married to my father and McBurney was our son, but he looked very much like my brother Robert too. At times he had Robert's face but he still wore his own ragged blue uniform and, of course, he had only one leg.

And yet he was a child, a very small child, a baby really. He was sitting on the floor of the library, staring at me with his wide blue eyes, and when I tried to approach him to put him in his crib he grinned knowingly at me so that I was afraid to touch him even though he infuriated me with that terrible way he grinned. A child should not look at his mother that way, I told him. I pleaded with him, begged him to close his eyes or at least turn his head away from me, but he wouldn't. He just continued to stare and grin. At last I couldn't stand it any longer and so I took the poker from the fireplace and threatened him with it, not really intending to hit him, but he still wouldn't stop grinning so I did hit him. I struck at him and beat him for a long time, until at last he disappeared. Perhaps I should add, I cried all the while I was hitting him. . . .

Edwina Morrow

No further unpleasantness occurred during the rest of that day on which McBurney was alleged to have attacked Miss Harriet—or at least I have no knowledge of any such incident taking place during the daylight hours. As far as I know he left Miss Harriet's room and went back to the parlor and stayed there.

I know Mattie took his dinner tray in there while the rest of us were at table. I remember this particularly because he had been taking his meals with us for several days—of course, not on anyone's invitation—and his absence that evening was commented on by several students.

Part way through the meal, Miss Martha directed Mattie to fix a plate for him, maybe partly in the desire to keep him out of the dining room. I remember also that Miss Harriet, who had managed to make it to the table and partake of as much dinner as the rest of us in spite of her travail, suggested that possibly the household could spare our visitor a little something extra on that evening.

"As a reward for his conduct?" inquired her sister, looking at her as though she were slightly mad.

"No, no, of course not," Miss Harriet replied, "only to show him that we harbor no ill feelings—that we have the proper Christian attitude."

"I believe Christian attitude in a situation like this depends on what kind of Christians you're referring to," remarked Emily. "For instance, I'm told that Christians of the Roman Church tortured their opponents severely during the Spanish Inquisition."

"And Northern Protestant Christians up in New England or somewhere burned quite a few old ladies at the stake, didn't they, because of some disagreement over worshiping the devil," put in Marie who is always quick to counter any attack on her religion.

"It's about all you could expect of Northern people of any extraction, Christian or otherwise," stated Alice, revealing a patriotism of which she had never previously been suspected. I presume she was making a rather late attempt to win some favor with those in power, against the seemingly rapidly approaching day of her expulsion from the school. I realize that Miss Martha will try to make me pay my share for the McBurney episode too, although as yet she has not managed to find a way of doing it.

Anyway Miss Harriet offered to sacrifice her next ration of salted side meat, whenever that delicacy was scheduled to be doled out, in order that he might have it for that evening's dinner. Miss Martha regarded her coldly for a moment, then assented and ordered Mattie to prepare it.

"If future rations are being apportioned out now, I'd just as soon have mine also," Marie declared.

"Then next week or whenever other students are having their meat, you will go hungry and your pangs will be all the greater for watching them enjoy themselves," Miss Harriet told her.

"We'll suffer together, Miss Harriet," said the child coolly. "And who knows . . . perhaps the war will be over before the next time Miss Martha decides to pass out a little meat. As far as that goes we could all be dead, and then you and I would be the winners, Miss Harriet."

"Be quiet, if you please, Miss," ordered Miss Martha. "No meat or other scarce food is being served out of turn to students. If Miss Harriet is foolish enough to give her ration to a person like that—well, she is an adult, supposedly, and I'm tired of being responsible for her."

Well this comment of her sister's resulted in Miss Harriet leaving the table and going to her room, which might possibly have been Miss Martha's objective in the first place. Sometimes it seems that our headmistress just causes unpleasantness for its own sake—purely for the joy of it—as I am well qualified to testify, having often been myself the victim of her spite.

Anyway the meal proceeded without further interruption after Miss Harriet's departure and when it was completed we were all dismissed and sent to our rooms. Normally we would have spent the hour or so before bedtime in the parlor or in the library but since McBurney had taken over the former room as his full-time headquarters and since he had been seen to hobble into the latter room occasionally—where he would stand with what I suppose he considered a scholarly frown as he read the titles of the books on the shelves, forming the words with his lips as he did so—we were apparently going to be forbidden the use of either room and possibly the whole downstairs area, except when under the direct supervision of our teachers.

I can tell you the whole thing made me good and angry and I remained that way during the several hours I spent in my room. I tried to study my History of the Bible for a while and then tried to work on my French verbs, but all to no avail. I just couldn't keep my mind on it.

You see it was the injustice of the thing that bothered me. I just couldn't see why the students in this place had to be discriminated against in order to accommodate McBurney. I couldn't understand why a fairly good student like myself, who ought to have been allowed to do her studying in the library where plenty of reference material was available, was being penalized in favor of a person like that.

And so, after brooding about it for a while, I couldn't contain myself any longer and I arose from my bed and left my room. Being so irritated over the business I hadn't even undressed but had only removed my shoes which I didn't bother to replace before slipping out into the hall.

Naturally we wear our shoes as little as possible in this place in order to conserve them, since they're impossible to replace or even repair in these times. Of course, very early in McBurney's sojourn here we were ordered by Miss Martha to remain shod in his presence, apparently in the belief that the sight of our bare and often dirty toes would send him into some excess of passion. Anyway the order caused little grumbling among the girls since most of them suffer from tender feet and are always complaining about nails, slivers, thorns and what not. These things don't seem to afflict me and I can go barefooted for days without being bothered by anything more than the uncleanliness of it, which is a problem ignored, unfortunately, by most people here. Of course I suppose I should add that Amelia Dabney seems to be more comfortable without shoes also, little barbarian that she is, and likewise old Mattie who owns but one ragged pair of hide slippers which flop and flutter disgustingly when she shuffles around in them—which, thankfully, is usually only in wet weather.

Well to return to the matter of the moment, I went quickly and silently down the stairs to the library, carrying my candle and my books. If I may be permitted one more deviation, I want to state that my possession of a candle during this time of great scarcity was due entirely to foresightedness and frugality on my part. When other students were wasting their candles on late night frivolities, I was conserving mine, even to the point of studying by the moonlight through my window.

Anyway with nothing on my mind but my schoolwork I found my way to the library. All bedroom doors had been closed as I passed and I assumed that the rest of the household was asleep since I judged it to be past ten o'clock. The parlor door was closed also when I went by and if I gave this any thought at all, it was only to presume that McBurney had retired, too—not that I cared, certainly, one way or the other.

Well I had put my candle on a shelf and was looking for some texts on Biblical scholarship of which there is a great abundance in our library—too great a supply, I think, in comparison with the number of books on more modern and worthwhile subjects—when I heard loud voices, seemingly an argument, coming from the parlor across the way. One of the voices was obviously McBurney's and so I ignored the sound for a while because I was simply just not interested in anything which concerned him—or in anyone foolish enough to be concerned with him.

Then suddenly it occurred to me that after all it might be one of the younger students—Amelia or Marie perhaps—in there with him and that I therefore ought to see about it. Now maybe I ought to explain that I wasn't afraid that he would harm the person, whoever she was, or at least I wasn't afraid he was going to hurt her physically, if you want to accept the notion advanced by some people here later that McBurney had corrupted our morals. I'll tell you truthfully what I was afraid of at that moment was that this unknown person might be in there telling lies about me to McBurney—not that I cared at all what he thought of me, but I couldn't have a person like McBurney spreading such lies further. And on the other hand it could have been the other way around. McBurney, don't you see, could have been telling lies about me himself.

And so I took my candle and came across the hall to the parlor door. Listening at key holes is not my favorite occupation, I can assure you, but in this case it seemed unavoidable. However I was determined to do only as much listening as necessary to determine the topic of conversation inside. If it didn't concern me, I was resolved to return immediately to the library and my studies.

Well it didn't concern me, or at least as much of it as I heard didn't. As a matter of fact I didn't hear much talk at all for the first few minutes that I stood there. I heard some mumbling and then what seemed like giggling, but which I realized as it continued was possibly sobbing.

I didn't know what to do—whether to burst into the room or not. The mumbling voice I presumed was McBurney's—and was wrong, as I'll reveal in a moment—but the sobbing voice didn't sound like either Amelia or Marie. The most obvious visitor to McBurney's room then came to my mind, but that person was eliminated very shortly too, as she materialized—yellow hair streaming—at my elbow.

"Go back to bed, Alice," I whispered sharply to her. "Clear out of here."

"Who's in there with him?" she demanded.

"I don't know," I replied, "and I care less."

"I don't really care either," said she. "I'd just like to satisfy my curiosity about whose skirts he's trying to lift this time."

"Is that what he did with you?" I inquired.

"I don't want to discuss him," was her answer. "I think we've all been treated shamefully by that devil."

"Could it be Emily in there?" I wondered then.

"Hardly. Even if he were willing to settle for almost anyone now, I don't know how he'd ever get her in there unless he dragged her, and we'd've heard that. Though I can't imagine Johnny overpowering a horse like that anyway, even if he weren't a cripple. Emily would knock him down with one blow."

"Then it must be Miss Martha or Miss Harriet," I said softly, "for I'm sure it's neither of the young ones."

"It's not Miss Martha either," declared Alice, "because I heard Miss Martha coughing when I came past her room."

"Then it has to be Miss Harriet."

"I expect you're right. They're probably having a gay old time, the two of them drunker than hooty owls."

"It doesn't sound much like a gay old time to me," I answered. "And if you don't keep your voice down they're bound to hear you."

"Well they won't come rushing out here, if they do," Alice remarked, "since they'll likely be afraid it's Miss Martha come to reprimand them. Anyway since it's only poor old Miss Harriet in there, it doesn't bother me. I was afraid it might be you."

"Thank you for the compliment," I told her coolly, "although I'm sorry I can't return it. I was never afraid it might be you."

Whether or not we made any more such disputatious remarks to each other at that time I can't remember. I confess I was also somewhat relieved to realize it was only Miss Harriet in the room with him because I felt that for all her faults Miss Harriet was the one person in the house I could trust not to spread any lying gossip about me. And so I think Alice and I were just about ready to leave the hall and go back upstairs to our beds, I having decided to abandon my studies for the evening.

Now perhaps I should explain why I felt that nothing more than a drunken argument was taking place in the parlor. It was the same explanation I had hit upon for Miss Harriet's fainting on that afternoon. I was sure it wasn't because McBurney had tried to choke her but only because he touched her. Believe me, I observed on many occasions how she would shrink away every time he came close to her. One time in the hallway, for example—this was before his amputation when we were all on the best of terms with him—he came in from the garden as she was coming down the stairs and he stopped her with what I guess he thought was a courtly gesture. He said, "My dear lady," in that stupid accent of his, bowed low and tried to kiss her hand. Well she snatched it away as though it had been burned. And then grew red and tried to explain it by saying he had startled her, or something of the sort.

Then another time at table, she did the same thing. She came in late and he arose to draw her chair and take her arm to lead her to it, and Miss Harriet pulled away with a look of horror on her face, but again recovered quickly, saying, "Oh, Mister McBurney, your hand is so cold." This on a warmer than usual evening when she was wearing her customary long-sleeved dress.

I know she attended to him after his operation, and I give her great credit for this because it was very likely an agonizing experience for her. However it must be remembered that he was in a very bad state then and expected by most of those around him to die before the day was through. Consequently, being inert he offered no threat to her, being unconscious he would not know that she had put her hand on him and if he died he would never even learn that she had done so.

Now I suppose you could say that what occurred then, if it didn't change the course of events completely here, at least brought matters to a climax. Two things happened really. The first was our decision to open the parlor door.

Whether Alice or I suggested it, I can't remember now. Anyway we had both started up the stairs when we decided to return and peek in quickly. "Just to make sure there's really nothing wrong," I think I said. "Just to guarantee that it's really Miss Harriet in there and not one of the little girls," I believe Alice said.

Well it was Miss Harriet all right, very drunk and completely unclad. He was too, or nearly so. They were on the settee.

Strangely enough it was McBurney who was weeping and cursing some-one or something through his tears. Miss Harriet seemed almost stupefied with wine. They had both evidently consumed a lot of it, judging by the empty bottles strewn about on the floor. Anyway because of their condition—and their preoccupation—they didn't notice us, and so we closed the door and went away.

I made no remark to Alice and she made none to me. I remember that she was very pale and biting her lip. When we arrived at the upstairs hall-way I went straight to my room, but instead of continuing up to her room on the third floor, she paused by Miss Martha's door and rapped. And that was the second event I mentioned.

I sat on the edge of my bed, not really listening but hearing vaguely any-way as Miss Martha opened her door and asked irritably what Alice wanted.

"I think you'd better go downstairs and take a look in the parlor," Alice told her. "I think you may find something there of interest to you."

That's all I heard because I noticed then that blood was dripping on to my dress front because, maybe in some kind of involuntary mimicking of Alice, I had bitten my lip too. I arose to find a handkerchief and in passing closed my door. Therefore whether or not Alice had more to say to Miss Martha and whether or not Miss Martha went downstairs immediately I cannot say.

Marie Deveraux

Well it was really an awful and rather upsetting story Johnny told me of how he had seen my father lying in the woods near here, bleeding to death of a terrible wound, and my father said to him, "Do a dying man a favor, won't you, Yank? Go to Farnsworth Hall and see how my daughter is gettin on there. There's a terrible lot of black Protestants there," my father went on according to Johnny, "and if you're a good practicin Roman Catholic, as I believe you are, you'll stop in there and see if you can do anything for her. I'll never be able to rest in my grave unless I know she's keepin the faith, Yank, and conductin herself like a little lady."

Of course I should have known right from the start that it wasn't true, because my father wouldn't have spoken with a brogue like that and also he'd be a fine one to talk about my keeping the faith since he doesn't keep it awfully well himself. Anyway I did halfway believe it at the time because I was somewhat upset about a little matter . . . about eating a piece of salted pork on Friday, if you must know . . . and Johnny knew about that and chided me about it and said that he knew I had been eating meat on Fridays quite often for a long time.

Well that was true, depending on what you consider quite often, although I think now he didn't really know it at all but was only guessing. Anyway I know it's very wrong to eat meat on Fridays and I've had a great many serious battles with my conscience over it. Unfortunately when it comes to a contest between my conscience and my appetite, the latter is nearly always the stronger.

Now Miss Martha, who I believe is secretly opposed to Catholicism although I think she would probably never admit it, makes things very difficult for me sometimes by having Mattie serve meat on Fridays when we haven't had any for a solid week or maybe longer than that. As a matter of fact I mentioned this to Johnny one time and he agreed with me, even though he never paid any attention to the Friday rule himself while he was here. Of course, he explained his disregarding it by special permission which he claimed the Pope had granted to all Irish members of the Union Army.

Naturally I didn't believe it. I'm sure if the Pope was going to play any favorites in this war he'd pick our boys to grant the special favors to rather than the Yankees. After all, in this part of the country we have only one or two kinds of Protestant heretics such as Episcopalians like the Farnsworth sisters and Baptists like Mattie. Up there in the North they have hundreds of different kinds of fallen aways, to say nothing of pagans and Jews and the Lord only knows what other kinds of heathens.

Well probably I ought to go back to the beginning of my disagreement with Johnny. I believe our troubles began on the day after—as Alice and Emily now put it—Miss Martha caught him in bed with Miss Harriet. Actually there's no bed in that parlor but only the old settee, which certainly does play an important role in this story, if you stop to think of it.

Unfortunately I didn't see anything of what went on that night. I heard a few things but I didn't see any of it because, although I started downstairs when the shouting began, Miss Martha was a little too quick for me. The way it was, she ran out of the parlor and shouted, "Any girl who comes down these stairs tonight is expelled from this school!"

"What about if there's a fire for pity's sake," I called back, but I don't think she heard me because she went back into the parlor instantly and slammed the door.

Well I probably would have taken a chance anyway and hurried down the stairs for a quick listen at the keyhole but the spy in our midst, Miss Emily Stevenson, grabbed me by the arm—wrenching it severely, I might add—and pulled me back before I could even go down one step.

The matter wouldn't've ended there, I can assure you, except that just then I happened to notice Alice Simms through Miss Martha's open doorway. She was seated on Miss Martha's bed, weeping as though her heart had been broken in at least nineteen different places. This, of course, caused Emily and I to forget our differences and the two of us went in to question Alice.

Thus we learned, between sobs, of what had happened downstairs. Now I still don't know how Alice happened to awaken and go down unless she had motives similar to Miss Harriet's herself and was rudely jarred to find our teacher there first. Naturally I was a little reluctant to believe Alice's explanation which was that she heard noises and began to worry about them and then went down to discover Edwina listening at the parlor door.

Well my private scoffing at that was due to the fact that I am usually one of the lightest sleepers in this house and I didn't hear anything until Miss Martha went down and the shouting began. Also to cast further doubt on Alice's explanation is the fact that her room is on the third floor and it would take a person with extraordinarily sensitive ears to hear a first floor conversation all the way up there.

Of course, even if you could poke holes in her reasons for going down, you couldn't doubt her genuine unhappiness at what she had discovered. It really and truly seemed as though that girl had been nursing just the most awful crush on Johnny and now her whole existence was shattered. In fact she was weeping so hard that it was almost impossible for me to even get the whole story out of her.

Anyway our questioning of Alice had to end just then because there was a new uproar from downstairs, and when Emily and I came out we found Miss Martha practically dragging her sodden sister up the stairs and McBurney, wrapped in his blanket like some poor bedraggled Indian, standing in the parlor doorway on his one leg and shouting, "Goddamit to hell I didn't invite her! Sufferin Christ, I didn't send for her! I ast her a thousand times to leave me be, but she wouldn't, Goddamit!" And more profane utterances like that.

Miss Martha paid no attention but continued trudging upward with one arm around Miss Harriet's waist and using the other hand occasionally for a little tug at Miss Harriet's hair, which you might have thought was to lift Miss Harriet's sagging head out of the way so that our headmistress could see where she was going, but which a more experienced observer would have realized was in the nature of a nice little reprimand. I should add that Miss Harriet was attired in her night dress and robe now, as Miss Martha had evidently spent the interval in putting them back on her. Miss Harriet certainly didn't seem at all regretful of her conduct but instead had just the silliest, lopsided grin on her face that you could ever imagine.

Of course my impression of the scene had to be a very hasty one because as soon as Miss Martha saw Alice and me she began yelling at us to get to our rooms instantly or be prepared to face some terrible penalty or other. Naturally, eager Emily pretended to assume that the order didn't apply to her and wanted to help Miss Martha with her burden but she received such a tongue lashing for her efforts that it did my heart good. Hearing Miss Emily put in her place in that way just contented me so much that I went to my room and closed my door as directed without complaining any more about it.

My roommate was awake, of course—she's even more alert to unusual disturbances than I am—but she hadn't bothered to get up and see about it.

"Well your friend is in trouble again," I informed her as I got back into my own bed. "It's rather serious trouble this time I'm afraid."

"I've told you biological situations don't interest me when humans are involved," Amelia said softly. "Also I'm rather worried about a problem of my own. My turtle is sick again."

"Do you think it's anything really serious this time?" I asked hopefully. Frankly I expected to awaken some morning and find half my toes chewed off by that crazy turtle.

"He didn't eat his dinner," Amelia replied, "and that's not like him if he's feeling all right."

"I don't think I'd be too eager to eat my dinner either if it consisted of dirty old leaves and dried up bugs and beetles."

At that time Amelia was a regular little scavenger, you know, the way she'd go searching the house and barns and fields for dead insects to feed that idiotic turtle. Naturally she wanted you to believe that she never collected any bugs that weren't already dead since she is so adverse to killing any wild thing, but I have always secretly suspected that on days when the supply of deceased bugs was scarce she may have stepped on one or two live ones and told herself it was an accident.

"If Johnny is in awfully bad trouble here and you're afraid some harm will come to him I could take him away from here," she said now.

"Where would we take him?" I emphasized the "we" because I felt the responsibility was as much mine as hers. She may have found him but he and I were of the same religion.

"We could take him to my hiding place in the woods," Amelia answered. "No one knows about that place but you and I."

"It mightn't be a bad idea," I remarked, rather taken with the novelty of it. "We could get food from the kitchen late at night and carry it out to him."

"And also blankets from our beds, in case he needs that kind of comfort."

"I don't think he needs it any more than I do," I said irritably. "Anyway we needn't worry about it until we see how Miss Martha plans to deal with him."

"Very likely she'll just try to send him away again," said Amelia drowsily.

I didn't see it that way. "He had his chance to leave and he didn't take it. Even if he'd go quietly now I don't think it would be enough to satisfy Miss Martha. She'll want to punish him severely now."

Of course, just how she intended to do it was beyond my comprehension. And at that time I certainly wouldn't have gone along with it no matter what the punishment involved, because up until then I had no grievances with Johnny.

In fact the next morning I arose very early and went downstairs with Amelia to discuss the matter with him—and also to try and get a few more details about what had gone on the previous night between him and Miss Harriet.

This was shortly after sunrise before anyone else in the house was awake. I'm not generally as early a riser as my roommate but that morning I opened my eyes almost as soon as she did and jumped out of bed, dressed and was ready in two minutes or less to follow her down the hall. All this was done without any conversation on our part. We knew exactly what we intended to do and there was no need to discuss it.

I did make one little remark to her however as we tiptoed down the stairs, just to remind her how difficult it is to put anything over on me. "It certainly was lucky that I awakened, wasn't it, because I don't really think you intended to rouse me."

"That's correct, I didn't," she admitted coolly. "It doesn't take two of us to warn Johnny. I brought him in here and I can take him out without your help."

"Don't be so selfish," I told her.

"It's not selfishness. It's just that you're liable to create some kind of disturbance and ruin the whole thing. He's much safer with me alone."

"That's ridiculous," said I.

"It is? You're starting to make noise already. The whole house will be awake if you don't stop talking."

"You're talking as much as I am," I let her know.

"Please go to bed," she begged me. "I can take him to the woods quickly and quietly. Then you can come out and see him later today."

"Absolutely not," I replied. "If anyone goes, we both go."

And with a few more such argumentative remarks like that we entered the parlor. Now to my surprise, Johnny was wide awake, fully dressed and completely sober. He was sitting on the settee with his crutch on his lap, and he was shaven and combed as neatly as if he were bound for church instead of the woods. There was only one thing at all unusual about his appearance, if you wanted to disregard the neatness. That was the fact of his nervousness. He was trembling very noticeably as he sat there.

"Well now," said I by way of jollying him. "I don't even see any signs of the famous party that is said to have taken place here last night. For one thing I don't see any of the hundreds of empty bottles that were supposedly strewn all over the floor and on which Miss Alice Simms was supposedly tripping and stumbling in her haste to escape from here."

"There was only the three bottles," he said in a low voice. "That's all Miss Harriet brought in here. I put them in the kitchen if you want to see."

"No, I'll take your word," I said. "I know Alice exaggerates terribly. Well what about Miss Harriet then?"

"I didn't ask her to come down," said he. "I tried to send her back upstairs. Honest to God I tried. She brought that wine in here and drank most of it herself, honest to God she did, and then she started takin off her clothes. I pleaded with her to stop but she wouldn't. She just laughed and carried on like crazy, and then began to tear the shirt and pants off me. . . . Listen, honest to God, it's not that I'm above a bit o' business now and then in the dark, but I'm not that daft to be foolin with old women. . . ."

"Oh I believe you, Johnny," I told him, "and I'm sure Amelia does too, but we can't speak for the others. As far as Miss Martha is concerned she probably wouldn't want to believe you even if you could prove it . . . because of family honor, you know, and things like that."

"Mightn't Miss Harriet tell the truth about it?" Amelia wondered.

"Hardly," I said. "Even if she remembers what actually happened—which is doubtful, considering how drunk she was—Miss Martha will never allow her to admit it."

"I've been thinkin," said Johnny. "I'd better get outa here. I want no more of this loony place."

"Oh well, things aren't so awfully bad, most days," I said, thinking perhaps I ought to defend the school a bit.

"You don't know anything about it," Johnny said. "You weren't here to see her and listen to her . . . the way she was thinkin I was somebody else, or maybe it was only pretendin that she thought so. . . ."

"If you really want to leave, that's what we've come down for," said Amelia. "We're prepared to take you to a wonderful place in the woods."

"And what will I do there?" asked Johnny.

"Hide. It's a marvelous place for hiding," Amelia told him.

"For how long?"

"For weeks," said I, "or months maybe. Until the rainy season begins or the danger passes."

"What danger now?"

"From Miss Martha's temper. I think you probably ought to stay there until Miss Martha's temper cools and that may take quite a while," I said.

"I think he ought to stay there from now on," Amelia said. "I don't think he ought to ever come back here at all. You'll find it's really very nice out there, Johnny. There's an old hollow log you can sleep in at night and during the day there's lots of interesting things for you to see. There are plants to identify and trees and birds and you'll see lots of wonderful natural activity. Squirrels and chipmunks storing food, various insects in their courting rituals, foxes tending their young.

". . . And there's plenty for you to eat . . . nuts and berries and wild honey . . . you could stay there forever, Johnny."

"You daft creature, what am I . . . some kind of animal?" he cried.

"Yes, certainly that's what you are," she informed him coldly. "Only sometimes you're not as nice as most of the other animals. However I found you and it's my responsibility to look after you. Now do you want to go out to the woods or not?"

"No, no . . . or at least not now, darlin," he said.

"Then I'll leave it to you to tell me when," said Amelia. "However if I were you, I wouldn't wait too long." And with that she marched out of the room.

"I think you may have hurt her feelings," I told him.

"I don't care if I have," said he. "She must be as mad as some of these others here, thinkin I'd be wantin to lie out there in the damp and dirt with all them worms and crawly stingy things."

Well I'll admit I wouldn't've cared much for the life myself, but I felt I ought to stick up for my roommate. "Amelia's a good friend of yours," I let him know. "You want to remember that."

"You're my best friend here, child, don't you know that? You see things my way. You ain't taken in by all this frippery and foolery around here. We're both of the same faith too, ain't we? Well then, you're the one I must count on to help me."

"What do you want me to do?" I inquired.

"Help me get away from here. And more than that, come a ways with me. I can't travel far alone on one leg and no money and wearin what's left of a Yankee uniform. If your boys get me I'll be sent to Andersonville or some place worse, and if my fellas see me wanderin around down here, I'll be shot before dark as a deserter. Will you come with me, Marie?"

"Before I decide, tell me a little more about what Miss Harriet did last night," I requested.

"I can't, I can't, you little imp!"

"Well then, what happened when Miss Martha came down?"

"She just hauled her sister outa here, that's all! You devilish child, I've said too much already! Ah now won't you come along with me, Marie. You know the roads around here, or at least some of them, and I could pass you off as my daughter, don't ye see, or maybe my little sister even, and we'd win piles o' sympathy that way."

"Take Alice or Edwina and pass her off as your wife."

"They wouldn't go, neither of them, after last night!"

"So I'm a third choice?"

"No, you're not, darlin. You're my very first choice and Amelia would be my second, but I know she'd refuse to take me anywhere but the damned old woods. I want to get far away from here, Marie. Dammitall, I want to go home!"

"Well naturally I can sympathize with that," I said. "All of us would like to get away from this dreary place. In fact I'm planning to go home myself as soon as my father comes by to fetch me. That's the reason I can't go anywhere with you right now, Johnny."

"But it wouldn't be for very long. Just until we got to the other side of the river and away from both armies. It wouldn't be more than a day or two or a week at most. I'd be safe then and I could go it alone and send you back here by the railway cars."

"I don't think there are any railway cars running in this vicinity at the moment."

"Well then you could come back by carriage or some other way. I'd find some quick way to get you back here."

"Where would you get the money since you don't have any now?"

"I'd raise it somewheres. A poor cripple with a sweet-lookin little girl wouldn't have any trouble raisin money."

"Do you mean we'd have to beg for it?"

"No, no. As long as we looked as though we needed it very badly, there'd be scads of folks to give it to us without us hardly askin."

"It still sounds like begging to me," I informed him, "and while I wouldn't mind giving it a try for a day or two, just for the novelty of it, I surely don't know what my father would say if he came by here and found I was engaged in that kind of activity."

"Listen, darlin," said Johnny. "There's somethin I got to tell you. I should've told you before but I didn't have the nerve to start. I'm only managin to do it now because I don't want to go off and leave you alone here at the mercy of the two old biddies."

And that's when he told me the outlandish story about meeting my dying father after a battle and being sent here to look out for me. Well, as I said, it seems ridiculous now but at the time I was very shocked by it.

The main reason I believed it, of course, was the way Johnny told it. That boy could really relate a story very convincingly. In this instance he talked so softly and he squeezed my hand so and he screwed up his face so and grew so sad himself in the telling that he actually managed to squeeze out a tear or two to keep me company when he saw me begin to cry.

In all fairness to him now, I don't think he anticipated my carrying on so about the news. I guess he didn't realize I had so much affection for my father because apparently there is something in my character that makes people assume that I am not capable of loving anybody. I guess maybe Johnny thought that I would be only momentarily disturbed by his story and that I would recover quickly and go off with him. Because that was part of the lie too, you see. That supposedly was what my "dying" father had wanted me to do.

Anyway I was so upset and making so much noise that Johnny grew very alarmed. And that was when he told me an even worse lie . . . I guess in an attempt to keep me in the room with him until he could calm me.

I was weeping very loudly, I guess, and had gone to the door, whereupon Johnny jumped up and hobbled just as fast as he could over there to block me. He was apparently thinking that he'd better not let me repeat the story about my father to other people. He knew that Miss Martha and Miss Harriet might attempt to convince me that the story was untrue, don't you see, and once that happened I might become his mortal enemy.

So then he told me the even more disturbing lie about my having been responsible for my father's getting killed. It was because of the Lord's being vexed with me, Johnny said, for eating meat on Friday. And then, things just went from bad to worse. I said I was going to ask Miss Martha to let me go home and see my mother and he said my mother wouldn't have me when she found out what I'd done and therefore the only thing left for me to do was to keep quiet about the whole business and go away with him.

He let go of me then, but followed me out into the hall. "Everythin will be all right, love," I remember he called softly as I went back up the stairs. "Don't worry about anythin, darlin. I'll take care of everythin."

You see I really think he began to feel sorry almost immediately that he had told me those terrible lies. I'm almost certain that if he had known how I was going to carry on right then, he never would have done it. And of course I'm absolutely certain that if he had known how it was going to affect my conduct later, he never would have done it. In that case, of course, he would've needed to be absolutely insane to take a chance on offending or frightening me.

Because you see I was very lonely then for my mother and, like Johnny himself, I wanted to go home in the worst way. It might be considered somewhat surprising that I felt like that because my mother has never been as sympathetic toward me as my father has and I gather I have always been much more of a trial for her than I have for him.

But when you think you have lost one parent, I guess it is only natural that your thoughts turn to the other parent and you hope that maybe this one will be a little more understanding and tolerant of you now. I realized, of course, that no new understanding was ever going to come about if my mother heard this terrible story about me from Johnny. My mother is just a terribly religious person who spends half her life praying and I was certain that she would accept my being the cause of my father's death as just one final act of devilment on the part of her wayward daughter.

And so it was plain that if I was ever to go home again, she couldn't be permitted to hear about my being such a sinner. It also seemed plain that I couldn't trust Johnny McBurney not to tell her unless I went along with him and became a guide for him and a beggar and maybe his servant too, for all I knew. And even then—even if I went with him and did everything he asked—I still wouldn't be able to trust him not to tell her some time or other, because he was such an impulsive spur-of-the-moment kind of fellow that he would be just liable to become displeased with me some day and do it anyway—sit down and write my mother a letter about it and ruin me forever.

For that same reason I didn't intend to say anything to Miss Martha or Miss Harriet about what Johnny had told me. There was no telling when one of them might become so upset with me over some trivial school matter that she would inform my mother about the whole story. Of course, I don't object to anyone knowing about it now since I found out the whole thing was completely untrue.

Anyway in the end it was all very bad luck for McBurney—my not telling our teachers, I mean—because it's quite possible that if I had told them immediately, Miss Martha—or perhaps even Miss Harriet—would have realized the ridiculousness of his story and would have marched right into the parlor and gotten the whole truth out of him. And then, of course, that would have changed my attitude toward him. I mean I undoubtedly would have been angry with him for lying to me that way but I would no longer have been frightened of his telling my mother.

Well, I went back to my room and stayed there for a long while, just lying there on my bed. Amelia had gone off to the woods or somewhere so I was alone with my troubles.

About a half hour or so later I heard the others arising and going downstairs to breakfast, but if my absence was noticed no one did anything about it because after a while I fell asleep and slept for hours.

I could tell by the sun that it was noon when I awakened and also I was beginning to feel a bit hungry. More than that I was also starting to feel a trifle vexed that no one had bothered to summon me for breakfast or morning lessons—not that I missed those, of course—or even, as far as I knew, to look in on me to see whether I was alive or dead.

Well I was lying there, comforting myself a little with these vexations and wondering what I could do to keep Johnny from informing my mother, when Emily Stevenson thrust open the door and sailed into the room— without knocking, naturally. Our student general is above such niceties.

"What are you crying about?" she demanded.

"I'm not crying," I yelled at her. I suppose I was crying but I was condemned if I was going to admit it to her.

"You certainly are crying and you have been crying for some time by the wretched sight of you. Your eyes are all swollen and your nose is all red and your cheeks are striped where the tears have washed the dirt away."

Well that made me very angry. "It's none of your business what I look like," I shouted, "and also you needn't come in here and tell me I have to go to lessons because I'm not going! I don't feel at all well!" And I ended with a small profanity which is really not such an awful word because my father uses it quite often but I suppose it's hardly something that ought to be repeated.

"You are going to have your mouth washed out with soap, Miss," said Emily. "We'll clean your tongue if not the rest of you."

"That will never happen," I informed her. "With the scarcity of soap nowadays Miss Martha doesn't even bother to threaten me with things like that anymore."

"Then I'll advise her to dose you with something else. If you're feeling ill we'll give you a couple of spoons of castor oil and tomorrow you'll feel better."

"Just try and give it to me," was my reply. "Don't forget what happened to Miss Harriet's finger when she tried to force castor oil into me last winter. She had her finger bitten, if you remember, and Miss Alice Simms got a good kick in the knee cap for trying to hold my legs down."

That seemed to give Emily pause for a moment because she just stood there and studied me. "You revolting child," she said finally, "I don't know why you should be included in any matter as important as this, but Miss Martha says you must be. We are all meeting in the library in a few minutes and you are required to be there."

"I told you I'm not attending any lessons today."

"This isn't a lesson. It's a meeting about McBurney."

"I don't want anything more to do with Johnny McBurney, now or ever," I said.

"That's the purpose of the meeting. None of us want any more to do with him so we have to decide what to do about him, since it seems just ignoring him isn't working too well."

"He hasn't done anything bad to you," I said, not really to defend Johnny but merely to continue the argument with Emily.

"Hasn't he though? He's only promising to give information to the Yankees which will lose the entire war for us, that's all. He informed me he was going to do that not two hours ago."

"Just where is he getting this information?" I inquired.

"He got it from me, if you must know. I very foolishly told him things, confidential things about our plans and strategies, because I thought he was a friend and also I was trying to take his mind off his own problems. Now this is how he repays me, by saying that once he leaves here, or once Yankee or Confederate troops are told about his being here, he intends to betray us . . . especially me and my father."

Well that mention of her father—who ought to have been betrayed, if you ask me, if he was stupid enough to tell military information to his daughter—set me to thinking again of my own father and I got caught up in a new attack of weeping.

"There, there, dear," said Emily, apparently thinking that I was worried about us losing the war. "Everything will be all right. We won't let McBurney harm us."

And so I guess because I had been waiting there for someone's shoulder to cry on, I cried on Emily's. That shows you how desperate I was, and feeling that way, I let her help me up from the bed and lead me down the stairs to the library where practically everyone was sitting waiting for the famous meeting to begin.

I believe everyone was there with one exception—Amelia—who I found out later spent the day in the woods tidying up the hiding place for Johnny. Of course he wasn't there either at the beginning although he came in later. Anyway I was rather glad of Amelia's absence because it explained why she hadn't come upstairs to inquire for me. At least I could think now that even though no one else in the place was interested in my welfare, Amelia might have been, had she been around.

Harriet Farnsworth

Note One. Most of the following conversation and testimony is reproduced exactly as it occurred on the afternoon of July 3rd although this is a fair copy made from my rough notes of that day.

Note Two. There has been some discussion between Miss Martha Hale Farnsworth and myself with regards to the proper nomenclature of the meeting which occurred on July 3rd for the purposes of this journal record. My position has been that the designation "Proceedings of Investigation" describe the situation best, since the word "Trial" which my sister proposes seems to me to presuppose some vested legal authority which we do not and did not possess. My sister's argument is that the conditions of the times and our extraordinarily isolated circumstances did in fact grant us temporary legal authority. She feels that since a decision was reached and a judgment made at this time, a trial, therefore, did take place. Perhaps she is right, at least in the lower case meaning of the word. However since this record is in my hand I feel it is my perogative to entitle it as my conscience dictates. It is a small matter in any case, since my sister and I are both aware that justice does not depend on the definition of a word.

Preliminaries of the Investigation

At approximately thirty minutes past the noon hour on July 3rd Miss Martha Farnsworth stated that she was ready to call our meeting to order. The time must be approximate because our library clock has run down on two occasions during the past year and had to be reset according to the sun, since we have had no visitors to bring us the correct time during that period.

Those assembled in the library were the following persons: Miss Martha Farnsworth, Miss Harriet Farnsworth, Miss Emily Stevenson, Miss Edwina Morrow, Miss Alice Simms, Miss Marie Deveraux and Matilda Farnsworth. One person was late in coming, Miss Marie Deveraux, which delayed the beginning of the meeting. One person did not attend. This was Miss Amelia Dabney, who was not in the house and whose whereabouts were reportedly unknown by any of the others present.

We were seated around the library table with Martha in Father's old chair at the head and myself to her left, Mattie at the end and the students in between. In front of me I had these pages—taken from one of Father's old tobacco account ledgers—a cup of blackberry ink which Mattie had made that morning, and, from Mattie also, a newly sharpened quill, the last remains of a wild turkey she had cooked for Corporal McBurney some weeks before.

There was some little frivolity involving Emily and Alice, but not as much really as I had anticipated.

Of course one reason for the relatively quiet response to the announcement of postponement of classes was the absence of our two youngest students, Miss Amelia and Miss Marie, who can be counted on to create some kind of disturbance on almost any occasion and especially at news of unexpected events. Oddly enough, Marie, who was present now, seemed very quiet and withdrawn and was seated with her hands folded, paying no attention to the rest of us. She was rather pale too, and I decided that unless she improved before nightfall, she would be dosed with castor oil and Mattie's herb medicine, just on the chance that she might be coming down with something.

Another chair, quite a comfortable one—the large, wing chair which is kept on the opposite side of the library fireplace from Father's chair—was placed at some distance from the table. This was to be for the use of Corporal McBurney if he decided to attend our meeting. At Miss Martha Farnsworth's suggestion a pair of cushions were placed on Miss Marie's chair so that Miss Marie might be on a level with the others at the table.

Proceedings of the Investigation

Miss Farnsworth: (rapping teaspoon on teacup to call meeting to order)
This meeting will please come to order. Miss Harriet, please call the roll.

Miss Harriet Farnsworth: (calls roll)

Miss Martha Farnsworth: (makes opening statement) I should like to make a brief opening statement. First, I want you all to understand the seriousness of what we are about to do. We are, in effect, setting up a little court here at Farnsworth School. We find this necessary because no other court is available to do what must be done. We are going to try to the best of our ability to discover the truth about certain matters and then act upon this knowledge in the way that seems best for all of us. As you all know, an individual here has been charged with very serious crimes. Other serious crimes are suspected of him. We must find out the extent of his culpability in these matters and, most important, we must consider to what extent it is possible, or perhaps probable, that these crimes will be repeated, or worse ones committed.

Miss Marie Deveraux: Are you going to punish Johnny?

Miss Martha Farnsworth: This court is not I alone, it is all of you. And we are not here to punish anyone. We are here to find a way or ways of protecting ourselves. Now I want to impress upon you that this meeting must be conducted in the same spirit of fervor and gravity as our meetings with God in church or during our prayers at night. Seeking the truth is seeking God.

Mattie Farnsworth: Amen.

Miss Martha Farnsworth: I want your complete attention to these matters. I want no giggling, no restlessness. I want you all to sit up straight in your chairs. I want no talking except when you are required to answer questions, or when you desire to make a statement to the chair.

Miss Marie Deveraux: What chair?

Miss Martha Farnsworth: The chair in which I am sitting. I might be called the chairlady of this meeting.

Miss Edwina Morrow: If it is a court, you ought to be called the judge, oughtn't you?

Miss Martha Farnsworth: If that is a cynical remark, Miss, it is out of place. If there is to be a judge here, it will be all of us.

Miss Alice Simms: Is Johnny going to be present?

Miss Martha Farnsworth: We are going to invite him to attend, if he so desires. His presence is not important to us, since we will not rely on his testimony.

Miss Harriet Farnsworth: Why not, sister?

Miss Martha Farnsworth: Obviously because we could not believe him.

Miss Marie Deveraux: You could ask him to swear on my Catholic prayer book.

Miss Martha Farnsworth: I'm sure no matter what oath he swore he would not hesitate to add perjury to his other misdeeds. However if he wants to join us, he is free to make any reasonable statements during this meeting and we will listen to him. That is his privilege in fair proceedings and we will not deny it to him. Now if he is present you must not smile at him or laugh at his sallies, with which we may expect him to try to disrupt this meeting. In the past we have been taken in by him. Let us be taken in no longer.

Miss Edwina Morrow: Will there be anyone to act as his defense representative? That is customary I think in court cases.

Miss Martha Farnsworth: If you, Miss, or anyone else here wishes at any time to speak in his defense you are free to do so.

Miss Emily Stevenson: In a court-martial a judge advocate is generally appointed to act as the prosecutor.

Miss Martha Farnsworth: This is not a court-martial. As we are all judges and, if we wish, defense attorneys, so we are also all prosecuting attorneys. Now is there anything else? Any more questions about procedure before we summon Mister McBurney?

Miss Harriet Farnsworth: (after a pause) I believe there are no more questions, sister.

Miss Martha Farnsworth: Very well then. Now generally we will conduct this meeting very much in the same manner as our lessons. When you are called on, answer quickly, briefly and truthfully. If you wish to speak at other times, or if you wish to leave the room for a moment, raise your hand. Let your questions and remarks be pertinent. Do not speak to the accused directly, but if he questions you, direct your answers to me. All right then, where is the accused?

Mattie Farnsworth: He's in the parlor. Leastways he was there this morning when I took his breakfast in to him and I ain't heard him stirring around since that time.

Miss Alice Simms: He's been out of the parlor at least once since he had his breakfast. I saw him coming up the stairs from the wine cellar with three bottles under his arm.

Miss Martha Farnsworth: It will be a mercy for all of us when that wine is all gone.

Miss Harriet Farnsworth: It may be all gone now, sister. If he had three bottles, that may be almost the last of it.

Miss Martha Farnsworth: Thank the Almighty for that. Mattie, will you go to the parlor and inform Mister McBurney that he is invited to join us in here.

Miss Harriet Farnsworth: Wait, sister. Since some of the matters which may be discussed here will be of a very private nature, do you think it is wise to have Mister McBurney in attendance?

Miss Martha Farnsworth: These matters concern him, sister. We intend to speak of nothing but what concerns him.

Miss Harriet Farnsworth: Even so, it may be embarrassing for some of these young ladies to speak of these matters in front of him.

Miss Martha Farnsworth: I don't care if they are embarrassed, they must suffer that. I do want to know if any of you are reluctant to the point of refusing to speak in his presence. Is this the case with any of you?

Miss Harriet Farnsworth: (after a pause) Apparently no one will refuse to speak, sister.

Miss Martha Farnsworth: What about yourself, sister?

Miss Harriet Farnsworth: I will not refuse.

Miss Martha Farnsworth: Very well then. Go along and summon him, Mattie.

(During this period there were some incidental remarks which I am including since they occurred while the meeting was still officially in progress.)

Miss Martha Farnsworth: What are you doing, Miss?

Miss Marie Deveraux: I'm trying to catch a fly which is pestering me.

Miss Martha Farnsworth: Sit quietly and he will not bother you. You, Miss, what is that picture you are drawing?

Miss Alice Simms: (putting aside her pen) Nothing.

Miss Marie Deveraux: It's a dagger piercing a heart.

Miss Martha Farnsworth: The question wasn't addressed to you, Miss. I would suggest, Miss Alice, that if you have the ink and the space in your exercise book to spare, you use it to practice your multiplication tables or your French verbs.

Miss Emily Stevenson: He may not come willingly at all. We may have to tie him up and drag him in here.

Miss Martha Farnsworth: There'll be nothing of that sort. If he doesn't want to listen to the charges brought against him, that is his prerogative.

Miss Marie Deveraux: I believe he'll come all right. Today happens to be his birthday and maybe he'll think we've arranged some sort of party for him.

(At this time Mister John McBurney did enter the room on his crutches

followed by Mattie. He was wearing his uniform, which Mattie had evidently repaired and pressed for him. He was clean shaven and neatly combed and nearly sober.)

Corporal McBurney: Good afternoon to you all, ladies. I thought maybe you were serving the lunch in here today instead of in the dining room.

Miss Martha Farnsworth: Mister McBurney, we have called this meeting to consider charges against you. Will you stay and listen to them?

Corporal McBurney: To be sure, Miss Martha. If people are going to talk about me, I'm bound to stay and hear what's said. There's not many young fellows get that chance, you know, to hear a lot of fine ladies open up their hearts about them. Of course, I may have to straighten you out though, if you say bad things about me.

Miss Martha Farnsworth: We intend to say nothing but the truth here, Mister McBurney, and if you are capable of it we would ask you to do the same. Is that clear, sir?

Corporal McBurney: Crystal clear, ma'am.

Miss Martha Farnsworth: Will you take that chair, sir?

Corporal McBurney: (sitting) If such be your desire, ma'am.

Miss Martha Farnsworth: Very well then, we will proceed. John McBurney, we are gathered here today. . . .

Corporal McBurney: To unite me and Mattie in holy matrimony!

Miss Martha Farnsworth: (rapping the teacup) Be quiet, sir! If you will not be orderly, you must leave! Now once again, John McBurney, we are gathered here to investigate the validity of several charges of grave and criminal misconduct on your part as well as several charges involving lesser offenses. *(Looking at charges listed on blank page of her Book of Common Prayer.)* The lesser offenses include dishonesty in speech, cursing and using vulgar language in the presence of ladies and children, drinking to excess and appearing in a drunken condition in the presence of ladies and children.

Corporal McBurney: I offer you all my most sincere apologies for those things, ladies.

Miss Martha Farnsworth: The major offenses with which you are charged include the breaking and damaging of school property, the theft of money and valuable articles, grievous assault on a member of this household, threatening violence to other household members and several criminal offenses of a sexual nature which we will not name at the present time.

Corporal McBurney: Oh why not name them, ma'am? We're all friends here.

Miss Martha Farnsworth: They will be identified at the proper time.

Corporal McBurney: It's all lies, all of that. I didn't steal anything or threaten anybody except as a joke. I did break a chair or two by accident. I'll pay for that as soon as I get work.

Miss Martha Farnsworth: Do you have anything else to say in answer to these charges?

Corporal McBurney: No, ma'am. I'll let you tell me all about the rest of it.

Miss Martha Farnsworth: Do you plead guilty to all the lesser charges?

Corporal McBurney: Yes, yes.

Miss Martha Farnsworth: Then with your permission we will not waste any time in discussing the lesser charges but instead turn our attention now to the more serious charges.

Corporal McBurney: It's all lies, all of that. I didn't steal anything.

Miss Martha Farnsworth: Very well then, we will take up the first offense in the second group . . . the breaking and damaging of school property.

Corporal McBurney: I plead guilty to that too.

Miss Martha Farnsworth: Do you wish me to name the various items of property?

Corporal McBurney: No, that won't be necessary. I'll take your word for it, Miss Martha. If you've put a few extra dishes or an odd wine glass or two in there, it's all right with me. I don't mind payin you a bit extra in return for the grand and glorious time I've had here.

Miss Martha Farnsworth: Very well then, we will proceed to the next item on the list . . . the theft of money and other valuable articles. This is a matter which concerns me personally, Mister McBurney. I charge you with stealing two hundred dollars in Federal gold coins from my room, a set of keys on a ring and a valuable gold ornament on a gold chain.

Corporal McBurney: You must be mad.

Miss Martha Farnsworth: Do you deny all knowledge of the money and the articles?

Corporal McBurney: You know I had the locket. I gave it to you in the wine cellar a few nights ago. It can't have much value for you the way you stepped on it and smashed it.

Miss Martha Farnsworth: Do you deny having the key ring?

Corporal McBurney: No, I admit having the key ring and I'm keeping it too for my own protection. Being a cripple and all and not able to move very fast, I wouldn't want to be locked up here anywhere, you know, in case there was ever a fire or an earthquake or something like that.

Miss Martha Farnsworth: Has anyone threatened to lock you up?

Corporal McBurney: They couldn't, could they, not as long as I have the keys. I'm keeping them safe and I'll give them back to you when I leave.

Miss Martha Farnsworth: Meanwhile you will use them to loot every room and cupboard in this house.

Corporal McBurney: That's not fair, ma'am. I haven't entered any room here yet without permission, except the downstairs rooms, which aren't locked, and the wine cellar.

Miss Martha Farnsworth: You entered my room in order to take the keys and steal the money and the jewelry.

Corporal McBurney: That's not so! I didn't take any money and the keys and the locket were given to me.

Miss Martha Farnsworth: By whom?

Corporal McBurney: By somebody here.

Miss Martha Farnsworth: You're lying, Mister McBurney.

Corporal McBurney: I'm not lying, dammit! I was never in your room! I admit having the keys but I've never used them except for the wine cellar and that cabinet over there where you had that old pistol. Hell, I'll give them back to you now if they mean that much to you and let you just try locking me up anywhere. I'll show you how fast I can break a door down if you try any tricks like that.

Miss Martha Farnsworth: And the money, will you return that too?

Corporal McBurney: I don't have your Goddam money!

Miss Martha Farnsworth: Then who does have it?

Corporal McBurney: I don't know!

Miss Martha Farnsworth: Very well, Mister McBurney. We seem to have reached an impasse in this matter so we will proceed to the next charge. I have questioned Miss Alice Simms privately this morning, Mister McBurney, and she admits to having improper relations with you. . . .

Corporal McBurney: Does she?

Miss Martha Farnsworth: Which she says were forced on her by you.

Corporal McBurney: She lies!

Miss Martha Farnsworth: She states that you threatened to inflict bodily harm on her unless she consented.

Corporal McBurney: That's a damn lie and you know it, Alice! Why did you say that? Answer me, Alice, why did you!

Miss Alice Simms: My name is Alicia . . . and I'm not supposed to talk with you. . . .

Corporal McBurney: She's lying, Miss Martha, and I'll tell you something else . . . she's the one who took the key ring and the locket from your room, and probably the money too.

Miss Alice Simms: I didn't, Miss Martha, I swear I didn't!

Miss Martha Farnsworth: Be quiet, Miss Alice. Mister McBurney, you are charged with having carnal knowledge of this fifteen-year-old girl.

Corporal McBurney: She's seventeen or eighteen for God's sake! Look at her! She told me herself she was eighteen!

Miss Martha Farnsworth: Do you deny the charge?

Corporal McBurney: Don't you see how she's lying about her age so's you'll keep her on here?

Miss Martha Farnsworth: Do you deny going to this girl's bedroom late at night?

Corporal McBurney: No, but. . . .

Miss Martha Farnsworth: Do you deny forcing your way into her room? Do you deny forcing her to consent to you?

Corporal McBurney: I didn't force her to do anything for God's sake!

Miss Alice Simms: He did, Miss Martha! He did everything you said. He made me do bad things . . . and he stole your keys and the locket . . . and the money too!

Corporal McBurney: It's lies, all lies! Listen, I'll tell you the truth about the keys. I asked her to get them for me, but nothing else! I didn't ask her to take anything else!

Miss Martha Farnsworth: Mister McBurney, do you deny having sexual relations with this fifteen-year-old girl?

Corporal McBurney: She's not fifteen, Goddamit!

Miss Martha Farnsworth: Do you deny the charge?

Corporal McBurney: No, no, I don't deny it!

Miss Martha Farnsworth: Very well, we will move on to the next charge. You are also accused of having an improper relationship with Miss Edwina Morrow.

Corporal McBurney: Who's charging me with that? Did Edwina say that?

Miss Edwina Morrow: (drawing pictures in her exercise book) I don't remember saying it.

Miss Martha Farnsworth: Miss Edwina, do you deny that anything of the sort happened between you and Mister McBurney?

Miss Edwina Morrow: (still drawing pictures) I'm not denying that it happened. I'm denying that I said it happened.

Corporal McBurney: (arising and leaning forward on his crutches) Nothing happened between you and me. You say that it did and I'll fix you, my girl. I'll fix you proper, I will!

Miss Martha Farnsworth: Pay no attention to him, Miss Edwina. Pay no attention to his threats. Now it has been stated that McBurney forced himself on you as he did with Miss Alice.

Corporal McBurney: Did she say that? Did Edwina say that?

Miss Martha Farnsworth: Miss Alice has said it. Miss Alice has stated that Miss Edwina told her about it.

Corporal McBurney: By God I'll say something about Miss Edwina!

Miss Edwina Morrow: I didn't, I didn't! Johnny, I didn't tell anyone anything!

Miss Harriet Farnsworth: Sister, it seems to me we are concerning ourselves with a lot of hearsay evidence.

Miss Martha Farnsworth: Be quiet, sister. We are not depending on it. Now, Miss Edwina, you must not be frightened by this fellow's threats. He is not going to harm your reputation or anyone else's. The evil he has done here will be forgotten by all of us. And I can promise you it's never going to happen again.

Miss Edwina Morrow: I swear I didn't tell Alice anything. . . .

Miss Alice Simms: I thought you did, Edwina. He did attack you, didn't he, like he did me?

Corporal McBurney: I didn't! I hardly touched her. And whatever I did, she consented to it!

Miss Martha Farnsworth: Is that your defense, Mister McBurney? We have heard already of how Miss Alice consented to your demands because of fear, and this young lady, Edwina Morrow, is likewise very obviously afraid of you.

Corporal McBurney: Lady? Lady is it?

Miss Martha Farnsworth: Pay no attention to him, Miss Edwina. He will not harm you any more. Now I think we can move on to the next charge. Mister McBurney's conduct with my sister.

Miss Harriet Farnsworth: Please, Martha . . . !

Corporal McBurney: Are you going to charge me with attacking her, too?

Miss Martha Farnsworth: I believe I am qualified to do so. I saw the event with my own eyes, Mister McBurney.

Corporal McBurney: And was that without her consent too? Did I go upstairs and haul the old biddy out of bed and drag her down the stairs by her hair, and rip the night dress off her skinny behind?

Miss Harriet Farnsworth: Please, please . . . I'm trying to write. You're all going too fast, and I'm trying to write.

Miss Martha Farnsworth: I think we can pass on to the next item . . . the physical assault on Miss Harriet which took place in her bedroom yesterday afternoon. Do you wish to deny that, Mister McBurney?

Corporal McBurney: No, I won't deny anything else. Go (UNPRINT-ABLE!) yourself, ma'am!

Miss Martha Farnsworth: Sister, do you want to say anything about that assault?

Miss Harriet Farnsworth: He was trying to kill me!

Corporal McBurney: You go (UNPRINTABLE!) yourself too, Miss Harriet.

Miss Martha Farnsworth: Mister McBurney, I cannot tolerate much more of this in the presence of these young ladies. There is just one more item here, Mister McBurney. What did you do to this child, Marie Deveraux, this morning?

Corporal McBurney: I didn't do anything to her, old lady!

Miss Martha Farnsworth: Mister McBurney, I saw her come upstairs from the living room at about six o'clock this morning. I saw you follow her to the stairs and call to her. She was in her night dress, very pale and weeping. What did you do to her?

Corporal McBurney: You dirty-minded old woman!

Miss Martha Farnsworth: She has spent the whole day in her room. This is the first time since she has been in this school that she has done that. This is the first time that she has missed coming to a meal. What did you do to her, Mister McBurney?

Corporal McBurney: Ask her, you bald-headed old bitch!

Miss Martha Farnsworth: What did he do to you, Miss Marie?

Miss Marie Deveraux: (weeping) Nothing, he didn't do anything.

Miss Martha Farnsworth: Don't be afraid of him, child. No one in this house need ever again be afraid of him.

Corporal McBurney: (starting out) Is that so, Miss Martha. Is that what you think? Well even with only one leg I'm a match for the whole bunch of you here. And don't forget I've also got the pistol. I'll tell you something else. I was planning to leave here today. All I wanted was your goodwill before I left. Now I'll stay 'til I'm ready to go. You think you've got charges against me now. Just wait until I really get started raising some hell around here. *(At this point Corporal McBurney left the room.)*

Miss Martha Farnsworth: Well, what are we to do with him?

Matilda Farnsworth: Send him off. Send him packing. Take a broom to him. Tell him, "Yankee, you clear out now! You clear out of here!"

Miss Martha Farnsworth: He has already been told that, Mattie, and it hasn't done any good.

Matilda Farnsworth: He hasn't been told that directly, has he? He hasn't been told in them exact words. Maybe you been too nice to him about his going away. Maybe now you got to get mean about it, and tell him, "Yankee, this is what you got to do. Right now, this minute!"

Miss Martha Farnsworth: That's enough, Mattie. You have the same right as the rest of us here to offer your opinion, but you mustn't persist with a suggestion when you are told that it is useless.

Matilda Farnsworth: Then if you can't send him away, go down to the front gate and holler. Everybody go down there and holler, "We got a no account Yankee in this house and he won't go away when we ask him nice to do it. Somebody come in here, please, and throw this no account Yankee out."

Miss Martha Farnsworth: Mattie. . . .

Miss Harriet Farnsworth: Let me explain it to you, Mattie, dear. There are none of our boys in this vicinity any more. The only troops on these roads now are Union boys and if we call on them for help we may find we have something worse than Corporal McBurney to cope with. Especially if he tells them that he has been mistreated here.

Miss Emily Stevenson: (emphatically) He certainly hasn't been! Of course I know he thinks he has been, because of the loss of his leg, I suppose, and possibly for other misguided reasons too. He doesn't stop to think of all our boys who've lost legs in battle and probably weren't half as well treated afterwards, as McBurney has been here.

Miss Harriet Farnsworth: If I thought he'd go away and not say anything mean about us, I'd even be willing to give him money to compensate for whatever injustice he feels he has suffered here.

Miss Emily Stevenson: You're too soft-hearted, Miss Harriet. What he'd do is take the money and betray us anyway. Miss Martha didn't even mention what I consider the most serious charge against him. If I had been called upon to speak, I would have accused him of spying and intending to furnish military information to the enemy.

Miss Martha Farnsworth: Stay to the point, young ladies. What shall we do with him?

Miss Alice Simms: We might take him back to the woods and leave him there.

Miss Edwina Morrow: What makes you think he'd go to the woods any more quickly than he'd go off down the road?

Miss Alice Simms: If he were asleep or unconscious we might put him on that stretcher we made and carry him out there.

Miss Harriet Farnsworth: I'm afraid we have no means of rendering him unconscious. If there were any such opiates or anesthetics here Miss Martha would have used them.

Miss Marie Deveraux: You gave him lots of wine to drink before his operation in order to put him to sleep. Couldn't we do that again?

Miss Harriet Farnsworth: It seems the wine is almost gone, dear. We think Mister McBurney has now taken most of it from the cellar.

Miss Edwina Morrow: What you all seem to be forgetting is that even if he were rendered unconscious with spirits or by some other means, he wouldn't remain that way indefinitely.

Miss Alice Simms: That's true. And then he'd march right back from the woods and we might be very much worse off than before.

Miss Emily Stevenson: He could be bound securely. Then he wouldn't be able to return.

Miss Edwina Morrow: Are you suggesting that he be left in the woods to die from starvation or thirst? I'm sure, Miss Emily, that wouldn't be a very pleasant way to die.

Miss Alice Simms: Of course if he did die it wouldn't be any worse than what has happened to plenty of other boys in the past three years, including close relatives of many of us here.

Miss Emily Stevenson: That's quite true, Alice, and I'm most glad to hear you say it.

Miss Marie Deveraux: I would like to hear Alice say which close relative of hers has perished.

Miss Alice Simms: I'll be glad to furnish dozens of names, but first I'd like this nasty child to give me the name of just one relative of hers who has sacrificed his life.

Miss Marie Deveraux: You think I can't do it, eh Miss Alice? Would you care to make a little wager on it, say perhaps our portion of meat at dinner, if we happen to be getting any?

Miss Martha Farnsworth: (striking the teacup with her spoon) Girls, girls . . . this is no time for private arguments . . . and that's not a suitable subject for argument at any time.

Miss Alice Simms: If her roommate hadn't brought him from the woods in the first place, we wouldn't even need to be bothering with this meeting. He'd've been dead long ago.

Miss Marie Deveraux: That's very nice! That's your usual cowardly way, Alice, attacking someone who isn't here to defend herself.

Miss Harriet Farnsworth: Girls, girls, you must stop this! And, Miss Alice, we cannot blame Miss Amelia for her act of charity. After all, if Miss Martha had not attended him during his two critical illnesses he would certainly have passed away, too. Indeed it causes us to pause and wonder, doesn't it, young ladies?

Miss Martha Farnsworth: At what, sister?

Miss Harriet Farnsworth: At how the Lord has brought him to the eternal door on those two occasions, and then permitted us to bring him back from it. Perhaps there is a sign for us somewhere in that.

Miss Martha Farnsworth: What are you suggesting, sister?

Miss Harriet Farnsworth: Nothing, sister. I'm just musing aloud.

Miss Marie Deveraux: If you're interested, I might be able to think of a way to get Johnny into the woods, but somebody else will have to find a way to keep him there.

Miss Harriet Farnsworth: How would you get him there, dear?

Miss Marie Deveraux: Well, Amelia has a secret hiding place out there. I won't tell you exactly where it is, but it's very deep in the woods. Now she has already suggested to Johnny that he go there, but he's refused up 'til now. However, I think he might agree if he had some good reason for going.

Miss Martha Farnsworth: And do you have that good reason?

Miss Marie Deveraux: Yes, Miss Martha. I think perhaps he would go if he was very frightened of us.

Miss Harriet Farnsworth: He's not though. It's just the other way around. We're frightened of him.

Miss Marie Deveraux: But we could change that. We could scare him by making him think we are planning to do something bad to him.

Miss Emily Stevenson: And what bad thing did you have in mind?

Miss Marie Deveraux: Well, maybe one of us could tell him that the others had decided to kill him.

Miss Harriet Farnsworth: Miss Marie, you mustn't say such things!

Miss Martha Farnsworth: Sister, we are in such a situation here that we cannot refuse to listen to anyone or any plan. We adults don't seem able to cope with McBurney. Perhaps these young ladies can think of a way to do it. You may continue, Miss Marie.

Miss Marie Deveraux: Well that was really all I had in mind, that I tell him a vote was taken, and it was decided to execute him.

Miss Emily Stevenson: I'm all for it! That's a fine idea!

Miss Edwina Morrow: How would we be planning to carry out this execution? Just in case he asks?

Miss Emily Stevenson: Firing squad.

Miss Edwina Morrow: That's ridiculous. Firing squad of what?

Miss Alice Simms: Hanging. We could tell him he's going to be hanged, like in the picture Edwina is drawing in her copybook.

Miss Edwina Morrow: (scratching out the picture) That's only scribbling and it has nothing to do with McBurney.

Miss Marie Deveraux: All the same, it isn't a bad idea. It would be a pretty scary thing to tell Johnny.

Miss Harriet Farnsworth: Do you think he would believe it?

Miss Emily Stevenson: Why not? It's a very common thing in wartime. He knows it's the usual punishment for spies and traitors.

Miss Edwina Morrow: Where would you be planning to carry out this sentence?

Miss Harriet Farnsworth: How about on one of the trees in the yard? Perhaps the apple tree near the barn would do.

Miss Martha Farnsworth: Are you getting into the spirit of it now, sister?

Miss Harriet Farnsworth: If it's only to frighten him . . . to drive him away. . . .

Miss Alice Simms: Who's going to be appointed to tell him this news?

Miss Marie Deveraux: I suppose I could do it. He might be more apt to believe me than he would some of you other people here, since we're of the same religion and all that.

Miss Harriet Farnsworth: Miss Marie hasn't had any difficulties with him either, as some of the rest of us have had.

Miss Alice Simms: It might be better to let Mattie do it. She hasn't had any trouble with him either and she'd be less likely to exaggerate than Marie.

Miss Edwina Morrow: If anyone could exaggerate a hanging, I suppose Marie could.

Miss Marie Deveraux: And why not, for pity's sake? The more colorful a story like that the better, I say. Besides I'm sure Mattie would be likely to get the whole thing all mixed up, wouldn't you, Mattie dear?

Matilda Farnsworth: Probably so, Miss Marie. It's more than likely I would.

Miss Edwina Morrow: What about Amelia? Johnny certainly trusts her.

Miss Marie Deveraux: She'd refuse to do it. I can tell you that for a positive fact.

Miss Martha Farnsworth: Well, Miss Marie, it seems that you're appointed. Now how do you propose to spread this news to him?

Miss Marie Deveraux: Well, I'll go and find him in a few minutes, and tell him that it's important that he leave the house with me right away. I'll say we have to go and find Amelia and let her lead us to this secret hiding place. I'll say that the sentence has been passed and that you all are preparing now to carry it out.

Miss Alice Simms: Then you might add that right now we're fixing ropes to bind him with.

Miss Edwina Morrow: What ropes?

Miss Emily Stevenson: There are those pieces of harness which we used on the stretcher. But what about the other rope?

Miss Alice Simms: Bed sheets. We could tear up sheets and other pieces of cloth and braid them.

Miss Harriet Farnsworth: Oh, I'm afraid we don't have nearly enough sheets for anything like that. You know how we've used so many of them for his bandages.

Miss Edwina Morrow: Well you don't really need the sheets, do you? I mean isn't the idea just to tell him that you're making his noose?

Miss Harriet Farnsworth: Of course, of course . . . that's all it is.

Miss Marie Deveraux: I'll tell you. It might be more convincing if you had really started on it. Maybe we could even fix it so Johnny would see you tearing up the sheets. That would really frighten him. Also that way I wouldn't be telling any lie.

Miss Alice Simms: That's certainly important. It would never do for Marie to be untruthful.

Miss Marie Deveraux: (who seemed to have regained some of her color and vitality) Especially since this house is just filled with honest people like Alice.

Miss Martha Farnsworth: That will do! You may go to McBurney now, Miss Marie.

Miss Marie Deveraux: And may I tell him that he has been condemned to death?

Miss Martha Farnsworth: Yes. *(At this point Miss Marie Deveraux left the room.)*

Miss Harriet Farnsworth: Do you think he will believe it, sister?

Miss Martha Farnsworth: I hope so.

Miss Harriet Farnsworth: And what shall we do in the meanwhile?

Miss Martha Farnsworth: Think about it. We shall sit here and think about it.

Miss Edwina Morrow: I would like to ask Miss Harriet a question before this meeting ends. I would like to know more about what really happened last night. For instance, why did she come downstairs?

Miss Martha Farnsworth: You needn't answer that, sister. We are judging McBurney here, not you.

Miss Harriet Farnsworth: Oh, but I must answer it, sister. You deserve to know everything I can tell you, although I'm afraid it isn't much.

Miss Edwina Morrow: Tell us what you can, Miss Harriet.

Miss Harriet Farnsworth: Well it was like a dream. In fact the beginning of it was a dream.

Miss Emily Stevenson: You mean you were walking in your sleep, Miss Harriet?

Miss Harriet Farnsworth: Yes . . . yes, perhaps I was. You see, I was dreaming about a person who was very close to me . . . and somehow I began to think that person was Mister McBurney. He kept calling me . . . and calling me . . . and when I awoke . . . if I ever did awake . . . I'm not sure now that I did . . . but when it seemed to me I was awake, I was sitting with him on the settee in the parlor, having a glass of wine with him. That summer . . . I kept thinking that summer had returned. But he wasn't looking at me, he kept looking away. And oh, I wanted him so much to look at me and tell me I was beautiful. . . .

(This is all I can report of the Proceedings of Investigation. I was very nervous and upset at that point and one of my bad headaches was coming on. Also, I think I may have wept a bit too loudly and my sister was disturbed by it. She and Mattie helped me up the stairs to my room, and then they returned to the library where, I understand, shortly thereafter my sister closed the meeting.)

Amelia Dabney

I really didn't know anything about the meeting although I probably wouldn't have attended if I had. What I did was spend the morning and a part of the afternoon in the woods. There is this little quiet place I have out there, which I go to quite often—perhaps I've mentioned it before. Anyway, earlier on that day the possibility of Corporal McBurney's going out there had been discussed by my roommate.

I cleared out all the old fallen branches and then removed one or two things which I thought maybe would annoy him. Some wasps, for instance, were starting to build a mud nest in a tree trunk, so I took the nest out very carefully and found another place for it, some distance away. I also resettled one or two spiders and beetles and a garter snake. Then I swept the dead leaves into a pile and put them on a bed of boughs for Johnny to sleep on.

Well I didn't hurry, so I wasn't finished until past noon. Then on the way back I stopped to pick a few mushrooms, because I knew Johnny liked them. Anyway when I entered the house I heard voices in the library, peeked in, and saw everyone seated around the table and trying to talk at the same time, and decided not to concern myself with it at all.

Then I came across the hall and glanced into the parlor. Johnny was seated there on his settee, drinking wine from a bottle and grinning foolishly, although a little nervously I thought.

"I have a nice place all fixed for you whenever you want to go to it," I told him.

"What could be nicer than here," he said, waving the bottle. "Good wine, fine women, and we'll have a merry song, too, in a minute as soon as I can think of a gamey one. How's about this?" And he crooned softly, "Come out from under your petticoat, Mary Anne my dear. The night is dark, the grass is warm, so what've you got to fear."

Then he halted abruptly. "Now I shouldn't be singin that kind o' song in front of you, should I, sweet? You're the nicest one here and you don't deserve that kind o' song."

"What is everyone talking about in the library?" I asked him.

"Me! They're figurin out ways to get back at me."

"What do you think they'll do?"

"What can they do? Two women, five girls and a darky. Four girls, I don't count you."

"You shouldn't count Marie either. She's on your side."

"I don't know," said he. "I ain't so sure about Marie. The only one I really trust here is you."

"That's nice of you," I said. "I'm glad you trust me, because I trust you, too."

"Why is that?" he wondered. "Why do you and I feel so sure of each other? For my part, I suppose it's because you helped me in the first place, and also since then you haven't seemed to want anything special of me the way some of the others have."

"For my part," I said, "it's because I know in your heart you're a kind person. I feel sure you'd never hurt anyone . . . or any animal . . . intentionally."

"Well then," he said, lifting the bottle again. "We're friends for life then, eh?" He swallowed a great gulp of wine and then sang: "Here's a toast to ye, darlin Amelia. If I was a thief I'd surely steal ya. You're still a bit young to be nippin on wine. So, I'll drink your share of the toast as well as mine." And he did so.

"Are you sure you don't want to come out to the woods with me, now," I asked him.

"Nope," said he. "If I did it'd be thought I was afraid. Even if I was afraid, I wouldn't give them the satisfaction of knowin it."

"Well you'd better come upstairs with me anyway," I told him. "I don't want to leave you alone down here."

"Can you protect me better up there?"

"I can keep a better eye on you. And also you'll be out of the way of those people. If you're not around them they can't say you're causing them any trouble."

"Well I'll go up with you then," said Johnny. "It's not that I need you to guard me, o' course, but I am glad to have a bit of company. I'm going daft here with only the four walls to talk to."

He lifted himself on his crutches, handed me the bottle of wine to carry and then followed me out of the room and up the stairs. He was getting around very well by that time, and I noticed he could move fairly silently as well as rapidly on his supports. I didn't ask him to be quiet, because I didn't care particularly right then whether or not Miss Martha and the others knew he was upstairs, but I guess he decided on his own that it might be better if they didn't know.

When we got to the room I share with Marie, he came in and sat on her bed, which was all disarranged, I noticed, as though Marie had spent the day there. I put the wine on the table near him and also my handkerchief full of mushrooms which still needed to be sorted.

"I have some things to do," I told him. "If you like you can take a nap there while I'm busy."

"I'm not tired," he said. "What is it you have to do?"

"Attend to my sick turtle." I reached under my bed and got the jewel box in which my turtle was staying. I had brought him a few dried insects from the woods, which I fed to him now.

"Do you pick those things up with your hands?" Johnny asked, making a little grimace.

"How else would I pick them up?"

"Oh don't get huffy. It just doesn't seem proper for a little girl, that's all. Also that turtle doesn't look sick to me."

"He's improving rapidly. He's much better now than he was."

"You're very fond of him, are you?" Johnny asked, drinking some of his wine.

"He's my dearest possession. I love all animals, but I love this turtle the best of all."

"Well then," said Johnny. "I certainly do hope he makes a complete recovery."

"Thank you, Johnny," I replied. "I know you're sincere about that. I'll tell you something else. If I had to go away from here and leave this turtle in charge of someone, that someone would be you. I know you'd care for him just as lovingly as I do."

"Sure I would. He's a great old turtle." Johnny took another swallow of wine, then selected a mushroom and began to nibble on it.

"Be careful," I said. "There are one or two bad ones in there."

"I know the bad ones," he said with assurance. "Don't we have these things growin all over Ireland. They're one of my favorite foods, you know. It's a wonder you wouldn't bring in a whole lot of them for Mattie to cook for dinner."

"Most of the people here don't care for them very much," I said. "Many of our girls are opposed to eating anything that grows wild in the woods. Now you've taken another one. You'd better watch out, Johnny."

"I told you I know them," said he, "and I don't see a false one in here. Why would you bring back bad ones anyway?"

"Well I can use them in my collection, and also they were growing with the others and I hated to leave them standing there alone."

He laughed. "God Almighty, you're a strange one, but I love you anyway. You're my heart's favorite, Amelia. Well maybe I will take a snooze for a minute or two. You wake me up, will you, if any of the mean ones come sneakin up here."

"Yes, I'll wake you," I promised.

He stretched out on the bed and was silent for a moment as he stared at the stump of his leg. "What is it do you suppose they'll try to do to me, Amelia?" he asked after a while.

"I don't know," I said, "but if it's something bad I won't let them."

"Thank you, Amelia," he said, and shortly after that he went to sleep. Now I'm not sure to this day whether he was honestly afraid at that time, or whether he was just pretending to be in order to make me think I was truly helping him.

Well I told Marie this, when she came in a few moments later. I was still attending to my turtle, and so at first I didn't pay much attention to her.

"I see the famous John McBurney is asleep," she remarked, sitting down on the floor beside me.

"Your powers of observation are becoming quite acute," I said.

"Don't be pert with me," she said. "I'm here on an errand. I'm supposed to tell Johnny something."

"What?"

"That Miss Martha and the others are preparing to hang him."

"Are they?"

"Well to be honest with you, I don't see how it's possible, although I'm sure they'd like to do it. Anyway I'm supposed to convince Johnny that they're getting everything ready and that they're going to do it tonight. That's supposed to frighten him into running off to the woods with us and never coming back."

"And that will be enough for them? That's all they want, that he goes off and never comes back?"

"Well they say that's all they want," Marie replied. "Actually, I believe most of them are afraid he may do more harm away from here than he's done while he's been staying here—by talking about various things, I mean. As a matter of fact, I'm a bit afraid of that myself."

"What could he say that would harm you?"

"Oh, we all have our little secrets," said Marie. "I'll tell you about mine a little later. Meanwhile, what's your opinion? Do you think it's worthwhile to try and frighten Johnny?"

"No, I don't," I said, "but if that's what you've been sent to do, I suppose you might as well try it. If it works, it suits our purpose as well as Miss Martha's."

And so Marie awakened him and told him that ridiculous story about how they were planning to hang him from the apple tree that very night with a rope made out of bed sheets or something. Johnny just laughed at first, or at least pretended to laugh, but after a few moments of Marie's very vivid description of all the details of the plan, he became noticeably less sure of himself and his voice took on a very definite quaver.

Marie described how they were going to wait until he was asleep that evening. Then they'd sneak into the parlor, bind him tightly with harness and drag him out into the moonlight. Finally they'd put the noose around his neck, throw the rope over the apple tree branch, and then tie the other end to Dolly and whip her until she bolted away.

Well, I guess it could have worked, although I certainly wouldn't have counted on it. Anyway, whether you believed that some girls and women could carry out a plan like that or not, just the fact that they hated you enough to discuss it would probably be enough to make most any person feel pretty nervous.

And Johnny began to get into a very excited state. He was mumbling curses and drinking wine with a trembling hand and a still more trembling lip, and spilling the wine all over the bed clothes in the process.

I guess it was a mistake to tell him, because it certainly didn't accomplish its intended result in the end, or at least not the goal announced for it. The thing was, Johnny couldn't make up his mind whether to be more frightened or more angry and as a consequence from the two emotions working on him together, he just lost control completely.

"Damn em, damn em all," he kept muttering. "Damn their dirty souls, the lot of them. Do me in entirely, would they? And after all the other rottenness they've done me here."

"It's going to be all right, Johnny," I told him. "Marie and I will take you out to my hiding place and you'll be safe."

"I'll fix em first," he said. "I'll fix em all. I'll smash every bit of glass and every stick of furniture in the house. Then I'll take care of every one of the biddies here, so I will. Like it or not, they'll get a bit o' Johnny McBurney. Then I'll burn the whole Goddam place down over the heads of all of you."

"You're getting nasty now," said Marie. "If you're going to keep on that way, you're going to make me disgusted with you. When you talk about burning down the house, you know, you're forgetting that my roommate and I happen to live here, too."

He didn't reply to that. He was trembling very violently then and I tried to think of some way to help him. "Here," I said finally. "Hold my turtle for a moment, will you, Johnny? I have to clean his box for him." And I put the little turtle in Johnny's hand.

You see, I was hoping that holding that friendly little turtle would occupy Johnny's mind for a few moments, and in the interval he might calm down. However, it didn't work out that way.

"Get the ugly thing away from me," he shouted. And he took my turtle and threw him against the wall.

Matilda Farnsworth

Now, if you ask me why I'd cook and serve bad mushrooms, I'll tell you it was because they was handed to me and I was told to cook em and that's what I did. I didn't look at em very hard and I didn't test em with a silver knife the way you're supposed to do. I just put em in a pot and cooked em like Miss Martha said to do.

And if you ask me if she knew that some of those mushrooms was bad, I'll say no, she didn't. She didn't know they was, but she was hopin they was and so was everybody else here, cept the one who ate them. And if you ask me what was in my own mind that day, I'll hafta say yes, there was a part of me hopin they was bad, too, and that's why I didn't drop the silver knife in the pot with them the way you always do to see will it turn black from the poison. See if I'd been sure they was bad I woulda had to do somethin, but as long as I wasn't sure I could keep on tellin myself that everything was all right and that nothing would happen and that the Yankee would be allowed to go away from here without bein harmed.

Well, there was a time when I wouldn't'a acted that way. There was a time when I woulda spoken up and said, "Look here, you people. You ain't in that much trouble with him. You say you're afraid of the things he does here and also of the things he might do if he goes away. Well then, treat him kindly here and maybe he won't do them. Don't argue and fight with him all the time and provoke him the way you do. Even when he provokes you and makes you mad, don't do nothin about it. Hold back a little on your feelins."

And then I woulda said, "If that don't work, if bein nice to him don't work, then lock him up somewheres around here. I know he's got the keys, but you can get them back from him. You can sweet-talk him into givin you those keys for some reason, or you can sneak em back from him some night when he's asleep. Or you don't even need the keys. You can lock him up in the wine cellar with that bolt that's on the door. He ain't gonna slip that bolt or break that door down, not that skinny little Yankee. Then you just take away his crutches and you keep him there long as you like. Take him food and water once or twice a day. Be nice to him, but keep him locked up. There's certainly enough of us here to handle him. It just don't make sense, all of us bein afraid of a one-legged frail little boy."

Well, I coulda said those things, but I didn't. And it wasn't because I was afraid to say them. Even if they was to send me away from here and sell me down the river, it wouldn't'a mattered. Fear of Miss Martha or Miss Harriet wouldn't'a stopped me. The only thing that could stop me is what did stop me, the lack of charity in my own heart.

And I'll tell you the reason for that, the reason I had a meanness in me toward that boy. It was because I was gettin back at him for a mean thing he said to me. That's why I was turned against him. That's why I didn't speak out for him at the meeting Miss Martha had. And that's why I didn't try to find out if the mushrooms was bad.

Here's the way it happened. A few days before his last day here he came into the kitchen late into the afternoon while I was shellin peas for dinner. Miss Martha was pokin around in the garden. Miss Harriet was takin a nap and the young ladies was at their studies, or anyway supposed to be.

Well he came swingin himself into my kitchen on them crutches of his and he says to me, "Mattie, I want to ask you a question. Is that all right with you?"

"Sure it is," I says. "You go ahead, Mister Yankee Soldier, and ask me any question you like. Thing is, o' course, I ain't gonna promise to answer the question, even do I know what the answer is."

"That's fair enough," he says, laughin. "I'll just have to take my chances then, I guess. Anyway maybe you won't even need to say anything. Maybe I'll know what the answer is just by lookin at your face."

"You think so?"

"Yes, I do, Mattie."

"All right," I says, "ask your question."

"You promise to tell the truth now? I mean if you answer at all?"

"I ain't promisin nothin."

He stopped and thought about that for a minute. "All right, Mattie," he finally says, "I'll go along with that. I know you're a good Christian and I'm sure you wouldn't lie about anything."

"I hope I wouldn't," I says.

"I know for a positive fact you wouldn't, Mattie. Now here's my question. Are you ready for it?"

"Shoot."

"Are you the mother of Edwina Morrow?"

"What, man? What you say?"

"Is Edwina your daughter?"

"You clear outa here, white man! You get yourself outa my kitchen!"

"Listen, Mattie, don't get upset. I'm only askin outa curiosity."

"Well she ain't, if that satisfies you!"

"Now, see, you're all excited and I can't tell whether you're lyin or not."

"Get outa here, white man, fore I call Miss Martha!"

"Look, will you let me explain what I've been thinkin. See Edwina told me one time that the thing she wanted most in the world was to be somebody else. So it came to me that maybe Edwina was your gal and Miss Martha was keepin her here and educatin her out of fondness for you. You tell me if I'm wrong, Mattie."

"I already told you that!"

"Wait now. Here's another thought I had. That maybe there was some relationship between the Farnsworth sisters and Edwina, you know? That maybe Edwina's father was somebody close to them . . . very close maybe . . . like their brother, Robert, maybe? Or maybe even their own father?"

"O, man, I'm gonna take this cleaver to you!"

"Now just a minute, Mattie," he says, backin off. "It's only because I'm very interested in Edwina, that's why I brought it up."

"Then you go ask her who her mother and father is!"

"She'd take it wrong, Mattie. She'd be offended."

"Well how come you didn't figger I'd be offended too, tell me that, white man!"

"Listen, Mattie, it's no disgrace, is it, for a darky to be pronged a little by the gentry, ain't that the way they look at it around here?"

"You listen, white man. That ain't the way I look at it! I had a man and he's dead and he's the only one I ever had. Now as for Miss Edwina, I don't know who her Mama and her Daddy is, but they sure ain't nobody from around here."

"But you do figger one of em is a darky, don't you?"

"Man, you git now! For the last time I'm tellin you, you better git!"

"See now, Mattie, I can read your face. You're tellin me all I want to know. All right, Mattie, I'm leavin. Put down your ax, old dear, and get back to your peas."

He went away laughin then on his crutches. Them was about the last words I ever spoke to him and I think they was the last words he ever spoke to me, cept for one little thing he did say to me on the night of his birthday dinner. Well, I tell you, I was real upset by those mean remarks of his. I don't know how he could ever have thought of such a thing. First, I even tried to figger it might be a joke, that maybe one of the young ladies had put him up to it. But then I decided it couldn't be that way, cause none of our young ladies would be that low-down mean to do a thing like that.

Anyway, I spose I shoulda waited a while for my temper to cool off, and for the mean thoughts to seep outa me fore I said anything about it. Because if I had waited a day or two it's likely that I wouldn'ta said anything at all. But I was just so downright mean mad about the whole thing that I couldn't wait. I told Miss Martha when she came in from the garden and then later in that same evenin I told Miss Edwina too.

Her I didn't tell as much as I did Miss Martha. Miss Martha I told exactly everything that the Yankee had said. And she didn't make no answer at all. She just stood there listenin and noddin and chewin on her lip the way she does when she's distracted. Then she threw the greens that she'd picked on the table and marched off without a word.

Miss Edwina I told only this. "The Yankee been askin questions about you. He wants to know who your Mama and your Daddy is and do I know them."

"Why does he want to know that?" Miss Edwina ask me.

"He didn't say why. If I was you, Miss Edwina, I'd stay mighty far away from him."

"Do you think I'd want to be anywhere near him?" she just about shouted at me. Then she marched away too.

Course I didn't expect her to thank me. Miss Edwina never took to me like most of the young ladies we've had here. What she acts most like is some of the Northern young ladies we used to have here sometimes before the war. Little white girls like that ain't too easy around black folks sometimes, cause they never been raised with them, you see what I mean?

Anyway, like I say, I had no more talk with the Yankee, or even with anybody else about him until that day of his birthday dinner when Miss Martha had a meeting about him in the library. She asked me special to go to that meeting. She say, "Mattie, in this matter you count as much as anybody else."

Well, it didn't seem like I counted for too much, cause they never paid much attention to anything I said. I told them they ought to drive the Yankee away from here, for instance, but they made it plain they didn't think that would work at all. Then Miss Martha went on to talk about the mean things he had done here.

And it was true enough, you couldn't argue against that. All you had to do was look at poor little Miss Harriet, how pale she was and tremblin, sittin there tryin to write with the tears runnin down her poor white cheeks, until finally she gave up altogether and just put her poor head on her arms and sobbed.

"It's no disgrace, it's no disgrace, dear," Miss Martha tried to tell her. "It wasn't your fault."

"You don't believe that, Martha," Miss Harriet say.

"I do believe it, dear. You're not responsible. You haven't been responsible for your actions for a good long time."

"Martha," cry Miss Harriet, "don't say a thing like that in front of these children."

"Marie isn't here now and neither is Amelia and the others are old enough to understand," say Miss Martha. "Now don't try to write any more, dear. You've put down all the essentials. Nothing else is needed."

"Martha, I'd like to tell you about last night."

"You've told us enough, dear. There's no need to tell us any more. We'll never speak of it again, and neither will McBurney."

Well she started into sobbin again and after a while Miss Martha say if she's gonna keep it up she's gotta go upstairs. Then long about that time Miss Marie come back down the stairs and into the library. She was carryin them mushrooms wrapped in a handkerchief and she dumped them on the library table.

"What are those for?" Miss Martha ask her.

"They're for Johnny's birthday dinner," Miss Marie say. "Remember I told you today is Johnny's birthday?"

"And where did you get these?" Miss Martha ask, poking them mushrooms around a little.

"From Amelia. She just picked them in the woods."

"Mushrooms of that sort are dangerous to eat," Miss Harriet said, wipin her eyes. "The dangerous ones are very like the good ones in that species."

"I'm sure Amelia knows that," Miss Marie say. "She knows everything there is to know about those matters. We really didn't discuss it though, because right now she's upset about something else."

"What is she upset about?" Miss Martha ask.

"McBurney," say Miss Marie. "I believe my roommate has come over to your side. From the way she looked at him a few moments ago, I'd say she's begun to hate Johnny McBurney more than anyone else here."

"Then why would she want us to have a birthday party for him?" ask Miss Alice. "And why would she gather mushrooms for him to eat?"

"Go ask her," say Miss Marie, "although I suppose when she gathered them she still liked Johnny."

"But now she doesn't like him any more?" ask Miss Emily.

"That's right," say Miss Marie.

"But she still wants to have a party for him and serve these mushrooms?" say Miss Harriet.

"That's correct," say Miss Marie.

"Well, she knows how fond he is of mushrooms," say Miss Edwina. "Maybe she just doesn't want to see them go to waste."

"Maybe so," say Miss Marie.

Miss Martha poked the mushrooms some more with her finger. "Well, young ladies," she say after a minute, "what do you think? Should we have a birthday party for Mister McBurney?"

"Of course," say Miss Marie.

"Why not," say Miss Alice.

"I'm in favor of it," say Miss Emily.

"It might be interesting," say Miss Edwina.

"It's been a long time since we've had a party here," say Miss Harriet, "an awfully long time."

"But do you think he'll come to it?" say Miss Alice.

"Yes, he'll come," say Miss Marie. "I'll ask him and I know he'll come. Now could we also have a cake?"

"Yes, I suppose so," say Miss Martha. "Can you manage it, Mattie, on this short notice?"

"I can manage it," I say, "if you want to spare the flour."

"And beaten biscuits? Can we have them?" ask Miss Alice.

"I don't see why not," say Miss Harriet. "We should have them at a birthday party."

"And meat?" say Miss Emily. "Would it be possible to have meat?"

"Yes, I think we might use the ham from the cellar," say Miss Martha. That was the ham she tricked Mister Potter out of in the spring, the time she went into his store, and caught him tryin to hide three or four of em away and he gave her one in order to keep her quiet about the rest of them.

Well that announcement caused a lot of excitement among the young ladies. "Ham, ham, wonderful ham," they all started in to shoutin.

"Johnny will surely come to the party now," say Miss Marie. "No matter how annoyed he is with some of us, he'll certainly come now."

"Very well then," say Miss Martha. "Mattie, we'll plan to dine about seven. You get started on everything, and cook these mushrooms too."

"You want me to see if they all good mushrooms?" I ask. Truly to the Good Lord, I did ask that then.

"I don't think you need to bother, Mattie," say Miss Martha. "They look all right to me."

"And me," say Miss Emily.

"Me also," say Miss Alice.

Miss Edwina studied them for a minute while she chewed on her knuckles. Then she say, "Yes, they seem perfectly all right."

"I wouldn't know one mushroom from another," say Miss Marie, "so I'll just have to take everyone else's word for it."

Miss Harriet looked at them for a long time while too before she nodded. She didn't say anything, just nodded and then started into sobbin again against Miss Martha's orders. So Miss Martha and I took her upstairs to her room and Miss Martha tell her to stay there and not come out until dinner time.

Then I come back downstairs and got the mushrooms and went out to the kitchen and started into fixin the birthday dinner. I cooked some nice greens and some peas and I made a sweet potato pie and then I took that old smoked ham and I baked it so nice with apple slices and a sugar crust on it. I used the last of the sugar for the ham and the cake, but I thought, if Miss Martha don't care, I sure don't care.

Now the cake wasn't the kind I woulda made a few years ago, naturally, but it was the best I could do with what I had. I used a little of the sugar and I took what little milk I had and I churned that nice and made some butter and then I mixed it all with the last of the flour and it turned out to be a pretty fair tastin batter. Then I baked it real careful on a slow fire and I put a sugar frostin on it and when I was through I had me a pretty nice lookin cake.

Well the dinner was ready by seven like Miss Martha wanted. The table was all set with the two dinin room lamps lighted when Miss Martha and Miss Harriet and the young ladies come in. I tell you they all looked so smart and pretty it made me forget for a minute what was goin on. They was all dressed up in their nicest party dresses and they was all so clean and neat with their hands and faces washed and their hair combed and pinned so nice I most forgot where I was.

Miss Marie was wearin her little short white silk dress with the ruffled pantalets and she had a blue ribbon on her curls. Miss Alice was wearin that nice red velvet dress that belongs to Miss Edwina and which Miss Edwina had evidently loaned her. It was a mite long for Miss Alice, but it fitted her pretty good on the top. In fact she had pinned a handkerchief to the front of it so's it didn't look too trashy. Miss Harriet had on her apple-green watered silk gown and the last time she wore that, as far as I can remember, was that last Christmas before her Daddy died, while Master Robert was still to home.

Miss Martha was wearin her nice black taffeta and for ornament that locket that I found all smashed and bent in the cellar. The glass on the picture of Master Robert was broken when I found it and the little piece of his hair was gone, but Miss Martha had evidently spent some time in bendin the gold back into place and it didn't look too bad. Course she never did find that little piece of hair in the cellar. I heard her rummagin around down there again, lookin for it just a few nights ago.

Well, Miss Edwina was dressed up nice too, in her blue velvet ball gown and her pearl choker that she says her Daddy gave her. She just looked so sweet and pretty that you'd've hardly known it was Miss Edwina and you'd've taken her right into the finest affair at the Spottswood Hotel in Richmond without thinkin twice about it. Miss Edwina even had a shawl around her so's nobody could complain about her bare shoulders.

And Miss Emily looked sweet too, in her brown muslin, and so did Miss Amelia in the little pink silk, which I think belonged to Miss Marie. What few nice things Miss Amelia brought with her she's either torn on brambles or given away to other girls. Also, she ripped up three or four of her dresses to use for the Yankee's bandages before Miss Harriet caught her at it and made her stop.

Now, I tell you, it had been a long time since I'd seen them all so nice and I think part of the reason for that was the way they must've all helped each other get ready for the party. It seemed like they must've all got together and figgered out just how each one of them could look the nicest and then all the others just pitched right in and helped to fix her that way.

Well, the Yankee was the only one still missin when they sat down to table.

"Is he coming?" Miss Martha asked.

"Oh yes," say Miss Marie. "He's takin an extra moment to tidy himself. He was polishin the buttons on his uniform when I came by the parlor."

For a while there he'd taken to wearin some old clothes of Master Robert's which Miss Martha had given him cause his uniform was so torn and dirty. Anyway I had cleaned and patched it a little a day or two before that, and he finally came to the dining room wearin it.

He wasn't too easy at first, I'll tell you that. He was shaved and combed and neat enough, but he was actin pretty suspicious too, as he stood there in the doorway.

"Come in and sit down, Mister McBurney," Miss Martha say.

"What's the game?" he say.

"We decided to have a little party for you," Miss Harriet say. "Please come in, Mister McBurney."

"You ain't been in the habit of holdin parties for me," he say.

"But this is your birthday, Johnny," say Marie. "That makes it different."

"We've all made up our minds not to quarrel with you for this one evening, Johnny," Miss Alice say.

"It's a sort of truce, Johnny," say Miss Emily. "Look at it that way."

"All right, I will," he say then, smilin, "and I thank you for it, ladies." He came in and took the seat Miss Martha had left for him at the head of the table.

Then I brought the ham in and all the young ladies did a lot of hootin and hollerin when they saw that. It had been a mighty long time since those little girls had seen a ham like that and Miss Martha just sat there smilin and lettin them make all the noise they pleased for a while. Course it wasn't too long a time before they couldn't do any shoutin cause they was too busy eatin. And the Yankee too, he set right in to eatin just as hearty as the others.

"Where are the mushrooms?" Miss Martha ask me then.

I hadn't brought them in with the rest of the dinner. I don't know why but I waited. Maybe it was because I thought they might change their minds about it, or maybe it was just because I wanted her to order me directly to bring them in. And so she did, and I brought them.

"Miss Amelia picked these few mushrooms today," say Miss Martha. "Who would like some? Mister McBurney?"

"Yes, ma'am I'm fond of them," he say. "But what about the young ladies?"

"None for me, thank you," say Miss Marie.

"Nor me," say Alice.

"I never eat them," say Miss Emily.

"Mushrooms don't agree with me at all," say Miss Harriet.

"What about you, Miss Edwina?" the Yankee ask.

Miss Edwina shook her head and Miss Martha did likewise. Then the Yankee was about to take all the mushrooms on his own plate when Miss Amelia spoke up.

"You didn't ask me," she say.

"Well, I didn't think you cared for them either, Amelia," he say. "I thought you told me one time you only ate them sometimes raw and never when they were cooked."

"Well, I can change my mind, can't I?" Miss Amelia say.

"If you are going to be impudent, Miss Amelia," say Miss Martha, "you'll find yourself sent away from the table."

"I don't think her request is too unreasonable," say Miss Edwina. "In fact I believe I'll change my mind and have some too."

Well while this talk was goin on the Yankee had started to eat the mushrooms. He laugh now and say, "They're only doin it for spite. They don't want these mushrooms, neither one of them. They're tryin to spite me, that's all. Amelia's doin it because I accidentally hurt her turtle and Edwina's mad because of another matter. Well I'm gonna get Amelia another better turtle and I'm gonna make it all up to Edwina too. All right, come on now, the two of you. Take some of these mushrooms before I eat them all."

"On second thought," Miss Amelia say, "I guess I don't want any."

"Nor I," say Miss Edwina.

"Suit yourselves," say the Yankee, and he did what he say he's gonna do. He went ahead and ate them all.

Well everybody kinda slowed down in their eatin then, 'cept o' course the Yankee. When he finished the mushrooms, he went back to the ham and the greens and the sweet potato pie and all the rest of it, and pretty soon all the young ladies got their appetites back and they went to it again until the table was almost cleaned, and then a while after that Miss Martha told me to bring the cake in.

So I did. I lit a tallow candle from the kitchen lamp and I stuck that candle in the center of the cake and then I brought the whole thing in on a platter and that started up the ooin and the aaahin and the hootin and the hollerin again and it wasn't long before it seemed that everybody had forgot about the mushrooms.

The Yankee blew out the candle and cut his cake and then he got up and made a little speech.

"I'm twenty-one today," he say, "and I feel not only like a man but like a new man. That's what your forgiveness has done for me, ladies. I want you to know this is the nicest birthday party I ever had. In fact, come to think on it, it's the only one."

Then he sniffled a little and wiped his eyes and sat down. Some of the other people there had to wipe their eyes, too, I noticed. Fact is most everybody did, even me.

"Well, Mister McBurney, will you serve your cake?" say Miss Martha.

And so he did and they all say it was the best cake they ever had. The Yankee say that too. Course it was a long time since any of them had any cake at all and they was bound to be happy with most any kind of cake you make for them. On the other hand, I did try a mite of it myself, and I got to say it was pretty good. Then I brought in the acorn coffee and while they was drinkin that they started in to talkin about old times at the school. I don't know who started it, maybe it was the Yankee, but pretty soon practically all of them was laughin and carryin on like there was never anything wrong in the house.

They talked about how it was on the day the Yankee first came here, how sick he was and how they all took care of him. Then they talked about the good times they had when he started to get well, the stories he'd told them and the jokes they'd played on each other. Finally they talked about how sick he was the second time, after his leg had been cut off, and how they'd all worked so hard nursin him and tryin to make him well again.

"I know it, I know it," the Yankee told them. "I know how much care you all gave me and I want you to know how much I appreciate it, now that I've come to my senses and can look at it in the proper light."

Course two of the young ladies didn't take much part in the conversation and one of them didn't even eat much of her dinner. That was Miss Edwina who just sat there most of the evenin, takin a bite of somethin or other now and then but mostly lookin as though she was way off somewhere in another world.

The second young lady was Miss Amelia and she didn't talk at all with the Yankee but she did eat her share of the dinner. I didn't even see her look once at him. She just kept her eyes and her mind on her own plate, eatin very slowly until she had cleaned it off, which was around the time Miss Martha say the young ladies ought to get ready to adjourn.

"Aren't we goin to say grace tonight?" ask Miss Marie. "It seems to me we forgot to say grace before our meal so we ought to say it after."

"Who will lead it then?" ask Miss Martha.

"How about Johnny, since it's his birthday?" say Miss Alice.

"All right," say the Yankee, "that's fair enough," and he folded his hands and bowed his head and say, "Thank you for this nice food we've eaten, O Lord, and bless these kind ladies for offerin it to a stranger. Bless them for bein kind to him and for grantin him their pardon, which he really didn't deserve. Amen."

"Amen," say everybody, bowin their heads.

"Could you say one more prayer, Johnny?" ask Miss Marie. "Just to give the party a Catholic touch, why don't you say an Act of Contrition?"

And he obliged her by sayin the prayer she wanted. She had to correct him a couple of times before he got it straight but finally she was satisfied with it. I thought maybe Miss Martha would tell her to stop that foolishness, but she didn't. She let Miss Marie go on helpin the Yankee say the prayer until he finished it.

"Now I suggest we have some good old songs," say Miss Alice. "Let's go into the parlor and have a good old songfest, just like the one we had that night, a while ago, just after Johnny came."

"I think not tonight," say Miss Martha.

"Not even in honor of Johnny's birthday?" say Miss Marie.

"Let's leave it up to Mister McBurney," say Miss Harriet. "If he wants it, I'm sure Miss Martha will agree to it, since this is his birthday."

"I'll tell you," say the Yankee. "I've eaten so much of this grand food, and especially that magnificent cake—for which you have my undyin gratitude, Matilda—and I've talked and laughed so much, that I don't think I could sing one note to save myself. I'll bet you all feel the same way, so with Miss Martha's permission, I say let's save the evenin of song for tomorrow night."

"Very well," say Miss Martha. "If Mister McBurney still feels the same way about it tomorrow night, we will have the evening of song. Now I think we have all had a very pleasant party with Mister McBurney."

"Yes," say Miss Harriet. "Isn't it a pity that they couldn't have all been this nice?"

"They will be in the future, ma'am, I promise you," say the Yankee. "I don't plan to stay here much longer, but while I am here, I'll try my best to make it up to you for all the unfortunate things that happened in the past. I won't try to apologize to each one of you personally right now, but take my word for it, I am very sorry for everything bad I did here."

Then they all left the dining room and went upstairs to their own rooms, 'cept the Yankee. He went in the parlor, walkin pretty good on his crutches, and closed the door.

Well I was startin to pick up the dishes from the table when I noticed somethin by the Yankee's plate. It was Miss Martha's key ring. I guess he musta left it there. Anyway I took it upstairs and gave it to her.

She was sittin there by her mirror, starin at herself, when I walked in. "The Yankee left somethin for you," I say.

She picked up the keys and looked at them and then tossed them on her bed. "It doesn't mean anything now," she said, "anyway the keys are the least part of it."

"You and I both know the gun don't work 'cause the trigger spring is busted," I say, "and I don't think the Yankee got the money."

"It doesn't matter," she say to me, not lookin at me. "You go to bed, Mattie."

So I went out and closed her door and while I was startin down the stairs I heard her call out, "Thank you, Mattie, for a very nice dinner." That's the only time in her life she ever thanked me for anything.

Well it took me quite a while to get the work done in the kitchen, longer than she expected maybe, because long about an hour later I heard her come softly down the stairs and then she stopped for a minute in the hall. Then I heard her lock the door to the parlor. After that she went out to the garden through the hall and came back again in a few minutes.

I guessed what she did out there but I wasn't sure until the next morning. I figgered she went around to the parlor garden and locked them doors too. See old Master had em fix special locks on the outside of them doors to keep Miss Martha and Miss Harriet's Mama from runnin off when she began to get a little weak in the mind the way she did a few years before she died. Anyway most of our garden doors here are only bolted from the inside, but them parlor garden doors can be locked with a key from either the inside or the outside. Leastways they could be before the Yankee busted them.

I found him in the morning. Well I wasn't the first to find him because Miss Amelia was with him when I got there. He was lyin in the garden, stretched out on the grass near the arbor like he was asleep, and Miss Amelia was sittin there beside him.

"You gonna catch cold sittin there," I told Miss Amelia.

"I'm all right," she say. "Will you help me take him back to the woods, Mattie?"

"Just you and me, child?"

"Well I guess Marie could help but I'd rather that the others didn't touch him."

"He'd be too heavy for just the three of us, Miss Amelia."

"Oh I think we could manage it if we went slowly and rested. You see I think he'd want to go back there, Mattie. I think that's where he was headed for when he came out here last night."

"Maybe so," I say. "I guess there isn't nothin wrong with takin him back to the woods but it's too far and I'm too old to do it alone with just two little girls. We better get the others to help us."

"Perhaps you're right," she finally admitted. "I guess they can't do anything to hurt him now."

"We all hurt him, Miss Amelia," I say. "Ain't none of us can get away from that."

Well she didn't believe me, o' course, and none of the others woulda believed me either if I'da said it to them, so I didn't waste time sayin it. Fact is, nobody said much of anythin that morning. They all just came downstairs and out into the garden and stood around him there on the lawn. They didn't weep or nothin like that, just stood there very serious and looked at him.

Finally Miss Harriet say, "He doesn't really seem to have suffered."

"That's true, he doesn't," Miss Martha say.

"It could have been his heart, couldn't it?" ask Miss Alice. "He never was very strong, you know."

"That's right," say Miss Emily. "He was always rather frail. Perhaps all that excitement last night was too much for him."

"I'm sure his weakened condition must have contributed to it," say Miss Edwina, "even if it wasn't the primary cause."

"But we don't know what the primary cause was, dear," say Miss Harriet, "and I'm afraid we never will know."

"Considering his religious faith, it certainly would be nice if we could have a funeral Mass with a choir and everything for him," say Miss Marie.

"I'd be willing to have a military ceremony, if it comes to that, since he was a soldier—even though an enemy," say Miss Emily.

"Nothing of the sort is feasible here," say Miss Martha. "With all due respect for Mister McBurney, he will have to be content with the simple prayers of those of us here."

"Shall we take him back into the house for a while?" ask Miss Alice.

"I don't see any point in doing that," say Miss Martha.

"I have a place in the woods I want to take him," say Miss Amelia. "I found him in the woods and I want to take him back there."

"If anybody was to ask me," I say, "I'd tell em you better do somethin with him fore the sun gets any higher."

"All right, Mattie, get his blankets from the settee," say Miss Martha.

"Wait," say Miss Edwina. "Use mine." And she ran off to fetch them.

Then the rest of the young ladies decided that they wanted him to have their blankets so they all went back to the house to get them while Miss Harriet and I went to fetch some needles and some stout thread.

When we got back it looked like every blanket and sheet in the house was layin out there on the lawn. Miss Martha didn't complain none about it. I expected her to raise a fuss but she didn't.

Well we fixed him up a bit first before we put him in the blankets. Miss Edwina took her handkerchief and wiped the dirt off his cheeks and forehead. Miss Harriet combed his hair and Miss Alice buttoned his jacket and all the girls took a hand in brushin the grass and weeds off him.

"There's some papers in his pocket," Miss Marie say.

"Leave them there," Miss Harriet say.

But Miss Alice had to go and take them out. It was just two letters and a part of an old torn magazine.

"This letter was sent to Private Soldier John P. McBurney, Company C, The Twenty Fourth New York Infantry Regiment, The Army of the Potomac River, USA," say Miss Alice. "Shall I read it aloud?"

"No," say Miss Edwina.

"There might be an address of a relative in it," say Miss Harriet.

"Go ahead then, if you must," say Miss Martha.

And so Miss Alice read out, "Dear Son John . . . I hope everything is well with you. Things are much the same here. The potatoes were very poor this year. I do not know how I will manage unless you can send something, son John. Is it a good position you have with the American Army? Is the pay good? I hope it is safe and not too hard on you. I would have thought you might have found steady employment in the City of New York. You have always been a shy boy, John. You must learn to speak up. That is the only way to get ahead. Your sister Bridget's cough has been worse this winter. Maybe when the spring comes she will improve. Did you go to Mass on Christmas Day? Have you made your Confession lately? I will close now, John. I know you are a good boy and will come home to your mother some day a rich and successful man. Your mother, Mary Anne McBurney."

"Is there a sender's address?" ask Miss Harriet.

"No, that's all there is," say Miss Alice. "Now this second letter has no address of any kind and it seems to be written in the same kind of black-berry ink we have here. Shall I read it?"

"You might as well," say Miss Marie.

And Miss Martha didn't argue so Miss Alice read out, "Dear Mum . . . I came to this place a few days ago and am being treated fine here. This place has some nice young girls in it and two ladies who are also very nice. My leg was hurt bad when I came but it is getting better now. These ladies are wonderful, Mum. It is just like home. The youngest girl here tells me to put this in. She says to tell you that she has the true faith like us and will look out for me and see that no harm comes to me from the others here who don't have it. Ha ha. Well they are all nice people here, Mum, no matter what they believe in."

"Is that all?" ask Miss Martha.

"Yes, that's all," say Miss Alice. "Now this old Harper's Weekly doesn't seem to be of any value at all. I don't know why he was keeping it."

"I believe I know why," say Miss Marie takin the magazine. "Look here on the back page," she say. "Do you see where this notice is circled with our same berry ink? The notice says, 'Genuine French Dolls, Imported From Paris. Just The Thing To Delight The Little Girl.' And do you also see what is written underneath? 'July eighteen, Marie's birthday.'

"Did you write it or did he?" ask Miss Alice.

"What difference does that make?" say Miss Marie. "He was preserving it wasn't he. He promised to get that doll for me when he went back to New York."

"You have no need of dolls in these times, child," say Miss Martha. "Now put those papers back where you found them."

"Do you want to look in his other pockets, sister?" ask Miss Harriet.

"No," say Miss Martha.

"The money you are missing might be in one of his other pockets."

"If it is," say Miss Martha, "we'll leave it there."

So Miss Alice put the papers back and straightened his jacket a little bit again. Then we rolled him on to a blanket.

There was a little bother there for a minute or two over which blankets to use, but Miss Martha finally decided to pick two of the least worn ones. Then I got my needle and carpet thread and Miss Harriet took hers and we sewed him up in there.

Before we put the last stitches in, Miss Harriet took off her Spanish lace shawl and covered his face with it. Then I folded up the top and bottom blankets and sewed them up tight. Last we rolled the whole bundle on to that old stretcher we made for him at the time Miss Martha cut his leg off.

"Now we will do as Miss Amelia has suggested," say Miss Martha, "and take Mister McBurney back to the woods."

So Miss Harriet and Miss Emily took the front poles and Miss Martha and I took the back poles and with Miss Amelia aleadin us and the other three young ladies followin and carryin the diggin tools we set off for the woods.

Well I'll tell you it wasn't easy gettin there. Miss Amelia musta took us through the deepest mud holes and through the thickest brambles and creeper vines and over the highest rocks and logs and up the steepest hills and down the slickest banks in the whole state of Virginia. Miss Alice and Miss Emily spelled off on the two front poles every now and then but Miss Martha and me on the back poles went the whole way ourselves.

The worst part of it was the last part when we had to crawl through what looked like a solid wall of thorns and brambles, pullin and pushin that stretcher along the ground. Then we came out into a little clearin and after we catched our breaths we started in to diggin.

The ground was soft and everybody helped so it didn't take too long, When it was deep enough to satisfy both Miss Martha and Amelia, we put the Yankee in. Then we busted the poles off the stretcher and put that in too cause Miss Martha say we wouldn't have no more use for it. Finally before we started fillin in the dirt Miss Martha said a prayer.

I didn't hear much of what she said cause right then I went off a little ways and had myself a good cry. I don't know if I was the only one who did it but I just couldn't help myself. It wasn't only that the whole thing needn't have happened at all. It was the fact that buryin that boy that way made me think of my own Ben who had to go off and die in a place that was strange to him.

See right then I wasn't blamin anybody for what had happened, and I'm not even sure I'm blamin anybody now, cept myself. I take the blame for whatever part I had in it, but the thing is I ain't sure how much that means. I had a reason for what I did at the time and I ain't sure but what I'd find another reason if the boy was to come back here right now and the whole thing was to happen over again.

Anyway what little of the prayer I did hear had the word "forgiveness" in it, but whether it meant that Miss Martha was sayin she was sorry for what had happened and what she'd done or whether she was just askin the Lord in a general way to have mercy on us all poor sinners, the way you generally do in prayers, I just don't know. After that Miss Marie said a little prayer she said was more suitable for dead Catholics and then Miss Harriet and some of the others threw clods of dirt in and then I dried my eyes and went back to help shovel in the dirt along with the rest.

One more thing. Before we got started shovelin, Miss Amelia bent down and laid an old jewel box in on the blankets.

"What are you putting in there, child?" ask Miss Martha. "What's in that box?"

"It's her turtle," Miss Marie say. "That turtle and Johnny were the two dearest things in the world to her and she wants to bury them together."

"All right," Miss Martha say. "Go head, Mattie."

So we filled it in and then Miss Amelia showed the young ladies where to get some pine branches and we put them on top of the dirt and then on top of that we put some wild flowers that Miss Harriet and Miss Edwina picked.

Then we went back to the house. It was maybe ten o'clock, I judge, and it was startin in to be a warm day.

On the way back Miss Marie ask Miss Martha if lessons were goin to be given and Miss Martha says she don't know why not. "You young ladies are at Farnsworth to learn," she say, "and Miss Harriet and I are here to teach you. That is our duty and we must get on with it."